Martin Kongstad has worked for many years as a journalist, columnist, culture writer and food critic at Denmark's leading newspapers and magazines, and has written for film, television and theatre. His debut collection of short stories *Han danser på sin søns grav* (*He Dances on his Son's Grave*) won the 2009 Debutant Prize. He grew up in Copenhagen and lives today in Nørrebro. *Am I Cold* is his first novel.

Martin Aitken is an award-winning translator of Danish literature. His most recent work includes novels by Kim Leine, Helle Helle and Simon Pasternak. He lives in rural Denmark.

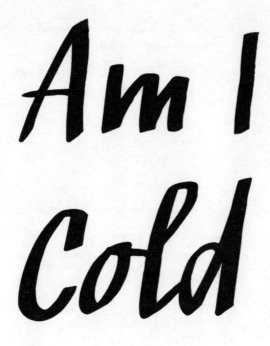

Am I Cold

a novel

Martin Kongstad

Translated from the Danish by Martin Aitken

Serpent's Tail gratefully acknowledges the financial assistance of the
DANISH ARTS FOUNDATION

First published in Great Britain in 2015 by Serpent's Tail,
an imprint of Profile Books Ltd
3 Holford Yard
Bevin Way
London
WC1X 9HD

www.serpentstail.com

First published as *Fryser Jeg* in 2013 by People's Press, Copenhagen

1 3 5 7 9 10 6 4 2

Designed and typeset by Crow Books
Printed and bound by CPI Group (UK) Ltd, Croydon, CR0 4YY

A CIP record for this book can be obtained from the British Library

ISBN 978 1 78125 333 5
eISBN 978 1 78283 100 6

To my best friend, Søren Korsbæk Fischer

On 11 June 2008, I resolved to turn my back on coupledom forever.

It is important for me to point out that I was not led into this campaign by disappointment. Yes, Helene and I had divorced and I was no longer living with my son, Charlie, but remarkably, all of that had occurred quite without conflict, as a matter of course, even. I gave up, and that was that. If ever I had wanted to find my place in coupledom, with all its trappings of vaguely satisfying kitchen-table natter, dreams of knocking through walls for that extra space, imagination construed as the ability to cook chicken in a variety of exciting ways, then Helene was the woman for me. The fact that it fell apart should in no way be made her burden, it was my fault entirely, and here I shall permit myself the right of recourse.

The fact that I had never stayed in any relationship for more than five years could be ascribed to a number of factors. When I was younger I was constantly on my way out of relationships. Like so many middle-class youths, I idolised Henry Miller and his amalgamation of Eastern thought and unbridled shagging, the myth of New York's disco revolution of the seventies, the warped, gender-confused goings-on backstage at Studio 54, and Capri at the beginning of the 1900s, where English homosexuals mingled with exiled Bolsheviks, disgraced German nobility and gossipy writers. I have always bemoaned the fact that the sexual revolution ended with the women's movement and miserable Marimekko-clad cows and men wandering about in confusion, trying to find their own footprints.

In the West, challenging prevailing conventions of love between individuals has always been a privilege reserved for artists or eccentric members of the upper classes, while schoolteachers and nurses, to name but two examples, have had far too much to do to ever seriously devote themselves to such existentially perilous experiments. But I had this niggling feeling that it was time for a radical change for everyone. Instead of wasting colossal amounts of energy embracing coupledom and trying to keep it alive in the face of its inherently decrepit nature, could undreamt-of happiness be attained by simply letting it go?

I realised all of this on the night of Wednesday, 11 June 2008 for a number of circumstantial reasons, but what really made the difference was a series of events and encounters with new people. One in particular.

It is Christmas Eve 2008, and I'm sitting at the kitchen table in my flat on Klerkegade. To my right is the chopping board, reeking of onion, as it has done ever since I was going about in grey charity-shop jackets and listening to *Steps Ahead*. I've had the place more than twenty years, thirty-seven square metres, or one hundred and eleven cubic metres of stale air, in a corner of the historic cluster of row houses called Nyboder.

It is Christmas Eve 2008, and I am in no mood.

In three and three-quarter hours my best friend, Søren T-shirt, will be here. Punctuality is a virtue he has retained, which is remarkable given his lifelong commitment to escapism, hedonism and drug addiction. I have just wrapped up his present, and for once I have made an effort, grey paper and pink ribbon.

It has been a tumultuous year, and though by definition I am back where I started, I nonetheless feel changed, a fact Søren is definitely not going to be arsed hearing about. The unctuous side of my character is not something he takes seriously, and whether that is a good or a bad thing I am unable to judge, but I do know for certain that the story this year brought with it is not one that will make him sit still. He will be here at twelve, and if I resist painting vivid landscapes I may have it told by the time he arrives. As I proceed, I shall swing my legs, to raise the pulse and firm up more infantile passages. I promise, to the extent that it is possible, to be utterly and completely honest. Even, or perhaps especially, when the story puts me in a less than flattering light.

'Everything escapes you.'
FRANCIS BACON

DENMARK, JANUARY 2008

It began in fog. The trees were blurred pencil sketches in a slush of landscape. One godforsaken town after another, condemned station buildings, depopulated platforms, not a fucking bird in sight. At Fredericia I realised I hadn't even noticed the other passengers, nor had they noticed me.

Nothing can be quite as disheartening as a train journey through Denmark in January.

Because I'd been a restaurant critic for a number of years, I had been invited to Aarhus by Thorbjørn Rasmussen, a foodie PR consultant in his fifties who was always rubbing his hands and heaving his neatly ironed jeans all the way up the crack of his arse. He had got his hands on the promotional account for an upcoming Aarhus Food Festival, about which I could have given less than a shit, but then he had beguiled me with the prospect of a truffle evening at Restaurant Frederikshøj and a night at the Hotel Royal.

A refugee was talking to himself on the city's main pedestrian street. He had a wild look in his eyes, staring into the dismal chain stores on either side of him. In the central square was a pathetic attempt at recreating a Roman coffee bar, complete with oversized sugar bowls and signs in Italian. When the chance comes around they always end up overdoing it in Aarhus. They grab the whole catalogue. There was a word for the place, I just couldn't think of it.

Some boys were running about after a deflated plastic football in front of the cathedral and I found myself standing there missing Charlie and trying to suppress a rising feeling of self-loathing.

I had just dropped my bag down on the hotel bed when my phone rang.

It was Søren T-shirt.

'I've been in Hvidovre Hospital for a week.'

'What's the matter with you?'

'I was pissed off. I fixed some rat poison.'

'Are you okay?'

'They might have to take my leg. My calf looks like a pumpkin.'

There was an abstract painting above the bed. Yellow, orange, white.

'You're going to come and see me, aren't you?'

I laid out the clothes I was going to wear – grey pants in a sixties cut, pale blue shirt, the red silk cravat again – and was about to have a shower when there was a knock on the door.

'We're so happy you could find the time to come over and see us.'

It was Thorbjørn Rasmussen in a loud new suede jacket. He squirmed his way in, apologising on the one hand for turning up unannounced, ignoring on the other the fact that I was standing with a towel around my waist.

He'd just popped up on the off-chance, he said, with the press folder that he reckoned in all modesty had turned out really well. He began to present it to me in the minutest of detail. First the logo on the front, wanting to make sure I noticed how his clever, outside-the-box-thinking graphic artist had implemented a fork. Then a prolonged sales pitch taking in gastronomic initiatives and regional dishes 2.0 with all the sports metaphors: everything to play for, best form of defence is attack, killer ball.

But it ended well. 'I'm afraid I can't make it tonight', he said, 'but let's have a spot of lunch tomorrow at twelve, I'll fill you in on the game plan.'

He turned casually in the doorway:

'Oh, and when do you reckon we can expect something in the paper?'

I gave him a non-committal answer and he made an effort to keep smiling, stuck an unconvincing thumb in the air and left.

Respectable! That's the word. Even something as outrageously luxurious as a truffle evening becomes moribund in Aarhus. None of your Chanel earrings here, not a blasé air in the house. The speaker at the truffle evening was a social democrat with a line in repartee, his mission to bring the truffle down from its pedestal. He went on in his Jutland drawl about how truffles found nourishment in the vicinity of new oak trees and lavender, and presented slides of men from Provence in waistcoats with their brainless fucking hounds, and then when he sent a genuine black truffle round the tables all the schoolteachers got their little digital cameras out and took pictures.

I was the only one eating alone, and so I produced a notebook to fend off pitying looks. On my plate was a poached egg with black truffle, lumpfish roe and a truffle *beurre blanc*.

Helene had always had this rather frenzied way of wanking me off. Maybe she had once read that was the way to do it, or maybe it was the way one of her old boyfriends had preferred. In general, I didn't much care for high-speed sex, but it did the job surprisingly well. Until one day it didn't. After a year I suddenly realised that my hands followed the same route every time and I found myself looking for signs of wear: first the shoulders, then down her back, across the loins to the outer thighs, buttocks, inner thighs, and finally the cunt.

Four men stuck out from the homogeneous mass. They were in their early thirties, without the sheepish deportment of the rest of the party, and they held their wine glasses properly. They were dressed like Aarhusian senior creatives, in sneakers and suits with untucked shirts. One of them in particular had his attention directed towards my table. I went out and found a book of recipes in reception behind which I could hide and prayed not to be accosted, but halfway through the second course he got up and came over and stood in front of my table until I lowered my book, then presented himself as Morten Levinsen.

'We're with you all the way, Vallin! If you don't mind me saying?'
His smile was at once timid and sceptical.
'All what way?'
'We kiss your feet, Vallin, but you know that, don't you?'

Immediately I was in trouble, unable to muster a reply. I received his smile with a mixture of offence and embarrassment, then found myself feeling guilty, and began talking away in an oddly lecturing tone of voice, and even heard myself plug the Aarhus Food Festival before he cut through my act and did a frighteningly good imitation of Thorbjørn Rasmussen, to whom, it transpired, he had served hectolitres of house red the time he had a student job as a bartender at the Café Casablanca.

'Come over and join us!'

I was too gobsmacked to say no.

'We're *good times*, Vallin. You'll love us!'

They knew each other from the second intake of KaosPilots, the alternative business school in Aarhus, back in the early nineties, and told stories of all the projects they had got started: a red-wine disco for unrepentant hippies, an African restaurant whose profits went to Somalia, a singing car park. They'd all done well for themselves since: one owned a minor empire of restaurants, another was something big to do with the Aros art museum, and a third was one of the driving forces behind the Aarhus Festival. Only Levinsen had decided to move to Copenhagen, where he quickly made a name for himself in advertising. First an account manager in a small agency, then planner in a bigger one, strategist in one of the well-respected ones, and eventually partner.

'So now you're in Aarhus stuffing your face, Vallin?' he said.

After the food we drove into town and it wasn't only for the sake of politeness that I went with them to Pinds Café, and though Levinsen kept feeding me with flattery it wasn't entirely for reasons of vanity either. The others found a corner to sit in and carry on their reminiscing, while Levinsen and I stood with pints of Ceres Royal at the bar. He kept looking at me and I couldn't work out whether it was psychological interest or lack of tact, so I began, for want of a better idea, to evaluate the meal and praise the three variations of roasted foie gras with cauliflower. He did nothing to help me along and simply kept smiling at me overbearingly. My calves were aching and

I wanted to sit down, but I kept talking. Without invitation I began to plough through the story of my divorce, and as if that wasn't enough, I quickly became categorical and self-critical to a point far in excess of what was reasonable.

'All that stuff about how it takes two to split up, that's just crap,' I said. 'The lamb doesn't ask to be eaten by the wolf. It just lies there in the meadow. Looking delicious doesn't mean it's to blame.'

He leaned so close I could smell his aftershave.

'My life's an open book!'

Apparently, he couldn't care less about my divorce.

'Do you understand what I'm saying, Vallin?'

'Your life's an open book, you say.'

'A year ago I sold my share in the agency with a view to opening up my life.'

He placed his hand on mine. It was highly unpleasant.

'Now is when we start to close in on ourselves, Vallin. Now, at our age. Do you follow me?'

I removed his hand and reached for my beer.

'When was the last time you danced with your arms above your head?' he said.

'I don't dance at all anymore. I hang around at the bar.'

'We mustn't become small and embittered, Vallin. It happens by itself, unless we choose another way.'

'And what way did you choose?' I said.

'I met my wife straight after school, right? We've got the whole package, *the lot* – three kids, big house, two cars, but we've shaped it in our own way.'

'Wouldn't most people say that?'

'Ours is an open relationship, Vallin.'

'You shag other people?'

'We share our love with others. It's a revelation!'

'So how does it work?' I said.

'We do what we feel like, and we don't tell each other. Come on, Vallin! It's a total turn-on. I know she's having sex with other people, but I don't know when or with whom. We get off on each other just thinking about it!'

He maintained eye contact longer than I was comfortable with.

'Openness is my mantra. It's even how I run Levinsen Open!'

'A tennis tournament?'

'Levinsen Open is my gallery. You're into art, right?'

'Of course,' I said. 'In the eighties you had to play in a band, in the nineties you had to make films, now it's art.'

'The artist seeks to expand the world, Vallin! It's the only ambition worth having. Artists make our lives bigger.'

He suddenly wanted a Moscow Mule and talked the bartender into popping out to the nearest kebab shop for some mint and cucumber.

'Did you know that the word *amateur* comes from *amour*? I'm a happy amateur, and the art world has so many rules, so many ossified ways of going about things. Artists are always in flux, but the galleries haven't moved an inch since the eighties.'

'So what do you do?'

'I enter into a process with my artists. I call them daily on the phone, stop by their studios and tell them what I think. They have to adapt themselves to the market. We're in this to make a living, and I know what my clients want. For Christ's sake, Vallin, I know them! I used to go out on the piss with all the upcoming marketing boys in the nineties, they're all handling massive budgets now, and they want art!'

He listed his artists and there were a couple of representatives from the peripheries of De Unge Vilde, albeit not quite as young anymore, and one from the Fluxus movement who was rediscovered every few years. The others I'd never heard of but the drink was good. The cucumber set it off nicely.

'You *must* have heard of Henrik Høeg Müller, Vallin, surely! He's the new Hammershøi. Huge, wide-format things, rich kids on junk, flat out in des-res apartments. I've just sold two of them to this major collector in Germany.'

One of his friends came up, mobile in hand.

'Janus Doubletooth says he's over at Sway with a whole bunch of girls.'

I tagged along in the slipstream with a bottle of Havana, through the town, jumping the queue, past the black doorman and into a time warp. Broken glass on the floor, sloppy lighting. Everyone in black, bottles of Gold in their hands. There were the side partings again, the caps, the braces, even the Doc Martens were out in force.

'It's like being back at the Bonaparte Club in 1982,' I said.

Levinsen put his hands on my shoulders.

'Let yourself go, Vallin, be a part of it. You can hang out at the bar some other time.'

My cheeks died on the spot, and then he wanted to hug. Ahh, he said as we let go, and I wasn't too keen, but who was I to criticise a man who had so obviously managed to turn things around, and he was right, as well. One of the others had ordered a tray of Snakebites and Gold, so we found a corner where we could sit, and there, sure enough, was Janus Doubletooth surrounded by girls, a couple of token blondes, a brunette with plucked eyebrows, the inevitable Jutland biracial, and a redhead with a certain poetry about her.

We hurled shots down our necks, and Levinsen dashed his glass to the floor.

'Come on, you gorgeous people!'

My feet still couldn't dance to Joy Division's 'Love Will Tear Us Apart', and certainly not to Nitzer Ebb. My hips locked and I was planning to drift off towards the exit when the DJ switched to Balkan. 'Disco Disco Partizani'. The room exploded into semitones and there was no way I could keep up at that level. Levinsen had everyone dancing with their hands above their heads, and they all cheered him on as he came writhing towards me, thrusting forth his gyrating pelvis. They whistled and whooped as he lifted my arms in the air. Dancing with your arms in the air is more than a physical action. It forces you to let go. It was an overwhelming psychological strain, laying myself bare like that, but once I'd got through the first song I found myself wanting more. I made eye contact with the poetic redhead and followed the twisting of her body. Her milky waist was smooth and soft, we danced to Depeche Mode and the Human League, and then it was Levinsen and not me who was standing at the bar, and when I hugged him, drenched in sweat and blissfully bleary eyed, he understood it was my way of saying thanks.

The idea came as a natural extension of the dance.

'I'm going to write a novel, a romance,' I said.

'That's the spirit, Vallin! Way to go! It's a love thang!'

They played 'Life's What You Make It' by Talk Talk, and normally it would have been way too much.

'1986,' I said.

'We're talking shoulder pads and Wham!,' he said.

'We're talking the last great relationship. The best couple the world has ever seen,' I said.

'Eighties to the bone, you are, Vallin. It's *so-o* beautiful!'

We stood with our arms around each other and let it happen, and it was only when the poetic redhead went past that I thought better of it.

It was ages since I'd last been naked in bed with a girl, and her breasts looked so soft.

'Next step, Vallin. Time for the next step,' Levinsen said.

'What do you mean?'

'Let's get Mimi back to your hotel room.'

He strode through the shards on the floor, sat down beside her and whispered something in her ear. Fifteen minutes later all three of us were in a taxi.

I couldn't get the key card to work, but Levinsen seemed close to sober and found drinks in the minibar and smoochy samba on my laptop. I sat down opposite Mimi in a low chair. But dancing about in broken glass was one thing, sitting there in Room 211 was quite another.

'I ran into Levinsen at a truffle event,' I said.

He was already getting the bed ready.

'We had three varieties of roasted foie gras with cauliflower.'

Levinsen put the duvet up against the wall.

'Vallin always talks food when he's nervous,' he said, and patted the mattress three times. She got on to the bed.

'Mimi's promised to show us how she masturbates.'

There was a delay before I registered what he had said. Masturbates? She smiled and looked down at the bed.

'Welcome to paradise, Vallin!' he said, and gave her a nod.

Mimi reached her hands up under her dress and pulled her knickers down. She drew the floral-patterned dress up around her hips. Her cunt was trimmed and partly shaven, only a narrow band of pale red hair remained. A pimple blared out from the white of her inner thigh. 'Touch yourself!' said Levinsen. She hesitated for a moment before putting a hand down to her cunt and slowly circling her index and middle fingers around her clitoris. She could have been washing dishes or kneading dough.

Her eyes were fixed on a point to my left, which I later discovered was a maritime scene of mediocre quality, and her breathing remained pretty much unaltered until after three or four minutes she gasped almost unnoticeably and eventually exhaled in small stages. She looked down at the carpet for a bit before finding the courage to look up. I could see then she'd only just got the braces off her teeth.

It was ten to twelve when the maid knocked on the door. I was lying on the floor in my shirt and tie, the minibar was open and there were bottles and glasses all over the place. I legged it through the town in a cloud of alcohol fumes and was only fifteen minutes late.

Thorbjørn Rasmussen was seated on a sheepskin-covered chair with a glass of white wine in front of him. I drank a litre of water in five minutes.

'Did you enjoy the truffles?' he said.

Grissini steeped in mackerel oil. Salmon skin, herring mayonnaise.

The room was spinning so much I had to grab hold of the table.

'And someone else paid for the binge afterwards, I trust?'

It took me a while to navigate through his questions.

'Do they still teach decent behaviour at journalism school?'

'I didn't go to journalism school,' I said.

'You don't say,' he said. 'You don't say.'

'You sound pissed off,' I said. That much I'd grasped.

Thorbjørn Rasmussen took a sip of his wine and cleared his throat.

'I called your editor this morning to have a chat about photo coverage for this article of yours.'

I said nothing.

'He tells me it's five months since you worked there. I think I've had the wool pulled over my eyes, don't you?'

Søren T-shirt was livid by the time I went to see him at Hvidovre Hospital. Like a little kid with a grazed knee who had been holding back the tears, he started whingeing and whining as soon as I came through the door, babbling his free-ranging conspiracy of broken promises, malicious-minded incompetence and terror of which he believed himself to be victim.

Someone had cut his hair down to the pasty roots.

'Where the fuck did they dig those nurses up?' he said. 'They're not trained, I can tell you that much for sure. I recognise one of them. Pill-popper, she is, and talks to herself.'

'Did they operate?'

'They cut my bloody calf open!'

He squirmed in his big white smock.

'Are they giving you anything?'

'No, that's just it, for fuck's sake. The quack was here, pissed as a fart with a fag-end in his gob, and stuck this in me.'

He showed me a drip that ought to have been inside him, dispensing painkiller at intervals.

'Only the dosage was way too low. I mean, it says in my notes I've been a junkie for twenty-five years. They can't expect to give me the same as some little schoolgirl with pigtails, can they? Ow, ow, ow!'

He pulled on the cord and yelled towards the corridor. After about five minutes a nurse turned up, not exactly bubbling over with warm feelings for him.

'What do you want now, Søren?'

'I want you to do your job. Is that too much to ask?'

'I'm doing my job, Søren. There's a lot of people besides you needing attention.'

'You've got to give me a decent whack of something. Now! I'm in agony here.'

'The doctor's already had a look at you, Søren. We can't give you anymore than you're getting.'

With that she left, and Søren hurled a mouthful of abuse after her until something made him stop. Something outside. I looked out. There was a man in a wheelchair, smoking. A man with one leg.

'I could do with a bit of fresh air,' said Søren.

I helped him into a wheelchair of his own.

'Bring the ale with you,' he said, indicating the carrier bag from the minimart that I'd brought just to be on the safe side.

The one-legged man was called Poul and was somewhere in his sixties. The doctors were wondering whether they should take his other leg too. Søren handed him a beer and asked what was wrong with him, and after about half an hour we were well in the picture.

We raised our cans in a toast and looked up at the sky for a bit, and then it was Søren's turn to talk about his fierce infection and the risky operation he'd undergone.

'You must be in quite a bit of pain yourself, eh, Poul? What are they giving you for it, anyway?'

Poul produced a handful of tablets from his pocket. Søren looked at them the way the wolf looked at the three little pigs.

'I'll give you a couple to take back up with you,' said Poul.

He handed Søren three of these most desirable pills.

'Are you sure? That's very decent of you, Poul.'

'One at a time, mind,' Poul said. 'Knock you sideways, they will.'

Søren took all three on his way back to the ward.

'Can I write a book about you and Signe?' I asked.

Søren was back in his bed.

'Yeah, sure. As long as it's an adventure book and I'm the hero.'

His eyes were half gone, but he pulled on the cord anyway.

'What now, Søren?' said the nurse.

'I need something… for the… pain.'

'You're asleep,' she said.

His contorted expression vanished. He looked like an innocent boy.

There's no doubt that Helene left me for a better man. She was Tue Nissen's publicist and they'd gone on a book tour together. He stuck his bony dick inside her, then got shot of his small village domicile in Jutland and closed the deal on a house on Ceresvej. A month and a half after their first shag – and three weeks after she'd left me – the happy couple stood in Galleri Nicolai Wallner's back room skimming through the folders of accessible paintings to find art for the pristine walls of their beautiful new home. The Polish builders had been in, as had the kitchen designer, the lighting consultant from On the Spot, the carpet man, all sorts of men whom Tue, by virtue of his eternally bestselling trilogy about World War II resistance fighters in southern Jutland, hired without so much as a glance at his bank balance.

In the three months since he'd moved in with Helene, he had established what I spent four years trying to avoid: a decent home with shelving and lamps, inviting rooms in which to dwell, and fixed mealtimes. It was a delightful place, lovely garden too. There's nothing wrong with buying good Danish art, subscribing to intellectual newspapers or selecting furniture of timeless design, but I was certain neither Tue nor Helene had reckoned on the consequences of doing everything right.

Occasionally, being on your own is hard, but it's nothing like as bad as the horrors to which a person may be exposed within the confines of perfectly functioning coupledom.

When they suggested we have dinner together at their house once a month, on a Tuesday, I could only accept. It was the kind of terrible but well-intentioned idea that summed them up. They met doing the wrong thing; he was high on his own success, cocksure of himself and looking to test his limits, she was unfaithful right under my nose.

When I arrived, my son Charlie ran on ahead up the stairs to his big bedroom on the first floor without so much as noticing the great Christian Schmidt-Rasmussen canvas above the landing or the elegant marine-blue stair carpet. Tue was standing in the doorway with a bottle of Hubacker from Weingut Keller. I liked Tue, I actually did. He carried his wealth with assurance, strolling about in cashmere, having lunch meetings for the sake of the food alone. He had started going to openings at the hip galleries, had his hair cut once a month at Frisør No, and was a frequent premiere-goer at Dagmar, Grand and the Betty Nansen Teater.

Until he moved to the city he was writing twelve hours a day, but now he put in the bare minimum, for Danmarks Radio. One reason was they had purchased the TV rights to his books and kept calling script meetings all the time, the other was that owing to his refreshing opinions, pleasant demeanour and irrefutable popularity he had become, in a public debate governed by academics, the voice of the ordinary man, so he was always in taxis, on his way to and from another radio discussion.

Helene stood chopping shallots in their huge kitchen and I could tell by her shoulders something wasn't right. She smelled of underarm sweat.

'What do you think of the rendering?' said Tue.

'Mikkel doesn't notice that sort of thing,' said Helene.

'Slaked lime, twelve-year,' he said.

Helene put the fish in the oven.

'You must have seen the scaffolding was gone?' Tue said.

He dragged me outside. They'd got a trampoline since I was last there. Tue pointed up at his house. Now I could see, they had restored the life out of the brickwork.

'Ask me about lime,' he said.

I didn't.

'French earth colour. Ochre.'

The house was the colour of cunt. No two ways about it.

The food tasted slightly of fish and mostly of nothing.

'I want to write a novel about Søren T-shirt,' I said. 'It'll be the last great love story. *The Ballad of Signe and Søren T-shirt.*'

'That's a brilliant idea,' said Helene.

'It'll be more or less documentary style.'

'Even better,' she said. 'I know I sound really annoying now, but docufiction was trending at Frankfurt this year.'

She was all go, and either she didn't think I could see through her act to what was really going on, or else – and I thought this was more likely – she was too absorbed in her own situation to pay much attention to what I was noticing. The encouragement she bestowed on me was at the same time a dig at Tue, and as though by some quadratic equation, Tue seized the intiative from the other side of the table.'Do you think you can write a happy love story?' he asked.

'Didn't it all go wrong between Søren and Signe?' said Helene.

'Yes, but that's not the point,' I said.

Tue laughed and took a bottle of white out of the fridge.

'What are you laughing at?' said Helene.

He tried to hold her hand.

'Helene is a bit upset that I've agreed to be in *Do You Know the Type?*, that harmless TV programme.'

'It's fine by me that you go airing your opinions about everything all the time, but no way am I having a TV crew in here rummaging through my underwear.'

Tue downed his glass of white wine.

'As publicity director you ought to be over the moon, prime-time exposure for one of your writers?'

'As publicity director I'd prefer you to be writing books.'

'You always hear writers saying they write because they can't help it,' said Tue. 'Well, I can help it.'

He leaned back with a smile.

'Who needs more books, anyway?'

'That's a rather stupid thing to say now that Mikkel's about to write his first novel.'

Tue straightened up.

'Okay, let's talk about Mikkel's novel. Let's say you want it out in time for Christmas this year. That'd be a deadline of, what, the first of August?'

Helene nodded.

'Can you write it in six months?' Tue asked me.

'I suppose so,' I said.

'Given your profile and the subject matter, we as publisher will definitely want to take it on, but they won't give you more than twenty thousand kroner up front. And you don't even have your newspaper work to fall back on anymore. You can't live on that,' Helene said.

Tue leaned forward. 'Tell you what. I'll lend you fifty,' he said. 'Have you heard of San Cataldo?'

'That stuck-up retreat near Amalfi?'

'There was an autumn deadline for applications,' said Helene.

'I wrote half of *The Raspberry Bush* there. They're not usually full in early spring. I'll give the director woman a call.'

C ycling back towards town I found myself thinking about when it had all begun to go wrong between Helene and me. Charlie was eighteen months old, old enough for us to feel we could leave him with a babysitter. I spent two workdays finding the right restaurant, eventually settling for Le Sommelier: good food, not too formal and with decent drinking establishments nearby for afterwards. Helene had too much make-up on, I was in a pinstriped suit. We were tense in the taxi and it wasn't because we'd rekindled those first feelings of being in love, it was because we were both so aware of the importance of what was coming up. It was more than just dinner in town. We were trying to prove to ourselves that we were still a happy couple.

They served us Dom Perignon by the glass and we talked about one of the staff at Charlie's crèche and agreed it was a subject that belonged to some other occasion.

The bread came, and after we had eaten it all and our different starters the edge had come off our appetites. The evening was entering its crucial phase.

I caught sight of a guy who looked like someone I used to know from college called Thomas and was reminded of a daft anecdote from the Saltlageret music venue. She laughed in the right places, and I was very particular about the details, building up towards the punchline, but just as I was getting there I happened to look at her, and saw that no matter how much she wanted to, she couldn't hide the fact that she'd heard it before. I pretended I hadn't noticed and rattled the story off to its conclusion. She got drunk on the thick-bodied Rhône and started going on about her dream of one day settling in the south of France and running a little hotel, and I repaid her confidence by asking the exact same encouraging questions as the last time and the time before that.

We had a beer at the Borgerkroen afterwards, but she couldn't drink anymore after that.

I gave the babysitter a hundred kroner more than we'd agreed, and when Helene and I flopped apart on the bed after twenty-three minutes of sex we both said we ought to make a priority of nights like that.

Neither of us had any idea how fragile it all was.

A new caress was all it took. Another kind of kiss.

I put off going home to my unmade bed on Klerkegade and went instead to the Byens Kro, where there was a surprise birthday party on the go for a stoned Swedish artist, and the painter Christian Finne was deejaying acid rock with ringing cymbals. I recognised a designer

with flat hair and baggy trousers, and a former member of De Unge
Vilde in workwear, but whether all the young street-looking guys were
artists with a *courtesy of* some Valby gallery stamped on their arses, or
whether they had just stepped down from a podium in Milan, I was
unable to judge at the time. It was all starting to blur into one. The
fashion mags were writing about art and hanging out at openings, the
artists were displaying their wardrobes and sitting front row at the
fashion shows, and at weekends they all celebrated each other's wed-
dings or met over the kids at the playground in the Østre Anlæg park
in their black get-ups and Tom Ford eyewear.

I got an Urquell at the bar and a group of girls in their twenties
caught my eye.

They were swarming around a tray of shots, dressed like spoiled
kids, gestures all sophisticated, chain-smoking and loud. They looked
like they'd seen it all but hadn't learned a thing. I thought they were
great.

1985 saw the demise of the radical feminist mouthpiece *Kvinder*,
mainly because the older activists lacked confidence in their younger
sisters and were reluctant to pass things on, and of course because
apparently the struggle for women's rights was over. Free abortion
had been introduced, women were working and went to university.
Journals from the Femølejren women's camp document how the
oppressed tore off their bras, took their sisters by the hand and found
themselves a new life. They mended their own bikes, earned their
own money and cast off their roles as sex objects. This had serious
aesthetic repercussions: make-up, clingy clothes and visits to the hairdressers were oppressive, reactionary and disloyal; women were either
free and naked or else shapelessly hidden away in tent-like smocks
and baggy trousers. For fifteen excruciating years, the author Suzanne
Brøgger was the only one around who managed to be intelligent and
feminine at the same time, but in 1986 a miracle occurred: young
women wanted their bodies back. Søren T-shirt's girlfriend Signe
wouldn't have been seen dead in woolly jumpers or crushed velour,
only in short black skirts and nylon stockings; she used perfume, too,

and washed her hair more than once a week, and she wasn't the only one.

The young women of the eighties retained their mothers' insistence on independence, but rejected their tiresome aesthetics and the two generations remained joined together as each other's polar opposites.

It sounds pathetic now, but back in the eighties I collected misfit women. I celebrated whenever I finally ran into one who set aside the dogma and took risks. Today, interesting, humorous women have increased in numbers. The granddaughters of the radical feminists are the first generation of women to live out the liberation. These days, it's the men who stand preening in front of the mirror for hours on end, then slouch against the walls in the ever-forlorn hope of attention, while the women snigger at the bar.

It was impossible to imagine that the group of girls I stood staring at would one day have little wrinkled mouths. On the pretext of mustering vitality I ordered another Urquell and decided on the spur of the moment to have an old Caribbean rum as well, since more than likely it was my last round.

Søren T-shirt and I had agreed to get together for two days to do some interviews after he got out of hospital. I knew the story of him and Signe, and parts of it were included in my arsenal of anecdotes, but I had yet to hear him tell it himself in its entirety and I'd prepared some questions to get him to delve further into the details.

Søren lives in a part of Østerbro I was afraid of as a child. The staircase still smelled like the seventies: cooking fat, dirty washing and filled ashtrays. He had just got out of the bath, seemed energetic and together, and the floor of his cramped living room was tidy. He mentioned he was thinking of going into rehab at some place in Nordsjælland, but apart from that we stayed off the subject, God knows we'd been there before. At one point in the nineties I realised he could drop dead any day. It's all been bonus since then.

When Søren and Signe were together, they shone, and it would be no exaggeration to say we mirrored ourselves in their life together and forgot about our own whenever she stroked her hand over his hair.

At one end of the scale were his great, hectic strides, the eternal quest for the highs, at the other the graceful way in which she could reach for her glass. She brought him to rest in the moment, and so it seemed quite inexplicable, even to Søren himself, that his weekend speed habit escalated into smoking heroin and later to injecting the stuff. Signe was absorbed in her law studies and hadn't learned to recognise the clues, and for a year Søren lived a double life; on the one hand a lovestruck young man enjoying the Rioja-fuelled dinner parties of coupledom, on the other a junkie traipsing the pavements of Istedgade. One day she found out, and that was it.

He hadn't shot heroin in five years. Now he relied on methodone and excessive alcohol consumption, topped up with whatever happened to come his way in the line of Rohypnol, coke, ecstasy and MDMA, and though there was no denying his physical decline, he continued to play the hedonist with remarkable gusto. The real world could look after itself. He had never really wanted it anyway.

'I never thought you were that stupid,' he said when I presented this interpretation of his life to him. I'd brought fishcakes.

'I'd be over the moon if I had a wife and kids. You know how much I love a plate of hot food.'

'Why don't you cook, then?'

He gave me a proud look.

'You really want to start with Adam and Eve?'

'Yes, I do.'

He lifted his shoulders to somewhere near his ears and began to talk, and we didn't stop until his weary bookshelf had all but dissolved into darkness.

Later we went out. I wanted to take him to Karriere Bar, a new artist's hangout in the meat-packing district, but Søren insisted on going to Floss first. As usual, he was received like a veteran returned home; apart from that, the place was business as usual: Peter still monitored everything from behind the bar, the Faroe Islander couldn't get his words out right, the fifties freak was asleep on his bar stool, and Søren introduced me to a young female poet from Latvia with pockmarks on her cheeks and a pair of breasts that looked like they were on their last legs.

We touched down briefly on Istedgade, where Søren cadged his usual two hundred and scored a little lump off an African, and then we got to Karriere. It resembled a canteen with curated tables and futuristic lamps. If the artist crowd were there, they were keeping a low profile. Marketing types with bleached teeth, cutaway collars and drinks on expenses dominated the place, creating that characteristic buzz of unfinished sentences and tedious territorial behaviour.

Kreuzmann was there, and I hadn't seen him since the disastrous evening at Noma several months ago. He was flanked by a pair of East European tarts whose eyebrows were plucked to the last hair; his face was swollen, he looked like a corpse washed up on a beach, white shirt stuck to his skin. I had known him since we started school, we were almost friends, but there was this latent mutual scepticism between us, and it had been like that ever since we first met. Søren, however, couldn't put a foot wrong as far as Kreuzmann was concerned.

'You're looking good,' said Kreuzmann. 'Have you stopped shooting junk?'

'I'm fit as a fiddle,' said Søren. 'I can do backflips.'

'I got divorced,' said Kreuzmann.

'What for?' said Søren.

'I shagged the neighbour.'

Søren squealed with laughter.

'A good thing, if you ask me. Getting divorced,' I said.

'Read a new book, have we?' said Kreuzmann.

'Why should anyone want to talk to the same person every night?' I said.

'I was never home!' said Kreuzmann.

I swayed to the music and sensed how annoying I looked.

'You were probably working to be away from it,' I said.

'You know how hard a divorce can be, Mikkel,' said Søren.

'Having a partner's a lot harder,' I said.

Kreuzmann put his glass down and scanned the room with a look of bereftness. A receptionist was entertaining the marketing guys with some zumba steps.

'I went to see the pastor in Taarbæk last week,' he said. ' I wanted to say sorry.'

'For what?'

'I promised Claudia I'd be faithful, until death do us part.'

'Did it help?'

'He was out playing tennis.'

Kreuzmann stood sobbing beneath a Jeppe Hein lamp, and Søren held him tight all through the twelve-inch version of 'Blue Monday'.

'Has anyone seen my black knickers?'

It was Inger asking, and there was every reason to take her enquiry seriously. Up until that point she had spoken only of buses she'd missed or which hadn't come. San Cataldo is a Danish-owned former cloister dating back to the twelfth century and situated 1,670 steps above the town of Amalfi. From my sparsely furnished cell I could look out across the Valle de Dragone with its lemon groves and donkeys. The long, cool corridors smelled reassuringly of Italian detergents. The walls were thick and whitewashed.

I arrived mid-month, and since the eleven other guests had already been there a fortnight I found myself part of what was already a well-established hierarchy.

There were only two strong characters: Lea Winther Jensen was a visual artist in her early thirties, with thick, flaxen hair, prominent eyebrows, dark, finely curved lips and a pair of large, oblong front teeth that lent her a rather girlish appearance. She was quick on the uptake, analytically gifted and seemingly extremely well read, and yet there was also a certain sweetness about her that perhaps – and now I am guessing – was more down to shaky self-confidence than purity of heart.

As for Peter Borch-Jensen, there was little doubt about his confidence. Here was, in every sense, a thoroughly unpleasant man. Exemplarily stylish and costumed as if by the Brasserie Flo back in the sixties: tweed, handmade brogues, fastidiously ironed shirts and a flourish of silk scarves in bold colours. He was about sixty, but his long hair and agile physique made him seem younger. He was there working on a monograph about Holberg and was most certainly a first-class scholar. Laid back and yet ever vigilant, a sarcastic smile on his lips, and with a turn of phrase that could floor an opponent in an instant. While he was not without humour, his wit was invariably aimed at some hapless individual who suffered injury as a result.

'I can't find my knickers in the laundry. Has anyone seen them?' said Inger.

Lea tried not to laugh.

'They're sort of nappy. What's it called?' said Inger.

'Towelling,' someone said.

'Towelling, that's it!' said Inger.

Lea cracked up laughing, blushed, then cracked up again. Peter Borch-Jensen put his hand on hers and smiled indulgently. Inger immediately went livid and was suddenly speaking with an accent. Southern Jutland, Als perhaps. She was thin from too many carrots, too much pumpernickel and cheap Earl Grey.

'Can't you two keep your flirting to yourselves?'

She pronounced flirting as if with a *d*.

'It's quite a nice word said like that,' said Peter Borch-Jensen. 'Ravishingly innocent.'

We retired to the drawing room after dinner. Some of the furniture looked like it was from the time in the 1920s when the carpet and rug dealer Carl Wiinstedt placed the property at the disposal of Danish artists and scholars. An uncomfortable art deco chaise longue, a large Sigurd Swane canvas in a gold frame, the classic pieces of Danish modern, naturally. The heavy, leatherbound visitors' books in the corner were filled with decades' worth of finely slanting handwritten acknowledgements, watercolours depicting the cloister gardens, stirring odes to the view and the benefits of absorption. Lea and Peter Borch-Jensen danced in front of the sofa area while conversing. She was in a brown jersey dress and long purple boots and ought to have been sexy.

When they stopped she made a beeline and sat down next to me on the Børge Mogensen. She started off making some flattering comments about my stuff in the paper that she claimed to have read with pleasure, despite her lack of interest in gastronomy. I outlined my current project and she expressed admiration for my resolve. She had left the Academy of Fine Arts and confided in me that the sheer amount of discussion, the degree of *verbalising*, had been getting in the way of real art.

'So what are you doing now, artistically?' I said.

She smiled and lined up her sentences.

'While I was there I began to investigate the interaction between conative and non-verbal communication, in particular gestures. That's probably still my main theme.'

If I was supposed to understand fuck all, then I was getting along nicely.

'Could you be a bit more specific?' I said.

Apparently, she felt rather shameful about having to talk about her art.

'The conative function of language is to make us act or refrain from acting. An order is conative, a piece of legislation is conative, adverts, prayer, a flirt. I've spent a lot of time investigating how our gestures input into that kind of discourse.'

'So what sort of work is coming out of that?'

'I've been very much focused on hands.'

'You've been painting hands?'

'Mostly I've been doing video.'

'You mean videoing people's hands while they were being conative?'

'Yes, it sounds rather simple, doesn't it?'

'But that can't make you a living, can it?'

'If only you'd been there to say that at the academy.'

She buried her face in her hands.

'Have you got a gallery?'

'No, there's no money in video. It has to be for walls.'

'For walls?'

'Yes, something you can hang up. My work's far too geeky for galleries.'

'So you've never actually sold anything?'

'I've sold some stills from the videos, but not exactly at Tal R prices.'

Peter Borch-Jensen sat down with a generous grappa.

'Have you met my good friend Peter?' said Lea.

We shook hands, though neither of us wanted to.

'Peter's writing a monograph on Holberg.'

'And now I've included gesture in my analyses.'

Analys*es*! Ar-tic-u-la-tion!

Peter Borch-Jensen took a large gulp of grappa.

'Why do we drink?' he said.

'I drink to escape,' I said. 'How about you?'

Lea put her hand on Peter Borch-Jensen's arm.

'I don't believe Inger's lost her knickers at all,' she said.

'We wish Inger well,' said Peter Borch-Jensen. 'And not least that she may find her towelling knickers.'

'What does Inger do exactly?' I said.

'She's a painter. I thought you knew,' said Lea.

'She's a pest,' said Peter Borch-Jensen. 'It does require a certain amount of talent, I suppose. Which brings us back to good old Holberg.'

'Be nice, Peter Borch-Jensen,' said Lea, and stroked his arm.

'But I am *not* nice, and I should very much like to remain so.'

Lea took the glass out of Peter Borch-Jensen's hand. 'No more grappa for this gentleman!'

'Whatever would I do without you, dear Lea? Work, most likely.'

When the so-called punk poet Michael Strunge jumped out of that window in 1986, he took the last of the eighties with him. The rest became a parody. The painters and the poets parted company to pursue careers, the squatters' movement lost its imagination, and even Danish pop-rock, whose oddly backward rebellion had been to sing about absolutely nothing, had run out of trivialities. We looked half-heartedly for something to live for, and in the meantime we had binding, unimaginative sex in couples. Friends became boring when they were with their partners, and strange as it was, the solution seemed to be to get married, take out a mortgage and allow one's social life to be filled with other people who had been just as stupid and for that reason had now become one's neighbours. My friends turned into other people's neighbours.

L ea and Peter Borch-Jensen had been on a daytrip to Salerno and came strolling in to dinner arm in arm. Judging by their buoyant mood it had been the kind of day that would be fondly recalled from the confines of some future care home.

She giggled like a Japanese schoolgirl, and we were served a rustic regional pie in a copper pan with wild spinach, pine nuts and raisins.

'I still haven't found my knickers,' said Inger.

'I'm sorry, I wasn't laughing at you, Inger,' said Lea. 'It's Peter's new trousers. Hasn't anyone noticed them?'

'I thought my time in corduroy had passed,' said Peter Borch-Jensen.

'*I* noticed,' the cloister director said. 'They're very swish.'

'Well, stand up, then,' said Inger.

Peter Borch-Jensen got to his feet and did a twirl.

'They make his bum look good, don't they?' said Lea.

They were the kind with thick cord, cognac-coloured and with the additional refinement that the cord ran diagonally across the thigh.

'He looks like a bloody rent boy,' said Inger.

We had coffee in the drawing room, and the director asked about Salerno, thereby to receive a talk for her edification on all that was worth knowing about the region. Peter Borch-Jensen sharpened his knife: Salerno was Italy's net curtains, the duomo was a jumble sale of a dozen different styles, and the bell tower had no idea what it was doing there.

'The only interesting thing about Salerno is that Holberg visited the place in 1715. Was there a little brass plate on the wall outside number thirty on the Via Antonio Mazza? No, of course not, though there was a soft drinks machine, for want of anything better.'

'Don't you ever tire of all those old stories?' Inger said.

Peter Borch-Jensen took his time before smiling.

'There are no new stories,' he said. 'Only new people to tell the old ones to.'

I began to dread the sittings at dinner. Lea and Peter Borch-Jensen held their dumb audience in a vice of academic observations and clever puns, while I contributed nothing and excused myself with having come to San Cataldo to write, not to indulge in team-building with a group of dysfunctionals.

Many tyrannies have found nourishment in such cowardice.

Even the cloister director had become unsure of herself. She cleared her throat:

'I'm to say from Inger that the work she's been doing here will be on show tomorrow at four o'clock.'

Inger smiled like a beachball.

'Furthermore, we shall be receiving a new guest. She'll be in number eleven for a week. She, too, is a visual artist, with the rather striking name of Diana Kiss.'

I escaped outside on to the patio with a cup of robust coffee. The air was warm and aromatic, and Lea was wearing a rose-coloured cardigan.

'Peter and I were thinking of going to Ravello and having dinner there tomorrow night. Would you like to come?'

A decent person would of course have declined.

After Charlie was born Helene and I began to talk differently. For instance, she was annoyed by the fact that all the new *in-conversation* books in which well-known people exchanged banalities were selling a hundred times better than Sartre, and of course I could only agree.

On the other hand, she agreed with me that the Irma supermarket chain, in spite of its volume, was useless when it came to finding interesting wines. We agreed that *Once Upon a Time in America* was a tacky Scorsese pastiche, and that Woody Allen might fruitfully cut down on quantity, and if by any chance there wasn't a piece of theatre overdoing things even on the poster, a serious band whose lyrics were not utterly mundane, a TV host too full of himself, or some writer posing hand under chin, I still had my pet hates about the intellectual left and cocktail Buddhism, and Helene hers about the descent of Østerbro mothers into organic nappies and baking recipes, or the widespread degeneration of the language; all issues and heads-ups and touching base, etc. If we failed to reach consensus on these topics, we moved on to our circle of friends, which was a treasure trove: why did they go to couple therapy when the only thing he could think about was that it cost twenty-five kroner a minute? Why after ten years was she still threatening to leave him instead of finding a hobby? Why didn't she like him being funny, and why did he stop talking every time she came back from the buffet table? Why did he get so annoyed over her always pausing to pick flowers when it was one of the reasons he fell in love with her to begin with?

Every day I made the decision to turn things round and be positive instead, but then Helene would come home with minced beef, and what had they done to the quality since now you couldn't keep it from boiling in the pan?

Peter Borch-Jensen strutted about the Piazza del Vescovada with his hands behind his back and his semi-professional Canon slung over his shoulder. Lea was wearing a shawl, of all things.

Ravello was a trade centre back in the thirteenth century and we admired its imposing mansions, villas with soulful gardens and town houses with meticulously ornamented cornices. Wagner composed parts of his *Parsifal* there, and we *had to* see the Villa Rufolo before dinner. In the extensive park were a Moorish cloister, a tower and a multitude of flowers and shrubs in strict rows and formations. Dinner was taken at the Hotel Maria, whose restaurant looked to be of decent standard, though we kicked off with three rather pedestrian pasta dishes.

'Diana Kiss,' I said. 'The name rings a bell.'

'Diana Kiss is legendary,' said Lea.

'We used to love discussing her at the academy. She came to Copenhagen in about 2002, I think. She's Hungarian originally.'

'Sounds plausible,' said Peter Borch-Jensen. 'Kiss is a common name in Hungary. Much like Poulsen in Denmark.'

'All of a sudden she had a piece in a group exhibition at Galleri Moritz. That was when he was still on Herluf Trolles Gade. Kaspar Moritz is known to be a very fastidious gallerist, so there was quite a stir about him taking a completely unknown artist in, and Minna Lund bought the piece at preview.'

'Preview?' I said.

'The major galleries usually throw a dinner for collectors the day before an opening, where they're allowed to reserve. Selling something to Minna Lund is a mark of quality.'

'What does Diana Kiss do?' I said.

'She does tapestries, rather pornographic ones. I've never quite been able to fathom her work, but you have to respect the way she exploits her market.'

'How do you mean?'

'She makes use of strategies that in my part of the art world are totally no-go. For instance, she cultivates an image.'

'Which is what?'

'She wears men's clothes. Quite simple, really. But it works.'

'She sounds like what used to be called a pseudo,' said Peter Borch-Jensen.

'Well, that's been the subject of many a late-night discussion,' said Lea.

'So her stuff's crap, then?' I said.

'It's highly decorative,' said Lea.

'Did I hear a stag in the glen?' said Peter Borch-Jensen.

'She has tremendous aesthetic sense, and it's definitely a brilliant idea commercially to bring porn into weaving.'

'What was the piece she sold to Minna Lund?' I said.

'A girl with semen on her face.'

'That's quite sufficient for me, thank you,' said Peter Borch-Jensen.

'Her first solo had this tapestry of a man with semen in his beard. All the rich new buyers love her stuff, because it's so decorative and yet so *risqué*.'

There was no need for the air quotes.

'Diana Kiss has had four solos and sold the lot.'

The main was a sad lamb *al forno*. We ordered more wine.

'You're in for something when she gets here. She's *una bomba*!'

We strolled around the piazza; they threw caution to the wind and held hands.

I suddenly wanted to encourage them and so I asked about Holberg, whereupon Peter Borch-Jensen dominated the three-kilometre walk home with miscellaneous considerations of Holberg's divided self, on the one hand chancellor of the university, on the other a baron and manor owner. Only after two bottles of crude red on Lea's balcony did we seem to be approaching any kind of conclusion, and I actually thought Lea had gone to bed.

'Look what I found among my clothes!' she said.

In her hand was a pair of black towelling knickers.

'Have you got your camera, Peter?'

I had the most despicable hangover the next morning, the sort that comes of drinking without laughing.

I was sitting in the sunshine writing when Lea came out on to the patio. She nipped a leaf from a plant and began methodically to pull it apart.

'Peter's married.'

'Are you surprised?'

'Do you think he acts like he's married?'

'He's a long way from home, and you're beautiful and intelligent.'

'And young,' she said. 'Peter's sixty-four.'

Peter Borch-Jensen apparently had few scruples. He finally surfaced at lunchtime, prancing in with the *Herald Tribune* under his arm.

The director tapped a spoon against her glass.

'In case anyone had forgotten, we are all invited to a little opening today. Watercolours, am I right, Inger?'

'The view from the studio, as seen in all weather.'

'A cliffhanger, indeed,' said Peter Borch-Jensen.

The exhibition was in the music room and Inger had put some rouge on. Quite a lot, in fact. A serving girl came round with prosecco on a silver tray.

At the window was a Steinway piano, and on the walls hung twelve pieces of paper that dissolved into the whitewash. You had to step up close to notice there was anything there. Clouds, the sea and gulls in the sky were painted with such caution it all resembled a suicide by sedatives. No one knew quite what to do with themselves, and Inger was visibly affected by the fact that Lea and Peter Borch-Jensen were the only ones who hadn't come.

I was planning my retreat when I heard an unfamiliar voice.

The first thing I noticed was that it contained more than voices normally do. There was a way out in its melodious tone, the suggestion of other possibilities. Diana Kiss went up to everyone present in turn and introduced herself, carefully repeating each name as she moved on to the next.

It seemed as if she knew me, but the odd thing was I had absolutely no sense of her at all. I consider myself to be relatively analytical by nature, and yet I found myself unable to apply the usual references, for while Nordic in colour, with fair hair and bright blue eyes, she nonetheless seemed unmistakably exotic. Only her eyes were there to relate to, her words, her breathing and the broad smile that took up her entire face.

Oddly enough, I wasn't scared.

Danes think you need to be great in number to change anything:

you need an association with an agenda and a committee. Diana was on her own, and when Peter Borch-Jensen and Lea came striding in, she had already seized all the attention and passed it on to Inger's pale brushstrokes, the vines and the director's blouse. The oppressive atmosphere that had prevailed until Diana's arrival was completely eliminated in less than half an hour. Even Peter Borch-Jensen became accommodating and wanted to know all about Diana's passage by boat from Naples, and I noted how all the time he spoke to her she made sure to make eye contact with Lea and include her in the conversation.

Everyone talked at dinner, and the director had to ask for a moment's attention:

'In front of you, Diana, is a little sheet of paper on which you will find printed this evening's menu. As you can see, it says *Prosciutto e mozzarella di buffala*, Italian dry-cured ham with fresh mozzarella cheese from buffalo milk, and here at San Cataldo we are to be taken at our word. Fresh means made today. Tomorrow it will be used only for pizza.'

Diana was wide-eyed; she giggled with delight and clapped her hands.

Everyone brought to the drawing room whatever they had stashed in their rooms: dregs of grappa, inferior red and unfamiliar dessert wines. Peter Borch-Jensen had got stuck in during dinner, and his second day pissed made him look older.

Diana poured spumante from Franciacorta, and Lea had a single glass before getting to her feet, whispering something in Peter Borch-Jensen's ear and bidding the party goodnight with a finger kiss. Hardly had she closed the door behind her before her noble knight had settled down next to Diana and was offering her a grappa.

'So, you're Hungarian, I believe. The Hungarians have such an understanding of their own culture.'

He placed a hand on her arm.

'We Danes do best to keep a low profile if we should ever presume to be knowledgeable. Are you from Budapest?'

Inger was thrilled about the day and needed to express how happy she felt about San Cataldo and its marvellous atmosphere, and I caught enough to nod in the right places.

'What are you working on here?' said Diana.

'I'm writing about Holberg,' said Peter Borch-Jensen. 'He founded Danish literature. All of it!'

'I know Holberg,' said Diana.

'You know old Ludwig? How refreshing to meet a person of refinement!'

He was staring stiffly at her breasts. She had taken off her grey suit jacket and had on a thin white shirt with a narrow, navy blue tie.

'Have you ever been to Buenos Aires?' he asked.

She shook her head.

'Lea tells me your art is highly passionate.'

He paused for a second to savour the word's effect.

'I've always had a weakness for straightforward girls, Diana.'

Now he was doing intimate. Now he was doing frank.

'Academia is hell for a man like me. Buenos Aires would be more like it.'

Peter Borch-Jensen poured himself another grappa.

'How about some music? Anyone?'

He got to his feet and began to hum '*Køb bananer*'.

'Marvellous song,' he said.

'Kim Larsen, isn't it?' said Diana.

'You know him too? You're certainly assimilated, I'll say.'

He took her hand and swayed. His eyebrows bristled.

'If I were a young man, Diana Kiss, we two would be on the first plane to Buenos Aires, tucking into a pair of great, juicy steaks.'

He was holding both her hands.

'It's hot in Buenos Aires. Sweltering!'

He ventured a couple of tango steps, then lost his balance and careened sideways, cracking his head against the mahogany of the chaise longue on his descent to the floor. We got him laid out on the Børge Mogensen and he came to and started rattling on about a swimming pool when Lea poked her head round the door.

'Can you carry him along to mine?'

She stroked his brittle, grey hair.

Inger was talking shop with Diana when I got back from Lea's room, and I tried to engage in conversation with a thin professor who was researching the history of cartography. When Diana said good-night she took all the energy from the drawing room with her, and I masturbated myself to sleep, ejaculating over the centre spread of *Weekendavisen*'s book supplement. An interview with Amos Oz.

At breakfast the director said Diana had gone to Salerno. I skipped lunch and spent the day writing about Søren and Signe at the opening of U-matic, the legendary eighties club in Copenhagen. I rubbed Kiehl's into my skin from top to toe before dinner and selected a pair of navy blue Mads Nørgaard trousers, cigarette silhouette, a chunky sixties shirt in white cotton and the red cravat, endeavouring to leave my hair correspondingly casual.

'So what do you think of Salerno?' the director asked.

Diana talked about the cranes and the stacks of containers on the docks, the decrepit market behind the station and the thick black espresso she drank among toothless men in dirty striped shirts.

'Yes, it's a wonderfully uncomplicated place,' said Peter Borch-Jensen.

Inger raised a finger in the air.

'Did you want to say something, Inger?'

'Where did these come from?' she said, holding up the black towelling knickers.

'Oh, they turned up!' said the director.

'Who hung them on my door handle?'

'I did,' said Lea. 'They'd got mixed up with my own.'

'What have you lot been doing with them?' said Inger.

'A slight error in the laundry department, that's all,' said the director.

'They're private,' said Inger. 'My cunt lives in them!'

Lea started to laugh, but this time she stopped herself.

Diana had bought wines in Salerno and was generous with them in the drawing room. All were from the region's oldest grape, Falanghina, and she had even chosen the right wineries: Vinosia Campania and Feudi di San Gregorio. Intellectual leftists are reflexively sceptical of hedonism, but they set store by quality, and the fact of free alcohol of superior provenance added to the pleasant mood.

Someone put on *Moondance* by Van Morrison.

'Can I ask you something, Mikkel?' said Diana.

We went out on to the big balcony and shut the door. The sea could be heard down at Amalfi. A cockerel crowed, despite the hour.

'What's all that about her knickers?'

I told her about our photo session a couple of nights before, how Lea had stolen Inger's knickers and put them on for Peter Borch-Jensen, posing in schoolgirl postures as he issued gruff orders.

'They were the knickers Inger's cunt lived in,' said Diana.

She made it sound poetic.

I went to bed feeling bright about the future, with a vague sense that something new was about to emerge.

Diana waylaid Peter Borch-Jensen after breakfast.

'I noticed you've got a professional camera with you.'

'Rather inadequate, I'm afraid,' he said.

'I'm working on a new exhibition and need some photos of myself. Would you like to do me some, by any chance?'

'Peter's not a professional,' said Lea.

'I have spent a lifetime taking photographs,' said Peter Borch-Jensen.

'It's pure documentation, that's all,' said Diana.

They agreed to meet in the music room at three o'clock.

'Can anyone come and watch?' said Lea.

'I think I'm too shy for that,' said Diana.

At a quarter past three I got myself settled on the patio with Grethe Zahle's memoirs. At a quarter to four I was joined by Lea.

'Peter and I are supposed to be going to Amalfi before dinner,' she said.

She sat down on a marble bench and was too upset to hide the fact that she was biting her nails. At a quarter past four they emerged. Peter Borch-Jensen's face was flushed.

'Thanks for your help,' said Diana.

'I'll send them in an e-mail,' he said.

'If we're going to Amalfi, we'd best be on our way,' said Lea, and strode off.

'What about us, what should we do?' said Diana.

'I'm taking you to Capri,' I said.

I tried to get a grip on what was tangible. The deck of the boat under our feet, the sea, a gull. Two gulls. The man on the seat in front, and the goosepimples on his legs. Diana was in a mint-green polo shirt and mousy-coloured trousers.

'I've always wanted to see Capri,' she said.

At the beginning of the millennium I wrote a lengthy article from the island and possessed a treasure trove of decadent tales, and I longed to tell Diana a few of them over grilled tuna.

We put in at the Marina Grande and took in the smells. The taxis of Capri are all convertibles, and as we drove past the white villas from the twenties with succulent purple bouganvilleas cascading over their walls, I began quite unconsciously to hum 'Against All Odds'.

'Oh, I love that one,' she exclaimed, and began to sing out the words as we negotiated the hairpin bends.

The town of Capri is hardly bigger than a fishing village in Denmark, but the mindset is a different thing altogether. Every prominent fashion house you can think of has grabbed itself a share of the island's precious square metres: Gucci, Prada, Zegna, Roberto Cavalli, Dolce & Gabbana, Moschino. We went down to the Piazzetta, the very heart of the island, animated by the Chiesa di Santo Stefano and its domes, corrupted by the life that is played out around it.

The Gran Caffé is the finest and most azure blue of the establishments, and we ordered Campari and soda, served in thick, chunky glasses with ice and lemon.

A woman with white-wine legs in a pair of leopardskin trousers passed by. Her breasts were large and immovable, her lips inflated into a beak.

'Here they stood and recited their poetry a hundred years ago,' I said. 'Now it's for rubber ducks.'

'First come the artists, then comes the money,' said Diana.

'And then we come and yearn for what went before.'

'I don't,' said Diana.

We strolled along the Via Cammerelle, and I noticed a little poster in the window of a sandal-maker's shop. There was an opening for a photo exhibition taking place at five o'clock.

'I know where we can stay,' said Diana.

She stopped in front of the Hotel Quisisana. Three elderly well-heeled couples were sitting on the terrace, each staring dolefully at a point on the horizon.

'I don't think I can afford it,' I said.

'I've got money,' she said.

A waiter paused to adjust a sumptuous floral decoration in the hall.

'Can you tell me which room the author Norman Douglas used to stay in?' Diana said in English.

How on earth did she know about Norman Douglas?

The receptionist looked at her in bewilderment.

'Author? Just a moment.'

A great leather sofa of a gentleman came out from the back room. He was in no hurry.

'So, you are an admirer of the late Norman Douglas?'

Diana nodded and leaned her arm on the counter.

'Room 41,' he said. 'I will make you a fair *prize*.'

He turned and barked out an order. Room 41 was a suite.

'Norman Douglas must have sat writing there,' she said, indicating the mahogany desk.

I opened the bottle of Moët et Chandon that had been placed in an ice bucket on the meticulously carved bureau.

'How come you know about Norman Douglas?'

'Your article made me read him. *South Wind* is an amazing novel.'

I poured champagne into her glass.

'You read my article on Capri?'

She nodded and smiled.

'Let's go to the bar,' she said.

The interior was a shock of black and white, and after lengthy discussion with the bartender she ordered a Krug Vintage 1995 and asked to have it served by the pool.

'Why did you come to San Cataldo?' I asked.

She took her trousers off and lounged in her polo shirt and white knickers.

'I've got an exhibition in October.'

'Do you know what you're going to put in it?'

'I might tomorrow.'

The champagne tasted quite singularly of rye bread and befuddled rodent.

She took off her polo, and until then I hadn't even thought about her age.

'Let's have a swim,' she said, pulled off her knickers and loped off towards the pool. I kept my underpants on.

The bells of Chiesa di Santa Stefano wouldn't stop ringing.

The exhibition was in a former fruit warehouse and consisted of photographs of the *favelas* of Rio de Janeiro. Men in drag, gangsters, alluring children with grown-up eyes. Pain and tragedy all done up in the aesthetics of monochrome.

A short, stocky man wearing expensive glasses, short hair and an untucked pale blue shirt came towards us with two glasses of spumante. Maurizio the host was an antique dealer from Rome, but he and his partner Salvatore, the photographer whose exhibition it was,

loved their outlet on Capri, and as soon as autumn came they took off
to New York and their little apartment on Bleeker Street.

Diana was shown round by Salvatore. Maurizio looked up at me.

'She has that striking aura of beauty and disaster that makes a real
diva,' he said. Diana was in a pigeon-blue suit.

I felt uncomfortably ordinary in my white shirt.

'Where do people eat here?' I asked.

'For a real romantic dinner you *have* to visit the Hotel Punta
Tragara.'

He flipped open his mobile and booked us a table.

We walked along the cliff edge outside and I was too absorbed by it
all to notice anything other than that the air was heavy with the scent
of flowers, and the tiny lanterns of the ships that bobbed two hundred
metres below us. We were received by the owner himself, who showed
us to a table right at the edge. There was a pianist and we had grilled
swordfish and a Pinot Bianco.

I Faraglioni rose up out of the sea, three jagged rocks from the
postcards.

'What got you to Copenhagen anyway?'

'Bjarne Riis,' she said.

'Bjarne Riis?'

'When I was fifteen I happened to see the Tour de France stage
to Hautacam when Bjarne Riis left them for dead on the mountain. I
didn't know anything about cycling then, but I did realise that a man
from a small, flat country had conquered the entire world.'

'That day changed the way the Danes look at themselves,' I said.

Diana told me how her fascination with Bjarne Riis made her take
up cycling. She trained hard with the discipline of a professional and
won a silver medal in the Hungarian road-racing championships. At
the same time, she took lessons in Danish language and culture from
a Danish violinist living in Budapest, and in 2002 she got on a train
to Copenhagen.

'Did you know anyone?'

'The very first evening I met Ida-Marie at Bang & Jensen Bar.'

'Who's she?'

'She's a visual artist. We still share a studio together.'

'Are you a couple?'

'I'm not in couples.'

'Why not?'

'I'd rather be doing other things.'

We drank coffee and grappa on the piazzetta and watched and listened in as an English writer with long grey hair tried to win the attention of two spoiled daughters of wealthy Italian parentage. I tried to envisage Diana's record collection. With most people I could do this very easily. I knew for instance that Lea would at best have a bit of B52s, some mouldy trip hop, Portishead most likely, maybe an early Talking Heads, but the rest would almost certainly be cerebral and mood-oriented white music: Cocteau Twins, Jeff Buckley, Mazzy Star, Mozart's *Requiem* out of obligation, and everything by David Sylvian, including *Japan*. After you'd sussed someone's record collection, figuring out the rest of their life was easy: the minimalist furniture with arty undertones, the big industrial lighting, the books in well-ordered stacks on the floor, the futon, the poster of Before's LP cover, the black Arne Jacobsen Series 7 chairs at the little kitchen table, the sachets of miso soup, the green tea with the intrusive lemon, Red-Green Alliance, Swedish literature and shoes outside the door.

Helene's record collection was what you would call honest when I met her: *En underlig fisk* by Gnags was there still, Helmig's *Kære maskine*, a small selection of Tom Waits after she was taken in by the feel of *Down by Law*, the Beatmasters' 'Who's in the House', the twelve-inch maxi, Anne Linnet's *Kvindesind*, nicked off her mum, a decent *Best of Disco* containing a never-ending twelve-inch version of 'You Can Do It', Bach's *Goldberg Variations* played by Glenn Gould, the obligatory Satie and Keith Jarrett. A gigantic mahogany bookcase stuffed with volumes: Marcel Proust, the Russians, Mann, the Alexandria Quartet, poetry and an extensive selection of modern American, all books she had actually read, otherwise a bit of old teak marred by candle wax, black leather sofa aspiring to be design, IKEA bed with stains on the mattress, rice-paper lampshades, half-decent muesli, brown beans she never got round to soaking, blue Irma coffee, Socialist People's Party, and then, pretty much dovetailing with her becoming publicity director, the Social Liberal Party. You could keep your shoes on.

But in Diana's case I was completely blank.

'What sort of music are you listening to at the moment?' I asked.

'Do you know "Borderline"?' she said.

'You mean Madonna?'

'Yes, doesn't it put you in a very special mood?'

I sat with my grappa glass resting between my fingers, wondering whether she was stupid or simply insistent on pretending to be. I wondered in all seriousness whether the success she had achieved might merely be attributed to her being in a better mood than everyone else and attacking life as a hungry boar might take on a lunch buffet.

Diana had produced a little sketchpad, and the owner came with Campari and soda on the house, for she was so truly delightful, the way she sat there keeping the island's artistic myth alive. She had a diminutively underhung jaw and might have spoken with a lisp as a child. As such, she confirmed my theory that women displaying even a suggestion of underhung jaw very often possess extremely lively breasts.

She was twenty-seven, and I was fifteen years her senior.

I wondered whether Diana saw me as easy prey, that in six months' time she would be able to introduce her young artist friends to me, the man with the lined face and the silk cravat, and to be given an authentic little talk about life back in the day when the tables of the Byens Kro had been covered with brown-and-white checked tablecloths and Pat Boone ruled the jukebox.

She was flirty in a natural way, and possessed the kind of optimistic outlook that led her to believe everyone she met had only the best of intentions. By contrast, when she was working she took on a rather stern appearance.

'What are you drawing?' I asked.

'It's for you.'

She tore off the page and handed it to me. It was me. Leaping across a mountain range, arms outstretched.

'It looks like a women's poster my mother had on the wall. *Was there anything else?* That was the caption.'

We kissed in front of the sandal-maker's on the Via Camarelle, and it was not like any kiss I had ever received before.

I live to forget myself. When I watch a good film I don't think about whether the dialogue is strained or whether it was filmed on location. Music can have the same effect, but it's one thing to shed your ego, quite another to do so in the company of others, which is why musicians load their gear into old Hanomags to drive to Aalborg and come home again the next day with a miserable four hundred kroner in their pockets. They play for that briefest of moments in which togetherness lifts them up out of their egos and into something that is indefinably greater.

Sex is the most intimate and intense way in which to forget oneself in the company of others, and I don't know whether it was because of Diana's own singular ability to transcend reality, or whether it was a state of mind we managed to attain together, but I was absolutely out of myself from the word go.

I woke up as she was stepping out of her bath, and I had difficulty connecting the sight of her with my own life. The way she swung her hips. Her waist, her long calves and muscular thighs. If it hadn't been for the smell I would have been completely gone. We smelled of meat together. Of open muscle and blood.

Two waiters knocked on the door and rolled in a trolley. They got our breakfast ready – grapefruit juice, a variety of hams, omelette, fresh-baked bread, fruit and great crimson tomatoes, *machiatto* with thick brown foam. Diana bit off half a tomato and kissed me with her mouth full; the other half she pressed down on my bell-end. With a cool slice of mozzarella on each side of my cock, she began to wank me off, her soft breasts brushing against my balls, and I came so intensely my legs lost all feeling. The sun shone down on to the bed, and we lay naked for half an hour, eating and talking about whatever came to mind.

'I need to check and see if Peter e-mailed me those photos,' she said.

She was allowed to use the manager's computer, and there were six e-mails with photos from Peter Borch-Jensen. Diana popped her head out of the door to make sure we were on our own before clicking on the first image.

A close-up of her cunt appeared on the screen. It was so proximate and so sharply in focus you could see every fold. She opened one of the final images, and the setting was the same, but whereas in the first photo her cunt had been closed and chaste, in the second it was open and wet.

She leaned back in the expensive leather swivel chair, looked at me and laughed until tears came out of her eyes.

We met Maurizio and Salvatore down at the Marina Grande at one o'clock.

The boat was relatively small and oblong with a chugging engine, and the deck was one big towelling mattress. We put out of the harbour and sailed for a quarter of an hour or so. Maurizio dropped anchor at a lagoon. I put my head against Diana and she stroked my hair gently.

Maurizio unpacked the cooler box.

Fresh mozzarella, white wine, bread, olives, ham and tomatoes.

'This is Capri,' he said. 'Do whatever you want. Swim! Eat! Sleep!'

The water was still, clear and deep. I jumped, and all sound disappeared.

'Why do people build bridges?'

Diana's flatmate, Ida-Marie, slouched in the chair in her black Ramones T-shirt, her long legs in skinny jeans. She had grown up in the so-called White Houses in the Frederiksberg district, a neighbourhood populated by Volvo-driving child psychologists and professors, and since she was too lazy to embark on any serious course of education, she took the easy way out and became an artist. She painted, so they said, souls: portraits of her friends' ethereal substance.

The apartment was a former plumber's depot. The place consisted of two rooms and Ida-Marie's space was off limits. She locked her door behind her when she came home. Diana's area was about a hundred and fifty square metres. The rows of steel shelving on the walls had once been home to pumps, thermostats and taps of stainless steel, but Diana had transformed them into a kind of mantelpiece gone mad, a display of scowling elves, champagne glasses, leather masks, books, disturbing photographs, little superheroes of plastic, and chunky candles. When the candles were lit you didn't see the tired grey-green lino on the floor, the crumbling plaster on the walls or the accumulated junk in the corners; an ugly teddy bear cut out of plywood, some rusty iron piping, a bright green bass drum, crap salvaged from skips. In the midst of it all was a square pillar with faces on it. Forty-one Polaroids of all her buyers. Minna Lund was there eleven times over, the same unrelenting gaze.

Along the big windows facing the rear courtyard of Lyrskovgade she had set up an industrial kitchen with steel counters and two enormous gas burners. At the far end, a thick velvet drape in midnight blue hung down from the ceiling and served as a partition behind which was her double bed and the racks containing her suits and shirts, arranged according to colour. The focal point of the room was the six-metre-long table with a laminated grey surface; the chairs had been salvaged from a school, and her handmade mint-green racing bike stood in a frame by the door.

Diana worked from the moment she woke up, consuming an apple or the odd carrot along the way, but never putting down her stick of charcoal. Peter Borch-Jensen's sharp photos were transformed into pitch-black drawings that lay smouldering on the table, until she decided the day was over, arranged them in order and placed them in folders. I wrote while lying in bed with the computer in my lap; the sounds from the street didn't bother me, and whenever I went over to the table to butter a hunk of bread I would look across at her and dwell upon the expressiveness of her neck.

'What's so attractive about the other side of the bridge?' Ida-Marie continued.

'What bridge?' said Diana.

'Any bridge. That's what I don't get. Why can't people just stay where they are?'

'Let's leave that for another day,' said Diana, getting to her feet and starting to clear the table. She took Ida-Marie's teacup too.

'I've got to present my new work to Moritz in an hour.'

She picked up the pile of drawings.

'Mind if I have a look?' said Ida-Marie.

Diana thought for a second, then handed her two off the top of the pile.

'Ah, the cunt,' said Ida-Marie.

'I've thought about keeping the tapestries black and white,' said Diana.

'Are you pleased with them?'

'I've always had confidence in my work,' said Diana.

'I'm not sure this time.'

They exchanged glances for about half a minute, then kissed each other goodbye on the mouth. Ida-Marie turned in the doorway.

'Make sure Moritz pays you money up front. I can't afford to keep laying out.'

'How much do I owe?'

'For three months. Twenty-four thousand nine hundred.'

'You'll have it tomorrow, darling.'

Diana selected nine drawings and placed them carefully on the table.

As she bent forward, her light blue shirt rode up, and that was all it took. My dick was red and deformed from all our shagging and so chronically being kept on alert. Of course it was animating with all that soft, elastic skin, but the way the darkness enveloped us was the most important thing. The rush of it.

With Diana I didn't have to behave. I'd never understood the parties Helene and I went to every other weekend. Twenty couples either heading for divorce, or else caring so little they could no longer be bothered to argue. All that talk about timber decking and food; women whispering about their problems after dinner or discussing the price of kids' clothing while their perspiring, alcohol-steeped men sneaked themselves another beer.

I only used the flat on Klerkegade when it was my turn to have Charlie, and my Burberry trench coat mouldered on its hook there. I took to wearing the army-green college jacket Diana had found in Naples.

On the table were nine almost identical drawings of her cunt. Labia closed, labia slightly open, clitoris at different stages of excitement. The ninth stuck out from all the rest: from the lower curve of her cunt-opening a droplet of semen dangled, about to descend and trickle down her inner thigh.

Sune, the wine merchant, stood in the doorway in his cloth cap, with two cases of spumante.

'You've got cunts on your table!' he said.

'Are they any good?' said Diana. 'The cunts.'

'Better, they're gorgeous.'

He looked up at me.

'So your jizz is going to be decorating the walls of Galleri Moritz, is it, Vallin?'

'It's not my jizz.'

'Whose is it, then?'

'An associate professor of Danish literature,' I said. 'He's writing a monograph about Holberg.'

'He photographed my cunt,' said Diana.

'And got paid in kind?'

'His cock was surprisingly handsome,' she said.

'Not to change the subject, but I'm afraid you've got to pay this time.'

'I'm getting an advance from Moritz today,' she said.

Sune unfolded an order sheet.

'It's nearly eight thousand now.'

A woman came staggering in, drunk and on the brink of blackout. She clung to the pillar and spelled her way through the most proximate visual stimuli: floor, window, lamp.

Lisa was in her late twenties; her hair was cut short in a 1920s pageboy style, and her teeth were remarkably small and uniform. It would have been inaccurate to call her Diana's friend, friend being another category with which Diana did not operate, but it was a fact that they saw each other often and enjoyed some form of interdependence. I had met Lisa twice, and she reminded me of a trip across the FM band: dance music, debate, opera, local radio. Moods that came and went.

It wasn't hard to imagine where she was headed if she carried on like this: a small drinking establishment in the old part of town, a place with frosted windows, moderately good jazz and the house white, where now and then the odd fashion student would happen by and declare that she, Lisa Zöllner, had been their inspiration when applying to the school, and they would invite her out to dinner, an invitation that would be declined with increasingly slurred speech, because she would rather stay put on the round leather seat of her bar stool and forget that she had ever been worth looking up to.

But it had yet to go wrong for Lisa. In fact, it could hardly have been going better. The media had pronounced her to be the decade's greatest talent, and though her own brand collapsed owing to irregularities in the accounting she remained out on her own and the air was thick with rumours about her being appointed new head designer for Jill Sander or Chloé, but until that happened she was her own model.

She stood swaying in her clingy, asymmetrical black dress and had finally recognised the place and us, when a square-built man came in and joined her.

He had bandy legs and was extremely short, in suit trousers of uninteresting cut, black shirt, black windcheater with leather patches on the elbows, over-designed glasses and cropped, football hair.

'This is Stig,' said Lisa.

'Stig Nissen,' he said, and shook hands.

'And there we have the cunts!' he said.

Diana got busy putting them back.

'I'm from Brande,' said Stig. 'The town with all the murals, that's us.'

'We don't know Brande,' I said.

'Of course not, what would you be wanting there when you can mooch around here in your bare arse with a glass of red, in a proper artist's pad. *Spitzenklasse*, that is!'

'We don't mean to be impolite,' said Diana. 'But my gallerist will be here soon, and I haven't spoken to him for quite a while.'

Stig Nissen produced a bottle of Dom Perignon from his black leather briefcase.

'I've got a proposal for you, Diana. Have we time for a glass?'

Diana took champagne glasses from the plumber's shelving.

'I've got these two brands: *Leader of the Pack* for those with knobs, *Cheerleader* for those without. And they're doing so well I have to keep rubbing my eyes. We just opened store number two hundred. Two floors on Ginza Street in Tokyo, escalator, the works. At this very second my people are handing jeans and sweatshirts over counters in Paris, Rome, Barcelona, Munich and London, and when we're all snuggled up in bed they're slogging away in Sydney, Kuala Lumpur, Singapore and Beijing.'

I knew all about his rubbish clothes. Stig Nissen had made a fortune fucking the life out of fine, all-American tradition. Thin sweatshirts in lifeless colours, shapeless T-shirts with ghastly prints, jeans of despicable cut and horrendous back pockets.

'I've made so much money I could float about in an indoor pool and stuff myself with caviar from morning till night, but I'd rather be doing something worthwhile!'

He paused briefly for effect and looked about.

'I've booked the suite at Hotel Petri, and by the time I get back to Jutland on Monday I'll have my dream team, and then there'll be only one way forward and that's forward!'

'Towards what?' said Diana.

'I'm going to create Denmark's first high-fashion brand. Giant flagship on Østergade opening in time for fashion week, sexy gear in the right quality. We want tits and arse, but with edge and style. Lisa is finally getting the opportunity to show us what she's made of. No holds barred!'

Lisa hiccupped and blinked slowly.

'I've just bought an apartment in Prenzlauer Berg,' said Stig Nissen. 'Think Berlin! Raw and artistic, and what we need is a house artist. Lisa suggested you straight away, Diana. What do you say, are you in?'

Diana said nothing.

'Nothing wrong with the money, is there, Lisa?' said Stig.

Lisa reached for the champagne.

'Nikolaj Krogh's agreed to do the interior,' Stig went on.

I couldn't see it. Nikolaj Krogh was a man of impeccable taste and involved himself only in first-rate ventures.

'I'd like to invite you for a bite to eat on Saturday,' said Stig Nissen.

'Come,' said Lisa. 'Please, please!'

'Can we call you back in the morning?' I said.

'I was thinking of Noma,' said Stig.

'Have you booked a table?' I asked. 'It's impossible these days.'

'But you know them, don't you, Mikkel?' said Diana.

Why was she warming to this?

'You're on the Berlin bus, too, Mikkel,' said Stig. 'What does a bloke like you do anyway?'

'I write,' I said.

'And you know everyone who's anyone in this little goldfish bowl, I bet? Wait a minute, I've got an idea. We launch on the seventh of August. How about you coming over to Brande and telling us bumpkins a bit about what it's like to be a front-of-the-bus Copenhagener these days? Fifteen large for an hour's natter. What do you say?'

I was just about to open my mouth when there was a knock on the door.

Kaspar Moritz was in his mid-thirties, his curly blond hair was in a rockabilly cut, and his cobalt-blue jacket clung to his boyish torso. Tight jeans, moderately baggy-arsed, a T-shirt with some neon-coloured print and black clown shoes. Big black glasses.

Stig Nissen clasped his hand.

'You look like the sort of man I'd give the sack. Did you go to university?'

'History of ideas and civilisation studies,' said Moritz.

'What did I tell you!' said Stig Nissen. 'I'm from Jutland.'

'Is that a mental condition?' said Moritz.

'He's quick, this lad!'

'Kaspar's my gallerist,' said Diana.

'In that case he's a shopkeeper like your Uncle Nissen here.'

It wasn't what Moritz would have said.

'Who the fuck's Stig Nissen?' said Moritz. We were seated at the low tables of the Tokyo restaurant, eating udon noodles. Kaspar Moritz could easily have been from Virum or some other safe middle-class suburb. He didn't bat an eyelid when Diana produced her drawings, and now he was talking practicalities.

Diana had her tapestries woven in Vietnam and the drawings had to be finished and ready within the fortnight if the weavers in Hanoi were to have the work done by October.

'Is there any one of these drawings you're unsure about?' he said.

'The one with the semen,' said Diana.

'I'll get them to do that one first,' said Moritz.

He made a note in his moleskin. Neat handwriting, of course.

'Carlsberg Kunsthal opens in November and they're kicking off with a big women's exhibition. We need to get you in there,' he said.

'Women? Couldn't they have done dwarves or spastics instead?' Diana said.

'Rumour has it they've got Gillian Wearing in, which will make an impact on the ArtFacts ranking.'

'What's that?' I said.

'ArtFacts compiles a list ranking all the artists in the world according to a very intricate points system,' said Moritz. 'Participating in a group exhibition with a highly ranked artist gets you good points.'

'Who's curating?' said Diana.

'Nynne Willer, Charlotte Breum and a girl who does video, Lea Winther Jensen.'

'She hates me.'

'Why?'

'I don't want to talk about it while we're eating.'

He had *agedashi dofu* for his main. We had *sukiyaki*.

'I need a small advance,' said Diana.

'I'd like to purchase one of the tapestries up front,' he said.

'Forty thousand's not enough,' said Diana.

'Forty-five,' said Moritz. 'We'll put them up at ninety.'

'It's the summer,' said Diana.

'People are talking crisis,' said Moritz. 'I need to step carefully.'

'You don't believe in my cunts!'

'Of course I do, they'll sell.'

'But you don't like them.'

'I'd been hoping for a surprise.'

'Such as?'

'Something surprising.'

'Aren't you supposed to encourage me, Kaspar?'

'I'm behind you one hundred per cent, Diana. But you did ask, and I'm thinking this is your fifth solo and you're doing pornographic tapestries as you've done four times already.'

It was the first time I had seen Diana in a bad mood. She was silent all the way to Jolene's, and it annoyed her that Moritz tagged along when he so obviously would rather be at home tidying up his desk.

We arrived in the middle of a gig and the audience listened intently as only architecture students can. The women had dresses on over their trousers and the men wouldn't have known what to do on a football pitch. There was a cello, the girl singer had a diagonal fringe and a guy fluttered his hands at some congas. The song was about getting lost in Husum and finding something completely other than a house, and it was all so twee and irrelevant.

Diana ordered three Elephant Beers with aquavit chasers, and Moritz sipped. Later, I found out he was actually from Lejre and had grown up in a lefty cult, all of which at least explained why he was so literal. I felt a clumsy hand on my shoulder.

'Why am I not surprised, Vallin, as soon as there's a bit of art pop going on!'

It was Levinsen, wearing a closely trimmed beard, lumberjack shirt and Acne jeans.

He hugged the life out of me.

'Can I get you all something?' he said.

'We're fine, thanks,' said Moritz.

'Who are you?' said Diana.

'Morten from Aarhus,' he said. 'Do you like the music?'

'No. What do you do, Morten?'

'Ask your husband.'

'I haven't got a husband.'

'I'm in the same business as Kaspar Moritz. Major respect for your work, Kaspar! My gallery's called Levinsen Open.'

'What are you here for?' said Diana.

'The music.'

'I don't know who you are, but you're lying.'

Moritz pulled Diana aside before he left.

'I'm not asking what that Stig guy was doing at your studio, but promise me you'll stay away from him, Diana.'

Levinsen laid his jacket on the bar stool.

'How about welcoming the summer in,' he said, and ordered a bottle of spumante, and with it all the rituals. The glasses, the ice bucket. The cork popped and Diana couldn't help but join us in the toast.

'Do you mind if I heap some praise on you, Diana?' he said, and then seemed oddly shifting in mood. First he stared into the air for a bit, searchingly, then appeared almost submissive before a look of fanatical madness lit up his eyes and he cracked a smile.

'Listen,' he said. 'I love the way you've reinvented tapestry, and I'm just totally owned by your presence.'

'You're owned by my presence?'

'Have you ever noticed how much everyone at a Vi opening always looks the same?'

'They look like you,' she said.

He glanced up and down her pin-striped suit.

'A lot of people get confused about your image. They see the suits, but what they don't get is that the clothes are just the aesthetic expression of an attitude. You are so immensely important to the Copenhagen art scene, Diana Kiss. You generate latitude. All of a sudden we glimpse the sky.'

'I can tell you're from somewhere else,' said Diana.

'I'm way over the top,' he said. 'Everyone says so.'

It annoyed me somewhat that it was Levinsen who got Diana back into a good mood, and on the pretext of getting into the music I moved up closer to the stage. Miss Diagonal Fringe had been clapped back for an encore. 'Letter from Uncle Bilegger', a song about her schizophrenic uncle and his poetically distorted outlook.

When I returned, Levinsen was filling Diana in on his open marriage.

'She likes girls. And so do I.'

'How do you actually go about it?' said Diana.

'We throw small parties for friends. Good food, nice wine. People are dressed up and we hand out dance cards.'

'What if no one puts any names down?'

'That's not an issue I've run into.'

'So they like you, these wives?'

He chewed his lip.

'They're wild about my wicked Jew cock.'

Diana recoiled on her bar stool. Levinsen shrugged and emptied his glass.

'Anyway, I'm off home for a shag. Besides, I've got a ZeZe meeting in the morning.'

'It was fun meeting you,' said Diana, and then they were hugging too.

On the way home we passed by Chicky Grill.

'You're not the kind who gets jealous, are you?' she said.

A sign in the window said they had rolled pork loin on Thursdays.

'No, I'm not,' I said.

We walked along Sønder Boulevard and I wasn't jealous, but I did start wondering about the question.

When she was a teenager, my friend Clara had grasped that her legs were her best asset, and ever since it had been my job to make sure she remembered this, and talk her down whenever she tried to wriggle into a pair of jeans that turned her arse into a flatscreen, or tell her that a full orange skirt that cut her off at the shins didn't suit her any better just because it was Marni with fifty per cent off.

This time Clara ended up with a mini, and I assured her she was charting new waters by this time choosing navy blue over black. Afterwards we went up to Illum's cafeteria, as we always did, and she started asking me about Diana.

'What's her body like?' she asked. 'Boobs first!'

'Round and firm. I've never seen any as gorgeous.'

'She's got a good bum, though, hasn't she? Did she used to be a dancer?'

'A bike rider. Road racing.'

Clara ignored this information so I wouldn't feel embarrassed by it.

'She's got nice eyes and a really lovely smile,' she said. 'I was looking at some photos of her. Her jaw's ever so slightly underhung, isn't it?'

'Just a hint,' I said. 'It's sexy.'

'And she's from Hungary, isn't she? Does she talk circus language?'

'She speaks perfectly fluent Danish.'

'It's amazing how kids learn a language so easily, isn't it?'

'I don't think about her age.'

'You didn't laugh!'

'It wasn't funny.'

Clara leaned back and studied me.

'Are her parents artists too?'

'We don't talk about the past,' I said.

'What do you talk about, then? What did you talk about this morning, for instance?'

I shouldn't have been telling her.

'We talked about something I've been thinking about for quite a while,' I said.

'Okay, explain.'

'It goes back to the time I played samba in a carnival group.'

She started to laugh and apologised profusely.

'We played these long sessions where we used to play the same figures over and over, and I discovered you stopped hearing your own rhythm in isolation. You listened to the bigger pattern.'

'That's what they call ensemble,' she said.

'But there's more to it than that,' I said. 'The progression of the day, the seasons, birth and death. Take a leaf off a tree and look at it. It's all patterns and repetition. Everything is rhythm.'

'So you were all cosmic over your miso soup?'

'Rice and beans,' I said.

Clara was normally a refined eater, but now she was shovelling roast pork into her gob at an astonishing pace. A dribble of gravy ran down her chin. She put her cutlery down.

'I shouldn't say this, but it worries me that my best friend has found a girlfriend who's made him lose his sense of humour.'

'We're not a couple,' I said.

'Have you started skateboarding as well?'

'I've stopped listening to "Billie Jean" anymore, Clara, is that okay?'

'What does it mean, anyway, you're not a couple?'

'I'm not sure yet. We've only been together a month.'

'It's not you at all, Mikkel.'

'That's for me to decide.'

'She's going to be leading you round the ring. She already is.'

'I think the way we're together is going to get more and more common.'

'You're in love, and that's wonderful. But everything has its time.'

'How long does it last, being in love?' I said.

'Actually, there are strict rules about that: six months.'

'October,' I said. 'What if we're still together?'

'Then I really will be worried.'

It was hard to find an objection to my being fired from the newspaper, the only one being, perhaps, that it came a couple of years too late.

It happened last November, and it was supposed to have been just another food write-up. I wanted to find out whether Indian Corner, Copenhagen's best Indian restaurant of the nineties, could still deliver a chicken jalfrezi, but it was one of those balmy nights in late summer, the kind that need handling with care and attention, and so I went by way of the floating bar at Christianshavns Bådudlejning and sat down at the bulwark with Stendahl's *Walks in Rome* and a ginger ale.

I ran into Kreuzmann, who I hadn't seen since a disastrous dinner in Taarbæk, and I knew from Clara that the evening had proved decisive for his and Claudia's divorce. Now here he was, broad as a pillar box in an untucked, short-sleeved shirt, the trousers of one of his old business suits, and bare feet in white Adidas.

'Have a seat,' I said, pulling up a café chair.

'If you ask how I'm doing, I'll headbutt you,' he said.

'How was your yoga class today?' I said.

He took my ginger ale and poured it in the canal.

'I want to have so much to drink I won't be able to feel my legs.'

He went up to the bar and was audibly stroppy about the wine menu for some time before returning with a bottle of white and pouring a couple of glasses like he was Russian.

'Are you with me, Vallin? All the way?'

We hugged, and he smelled of sweat and old newspaper.

He only used to drink with Botox Barbies and men in box-fresh white shirts; now he wanted to go on to Café Stærkodder. Elephant Beer and Jägermeister, naturally, the so-called safari suit.

He was stuck in the aftermath of ten years of fatal decision-making and was desperate to unload the lot. People he'd stabbed in the back, tarts he'd shagged while expensively out of his head, all the foie gras he'd wolfed down without ever pausing to taste. Kreuzmann is a man of conscience, with a singular ability to ignore the fact.

'Do you realise how cold a place the world is, Vallin?'

I reckoned I did.

'Of course you don't, you great knobhead. I can tell just by the way you're sitting.'

I was sitting with my legs crossed, as one does if one happens to be the kind of guy who stayed behind with the girls while the others went off climbing tall trees.

'You wouldn't even make the effort to get wrecked, Vallin.'

At some point a full bottle of Nordsøolie appeared on the table, and from then on things went rather awry; we danced to *Ensomhedens Gade nr. 9* with the fantastic horn arrangement and found ourselves back in the seventies, with Bent Jadig and Perry Knudsen and brilliant, utterly uncomprising drinking, and we made friends with Preben, who had worked on the Norway boat.

We drank so fiercely we transcended intoxication.

'Claudia knew what she was getting into, of course she did,' said Kreuzmann. 'Have I ever told you about our first date?'

He knew perfectly well he had.

'I took her out for a meal at Sankt Gertruds Kloster. That place was really the shit in 1986, as you well know. All caviar and salmon, and steaks in red-wine sauce, and of course I'd got the Boss suit on with the white shirt and the floral tie from London House. Claudia saw herself as a bit of a bohemian, so she was like seriously down about Strunge's death, but you know me. I didn't even know who Michael Strunge was until you could get him on a bedspread from IKEA, did I? Anyway, I told her I'd got plans for the two of us, big house and two kids, which understandably she was a bit taken aback about, seeing as how it was only the second time we'd met. But I was really going for it in those days, so when I realised part of the problem was the yuppie togs, I took them all off in front of her and ended up sitting there in the buff. How about that, then?'

We had a good long laugh. He deserved it.

'I've always been up front, Vallin, you've got to give me that, haven't you? What you see is what you get, do you know what I mean? So how, after twenty-two years, she can get the idea she'd come away with a pig in a poke, it's beyond me. She had *nothing but* high-quality pig!'

I patted the reviewer's notebook in my pocket.

'Indian Corner?' said Kreuzmann. 'No more curry, Vallin. We need to reach up into the light. It's Noma tonight. Can you feel it?'

I called up the restaurant manager, Anders.

'Just a quick stop-off at Taarbæk first.'

I tumbled into the back seat of the cab like a sack of potatoes with no questions asked. The night was dictating its own terms anyway.

At Bellevue people sat around their barbecues in the sand and I didn't suspect a thing until we turned up on Taarbækdalsvej.

Kreuzmann asked the driver to wait and got out in front of the big house that had been his home for eighteen years. Was that Claudia at the kitchen window? She'd lost weight and her hair was cut short and dyed red.

'Are we going inside to your family?'

'No, I just need to sort something out about Oliver's football trainer.'

He pulled the bottle of Nordsøolie out of his inside pocket, and just as we'd each knocked back a slug, Oliver came round the corner. He was with this pretty-looking guy of about thirty, medium-length wavy hair, local yachting teint, swaying gait. Oliver came running up to his dad, and the black taxi idled.

'Have you moved in?' said Kreuzmann.

'I need a word,' said the guy. 'Only not like this.'

'I bought that house for my family,' said Kreuzmann.

Oliver was standing two metres away.

'You used to be polite enough to only come creeping at night,' said Kreuzmann. 'But now it's all in broad daylight, I see.'

He raised his voice so much I wondered whether I ought to step in.

'Public knowledge now, is it? That you're shagging my wife?'

Claudia opened the kitchen window and looked out.

The flat-hander Kreuzmann delivered to the man's cheek was in the manner of a classic tennis forehand and shifted him a metre to the side. The one that followed sent him head first into the bushes. Through the taxi's rear window I could see Claudia come running. Oliver stood motionless.

'It's called a bitch slap, in case you were wondering,' said Kreuzmann. 'Drive!'

I was having second thoughts as we walked in through the door of Noma. The purposeful movements of the waiters across the floor, the low hum of discreet conversation. If it hadn't been for the interior

I would probably have turned around and left. The ancient floor-boards, the great ceiling joists of variegated patinas, a mellow white relief, the windows facing the harbour, N.O. Møller's model 62 chairs in stained south-German oak.

Restaurant manager Anders winked and led us down to the far corner.

At the neighbouring table sat two blondes, trying to look like they came here often. Kreuzmann ordered a bottle of champagne from Selosse and we had snacks with an absolutely stupendous creamy dressing reminiscent of mayonnaise. It was all looking up again.

I leaned over the table.

'So it's true, then, that businessmen visit tarts?'

'A man needs a bit of life,' said Kreuzmann.

'Have you been with any?'

'Of course I have! Loads.'

'And you've never had any scruples about it?'

'Why should I?'

'Because they sell their bodies.'

'All women do, don't they?'

'Helene didn't sell her body to me.'

'You didn't have any money.'

Kreuzmann asked for two more champagne glasses.

'Fancy a taste, girls?'

Monique was pretty in a business college kind of way. Full-cheeked, reasonably tanned, affected in gesture, firm breasts under a black blouse. Emilie was tall and shapely, with eyes like an old-fashioned film star, and held her glass by the stem as if it came naturally. She barely said a word, which was due either to healthy scepticism or basic damage control.

The waiter was about to get his palaver started about the first course, but Kreuzmann raised his hand.

'I prefer to speak to my friend here than listen to someone go on about beach weeds and rearing lambs in Lapland. There's a fucking great wad of tips in this pocket, but every word you say is going to cost you twenty.'

And with that he ordered a bottle of Meursault.

Monique got to her feet to take a photo of the snack set-up from above. Her figure was surprisingly delicate, considering the fullness of her cheeks.

'I'm going to shag her in the bogs,' said Kreuzmann.

I fumbled the greasy black notebook out of my inside pocket and began to catch up on the smoked quail eggs, the numerous cereals, flavoured lard with pumpkin seeds and savoury *æbleskiver* with pork. I was on thin ice, partly because I was now drunk for the second time that evening, partly because the raw ingredients and taste of the menu here were miles away from the Mediterranean flavours I usually wrote about.

'Did you notice the dip?' said Monique. 'It wasn't just a cold hollandaise. It was egg yolk, caper juice, chicken stock, boiled carrot, rapeseed oil and roasted peanut oil.'

'Are you a chef?'

'I blog about food,' she said.

'Are you going to be taking photos of all the courses?'

'I'm very thorough in what I do,' she said.

'Do you think I could borrow your photos and your notes?'

'I'll e-mail it all to you in the morning.'

'Won't you join us, girls?' said Kreuzmann.

He and Monique were visibly in agreement as to how their acquaintance was to develop, and the mood was approaching *après-ski*.

The chef came to present the main courses. His sleeves were meticulously rolled up in order to display his sculpted triceps, he had a bright-yellow mohican and old-school tattoos of naked girls and ships.

He crouched down and told the girls all about the reindeer.

'Yes, all right, Tarzan,' said Kreuzmann, and put a twenty on the table. 'Here, get yourself a tanning session and get back to your pots and pans.'

For a brief moment, the guy considered laying his job on the line, but thought better of it.

'Now, let's have some Jura,' said Kreuzmann.

And that was where it all went wrong. At that exact moment.

Flavour can do irreparable damage, and *vin jaune* from the Côtes du Jura is a wine in conflict with itself. On the one hand seductively sherry-like in body, on the other coldly dismissive with all its bitter orange, vanilla and pine. The disharmony sent a tingle down my spine and made the hairs on my arms stand to attention. I have no idea how I got home or why I woke up with two bruised ribs.

The last thing I remember is Kreuzmann marching back from the loos, foaming at the mouth and with Monique creeping along behind him.

'Filthy bitch,' he said. 'You go out to the bogs for a bit of fanny and she wants it up the arse. What the hell is it with young girls these days?'

The next morning, Monique sent an e-mail to Peter, my editor, revealing to him the details of how I did my job. By the end of that day, I was unemployed.

Tonight would be the first time I'd gone back to Noma since then, and though I'd spent the afternoon in my local bar, the Borgerkroen, writing and drinking, I hadn't drunk enough to stop me feeling nervous. Diana laced her fingers through mine as we sat in the back seat of the taxi on the way there. 'It's so romantic, you drinking during the day,' she said. I haven't mentioned Diana's bimbo side. It was classically done, wide eyes and a pout, and as far as I could figure, what triggered it was uncertainty. The odd thing is that it worked.

'I think you should be careful about Stig,' I said.

She looked down at the floor.

'I'm really looking forward to meeting your friends.'

'No one calls Nikolaj Krogh and Mille friends.'

The atmosphere at Noma had intensified since my last visit. The waiters were as intensely focused as chess players and the clientele were now European master chefs, foodies from all over the world and powerful business people.

Nikolaj Krogh was on his own at the table, and maybe I saw him with Diana's eyes, but it was striking how handsome he was: long legs and broad shoulders; he looked a bit like an an Italian racing driver with his thick, deliriously wavy hair, and pianist's hands. The best of all worlds, impeccable taste. His clothes were expensive, discreet and modern. And yet he exuded about as much life as half a bag of flour left behind in the cupboard of a summer cabin.

Mille wasn't feeling well, he explained, and the lie suited him.

Diana the bimbo besieged him with flattering questions and encouraged him to hold forth, and after he'd delivered the story of how his signature chair, the Black Egg, had ended up at MoMA in New York, he felt sufficiently certain of his footing to tell us why he had decided to get himself involved in Stig Nissen's dodgy enterprise: he wanted to get Mille singing again.

She had crossed over into jazz by the time he met her, which at best would be a harmless form of stagnation, but since then her career had run pretty much parallel to Rasmus Duck's in the children's song: first backwards, and then to a stop. It wasn't difficult to imagine how hard the fall from grade-one certified diva to Taarbæk housewife impacted on Mille's state of mind, but if I knew Nikolaj Krogh at all it wasn't merely for the sake of peace on the home front that he had decided to take action, but out of genuine love for his wife and a belief in her artistic capabilities that was quite disconnected from reality. He told us that he had been trying to get Mille a gig as sound designer ever since his first meeting with Stig Nissen.

'I think Stig Nissen has a fabulous ability to intuitively sense who he needs to hook up with,' he said. 'But I don't think he knows much about music. Mille's started doing this wild hybrid stuff, kind of a cross between folk and scratchy industrial.'

I wondered whether Mille even appreciated his loyalty.

'You know what Mille can do as a singer and composer, Mikkel, and I'd really appreciate your support tonight.'

Stig Nissen bustled in wearing a pin-striped suit and red suede shoes. Lisa followed on hesitantly, putting her feet to the floor like she was on the boat to Norway in a rough sea and grabbing all the attention in her rust-red satin dress.

'Have you been shagging?' Diana asked.

'I wouldn't know,' said Lisa.

'We set the Hotel Michala Petri alight, I can tell you that much,' said Stig Nissen, and rubbed his stubby fingers together.

'Have you got the food under control, Mikkel?'

I had stretched my acquaintance with restaurant manager Anders to the limit to get the table.

'It controls itself,' I said.

'How about a bit of bubbly to start off with?' said Stig.

We got two bottles of Selosse and a pep talk:

'Twenty years from now, business-school students will be sweating over assignments about this night. You can almost hear it, can't you? *The Noma Session.* This label of ours is going to be so big it'll dwarf everything else, and getting there is going to be pure rock 'n' roll. Lisa can do offbeat luxury like nobody's business. She's in a class of her own, two years ahead of everyone else's time. *Weltklasse!* And Nikolaj, those drawings you showed me. *Spitzenklasse!* Mikkel makes it all come together. Nice going with the table, Mikkel! And then we've got our gorgeous wild card, Miss Diana. Those cunts of yours are going up on the bloody walls, they are, in the flagship on Østergade! You'll see why once I reveal our name to you later tonight. Anyway, *skål,* and what a bunch of lookers we are!'

Lisa and Diana grabbed a bottle for themselves and held their own private party in the corner. Nikolaj Krogh handed Stig a CD he'd burned.

'I've brought Mille's new tracks along for you.'

Stig Nissen dropped it in his pocket without looking at it.

'Bloody hell, look at these little buggers!' The bread appeared wrapped in small pouches of felt tied up with a ribbon. 'It's enough to make you horny, that is!'

Diana and Lisa laughed, and Stig Nissen glanced uncertainly in their direction.

'What do you reckon, Mikkel? Can't you just see those cunts of hers blown up on the walls on Østergade? Five metres high. Wham!'

I considered my wording.

'Diana has an exhibition on in October to which those drawings are rather pivotal.'

'We'll be the talk of the town at fashion week, I'm telling you! Those cunts'll be famous by the time we get to October. Are they going to be sold, or what? It's called free publicity.'

Restaurant manager Anders served the first course proper. On the left side of the plate was a raw razor clam encased in a garishly green parsley gel. To the right of this lay a length of dry ice made of buttermilk and horseradish, over which Anders poured mussel stock. It was like sticking your head underwater in Thorshavn. It was an expression of the Nordic mindset, a poem, no less. I have never been one for mixing up food with art, but in this case it was relevant. The table fell silent and remained so for a couple of minutes.

'It's all too offbeat for me,' said Stig Nissen.

He took a swig of unfiltered biodynamic wine.

Then he stood up and waved Anders over.

'I'm not doubting this bog water is the latest thing, but do you think you could find us a really *spitzenklasse* Chablis?'

'Chardonnay would be a mite too exaggerated for the razor clam,' said Anders.

'I'm not having anymore,' said Stig, and handed him his plate.

I tried in vain to establish eye contact, but Anders had already gone to get another bottle.

'I've promised Mille she'll know one way or the other by tonight,' said Nikolaj Krogh.

'He's off again. Is she in the club?' said Stig Nissen.

Anders returned, poured him a splash of Chablis and swayed impatiently on his heels.

'I know you've told the wife you'll put in a word, Nikolaj, and, hey, I respect that. But wouldn't she be out of her depth here? I mean, it's ten years she was driving the bus. What say the girls?'

Anders had run out of patience.

'Would you care to taste the wine, please?'

'Are you still here? Just get pouring. Girls?'

Lisa was falling asleep.

'I'm from Budapest,' said Diana. 'Ask Mikkel.'

'I think Mille's new music would be just the job,' I said.

Stig Nissen lowered his head, then knocked three times on the table.

'Rock 'n' roll! Your wife just joined the team, Nikolaj!'

Nikolaj Krogh gave my thigh a squeeze under the table.

Diana took off her jacket, and I wasn't the only one to be thrown by her breasts. Stig Nissen looked like he'd been given a fright.

'Onion for everyone,' said Anders, and placed a hand on Stig's shoulder. 'It'll go well with your Chablis.'

'Onion?' said Stig Nissen.

It was masterful: onion compote with chicken stock, fresh stems of ramson, decorative onion leaves and a bouillon of onion and pearl sago. The taste was so deeply seductive you had to concentrate so as not to climax.

'Onion! They've got to be bloody joking!' said Stig Nissen.

He stood up and waved Anders over to the table again.

'Do me a double vodka and orange.'

Lisa was fast asleep. Stig Nissen was not.

'What do you say, Diana, do you need the go-ahead from your boyfriend, or can you say yes yourself?'

'I haven't got a boyfriend.'

'I think you need to make a little investment in the jewellery department, Mikkel,' he said.

Anders came back with his drink.

'Since you're dining at Noma, we've taken the liberty of doing our own interpretation of your vodka and orange. The vodka is from a small Finnish distillery south of Tampere, while the juice is sea buckthorn.'

Stig Nissen took a sip.

'Well, it's sour enough!'

Anders hurried away. Stig Nissen gave us a crafty look.

'Now, I'm going to pop off to the little house, and when I come back I'll tell you what we're going to call our new venture, okay?'

Nikolaj Krogh leaned across the table.

'It's rather liberating, all his grand designs.'

It worried me that Diana was still in bimbo mode.

'Do you want me to say no for you?' I said. She didn't answer.

Stig Nissen came back with a smile on his face.

'Are you ready for this?'

He leaned forward on his chair.

'Dusk,' he said, in Jutland English. *Dosk.*

'Dusk?' said Nikolaj Krogh and I.

'After my favourite Fleetwood Mac album.'

Nikolaj Krogh looked obliquely towards the ceiling. 'The double LP, right?'

'Monster album,' said Stig Nissen.

'Isn't it called *Tusk*?'

'Tosk? What's that supposed to be? It works in Danish as well as English. Sunset and tuft of hair. Can you see where I'm heading, Diana? That little tuft of yours?'

He was talking about her cunt.

The main course was reindeer, and not in my wildest fantasies had I imagined they would be able to keep up the standard. Two pieces of meat that melted in the mouth, wafer-thin slices of celery root, jellied discs of wild herbs, raw apple, beetroot and a sauce of browned butter and ramson. I am not capable of explaining how good it was.

'Have you had a look in your diary, Mikkel?' said Stig Nissen. 'We need a briefing over in the control bunker.'

'I'm afraid I can't find the time,' I said.

'We're talking popping over on the plane, an hour's spiel and back home again the same night with fifteen biggies in your back pocket.'

'I've got a book to write,' I said.

The evening was exhausted. We had an annoying dessert involving

73

freeze-dried hazelnuts, and Stig Nissen looked at his watch. Rolex, of course. Ugly, ugly.

'What do you want from me?' said Diana.

Stig Nissen leaned across the table.

'I want your cunts to be the concept. I want them on the walls, on the carrier bags. I want them on T-shirts, and I want all of us to be totally on board. Literally, in the picture.'

'How do you mean?'

'We're going to be the models in the photo.'

'What photo?'

'Ads in all the papers. You've nothing to be ashamed of, have you?'

'I'm not sure about photos.'

'How much do you want?'

'Can we give it some thought tomorrow?' I said.

'You can, but the bus'll be gone by then. Toodle-pip,' said Stig Nissen.

'How much?' said Diana

'A hundred big ones,' said Stig.

'A hundred and fifty!'

Stig Nissen produced a contract and entered the figure.

'Sign here.'

Like me, Charlie felt at home in the Borgerkroen. He sat next to me with a Coke and a glass full of ice cubes. He imagined they were sweets, and the nice bartender provided him with paper for his drawings. I made a rule for myself and stayed on coffee and mineral water until I'd written a thousand words. Then we celebrated, and I had a beer and Charlie another Coke.

The impossibility of constructing a perpetual motion machine is down to entropy. 'The amount of unavailable energy in a closed system can only increase,' says the second law of thermodynamics. No matter how cleverly such a machine might be constructed, the closed cycle will continuously transform a measure of the available energy into unavailable energy.

P lace your hand on the back of your fridge. It is made to create cold, and yet it is hot. A perpetual motion machine will in time run out of available energy, for which reason machines need energy from outside in order to perform. And still we kept on forming little closed systems of couplehood, promising each other to be faithful till death do us part.

Twenty years from now people might look back indulgently on our time and wonder with a smile why we so desperately clung to traditional coupledom when everything around us indicated its demise. There was a time when coupledom was of practical importance, but Dad no longer has to get up and milk the cows in the morning and Mum doesn't darn the family's socks anymore. Sentiment, children and convention keep us together. Everyone agrees that children need as much love and support as possible, but surprisingly few have the guts to contest the framework for this secure upbringing, despite the consensus that dysfunctional instances of coupledom can be quite as traumatic to children as divorce. The epicentre of the modern family is still monogamous coupledom. The perpetual motion machine. Supplying the energy is the man's and the woman's job, and this self-consuming state of inertia contrasts sharply with the changes that are occurring all around us. It is all in flux. Traditional media is dissolving, governments scramble to maintain national boundaries, and new generations feel equally at home in Tel Aviv, Brooklyn or Østerbro. Nationalism has been superseded by communities of reference, and where people happen to be in the world is insignificant. A weekday is no longer divided into eight-hour modules, work can be done anywhere and whenever, and companies sense there are advantages to allowing employees' work hours to integrate with family time and leisure.

Gender has levelled out, the word homosexual has all but disappeared from the language, and sexual preference is an utterly irrelevant distinction. Boundaries have melted away, barriers toppled around us, and yet we keep on with our units of coupledom as if nothing has changed.

My phone rang. It was Kaspar Moritz, he wanted to meet up right away and suggested the café in the Design Museum's garden.

'What's up?' I said.

We were surrounded by grandmothers from the intellectual left. I'd installed Charlie at a table just out of earshot to carry on with his drawings.

'I've worked with Diana for six years,' Moritz said, 'and as well as being talented she's really got her finger on all the factors that differentiate artists today: marketing, press, image, integrity. She learned fast. Right now she ranks just under Tal, Kørner, Ærtebjerg and young Bonnén, so it's essential she makes all the right decisions. It takes ten years to build an artist up, but only one exhibition to bring it all crashing down again.'

'You assured Diana her cunts would be sold at preview.'

'I know, and that's partly the problem, I'm afraid. It's like with music. Your favourite band puts out a new album, you buy it the day it comes out and give it a few listens, then realise it's not that good. So you never listen to it again, and when their next one comes out you don't buy it. Diana's new stuff lacks the kind of careless abandon that so characterised her first works, and I can't see anything unsettlingly new in its place. Art is merciless. Works give themselves away once they're up on the walls.'

He leaned across the table and lowered his voice.

'Diana has put everything she's got into her art. Literally.'

'What do you mean by that?'

'That's for her to reveal, I think.'

He looked out across the garden.

'In less than a fortnight those drawings of hers are off to Vietnam, and getting them woven is costing over a hundred thousand. If they're going there, they're going to exhibition.'

'Why did you want to see me?'

'I have a feeling she listens to you.'

He gazed into his coffee. 'If things start going wrong for Diana, they're going to go really wrong.'

I dropped Charlie off with Helene and hurried to Diana's place to find her in buoyant mood.

She had made goulash with genuine Hungarian paprika, laid the table with a fine purple tablecloth and lit all the candles.

'I've coloured one of the cunts today. I should have done it before.'

She threw her arms around my neck.

'I need to get to work.'

She straddled me. Polo jersey, no knickers.

'I've got this urge to be tied down.'

The staircase was an acoustic catastrophe. The metal banister reverberated and the stairs threw back all sound in an unfriendly echo.

'Not today, thanks,' said Søren, but let me in anyway.

There was snooker on the TV and his duvet lay in a sweaty heap on the smooth black leather of his sofa.

'You weren't supposed to be here until tomorrow.'

'We agreed on the third, that's today.'

'What did you have in mind?'

'I need a whole load of prosaic detail about your dealer back then. What the flat looked like, who he was, and all that about the difference between white and brown smack.'

He got that surly twist to his mouth again.

'Oh, great, just what I needed.'

'We agreed on this three weeks ago, Søren.'

He looked me straight in the eye.

'Can you lend me thirteen hundred?'

'What for?'

'I've got this extra heating bill.'

'I thought your bills got drawn from your benefit?'

'They do. But the twats never told me I have to pay any extras myself. It's got to be paid today, otherwise I'll get chucked out.'

'I've got no money, Søren.'

'What about that new girlfriend of yours?'

'She's got some coming in, but she hasn't got it yet.'

'Can't she borrow, then?'

I thought for a second about how best to tell him.

'I'm not having her mixed up in all this.'

He narrowed his eyes.

'All this? You mean me?'

'I mean your mess, Søren. Not you personally.'

He got up and put on a blue Ralph Lauren jacket.

'In that case, we'll have to go and see Camilla White Wine.'

I had met Camilla White Wine a couple of times before. Her consonants started to drift around about six in the evening, but it was only a quarter to twelve in the morning and her flat was in a well-run cooperative association halfway along Silkeborggade.

'Does she owe you money?' I asked.

We were on our way up the stairs.

'She's got my Ole Appelgreen print.'

Camilla was in a perilously see-through Indian robe. She had definitely been pretty at some point, only now it was hard to tell where anything began or ended.

'You could have said you were bringing Mikkel,' she said. 'I'd have done my eyes.'

She insisted on making us a proper cup of coffee and busied herself with a coffee grinder and an Italian espresso maker. For her own part she was halfway through a bottle of white wine called Sunrise.

'I grew up with Elizabeth David's cookery books,' she said.

'You're from Gentofte, we know,' said Søren.

'Have you looked at them recently, Mikkel?'

'Elizabeth David was ahead of her time,' I said.

'And such marvellous illustrations,' she said.

Søren had a sip of her wine and spat it out in the sink.

'Fucking hell, that tastes like petrol.'

'It's actually rather decent. It was best in a test.'

'Of what, paraffin and citric acid? It's a wonder you've still got so many teeth left.'

'Søren's a bit upset about being middle-aged and still a drug addict,' she said.

'I'm not a drug addict anymore. I'm a drinker, like you.'

'You're on methadone, Søren. And any kind of pills that happen to come your way.'

'And you puke over the furniture every night,' said Søren.

'I do apologise, Mikkel,' said Camilla. 'I used to be rather a respectable girl, you know. I went to Øregård Gymnasium School.'

Søren went into the living room with Camilla White Wine right behind him.

'You're not getting that picture, Søren!'

'It's mine!'

He took it down off the wall. It depicted a cow looking despondently up at a big black cloud. Camilla grabbed him.

'You leave that where it is, Søren T-shirt!'

Her voice was shrill. I got the feeling things could get out of hand.

'Hey,' I said, and stepped in. 'What's the problem, exactly?'

'That picture's with me as security, because Søren owes me two hundred kroner.'

'You can have your two hundred once I've sold it,' he said.

'Søren, Søren, Søren! You don't really expect me to believe that, do you?'

Momentary deadlock.

'Listen, is there anything you need?' said Søren. 'I can go and get you something. Wine? Coffee?'

Camilla smiled at me sweetly.

'Well, talking about Elizabeth David just before gave me the urge to do something nice for dinner. What do you say?'

'I'll go down and get a joint of beef,' said Søren.

'I was thinking about osso buco,' she said.

'Osso buco? Does it have to be so fiddly?'

Camilla ignored him.

'I've got tomatoes and fresh rosemary, and some of that good Muti tomato paste. You know Muti, don't you, Mikkel?'

We went to Netto and I assured him they wouldn't have osso buco, but he was round the place like a businessman on his way to an airport gate, and once he realised I was right he routinely slipped a couple of bottles of white under his jacket and was out again just as quickly. We got lucky in Brugsen. Søren lifted a couple of packs and somehow made himself invisible.

'There you go, love,' he said, and dumped the meat on Camilla White Wine's counter.

'But it's frozen,' she said. 'It won't have time to thaw. An osso buco needs to simmer for three or four hours. Mikkel knows that, don't you, Mikkel?'

'Do you know anyone who's got a microwave?' said Søren.

We went over to Clara's to use her microwave. She was listening to the radio – culture and current affairs on P1 – and baking rye bread when we knocked on the door of her flat on I.A. Schwarzgade, but at least she wasn't in her slippers.

'So when are we going to see your new girlfriend, Mikkel?'

'She's still not my girlfriend,' I said.

She popped our bricks of osso buco in the microwave and put it on thaw. Søren was put on a chair with a glass of red.

'I'm having difficulty taking it seriously, Mikkel,' she said.

'I know, what sort of bollocks is that?' said Søren.

Clara had heard all the stories about Søren and was always afraid he was going to make off with the plateware or inject something into his eye, and Søren responded to this lack of trust by becoming despicably anxious to please.

'Maybe we should throw a dinner party and invite Kreuzmann,' said Clara.

'Things go wrong for me when I'm with Kreuzmann,' I said.

'Brilliant,' said Søren.

Erik Brinch came in through the door in his long black leather coat. He had been with Clara for about six months and they made a truly dreadful couple. He was an architect in his mid-sixties and looked like a malicious tortoise.

'We've got another bottle, haven't we, dear?'

Søren and Erik got on like a house on fire, mainly because they were both in need of a plausible social situation in which to drink.

Twenty minutes later the bottle was empty. Søren obligingly offered to go down to the shop with Erik's money and was back with a carrier bag full of cans before we had even blinked. Clara stuck to tea with ginger and lemon in it, and it wasn't the first time she had heard Erik Brinch go on about Drop-Inn in the seventies; Stangerup, Peter Hjorth, the advertising man, and Per Arnoldi. Literary discussions that degenerated into fist fights, whisky drunk by the barrel, women picked up on the way home.

'Don't forget we're going to the theatre tonight,' said Clara.

'Oh, Christ. Do we have to, dear?'

'Bølle's left us some tickets on the door, Erik.'

'Can't we go out for dinner instead?' he said, meaning drink.

'I hate theatre,' said Søren.

'Me too!' said Erik Brinch. 'What a jaded art form it is!'

'The way they ponce about,' said Søren. 'Look at me, look at me, look at me!'

Clara put a carrier bag on the table with the meat in it that was now thawed.

'We fucked the women's movement out of them,' said Erik Brinch.

Now he couldn't be dragged from his orgies in the seventies, and Clara left him to it. She has always been inclined to jealousy, but in the case of Erik Brinch it was all backdated.

'The Red Stockings were horrible!' said Søren. 'Long boots, lipstick, short skirts and nylon stockings, that's what women should look like!'

Erik guffawed and opened three beers.

'All the hippy guys sat on the floor talking about their feelings,' he said. 'We buggered off with their girlfriends. I mean, they wanted a proper man, didn't they? With a bulge in his pants. Skirts up and mind the doors, sister!'

We had to get a taxi and made it wait outside while we dropped the meat off at Camilla White Wine's. She had wriggled herself into something romantic, off-white with little purple flowers.

'Don't be long, now,' she said.

The art dealer on Gothersgade was getting ready to close as we came bursting through the door. Søren put the picture down on the counter.

'Yes,' said the art dealer. 'Hm…'

'There's a little gem for you, eh?' said Søren.

'Is it a work of which you're fond?' said the art dealer.

'It's a good picture,' said Søren. 'Anyone can see that.'

'Because if you *are* fond of it, I would suggest you take it home with you and put it back on the wall.'

'Thanks, but I'm here to sell it.'

'I can't give you much, I'm afraid,' said the art dealer.

'It's a genuine bloody Appelgreen,' said Søren, indicating the pencilled signature in the corner.

'It's a lithograph, and as you can see it's number eleven of one hundred and fifty. Ole Appelgreen is a fine painter, that far I agree with you, but I'm afraid it's not quite sufficient on its own.'

'What's that supposed to mean?'

'His work isn't in demand at the moment.'

'You mean I should have brought you a turd on a stick?'

The man was about to lose his patience, but thought better of it.

'Okay, let's cut the crap. How much will you give us for it?'

'Five hundred,' said the art dealer.

'You must be mad!'

We left with the five hundred kroner and the bottle of aquavit Søren had noticed on a shelf. He was utterly miserable.

'Let's get back to Camilla White Wine,' I said.

'I can't be arsed now.'

'What are you going to do instead?'

'Sort out some business on the street.'

'What about your heating bill?'

'What about it?'

Jan Minetti lived in the next-door studio and was Diana's best friend. Though he had moved to Copenhagen twenty-five years before, his Jutland dialect remained intact. He was plump, in the way of a silent movie star, with black curly hair tumbling down his forehead which he constantly brushed away from his moist, puppy-dog eyes. If anyone was an artist, he was, and his big oil canvases depicted mechanically perceived intestines in distorted colours and would have been original had Francis Bacon decided on a career in bookkeeping. Jan wasn't represented by Galleri Wallner, Claus Andersen, Nils Stærk, V1 or Galleri Moritz, but by a gallerist up three steps on Smallegade. He was the son of Vejle's first pizza baker and insisted he was a *wop*, not an Italian.

'We're the only ones left in Copenhagen,' he said, sweeping his hand out across the city's rooftops. We were seated on his eighty-square-metre rooftop terrace, all little plateaus and exotic plants. 'Everyone's moved to Berlin. Tal R doesn't even want a Danish gallery.'

'I don't like Germans,' said Diana. 'They smell of cheap soap.'

'You're just scared you won't hack it there!' Jan said.

'And you've got nothing to lose,' said Diana.

'Delightful, isn't she?'

We had dinner at Jan's place every evening; his food was good and displayed variety with a minimum of components. Tonight had been grilled pork chops, green lentils with rosemary and halved bulbs of fennel braised in water, butter, oil and garlic. As usual, Diana had paid for everything. That same afternoon I had been leafing through an art book in her studio and had come across Carl André, the minimalist American artist whose most familiar work, one hundred and twenty bricks stacked two high in a neat rectangle, became the object of one of those debates all art historians depise when it was purchased by the Tate with British taxpayers' money in 1974.

'What do you think of Carl André?' I said.

'I adore him,' said Diana. 'His work is so fine and expressive.'

'He's a poor bricklayer,' said Jan.

'Let's take a hypothetical example,' I said. 'A Swiss collector buys a work by Carl André and wants it installed in his home. A carrier arrives with two big packing cases, and when the collector opens them all he sees is ordinary bricks. How can he be sure it's art?'

'He has the artist install it,' said Diana.

'That sort of thing makes me embarrassed to be an artist,' said Jan. 'What's the point of art questioning art? Can bricks be art? No, they can't. They can be bricks, in fact they're very good at it. Art should be about expanding horizons, not narrowing things down to some pointless discussion among a tiny elite. Do you know what Carl André's art begets? Jobs for dried-up fannies who have spent six years reading art history, that's what!'

'As I understand it, the work at the Tate was a hundred and twenty ordinary bricks,' I said. 'And what makes them art is that they are chosen by the artist.'

'No, the *idea* is the point,' said Diana.

'There is no such thing as good or bad art,' I said. 'There are people who are artists, trained or otherwise, and what they do is by definition art, and it's up to us to make of it what we will. Is that it?'

'Definitely,' said Diana. 'That's got to be it.'

'I miss Harlequin!' said Jan. 'Can't we go to the Tivoli Gardens soon?'

The longing I felt for a woman when she was asleep tended to disappear once she had opened her eyes, but with Diana it was different. I liked her better awake. She woke up and immediately embraced whatever reality was at hand. She had nothing resembling a standard routine.

We ate smoked cheese and radishes, and outside it was Sunday.

'I love the way we are,' she said.

'It's like a dream,' I said.

'But you're real,' she said. 'I'm real, and everything is happening.'

I made juice out of beetroot, chilli, lemon and ginger.

'Do you think it can go on like this?' she said.

'I want it to, in every way,' I said.

'But you know what I'm like,' she said.

'Do you believe in God?' I asked.

'Of course.'

'Should we go to church?'

I had always taken a romantic view of church and faith. I can't remember having heard the word God at any point in my upbringing, save perhaps for sentences such as: 'Oh God, we forgot to get wine in!' Church was then as now considered oppressive and viewed with ridicule by the intellectual left, and the protest generation of the sixties managed successfully to undermine all notion of faith that might have been held by the Danes, a fact that had to be lamented inasmuch as the epic narratives and profound thinking of religious faith enrich the spiritual constitution of any nation's people. Fundamentally, though, I acknowledged that one either had faith or had not, and I was unable, no matter how much I would have liked, to believe with anything other than my intellect, and at best only from time to time.

The church we entered looked like so many others: high, white walls, exhortative words painted on wood, a three-piece choir of disharmonious constitution and an organist who was only occasionally in contact with the melody. The pastor was called Andreas Møller. He was in his mid-thirties, with shoulder-length hair and a carroty full beard. He would have been hard to caricature, possessing no special characteristics beyond his ordinary appearance and Danish blue eyes.

'I've seen him somewhere before,' said Diana.

His sermon was about purgatory and he related the parable of the rich man who enjoyed life to the full and neglected to give food to the poor beggar at the gate.

One day the rich man died and found himself in the kingdom of the dead with a terrible thirst. From far away he could see the poor beggar receiving comfort in the bosom of Abraham. The rich man asked Abraham to send the beggar to him with water, but Abraham declined, and the rich man realised he was doomed to agony. He then asked Abraham to send the beggar, that his five brothers might be converted to the faith, but Abraham replied that if the rich man's brothers did not listen to the Prophets they would not be convinced even by someone rising from the dead.

'Is Hell a hole that gapes beneath us?' said Andreas Møller. 'Is there a Devil with a trident in his hand? No, Hell is right here, and it begins with the uncivil comment we make to the bus driver. Hell is having no time for others. It leads to bitterness, and we end up lonely and joyless, calling the police when the neighbours have a party. Ought God to save those who are on their way to Hell? Ought He to allow them to begin anew? That's what Jesus did for us. God does nothing! He leaves them alone.'

I shook his hand on the way out. He was mild and smiling.

'Thank you for coming,' he said. 'Would you like to come over to the parish hall and have a coffee?'

There was a poster of a local football team on the wall, and a couple of toothless old men sat drinking beer in a corner. The coffee was remarkably good, and later I discovered the beans were from Ricco's coffee bar. Andreas Møller flitted from table to table and seemed to be in the midst of ongoing conversation with most of those present. He listened patiently to people's problems concerning drink, illness and loneliness. Coffee went on for an hour. 'You're not in a hurry, are you?' said Andreas. 'I'd like to show you something. Five minutes!'

He came back looking like someone who was into Prefab Sprout.

Short jacket in soft calfskin, charcoal-grey trousers and brown Playboy shoes.

He took us to his apartment, which was diagonally opposite Al-Diwan on Vesterbrogade. 'This is where Handelsbanken's directors used to install their mistresses,' he said. The ceilings were four and a half metres high and decorated with some exceptional stucco. He led us through three enormous rooms, opening the double doors wide into a fourth before turning on the light by an old porcelain switch and looking up. Diana's tapestry of a man with semen in his beard.

'I *knew* I'd seen you before,' she said.

'I was going through a strange time when I bought your tapestry. I was rather unstable and I'd shaved my head completely. Are you hungry?'

He proceeded to concoct a curry from scratch, allowing the finely chopped onions to simmer in ghee, roasting the spices in the pan and crushing them in a mortar together with garlic and fresh ginger. The aromas filled the room.

'That was a harsh sermon,' I said.

'You have to make an example,' he said. 'We've got enough pop stars who've been on a yoga retreat to Kerala and found God in a stone they tripped up on. What would you like to drink? Riesling?'

He took a Battenfeld-Spanier out of the fridge.

'How come you can afford to live here on a pastor's salary?' Diana asked.

'The building belongs to me,' he said. 'My father bought it back in the seventies. He was a solicitor here in the Vesterbro district, his clients were all the smuggler kings and pimps of the day, and when they fell on hard times he bought up their properties.'

'So you're a true Vesterbro lad, then?' I said.

'Well, I grew up on Sønder Boulevard, but when I was eleven we moved to Hørsholm and my father gave vent to all his social ambitions and sent me to board at Herlufsholm.'

'Which you weren't happy about?' I said.

'The standard was appalling. They couldn't even sing their ABC in Year 6.'

His tiger prawn curry had the kind of intensity and multiple layers of taste found only in Indian restaurants in London.

'So, what made you go to church today?' he asked us.

'I grew up with it,' said Diana.

Andreas Møller had difficulty looking Diana in the eye. He addressed me, but was focused on her.

'What do you think, Mikkel?' he said.

'I think we're entering a new age,' I said.

'Aha! What kind of a new age?'

I told him my ideas about big community and how I believed love could be found outside coupledom, and though he seemed mightily surprised that I should be preoccupied by such matters, he listened attentively, something I suspected he didn't do very often.

'Have you heard of John Noyes?' he said, immediately disappearing into his library and returning with two books: *Without Sin* by Spencer Klaw and *The Man Who Would Be Perfect* by Robert D. Thomas.

We decided to go for a drink at Café 42, and as we walked along Oehlenschlägersgade, Andreas told us about the Oneida Community, an alternative society founded amid the piety of the Victorian age. John Noyes came from a religious home in Vermont and studied theology at Yale, but found it hard to come to terms with the restrictive values of the age: man sinned, found redemption and sinned again, and to John Noyes this seemed both illogical and lax. Jesus bore our sins on the cross, and Noyes considered that by bearing Jesus truly in our hearts and serving God to the best of our ability man would be eternally freed from sin.

Noyes married into wealth, his new wife sympathising strongly with his ideas, and together they founded a small movement that under Noyes' direction was to carry out his radical blend of Christian revival, socialism and free sex. Noyes believed God had given man the gift of sexual pleasure in order that he should exploit it to perfection, which in Noyes' conviction could not occur within the confines of monogamous marriage.

In 1848 he and thirty adherents moved to the state of New York, to the former Indian reservation Oneida, where they built the Mansion House, a huge complex comprising a very large number of bedrooms. By the time construction was completed, the movement had swelled to some two hundred members and its rules were as entrenched as they were simple. All women and men were in principle married to each other and exclusive relationships were not allowed. If, during work in the field, one met a person to whom one was attracted, permission to act on this desire had to be sought from Noyes, and if he deemed the applicant to be feeble in mind or uncommitted to the community, the application was rejected.

Coitus reservatus was obligatory, men were not permitted to ejaculate inside their partner, primarily because pregnancy rendered women unable to work. Work was central to the community and, like sex, it should be enjoyed, which meant frequent job rotations in order to avoid the monotony of routine.

He set up a nursery school so that women could return to work as soon as they stopped breastfeeding. Women were uniformly clad in functional short skirts, and all wore their hair short.

In frequent lectures given in the main hall, Noyes encouraged diligence and high moral standards, and placed the community before the individual. He was opposed to competition, believing that man was better served enjoying life to the full rather than competing with others.

The most academically promising youngsters were sent to Yale to be educated for the good of the community. At its peak, Oneida comprised three hundred and six residents.

As the 1870s drew to a close, Noyes passed on leadership to his son, who lacked his father's charisma. The community gradually dissolved after some thirty years.

I'd been listening raptly to Andreas Møller's story, but Diana looked vacant and said she wanted to go home and draw. Andreas Møller took her hand as she said goodbye, but could find nothing to say. We ordered safari suits.

'John Noyes sounds like he was a bit of a dictator,' I said.

'No. He was omnipotent, but the supreme authority rested in group criticism meetings. Aggravations were nipped in the bud, and problems were addressed by the assembly.'

Andreas Møller enjoyed my full attention, but although I was fascinated by his stories of Oneida, there was an odd lack of warmth between us. I was certain this came from him and it could have just been a simple lack of chemistry, but it felt more like distrust to me.

'My father used to wear an Ascot, too,' he said, and I had no idea what he was talking about until he indicated my silk cravat.

'Is it called an Ascot?' I said.

'You know full well it is, Vallin.'

'Isn't that some kind of inverted snobbery?' I said.

'Now you're being rude,' he said. 'I know you mean well, though. You're trying to figure out who I am, aren't you?'

I nodded. He chinked our glasses.

'You won't be able to, Vallin. I'll never be whole, but I am a very strong half-person. Is that good enough for you?'

We emptied our glasses and ordered two more suits.

'Let's talk about Diana,' he said. 'Such an intensely beautiful and divinely distracted woman.'

The latest American neurological research explains that the brain has three regions for love.

The first is primordial and is all about sex and ensuring the survival of the species: fuck her, fuck him. But in prehistoric times, people lived in small clans, and inbreeding became a serious problem.

Therefore the brain developed a new region and invented attraction, a state transmitted by dopamine, a hormone that activates the brain's reward centre to release a sense of invincibility.

A male member of the clan might see a female on the other side of the river, and attraction (or dopamine) made him capable of swimming across to the other bank, fighting off other males and mating with the female from the other clan, thus transcending the cycle of inbreeding, and conceiving offspring with the best possible genetic make-up. Clans mingled and produced healthy children.

With evolution the human brain increased in size, and in order to contain it our heads grew bigger. Unhelpfully bigger, as it happens. Whereas nearly all mammalian young are viable from day one, human babies are capable of looking after themselves only from the age of three, and since the skull of a three-year-old would be too big for women to give birth to, children had to be let out early, so the brain needed something new to make the male hang around until the child was strong enough to stand on its own two feet. Thus evolved the third region.

This was devoted to more long-term association, what we call relationships, and for these, oxytocin is essential. Oxytocin is a hormone that stimulates our desire to attach ourselves to others, for which reason it is also often referred to as the bonding hormone. The greatest concentration of oxytocin is found between the newborn child and the breastfeeding mother and serves to bond them inseparably together. When we hug another person, our levels of oxytocin, and thereby our desire to bond, are significantly increased during the hour that follows.

If a couple stops touching, their oxytocin will plummet, and with it their desire to bond.

Couples who stay together are either faithful to convention and willing to disregard their own individual wants and needs, and thereby, I suppose, each other's, or else they are good at producing oxytocin, which means they enjoy more frequent physical contact.

If a hug equals more oxycotin for an hour, I calculate that a shag must be good for at least twenty-four hours.

The fact that many couples do not desire physical contact with each other is attributed mainly to poor communication. To maintain positive communication, for each negative exchange you must have four good ones. If that balance tips, physical contact will be affected and with it the desire to bond. So staying together more than four years requires a concerted effort.

Or stimulation from without.

So the brain has three regions for love, and it is a remarkable and somewhat under-investigated fact that these three regions can function simultaneously and independently of one another. Basically, you can want to fuck one person while being in love with a second and more profoundly emotionally attached to a third.

The brain is able to handle love more dynamically than we let ourselves think, and the fact that we do not exploit the opportunities presented to us may be ascribed to culturally accepted rules and norms of behaviour that serve to generate stagnation, unhappiness and broken relationships rather than happiness, desire and new energy.

COPENHAGEN, JUNE 2008

The right cause had never really come along for me, though there had been plenty on offer: peace marches, No to this, that or the other, solidarity with peoples and places you had never heard of. The protest generation of the sixties had been enriched by a wealth of causes they could unite against or in favour of, and most of these had been relatively easy to relate to and win. I have always envied them for having been able to get together and break down the rigid structures of the fifties, for having had something they felt they could fight for.

They held meetings and discussed weighty issues. We held dinner parties.

So it came as a surprise to me that I suddenly had a cause of my own: my struggle against coupledom was directed at something concrete. I wanted to tear something down that didn't work, and what little I had revealed to my circle of friends, by definition radically minded, free-thinking people one and all, indicated to me that resistance would be fierce. But I was so certain there was a wealth of happiness to be had if my argument prevailed that I was ready to do whatever it took to win a new set of terms to live by.

The final spur to my resolve came at a Tuesday-night dinner at Helene and Tue Nissen's.

Being a boss did not suit Helene at all, and now she was a boss all the time. When I first met her she wore hoodies and jeans, now it was all knee-length skirts, midweek blouses in drab colours and shoes with leather soles. The zealous sound they made when she came striding across the parquet flooring was a fairly precise auditory encapsulation of her state of mind. Tue tried, more or less intentionally, to create an equilibrium by being in no hurry to do anything whatsoever. On the face of it he looked serene, which he wasn't. His enormous royalty cheques provided the foundation of a life without worry, but the brash and enterprising man Helene had fallen in love with was no longer in the building. The two people who less than two years before had cast all decency to the wind and fucked themselves silly under my nose were quite removed from the couple who now exchanged an arid kiss in the doorway.

I had got into a bad habit of skipping our Tuesday-night dinners, but for Charlie's sake, and because I at least in theory applauded the idea, I had dragged myself over there.

Helene did roast chicken with new potatoes. The organic fowl was near-atomised and the potatoes boiled to sludge.

'How's the writing coming along?' she asked.

'I've done fifty pages,' I said.

'Send them to Bernhard, Mikkel.'

'I remember the feeling of writing something important,' said Tue. 'But lounging around with a glass of wine in your hand isn't bad either.'

Helene stood up, pushing her chair back with such force it nearly toppled over. She went over and stuck her head in the American-sized fridge.

'Didn't we have some cucumber salad?'

'You used it in that Thai dish the other day,' said Tue.

'No, I bought a new jar at Meyers Deli. You didn't take it anywhere, did you?'

'Are you asking me if I took it with me to get my hair cut?'

She rummaged around, placing items from the fridge on to the counter and taking the opportunity to bin stuff that was past its sell-by date: pasteurised egg yolks for the mayonnaise that never got made, an unopened organic calf-liver pâté, a jar of vindaloo paste from a grocer's in Vesterbro. But the cucumber salad from Meyers Deli had vanished without a trace and in the meantime her dinner had gone cold.

I put Charlie to bed and Tue got the table ready with coffee, Armagnac and Rød Ravnsborg.

'Clara says you and Diana still aren't a couple,' said Helene. I was beginning to tire of it coming up all the time.

'Does that mean you're allowed to go to bed with others?' said Tue.

'Whatever we want,' I said.

'Sounds ambitious,' he said, gazing into his beer.

'You can do anything when you're in love,' said Helene.

'That doesn't sound right,' said Tue.

'Does she want children?' said Helene.

'She can't,' said Tue. 'She's carving a big career for herself. It doesn't go with children.'

'I'm carving a career too,' said Helene.

Show me a single couple who don't sound like a rubbish theatre piece.

A muffled bass was pumping away somewhere and I couldn't sleep. For a while I'd had the feeling my book was more than just a love story from the eighties, and now it was clear to me. The story of Signe and Søren was the demise of a dream, the very symbol of coupledom's legitimacy having come to an end. But the book was going to be about more than that. It would encapsulate my life and thoughts. It would be a manifesto.

Two hundred and thirty-five years before, Goethe and the young Werther infused passion into coupledom: romantic love, the notion of forever being complemented by another.

Our brains were designed to separate sex, attraction and deeper interdependence, and yet we made do with the monogamous relationship and all it occasioned in the way of jealousy, latent dissatisfaction and infidelity. The fear of losing each other kept us together, rather than the desire to give.

This wasn't about me wanting to satisfy some superficial desire to surf around for instant satisfaction. What I wanted was limitless love and sublime trust. We had to allow each other to do whatever we wanted.

Love becomes greater the more we share it.

We were going to rise up. We were going to fly together.

I was shaking. I sat down at the computer and wrote:

Goodbye coupledom, thanks for nothing.

S tig Nissen was in a dreadful Dolce & Gabbana T-shirt and was trying to high-five the photographer, who rolled his eyes behind Stig's back.

The shoot took place in a rear building off Sct. Gertrudsstræde: big studio, original Italian coffee maker, expensive clothes in brand carrier bags dumped in a corner, lamps and cables, catering crew from Grill Bar on Ny Østergade.

'Once the girls have got some slap on we're pretty much ready to go,' said the photographer. The music was Fleetwood Mac.

Diana's make-up was dramatic, Lisa was sober and her hair had been crimped.

Mille had brought her own entourage of minions, these numbering a stylist, a make-up artist, a hairdresser and a couple of assistants. Her hair was done up in waves like Lauren Bacall. She snapped an order at Nikolaj Krogh, air-kissed Stig Nissen, and delivered a jaunty comment to the photographer.

Everyone else she brazenly ignored. Stig called everyone to attention.

'This here, people, is fashion history. Here we have the team that's going to make Dusk Denmark's biggest high-street fashion brand since Margit and Erik ran Studio 54. Rock 'n' roll!'

'Right,' said the photographer, indicating where he wanted us, in front of a white canvas backdrop.

The first thing I noticed was how plump Mille had become. She looked like she'd been stuffing herself with ladlefuls of mayonnaise while confined to bed. Her ample cheeks had spread under her eyes, reducing them to small slits and making her look like a self-important pig.

'Let's have some bubbly,' said Stig Nissen.

Black-clad waiters handed out champagne glasses and filled them up.

'Where are the clothes?' said Mille.

'The collection samples have been delayed,' said Stig Nissen.

'So what do we do?'

'We think outside the box,' said Stig Nissen. 'Exploit the challenge actively. Before Dusk there was nothing. Do you follow me?'

'Not really,' said Nikolaj Krogh.

'We're doing it in the buff!' said Stig Nissen.

'Is this a joke?' said Mille.

'I'll respect anyone who's not up to it,' said Stig Nissen.

Mille muttered some obscenity to Nikolaj Krogh and stomped off with her entourage. Nikolaj Krogh had been mountain-biking all winter and had nothing to hide, and Lisa had already derobed.

'Let's have Diana in front,' said Stig.

'And if you, Nikolaj, would like to stand behind her and cover her boobs. Do you remember Janet Jackson?'

Nikolaj Krogh placed his hands over Diana's soft breasts.

'Lisa, you cover Diana's fanny with one hand.'

'We're flying,' said the photographer.

'This is going to be bloody brilliant,' said Stig Nissen. 'Lezzers are the new black.'

Afterwards, we sat and had some food in little clusters on the floor, and it was striking how much Nikolaj and Lisa had to talk about and how well they suited each other.

'Have you got any plans for the summer?' said Nikolaj Krogh.

'I'm writing and Diana's drawing,' I said.

'Why don't you come up to our summer house at Nordhusvej and set up an artists' camp?'

D iana did a little jig in the gravel outside the Grøften restaurant in the Tivoli Gardens. In her jacket pocket were two hundred and thirty thousand kroner. We had been to Bindesbøll's and bought Armani, we had been to Christiania and bought spliffs, we had eaten foie gras and oysters at Alsace, fucked each other against a tree and laughed our heads off by the lake in the Østre Anlæg park.

We yapped like little Pekinese lapdogs when Jan came striding up in an African smock and a wide-brimmed hat.

'I've been at the gallery for hours drinking white wine with the most gorgeous advertising man. He bought a big canvas and wants to make me house artist for his agency.'

We ordered large, jubilant draught beers, two substantial pieces of *smørrebrød*, each with fjord shrimps, and a bottle of Rød Aalborg aquavit, and I was just getting into my stride about Grøften being Denmark's original answer to the great Parisian brasseries, when I noticed Rie Becker, and if it hadn't been for her looking me up and down as though she were assessing me, I might not have bothered.

The perceptive, pigtailed MA in communication studies had mutated into a platinum-blonde glam bitch with garish tattoos and a leather waistcoat, and it was a mistake to wave to her and then disorienting to be suddenly exchanging cheek kisses, but the biggest surprise was that Jan invited her to join us and made room at the table.

'It must be so boring writing about art, surely?' he said.

It dawned on me that Rie Becker had crossed over, which explained why she was so obsequious to Diana.

Rie Becker possessed little more than the average gallery-goer's knowledge about art when her newspaper's powers-that-be decided to make the modern art scene a *focus area* and sent their star columnist off into the field. She worked sixty hours a week, she told us, approaching the art world from a sociological and business-oriented perspective rather than, as tradition prescribed, rewording gallery press releases or penning humble lines about this or another artist's relationship to birch trees.

Jan kept her going with questions, and she found it increasingly hard to conceal her smugness and had little issue at all with the sound of her own voice.

'It's a disaster for the Danish art scene that all of a sudden any old binman can afford to have art hanging on his walls,' she said, and not because anyone had asked her to have an opinion about it.

'Aren't binmen allowed to buy art?' I said.

'Certainly, but unqualified purchasers create stagnation, and artists submit to the temptation of reproducing themselves. There's prestige in owning a Diana Kiss. Aren't you tempted to give the binman what he wants, Diana?'

'Do you want a Rød Aalborg?' said Diana.

'Are your next works going to be tapestries too?' said Rie Becker.

'Down your neck,' said Diana.

'Did you go to the Christmas market at the Academy?' Rie Becker went on. 'The first-year students were selling kids' drawings for twenty thousand. Join the dots! If anyone's got any ambition at all besides peeing their pants to keep warm, they'd do well to get out and go somewhere else. Why aren't you in Berlin, Diana?'

'I'm moving there now,' said Jan.

'Are you an artist too?'

'Let's all go back and have champagne on the roof,' said Jan.

Rie Becker had an opinion about everything along the way: Latvian prostitutes, children's prams, energy drinks, the restoration of rear courtyards, Friday nights. and eventually Vesterbro.

'It's turned into Jutland. I got out by the skin of my teeth before it all went Buena Vista Social Club.'

Diana made sure to lag behind.

'I've got to deliver the drawings in four days,' she said.

'Don't listen to her,' I said.

'It's more me, really.'

Jan was already busy sorting out his canvases in the studio and had installed Rie Becker on the rooftop terrace, where to my boundless annoyance she sat back to front on her chair with a spliff in her hand and a glass of the Egly-Ouriet Grand Cru Jan said he was never going to open.

'Right, *vernissage*!' he called out.

Rie Becker sidled in with a New Yorker smile on her face, and Jan twirled his fringe in terror. She stepped up close to a painting to study a detail, took a blast of her spliff and spoke as smoke curled about her mouth.

'This is really good, Jan.'

'Thanks!' he said, trying to control his voice.

'Technically, it's very good indeed.'

'But?' said Jan.

'But you're out of sync.'

'You mean it reminds you of nothing you've ever seen before?' he said.

'It reminds me of Francis Bacon,' she said.

'I'll take that as a compliment,' said Jan.

Rie Becker stared obliquely into the air above in order to find her words.

'You hear a good joke and want to pass it on, but halfway through you realise you've forgotten the punchline. Does that make sense?'

She turned to Diana, a little pirouette.

'I'd like to see what you're up to at the moment, Diana.'

'I can't oblige, I'm afraid,' said Diana.

Rie Becker snorted. 'Oblige?'

'Don't snort,' I said.

'Oh, peeved, are we?' she said, and snorted again.

'You make a living out of writing about artists, Rie. Without Diana and Jan there'd be nothing for you to do, in case you'd forgotten.'

'I can write about whatever I choose, Mikkel Vallin.'

'You suck people's blood, Rie. You're a gnat.'

It was late afternoon and I was lounging around watching a film about Francis Bacon. He stared caustically into the camera and I was unprepared for what he said:

'Everything escapes you.'

Diana was drawing and Ida-Marie was drinking tea.

'Moritz will be here with the curators in half an hour,' said Ida-Marie.

I had a shower and watched the water run off my skin. Everything escapes you. I had thought it was me who always fled.

'What do curators eat?' said Ida-Marie.

'We're going out with them for a bite afterwards,' said Diana.

The three curators were visibly uncomfortable in the assessor's role, and Lea completely avoided eye contact. To begin with, Moritz said a few words about why Ida-Marie's and Diana's art was so vital to our understanding of contemporary urban life, and then one of the curator women explained some of the ideas behind their big exhibition of women's art, and it was impossible to listen. When eventually they went in to look at Ida-Marie's work, Lea plucked up the courage and stepped up to Diana with her cheeks blushing.

'I'd like to thank you, Diana.'

It was obvious she had rehearsed.

'Peter told me all about your photo session together. I even think he relished it. You saved me from the biggest prat on earth, so I just want to say thanks!'

L ater that evening, we had roast pigeon at Le Basilique. Lea got stuck in to the Rhône.

'You've found your style, Diana.'

'What is my style, Lea?'

'There's a congruity between your life and your art. I wish I could say the same for me!'

Lea laughed without reason.

'But you're a troublemaker, Diana Kiss!'

She pinched Diana's cheek. 'A bloody troublemaker, that's what you are!'

'I thought I was minding my own business,' said Diana, and removed Lea's hand.

'You let my man fuck you!'

The others tried to keep a conversation going.

'You documented his sperm dribbling out of your cunt. You're a troublemaker, all right.'

'Are you jealous?'

'I've wished you into the depths of hell, Diana.'

'You've no need to be jealous.'

'You're very full of yourself, aren't you?'

'Would you like me to get nasty?' said Diana.

She squeezed my arm under the table.

'Come on, let's go,' I said.

D iana had cycled to Buresø when Clara phoned the studio and invited us for dinner. She was sure we would just love the doctor from her road, with his artist girlfriend she insisted I remembered from Jazzclub Montmartre, and as she went on I happened to notice some drawings sticking up out of the drawer in the big dresser. They looked like any other kids' drawings: a house, a sun, a cloud, and they were dated on the back:

Nona, 7/12/2004. Nona, 6/9/2006.

Clara was still going on about the doctor's artist girlfriend, something about a difficult childhood and the old song about parents wanting to give vent to their dreams, but staying put until there was no more left in the bottle.

'People who grew up in happy homes are dead boring,' she said.

'I don't know anyone who did,' I said.

'Nikolaj Krogh,' said Clara.

'Oh, that's right, Nikolaj Krogh.'

'He's the most boring man in the world,' she said.

I thought about closing the drawer, but left it open.

An ageing secretary in a blouse and pleated skirt led me through the long corridors of the publishing house, eventually stopping at a corner office.

Bernhard put his pen down immediately and rose to greet me, polite in the way no one ever is anymore. I'd sent him the first fifty pages of my manuscript and they lay in a clear folder on his desk.

'The style is there, you've got a good grip on your story, and even in the bleakest passages the reader really feels for Søren T-shirt. But this second layer to the book, your reflections on coupledom, this rather surprised me.'

He jabbed at the folder.

'You're writing from on top of a bonfire. You've got something you're burning to say.'

'I want to abolish coupledom,' I said.

'The love story *is* touching, but it's the other stuff that's dynamite. In parts it almost reads like a manifesto. Goodbye, coupledom, thanks for nothing!'

The secretary came in with two Ramlösa mineral waters and a pair of limescaled drinking glasses.

'My advice would be to develop that part of it as far as possible. This is an issue everyone can relate to, whether they're in agreement or not. It'll be like an arrow to people's hearts, Mikkel. You could start a whole new paradigm.'

He reached down into a drawer and took out another folder.

'Here's a contract. Have a look and see what you think. My feeling is you've got a flow going. Could you deliver a completed manuscript by October the first? Does that sound realistic?'

'Definitely.'

'There's something I need to know. The couple arguing about the cucumber salad, Helene and Tue Nissen, right?'

I nodded.

'Have you got that cleared with Helene? Aren't you the father of her child?'

He gazed out of the window for about fifteen seconds.

'On second thoughts, just keep writing! We'll address that as and when it comes up.'

The secretary knocked and behind her hovered an author with saggy Rioja cheeks and a suit jacket that reeked of smoke. Bernhard shook my hand.

'We've launched a ship, Mikkel. Now let's sail her out to sea.'

And with that he bid the next in line welcome with an enthusiasm that seemed genuine.

Helene was sitting in the publishing house canteen with a cup of tea.

'What did he say?'

'He gave me a contract.'

'Congratulations! And he's going to do the edit himself? That's encouraging, but then Søren T-shirt and Signe do make a really good story.'

It was a relatively large canteen and someone at some point had decided to purchase a hundred good-quality wooden chairs. I imagined the decisive meeting, catalogues on the table, two representatives from the dealers, cold cuts and sesame buns, coffee in Stelton pots and a little bowl of shortbread biscuits.

Helene had a salad, I opted for pâté with sour pickle and frisée lettuce.

'Whatever happened to your country gent look?' she said.

I was in my new favourite trousers, narrow in the leg, with a large pastel check. We talked about Charlie's growing vocabulary and the kindergarten, and then she got to the point.

'I'm worried about you, Mikkel.'

'I've never felt better.'

She tilted her head at me and had another sip of tea.

When she got back to her office, the secretary would have stuck two Post-its to the edge of her desk. A women's magazine had called wanting any final adjustments to an author interview, and that freelance journalist woman with the dry hair who wanted to do a feature on some supposed trend among young female writers had called with a reminder about some free copies. Later, a photographer would be there to show her some graphically enhanced landscapes from Alaska and a series of black-and-white portraits of well-known people in the arts. She would cancel a spinning session too late and sit on the toilet for twenty minutes with her heart pounding, and when she got back the secretary would have stuck another Post-it to her desk: the freelance woman again, now with exclamation marks. Later still, there would be rump steak on offer in Irma on Gammel Kongevej, and she would give it a miss because someone or other had said the gastric system took weeks to break down beef. She would go to the vegetable section and stare blankly at leeks and spring cabbage, and end up grabbing a pack of chicken breasts without knowing what on earth to do with them.

Helene poured the last of the tea from the pot.

'It all seems so desperate, this playing the free bohemian. What's it all about, Mikkel?'

I didn't feel provoked in the slightest.

'I'm just trying in my own little way to avoid all the tedious rules and patterns. Isn't that okay?'

'You drink too much, Mikkel, you have done for years. Now you've found yourself a situation that makes it legitimate.'

'I drink less now than when we were together.'

It sounded good, but it was a lie.

'Are you saying it was me and my tedious rules that forced you to consume a whole bottle of white wine every night? Was it me who made you sit outside for hours on end, staring into space and going on about blackbirds, Mikkel?'

'I never said that, but living like that wasn't good for us, Helene. We were utilising about a tenth of our potential, at best.'

'Isn't one of the definitions of growing up that for a time you think less about your own happiness than that of others?' she said.

'Children are no happier for their parents discussing the rendering of outside walls.'

'Oh, come on, Mikkel. Now you're being mean.'

'I'm sorry if I sound harsh, but the truth is you and Tue argue about cucumber salad.'

She sighed through her nose.

'Our Tuesday-night dinners are an attempt to bring some kind of unity into Charlie's life, Mikkel. Why should I be afraid of not living up to your new ideals? Am I to be monitored in my own home?'

She raised her voice, and the author in the smoky jacket looked nosily across. It wasn't the first time she had spoken to me like this.

'You've got me snarling at you now,' she said. We both laughed.

'You're in love, Mikkel, but it's summer and she's young and beautiful.'

'And autumn will come around soon, is that it?'

'It generally tends to,' she said.

'It won't this year.'

We were due at Clara's for dinner at seven and I wasn't in the slightest bit worried. God knows, she had always been my most perceptive critic, but at the age of forty-two I had become immune to her judgement.

I didn't give a shit what she would make of Diana.

That said, Clara is not just anyone. Halfway through high school her family moved to Provence and when she came back a few years later, she was a fully fledged woman, more sophisticated than all of us. She was the epitome of upper-middle-class chic.

No one could do the Bodum cafetière like her.

The sun reflected in the cobbles, and the cluster of homeless men outside the hostel stood patting their dogs. It was half past six and no one had the energy to argue about anything. Rounds were bought and people sat on the steps with their legs tingling. It was the first evening of summer, and tonight everyone was beautiful.

Up on Jan's rooftop they were sniffing poppers and dancing to 'You Spin Me Round' by Dead or Alive. I made eye contact with a bony

Swiss performance artist in an army jumpsuit. Though I matched her
in my short-sleeved navy surplus shirt, she sussed straight away that
I'd never been keen on either Front 242 or The Young Gods, but I did
know the entire fretless bass solo from 'Brother to Brother' by heart.
Diana danced with a Brooklyn DJ with a bowl cut and heavily kohled,
beautiful eyes. Otherwise it was all dinner jackets and patent leather
shoes.

'My drawings have been sent to Vietnam!'

She threw her arms around my neck, and to avoid stealing any of
her thunder I refrained from telling her about my publishing contract
and sent her back to dance some more.

Lisa dangled about with a spliff and a Kir Royale and was generally out of time. As far as I could gather from her pretentious incoher-
ence, they were warming up for a big night at Jolene's.

'He's not my type,' she slurred.

'Who isn't?'

Her lights were on, but there was no one in.

'He's too perfect.'

'God, you mean?'

'Do you realise how gorgeous Nikolaj Krogh smells?'

She did a little jump like a girl with a skipping rope and began to
shout something into my ear. I felt the spray of her spit on my earlobe,
but heard only Tom Tom Club, and when I looked at her again her
face was a void of despair. I patted her shoulder like you're supposed
to, and she stepped back and smiled.

'We'll party all night!'

She grabbed my hand and swayed like a housewife on the Chianti,
only for tears to well up again. Rather appropriately, she chose the
twelve-inch version of 'Fade to Grey' as the backing track for her final
breakdown. Jan took her on to his lap.

'Why don't you stay here?' he said to me. 'It won't be Diana's
scene there. Let them keep their Steely Dan for themselves.'

Reluctantly, I went to drag Diana out of the seething international
scenario into which she'd mingled, preparing to have to coax her in

the direction of one involving feta cheese, Arne Jacobsen chairs and French flea-market items, but all she did was smile sweetly. Maybe she found the prospect of a dinner party for couples in the fashionable terraced dwellings of the Kartoffelrækkerne exotic.

'We're taking some poppers with us, aren't we?' she said.

We stopped for an absinthe at Krut's, then ambled along, flanked by the chestnut trees.

Diana looked down the rows of houses and I got the urge to tell her stories from my past. How on nights like this when I was a child, I would have been zigzagging my bike through the chewing-gum stains. The men wore grandad shirts back then, and the girls never said hello. I had a colour for each of the ten streets. Jens Juelsgade was still red-brown, and Eckersberggade a stand-offish blue. There was always a light on in the frosted window at the rear of the baker's shop when we cycled home from the Montmartre club, and two bottles of Tuborg would get you a huge bag of rolls and pastries. The prostitutes on Lille Farimagsgade wore negligés and tipped the grocer's delivery boy handsomely, unlike the widows in the spacious apartments of Malmøgade.

Østre Anlæg was the end of the world with all its forbidding hiding places and the bench by the football field where student types and dropouts smoked Afghan black.

Diana's eyes glistened. I noticed her eyeliner was smudged. We kissed madly.

Clara was immediately self-effacing. She'd had no idea Diana was *that* beautiful and what an elegant dinner jacket, and all *she* could muster was this old black thing from Filippa K, and how interesting about Diana's art, and do forgive me for not being in the know, I just file along with everyone else at Louisiana, and I only ever get to the meat-packing district when we need to buy in bulk at the cash-and-carry, there never seems to be time for the galleries there. She stopped us in the hall.

'We're having leg of lamb and it's giving goose pimples. Joke, ha ha!'

Diana had no idea what she was on about, which was just as well.

Kreuzmann was at the centre of things, as always. Champagne in hand, spotless white shirt and a silk polka-dot cravat.

'Here they come, Bonnie and Clyde!' His face was oddly stiff, his eyes glazed.

The doctor's name was Mosbeck. He was in his mid-fifties and made an effort to seem friendly. His hair was straight and swept back, and he was barrel-chested in an old-fashioned sort of way. His eyes registered everything. He was wearing a pale blue shirt and shoes that were scuffed and worn-looking. His artist girlfriend, Kathrine, had no hairstyle to speak of, just dark hair, and her threadbare denim jacket looked like it had been grown on her. I knew her type: Café Wilder, too much hash in the eighties, automatically left-wing, collector of seashells, cat lover, careless with her bikini line and just about able to pull off a kids' song with an easy G-chord.

Erik Brinch played the host, and when he realised I'd rather have a beer than champagne he drew me out into the hall.

'I've got to tell you this, Vallin.'

He glanced over his shoulder to make sure we were on our own.

'You know how worked up Clara gets when she's putting on a dinner, don't you? So what do you think I do while she's standing there julienning the fennel? I come up behind her, pull her knickers down and stick the cocky gentleman up her Fanny Adams. Can you imagine the state she's in? The neighbours! It'll never be ready on time! But then imagine how horny she gets not being able to do a thing about it. No escape! Do you know the feeling, being so far up inside a woman it feels like you're conquering new land?'

Clara called everyone to the table.

'Screaming and moaning, she was. Must have had five orgasms in the space of fifteen minutes. Fennel and pussy juice all over the place.' He tossed his head back and laughed, allowing me a view into his gullet.

The door opened and Clara came out.

'What are you two standing here talking about?'

'I think you know perfectly well, darling!'

She glanced at me and blushed.

'Dinner's ready. It's on the table.'

I was put next to Kathrine. She told me frankly that the art boom had left her and the other members of the artists' collective Pust behind.

'The times aren't exactly crying out for non-figurative painting,' she said.

The last two months she'd spent all her energy selecting and photographing paintings for her new website.

'Can you see the idea?' she said. 'In a month the site will be up and then everyone will be able to see all the paintings they don't want to buy.'

Clara was carving the lamb when Mosbeck raised his voice so that all conversation around the table stopped.

'Are you happy at Galleri Moritz, Diana?'

'Kaspar Moritz is sweet,' she said.

'No faulting his connections, am I right?'

Diana nodded and asked him what he was getting at.

'Have you heard of De Unge Vilde?' he went on.

'She's twenty-seven,' said Clara.

The tomato salad floated in its own juice.

'De Unge Vilde were the first major new departure after the Cobra movement,' said Mosbeck. 'Painting was dead throughout the seventies, but then all of a sudden these extremely talented and visionary artists appeared and claimed it back. Kathrine was part of that.'

'I met some of them later on,' she said.

'Being an artist then was all about creating *works of art*,' said Mosbeck. 'These days all artists seem to care about is creating *themselves*. Or am I too far out of line?'

'You've been saving that up, haven't you?' said Kreuzmann.

'I like anyone who creates a scene,' said Diana.

'Perhaps Kathrine's mistake has been that she has always concentrated on her art,' said Mosbeck. 'On the other hand, she can paint.'

'She's certainly competent,' said Erik Brinch. 'Fine sense of colour.'

'Enough about my art!' said Kathrine.

'Get to the point, for God's sake!' said Kreuzmann.

'What does one of your tapestries cost, Diana?' asked Mosbeck.

'The new ones are priced at ninety thousand.'

'Well,' said Mosbeck. 'I can tell you that Kathrine puts just as much energy into her work as you do into yours, Diana, and she has rather more experience. And yet your works cost more than three times as much as hers. Food for thought, I'd say.'

'Don't your paintings sell, Kathrine?' Kreuzmann asked.

'I've never sold anything, really.'

Kathrine poured herself some wine and spilled some in the process.

'People are starting to look for quality again,' said Mosbeck.

'You can't get anywhere today without a gallery,' said Clara.

Mosbeck straightened his shoulders.

'Do you think Galleri Moritz would be interested in an artist like Kathrine?'

'There we go!' said Kreuzmann.

'What's Diana supposed to say to that?' said Kathrine.

'She might be able to put in a good word.'

'She hasn't even seen what I do!'

'We could have a little walk down to the studio,' said Mosbeck.

'First dessert,' said Clara. 'I'm stuck in the eighties, as you know, so we're having baked figs. What would Mikkel and Diana say to popping over to the convenience store with me for some cream?'

Children were playing hide and seek in the street. Clara looked back over her shoulder.

'It was a mistake inviting Mos and Kathrine.'

'She's obviously uncomfortable being forced to be the centre of attention,' I said.

'It's his guilty conscience. Mos was away working in Norway all winter. Doctors can make a packet there, and Kathrine accidentally read a text message from a Norwegian nurse.'

'What did it say?' asked Diana.

'Something lovey-dovey and shaggy-shaggy.'

'He'd been bonking a nurse in Norway?'

'Kathrine's not exactly Mae West, is she?' said Clara. 'More like a mouse on a treadmill.'

'What are her paintings like?' I asked.

'Imagine. That's what they're like.'

Erik Brinch put some salsa music on after the fig dessert and swayed about, sloshed and full of food. Clara cleared the table and had blotches under her eyes. She was no longer in a position to insist on status and refinement in her relationships, and Erik Brinch only just made the cut: he *had* fallen asleep while watching Kurosawa, he *may* have known that Miles recorded *Kind of Blue* before *Bitches Brew*, and he *might* have been able to tell a Burgundy by the sloping shoulders, but as a future prospect he clearly fell short. On the other hand, they seemed to have a sex life.

But what about Kathrine and Mosbeck? She became grey in his company, and they seemed more like friends than lovers. Perhaps neither of them had the courage to go it alone.

Clara was drinking red wine now, which she never used to.

'Anyway, I must hear about this open relationship of yours!'

'What do you want to know?'

Thankfully, Diana was talking to Kreuzmann.

'Diana and Mikkel don't want to be a couple. Isn't that modern?'

'I'll say!' said Mosbeck. 'We're in 1967, right?'

'My conscience isn't cut out for more coupledom,' I said.

'What are you after instead?' said Clara.

'To try what I want.'

'So you don't want to be tied down as a couple?' said Clara.

'Animals are tied, tethered so they don't run away,' I said.

'What's it actually like having an open relationship?' said Clara.

'Are all other relationships closed? That doesn't sound appealing.'

'So you keep all your doors open,' said Clara. 'That must be draughty.'

'All my relationships died because they couldn't get enough air,' I said.

'Aren't you too old to be spouting such banalities?' asked Mosbeck.

'Letting go of the banal makes you old,' I said.

'Oh, for God's sake!' said Mosbeck. 'Pathetic.'

'That sounded old,' I said.

'I *am* old,' said Mosbeck. 'I'm past gallivanting. I've got experience and I draw upon it in my work, in my dealings with others, in my relationship.'

'And you both live out your potential and are happy together?'

'I live within it. Happy and not. I live within it.'

'Do you bring other people home with you, Mikkel?' asked Clara.

'So far it's just been us.'

'And what if all of a sudden Diana wants to go to bed with someone else instead?'

'Instead?' I replied.

Mosbeck laughed excessively. It wasn't that funny.

'You've got nothing to laugh about,' said Kathrine.

'No, I must take something for it,' he said. 'What do you do to stay miserable?'

'I live with you.'

'It's not forbidden to think before you open your mouth, Kathrine.'

'You live in an open relationship yourself, Mosbeck. You just forgot to tell me about it, that's all. You shag around.'

Mosbeck got to his feet.

'Perhaps we ought to go home and be old,' he said.

'Speak for yourself,' said Kathrine.

'I said *we* on purpose, meaning including you.'

'Poppers, anyone?' said Diana, shaking the little bottle in the air.

'I'm sick of being *included* by you,' said Kathrine.

'So you want an open relationship, too, do you?' Mosbeck asked. 'Well, I can tell you that opening up only makes sense if someone else wants in. Otherwise it's just you, wide open.'

Kathrine took the bottle of poppers, took a snort and was gone for a minute.

'You fucked my friends, Mosbeck! They've admitted it.'

'Drunken nonsense,' said Mosbeck.

'Clara didn't want to. Otherwise you'd have fucked her, too.'

'You're humiliating yourself, Kathrine,' said Mosbeck.

'Did Mosbeck ask you if you wanted to go home for a shag, Clara?' asked Kathrine. 'Come on! Did he ask you if you wanted a shag?'

'We were drunk, and it was three years ago,' said Clara.

Mosbeck put his jacket on and came over to me.

'Are you satisfied, Mikkel? Do you enjoy tearing people's relationships apart?'

His breath was dense from the wine, and droplets of spit sprayed into my face.

'Time for Doctor Jollycock to go home and sleep it off,' said Kreuzmann.

'You stay out of this,' said Mosbeck.

'Fuck off!' said Kreuzmann.

Mosbeck turned and wrestled off his jacket.

'Why don't you make me, you shabby little backstreet broker?'

Kreuzmann stepped towards him.

Mosbeck took a step forward and lashed out with his right fist. Kreuzmann ducked and punched him clean in the solar plexus. Mosbeck stood for a second, eyes wide, then crumpled up, gasping for breath. He lay on the floor for five minutes before cautiously getting to his feet. We could hear him throwing up in the toilet.

It was half past one by the time we staggered out of the door. The desirable residences of the Kartoffelrækkerne lay dead, but the rest of the city was alive.

'That was my past,' I said in the taxi as it drove us to Jolene's.

'Kreuzmann's good,' she said.

I put my arm around her delicate shoulders.

'Just the two of us now,' I said.

Jan was standing at the bar with that peculiar perplexity in his eyes a person can only experience by anaesthetising the body with booze and keeping the mind awake on coke cut with speed. His arms hung like a marionette's and his black shirt glistened with sweat. He smiled slowly as he finally managed to focus and haul himself up to the surface. The music was simplistic and pedestrian, the place as humid as Sumatra.

'I've been offered a publishing contract,' I said.

'Why haven't you said anything?' Diana replied.

'You two don't half go on,' said Jan. 'What are you rabbiting about now?'

'Mikkel's been offered a contract for his book!' said Diana.

Levinsen appeared in our midst. He'd lost the beard and was all in black, apart from a red knitted tie.

'Are we going to Tisvilde this year?'

'Mention of Tisvilde's prohibited here,' said Jan.

'Aren't you Jan Minetti?' Levinsen asked.

'You're not supposed to *know* me,' said Jan.

'I'm mad about your work,' said Levinsen.

'Who's this?' enquired Jan.

'That gallery owner from Aarhus,' said Diana.

'The one with the dick?'

Levinsen and Diana air-kissed.

'Well, get it out, then!' said Jan.

'Only if you'll all come and dance afterwards.'

Levinsen began to unzip his pants, and though I turned away on the pretext of getting something from the bar, it was impossible not to hear Diana's shriek of laughter.

'It's like something from a cash-and-carry!' Jan exclaimed. 'I don't like them that big.'

When I turned back with four superfluous beers in my hands, Diana and Levinsen had gone off for a dance.

'Diana's not going to Tisvilde,' said Jan.

'We've been invited.'

'She's going to Berlin with me. I've already bought the tickets.'

'Fine by me,' I said.

Diana and Levinsen danced well together. They were showing off, coming on to each other with no inhibitions, staring into each other's eyes.

'You've not got Diana under control!' said Jan. His eyes were narrow and yellow.

'How do you mean?' I asked. Why was I kidding myself?

Ten seconds later, I was outside in the summer night's air and I resolved to read Marcel Proust as soon as I sobered up. I failed to notice Istedgade, failed to notice Rådhuspladsen and the seamless alliance of Peruvian pan pipes and Burger King, stopping only when I found myself outside Floss. Inside, they were singing along to 'Stuck Inside of Mobile with the Memphis Blues Again', and Søren was seated at the bar with the Faroese scriptwriter.

'I'd quite like to go to Tisvilde this year,' he said.

'You hate Tisvilde!'

'It'd do me good, eating fish and relaxing. Do you reckon your new girlfriend will like me?

You know I'll come presentable, and I know more about art than the lot of you put together.' A young gnomish-looking guy with a pointy beard, fashionable drug habit and tight black Acne windbreaker enticed Søren outside. The spirits shelves were lit from behind, presenting an array of bottles of all shapes and sizes, each with its own alluring label. There was a surprisingly wide selection of grappa and a good stock of whisky and rum. I started thinking about Helene and Charlie. Maybe I ought to suggest to Helene I pick Charlie up from the kindergarten more often. Once a week? Twice? I felt a hand on my waist and the Faroese scriptwriter proceeded to pitch me a story. The beginning was original, but that was it. Søren came back to scrounge the usual two hundred, and when he encountered no resistance he put it up to five and assured me I wouldn't regret it.

Twenty minutes later we were sitting in the gnome's flat, plexiglas furniture, street art on the walls, expensive clothes on the floor and a couple of girls who seemed to never finish putting their make-up on. A mirror went round and Søren told the girls that I, his best friend, was writing a book about him. 'I'm a goddam hero!' he exclaimed in English, and flexed his biceps.

Three lines later, Søren and I found ourselves amid a group of ladyboys at Cozy Bar, dancing to Madonna. Someone put their arms around me from behind.

'You mustn't leave me like that!' said Diana

We French-kissed our way through 'Tainted Love'. She had been looking for me all over town. We went to the toilets, and I loved the reek of cheap aftershave.

The Internet has altered our psychology. What started out as a technological revolution, a sharing of knowledge, has now become an integrated part of our lives and has added a whole new dimension to the concept of community. Social networks have made it completely normal for us to share our lives online. We converge and diverge at will and without resistance. At the same time, we are forced to make choices quickly, we click yes or no, responding to one thing at the expense of another, and must keep our wits about us: wrong decisions online can be ruthlessly exploited, or generosity returned tenfold.

This new way of constructing our lives has already impacted on the way we experience love and relationships. The pursuit of unselfish, impassioned intensity is a driving force of life in the modern age – we are both freer and more accountable for the choices we make.

While I'd been working on the book, Diana had been down in the Haslev area, cycling through the country estates. When she got back she lay like a starfish on the mattress as I licked the salt from her. Her armpits made me insane and I ordered her to lie still while I went to work on her pussy with my tongue and fingers, and then my ferociously insistent cock.

I asked her whether she'd be willing to read what I'd written so far.

'If it'll help,' she said.

It would, for I was constantly battling with myself as to whether I was being a parasite, feeding on her way of life and exploiting her by writing about it for my own gain.

'It's ended up being a lot about coupledom,' I said.

'Couplet is a nice word,' she said. 'But coupledom sticks in the throat. Isn't there anything better to call it?'

'Pairing off, alliance. Too vague. Relationship, yuk!'

'Maybe we should invent a new word.'

'I'd rather invent a new way of being together.'

We went into the kitchen, where Jan was in a thick, white towelling robe, sipping ginger tea and making a noise about how he couldn't remember anything from Jolene's, which might have been his awkward way of saying sorry.

'I've got a present for you, darling,' he said, and handed Diana a ticket to Berlin.

'Why don't you come to Berlin with us, Mikkel?' she said.

I told them I needed to focus and spend a couple of days with Søren in order to make headway with the book, not admitting that Berlin, and its entire mythology, had annoyed me ever since the eighties on account of all the phoney depressives who went there to cultivate darkness and misunderstand Joy Division before plucking up the courage to do their degrees in librarianship. Also, I didn't want to go with Jan.

I kneeled down and shouted through Søren's letterbox. Even at Floss they were concerned. Occasionally he wouldn't turn up for a day or two, but never a whole week.

The neighbour opened his door, a flabby bloke with tits in an undershirt.

'Have you seen Søren?' I asked.

He shook his head and closed the door again.

Søren T-shirt had been in mortal danger at least fifty times, including three occasions on which he'd actually been dead and had been brought back to life with adrenaline.

I stopped by Camilla White Wine's place and she blushed.

'You must think I'm never decent.'

She was in her see-through robe again.

'Have you seen Søren?'

'Come in,' she said. 'He's starting to feel better now.'

A sickbed had been rigged up in the bedroom: puke bucket, moist compresses, painkillers on the bedside table. She opened a window. 'I found him asleep on my doormat,' she said, shaking her head.

Nothing animates an alcoholic more than a fellow boozer in deep shit. 'How long's he been here?' I asked.

'Four or five days, I suppose,' she said. 'He's been completely out of it. Sleeping and crying like a little boy.'

Søren turned in the bed. 'Shut the fuck up!'

His hair was pressed flat against the back of his head and he'd got one of Camilla's T-shirts on. Fruit of the Loom.

'Do you want me to make you some mint tea?' she asked.

'What do you think?'

'It'll do you good, Søren.'

'I've been having nightmares. They've been after me, and I don't blame them. Really, I don't.'

He sat up in bed.

'It hasn't all been a dream, though.'

Camilla drew the robe around her. Søren pointed a finger.

'She's been rubbing herself up against me, the horny cow. I ought to report her for rape.'

'I'm sure Mikkel will agree that it's hard to rape a man who isn't aroused,' said Camilla White Wine.

'There's always life in the old trumpet, and you've been taking advantage,' said Søren.

She smiled overbearingly in my direction.

'I would have said thanks if someone had been looking after *me* for a week.'

'Shove it!' said Søren.

'Tell Mikkel about the soup yesterday.'

'Delicious,' said Søren. 'Unforgettable!'

Camilla White Wine's cheeks shone.

'White wine heated up in a saucepan.'

'Don't listen to him, Mikkel! I made him a proper Thai soup with chicken, coconut milk and lemongrass, and he wolfed it down.'

Camilla's three-litre box of Sunrise beckoned to her from the kitchen.

'Can we talk about the old days on Istedgade some time?' I asked.

'I need to get out of the city,' said Søren. 'Let's go to Tisvilde, eh? I'll behave myself.'

'It's upper crust there,' I said. 'It'll be full of kids.'

'I love kids, you know that. I could teach them to spit.'

I knew I was behaving like a traitor, but I was afraid if Søren came with me he would ruin my reputation.

'Come on. Your old mate needs a break,' he said. 'They'll love me. The stories I could tell them.'

I went out on to the balcony and gave Nikolaj Krogh a ring. He was in transit at Frankfurt airport and I told him what was nearly the truth, seeing no need for him to know Søren T-shirt was celebrating his twenty-fifth anniversary as a substance abuser.

He was unconditionally accommodating. 'Will we be seeing Diana, too?' he asked.

'She's going to Berlin.'

'You'll have to talk her out of that. Diana's made a big impression on Mille.'

I played Diana the *Minefield Elite* radio montage about the pianist Klaus Heerfordt on the boom box. It was an original cassette from Danmarks Radio's store. She laughed and cried.

'Brahms was there, in our icy rooms!'

We kissed until our jaws locked.

'Søren's coming to Tisvilde with me,' I said.

'I would have liked you to come to Berlin.'

I looked into her bright blue eyes.

'We want to be together, don't we?' I said.

Oddly enough, it was a sentence I'd never uttered before.

Diana ran her fingers through the hair at my neck. I was immediately filled with yearning. I had no idea why.

'Come on!' she said, and we went to find Jan.

He had a white facial mask on and was listening to Albinoni.

'This is the most amazing music,' he said. It was easy to get your head round, certainly. No effort required.

'I'm going with Mikkel to Tisvilde,' said Diana.

Jan sat up with a snort.

'You don't normally make bad decisions, Diana.'

Helene displayed her annual smattering of summer freckles and was playing badminton in the garden with Charlie. The lawn was lush and thick, the big rhododendron was in bloom and the garden furniture was made of dark wood. I shelled fjord shrimps with Tue and drank Mosel from Fritz Haag. Helene was in a bathing suit and it was unfair, of course, to compare her with Diana.

Helene was still slim, but more square and practical these days. Tue was wearing designer sandals and had a little paunch beneath his untucked shirt. The neighbour had got a barbecue going and the smoke smelled of firelighters. Tue heaped mayonnaise on his open shrimp sandwich.

Charlie played with his soldiers in the grass and Tue went into the kitchen to get the veal *fricassee*. I'd already worked out that he'd chosen the dish because it goes with both red wine and white.

'Bernhard believes in your book,' said Helene. 'He talked about it at our Monday conference. He says you're expanding your idea.'

'I'm going to war against coupledom,' I said.

'So I've heard. Have you thought it through?'

'No, it's from the heart,' I said.

'But you realise you might piss people off?'

Tue carried the *fricassee* to the table and picked my brains while Helene went inside to put something warmer on, as women do.

'Will it be based on your own life?' he asked.

She came back in a fleecy jogging suit.

'Of course,' I said.

'Am I in it?' Helene asked.

'There aren't any names,' I said.

'Is there cucumber salad in it? she said.

'Yes, Danish literature is crying out for cucumber salad,' said Tue.

'Mikkel overheard us arguing about cucumber salad,' said Helene.

'Any couple would recognise the example,' I said.

'But we're not *any* couple,' said Helene. 'I'm the mother of your child.'

'I think we'll survive the cucumber salad,' said Tue.

'How are the curators going to understand my work if I don't understand it myself?' said Ida Marie.

For once she had joined us on the rooftop terrace.

'Only fools talk of content,' said Jan. 'John Kørner's paintings aren't good because of their message, but because he interferes with it.'

'How on earth can I paint souls?' said Ida Marie.

'I always loved paintings of real people,' said Diana. 'Faces and conversations and friends dancing. I would love to do that some day.'

'People are so boring,' said Jan.

I went off into the summer night.

Up on the first floor on Flensborggade they were singing along to Elliot Smith. I followed an impulse and went to Jolene's. And there I was, bright-eyed at the bar, when Levinsen came sidling up in a military shirt and narrow black tie.

'What have you done with Diana?'

'She's at home.'

'Problems?'

'Not at all.'

My composure seemed to stress him out.

'Can I tell you something?' he said. 'She flirts with me.'

I took a sip of my beer.

'How do you feel about that?' he said.

'I don't,' I said.

His eyes narrowed.

'People should know what a good bloke you are, Vallin!' he said.

When I got home, Diana lay reading my manuscript. Every now and then she laughed a bit, or seemed taken aback. Then all of a sudden she got up and put some music on, and I had absolutely no idea how my words could trigger a desire to listen to 'Daniel' by Elton John.

'I can't wait to find out what happens to Søren T-shirt and Signe,' she said.

'What about the rest of it?' I said.

'I skipped all that.'

On the Friday morning Peter Kiest phoned from *Berlingske Tidende* and was more cheerful than was called for.

'How's it going, you old libertine?' he said.

He was doing a piece for their MS lifestyle section about unusual couples, 'Coupledom 2.0', and had heard down at the Byens Kro that I was with Diana.

'From what I hear you've got an open relationship going on. Is that something you'd be willing to share with our prim lady subscribers?'

'When do you want to meet?'

'Yesterday! How about this afternoon?'

We got Dóra Dúna to open up Jolene's especially for us and the photographer stalked about.

'I've not actually got anything to say about relationships,' said Diana. 'Is it okay if I just sit here and look good?'

Peter Kiest came swanning in fifteen minutes late and leaned his old Raleigh up against the window. Stubble doesn't become a man in his condition: worn-out leather shoes of middling quality, a streak of dried-up dressing on his lapel. He did a little sidestep as he got off the bike.

'Are you a proper journalist?' said Diana, extending a ladylike hand.

'They don't come more proper than this. I've known your husband here for years.'

Diana looked at me with eyes wide.

'You mean Mikkel?' she said. 'He's cute, isn't he?'

'I don't suppose we could get a beer,' said Peter Kiest. 'I was at an opening at young Asbæk's yesterday and all I saw were the drinks. No expense spared, I can tell you.'

He got himself into a weakly plotted tale of his subsequent night of drink and debauchery, but there was nothing left of it by the time he reached what didn't happen at the bar at Wessels Kro.

'Anyway, Vallin, have you completely dumped journalism, or what?'

'It was mutual.'

'Rumour says you're writing a book.'

I nodded.

'Join the club. I've been working on mine on and off for four years. At some point I'm going to have to take that sabbatical and get the bloody thing finished.'

Indeed. It was a dark and stormy night . . .

'Still, it can't all be fun now, can it, as Rasputin said.'

'Boney M!' said Diana.

He produced a greasy little Dictaphone, placed it in front of us and altered his tone of voice.

'So what's wrong with coupledom today?'

Diana looked at me.

'Relationships haven't kept up with the times,' I said. 'Coupledom is reactionary, as the sixties lot would say. My feeling is that love will grow out of it and find new forms, and when it does we'll all have sex lives again.'

Peter Kiest chewed on his blue Bic and jotted down some notes on a crumpled notepad.

Dóra Dúna stood behind Diana, massaging her shoulders.

'You've been with women as well, haven't you, Diana?'

'I love girls, don't you?'

'And you two just met recently, is that right?' said Kiest.

'We've known each other for two and a half months,' I said.

'But it's hardly a revelation, is it, that two people who just met have more sex than a couple with two kids who need fetching while the spaghetti boils over?'

'Why become a couple at all, if all it comes down to is picking up kids and cooking pasta for dinner?' I said.

'You're a dad yourself,' said Peter Kiest. 'How often is your son with you?'

'Every other weekend.'

'Mikkel Vallin, you're with this beautiful, younger woman, and you've eliminated the drudgery of everyday responsibilities from your life. What if I said it's easy enough for you to say?'

'Would it be any less true?' I said.

'Diana, I've heard you've never had a steady partner, is that right?'

'I've never wanted one,' she said.

'So you can't promise Mikkel anything?' said Kiest.

'I can promise Mikkel I'll always be nice to him.'

'But what if you suddenly want to go to bed with someone else?'

'What if?'

'Would you act on that urge?'

'Of course.'

'Even if it made Mikkel jealous?'

'It wouldn't, I know.'

'Tell me about your younger days in Budapest.'

'I'd rather not,' she said.

'Why not?' said Kiest.

'I'd rather just be here.'

'But everyone comes with baggage from their past, even you.'

'I had nothing with me when I came to Copenhagen. Let's have some spumante, shall we?' said Diana, and then stalked off to the bar. Kiest eyed her bum without the slightest inhibition.

'You've found yourself a ball of fire there, Vallin.'

'Diana's like nobody else,' I said.

'You understand I've got to have a go at you, don't you? Free sex! Our lady subscribers are going to choke on their tea.'

He finished his beer and went back to rote journalism.

'Are we talking a new movement here, Vallin?'

'These thoughts aren't just mine. The movement has been out there for a long time, and I commit an offence against its autonomy by even attempting to put it into words.'

'What do you have to say about this movement, Diana?' said Kiest when she came back.

'I think we should stand in front of Anika Lori's DJ booth for the picture,' she said.

Helene called seven times as we posed.

There is something admonitory about the main entrance to Frederiksberg Park. Frederik VI with his hand on his hip and one foot splayed out to the side like a conceited ballet dancer, the sombre baroque gateway, the old herons that lurk by the bushes, the genteel poverty of the English lawns. A good place to meet and deliver bad news.

Helene was in frumpish lady's shorts and a short-sleeved blouse of indeterminable hue. Porridge-coloured, perhaps. 'I was working late at the office last night,' she said. 'When everyone had gone I sneaked into Bernhard's office and found your manuscript. So you finally found a cause, Mikkel.'

'Yes, and high time too,' I said.

'But you realise you're a laughing stock, don't you?'

'Who's laughing?'

'Anyone who can put two and two together. Old lech plus too much drink equals distorted self-perception. It's not original, you know.'

'Was there anything else you wanted, apart from throwing mud at me?'

'Actually, no. But let me spell it out to you, Mikkel. Our family dinners stop as of now,' she said.

'Charlie will be upset,' I said.

'Don't you dare use Charlie against me!' she said, going from zero to a hundred in nothing flat. Her voice rocketed off range.

'What you're writing is a public report from inside my home. How dare you! Have you gone completely mad? How can you play spokesman for some embarrassing drunken idea when you're incapable of mustering even a minimum of responsibility for your own child?'

She became increasingly hideous as she berated me. The area of upper lip between her mouth and nose swelled, her eyes grew small and her cheeks hollowed. I had written something that made her look ugly.

A well-heeled elderly couple sought cover behind their picnic basket.

'I've got a very good relationship with Charlie,' I said.

'You have occasionally noticed he exists, Mikkel. Since you got back from Italy you've been on your own with him a total of six days.'

'I was thinking I'd like to take him somewhere,' I said.

I was eating an open roast beef sandwich from the ferry's cafeteria and staring out at the horizon until I realised that sea and seagulls have never done a thing for me. Charlie had fallen asleep with his head in my lap. On the table was a half-eaten kids' pizza and a Coke in a plastic beaker. Charlie had put his toy men away in his little blue suitcase. The two of us were on our way to the Gæstgivergaarden in Allinge. Three days of fairground, beach life, local vegetables on the barbecue and live music in the evenings. Helene and I were tipped off about the place when Charlie had still been a baby, and we'd loved it, even if we hated being there together.

I got the day's *Berlingske Tidende* out of my bag. The photo editing had accentuated mine and Diana's blue eyes, making them stand out bright against the shocking pink figures on Anika Lori's DJ booth. 'Couplehood 2.0.'

'Artist and writer couple Diana Kiss and Mikkel Vallin allow each other the ultimate freedom!'

I read the interview for the third time, and it was almost quite good. The main thrust of my thoughts had been retained, but Kiest had angled it all rather more sharply than I thought necessary. We are a new movement, I read myself saying. Diana came across like a flitting muse, with me the great agitator whose declared aim was to destroy all Danish couples and introduce gang-banging on the village green.

He seemed to have fast-forwarded past my idealistic visions of love without limits.

We checked into our hotel room and were back in the seventies.

Framed LP sleeves of *Gas 2* and *Stakkels Jim* on the wall, an old Gibson repro in the corner.

'Nice interview, Vallin,' said Henrik, one half of the couple who managed the hotel. 'We're thinking of setting up a communal shagging room in the basement. Red Burgundy and wife-swapping. Have we got a concept or what?'

C harlie wanted to go outside and play football on the little lawn by the clothes line and I wasn't going to refuse him anything on this trip. He soon hooked up with Giovanni, a little terror his own age with thick brown hair, whose parents nodded obligingly and looked like the sort of people you ended up on a street party committee with. Lars was the type of man who attracted bewildered women. Solidly built, narrow-eyed and good at repair work. His wife, Suste, played the scrumptious little dolly bird and was effortlessly flirtatious by nature. Lars looked like a former spliff-head from a well-to-do suburb with the usual accoutrements: Jaco Pastorius, retro racing bike and knowledge of basic frisbee techniques.

We acted like we were acquaintances, which can easily become a strain, but thankfully they didn't ask whether I'd been to the parties on Anemonevej or whether I could remember Gulv Knud from the Musikcaféen.

The evening's band got under way with the sound check. Five young guys in lumberjack shirts. The lead singer's rockabilly quiff and tattoos didn't quite align with the tameness of their music.

Lars was, of course, a carpenter, Suste an out-of-work actress. They were a good match, as they say. He was rather dull, she rather dizzy, and this classic combination had held for seventeen years and counting. They bought their apartment in a large detached in the Dyssegård district at just the right time and were parents to teenage twins as well as Giovanni. We had dinner together.

'How much do you know about wild garlic?' said Lars.

'We were wondering about it yesterday, whether it was still in season,' said Suste, then started to laugh. 'We sound like a parody, Lars.'

To reassure her, I told them wild garlic was in season in the spring and that the chef here had almost certainly harvested lots and made pesto out of it.

Suste was curious and outgoing. Lars was more inclined to do everything he could to avoid confrontation. I'd hoped to avoid talking about the article, but they'd seen it and she peppered me with questions as Lars stared out over the red-tiled rooftops, shredding the label of his beer bottle.

The lead singer had a waistcoat on and his shirt wide open, and his arms were soft and muscular as they are only on men under thirty. His voice had a rough edge to it and he sang with feeling, and it was obvious the women in the audience who were spoken for were trying not to ogle him for too long at a time. Suste had progressed to talking about divorce and had drunk herself categorical, she wasn't going to put up with anymore bollocks and tossed her head, but when this failed to trigger any kind of reaction from Lars she gave up the confrontation and turned her attention to the stage.

I took myself by the scruff of the neck and went rather light-headedly to bed.

The next morning I rented a bike with a trailer and pedalled off into the countryside with Charlie. We sang for the fields and the sea, and after fifteen kilometres we stopped at a little ice-cream kiosk and were gloriously on holiday. This is our trip to Bornholm, I thought to myself. This is what it looks like. Maybe I had sat there like Charlie with my own father once. Maybe.

When we got back to the Gæstgivergaarden the chairs outside were draped with bathing towels and the golden light of evening accentuated everyone's rosy cheeks. The band had declared a party after the gig and a number of guests were wearing white. Suste was affectionate, she wanted rum and Coke and to sit on Lars' lap. What Lars wanted was not immediately obvious.

People were dancing in the courtyard and Suste was inventing some new steps in front of the stage. Lars was still sitting where he was before. He hadn't moved.

'Where did you two meet?' I asked.

It was the sort of question that usually got people talking.

'Musikcaféen, Thursday the fourteenth of March 1991. A Sko/ Torp gig. They'd had that hit.'

'And there she was all of a sudden at the bar, or what?'

'No, she was right in the middle of the crowd.'

I waited, but nothing more was forthcoming.

Suste lived with his silence every day. Their friends probably thought of him as down to earth, deep even, because he never opened his mouth, but I was done hailing the mute. Maybe he was shy. If he was, he could do something about it. Or maybe he just didn't have anything to say, in which case his unwarranted points would have to be deducted.

I missed Diana dreadfully. It wasn't our style to call and kiss good-night, which was fine by me, but on the other hand it seemed silly to resist, and so I rang, only to reach her answerphone and hang up without saying anything.

Suste danced over with three Havana Clubs. Of course she had taken salsa lessons. We drank in silence. 'That's me for tonight,' said Lars. 'I'm turning in. Remember we promised the kids that trip to Brændegårdshaven tomorrow.'

The band were soaking it all up at the after-party, women of all ages hanging on their sideburns, but the lead singer, who called himself King of the Night, had read the piece in *Berlingske Tidende* and wanted to discuss it with me.

'I don't give a toss for your theories, Vallin. You say the Net has altered our psychology, but my friends are going the opposite way. Closing down their Facebook profiles. Chopping firewood and reading poetry.'

'Where are your friends from?' I said.

'I'm from Bistrup, between Holte and Birkerød. Why?'

'Do you know those people who drive up and down the Strandvejen in vintage cars on a Sunday, with leather driving helmets on? That's you.'

He couldn't see the funny side. Maybe he was on coke. Suste was standing next to us, swaying. She had buttoned down her shirt.

'Your generation are the ones with all the *bon viveur* shit, Vallin, but it's all crap. Couples are here to stay. There's beauty in banality. We *want* to repeat ourselves. People are happiest with repetition. Think of Buddhist monks.'

'Have you got any children?' Suste asked.

'I'm twenty-fucking-six,' he said. '*No kids.*' The latter he delivered in English.

'Repetition's good for kids, but it's not for grown-ups. *Trust me!*' said Suste, echoing the linguistic shift.

She downed a Havana Club and poured herself another.

'That bitch is seriously frustrated,' said the lead singer.

'That bitch is going insane,' said Suste.

'How come?'

'Have you got the balls to listen?'

'*Hit me!*' said the lead singer.

'All I can think about is sex, but I'm not getting any.'

'I've got plenty for everyone,' said the lead singer.

'So kiss me,' said Suste.

The little blue disc on the table began to flash. Our chips were ready. The sun reflected in the swimming pool, off the little steel table and the wet tiles. I went to the counter and collected our tray. Lars was in a black, short-sleeved shirt from the nineties. The kids pounced on the chips. They stank of tired cooking oil and lacked salt.

'She didn't come back until after breakfast,' said Lars.

A waft of chlorine enveloped us. His face was lined.

'It's not on. Disappearing like that. It's exactly what you're going on about, isn't it?' he said.

'How do you mean?'

'Screwing around.'

'I prefer to talk about exploiting our potential instead of being bored together,' I said.

He stared out at the water slide.

'I'd rather just be a decent dad.'

D iana was out and the room was in chaos.

Over by the stereo a messy pile of CDs lay separated from their covers. She had been listening to Motörhead and Elis Regina. Ravel's *Bolero*. I put them back and put Bill Evans on, then went over to the washing-up and lifted a plate. There was something black stuck to its edge. I went over to the bin and rummaged through cigarette ends and banana skins. It was down at the bottom. Oscietre Caviar, 50g. Then there were all the empties: one gin, one vodka, a jar of beetroot, a large number of beer bottles and four ginger ales from Naturfrisk. And there, shoulder to shoulder, two bottles of Launois Millesime, much lauded by champagne oracle Richard Juhlin. Lisa and Stig might have been over, but his taste was too poor. This was for connoisseurs.

Who else was in the know?

'Autumn Leaves' was full of chase. Bass and piano. Where did he find those notes? Bill Evans can play anything, but finding the notes there, at that exact juncture, was beyond virtuosity. They revealed themselves only to humans who had placed themselves utterly at their disposal.

I was dancing when Diana got home. Teddy bears showered down from the ceiling. Brown teddies, yellow teddies. The big white one.

It didn't come back together again until I was lying there slobbering her juices.

Nothing is as breathlessly unreal as an open cunt.

I cried when I delivered Charlie back to Helene. They were going to Mallorca for three weeks. Deia, naturally. Helene's safe choice.

Tue had started writing again and now Helene could talk about fresh figs in the salad without fear of an argument. I had a clear feeling that Charlie was going to miss me the first week. I said my farewells and headed over to Søren's, picking up Diana on the way.

The taxi pulled up outside his building in Østerbro at five to eleven. Søren was standing on the pavement with his fishing rod and a tightly packed holdall, smiling faintly. He was putting his best face on, but the way he mumbled a humble hello to Diana revealed just how fully aware he was of how little he had achieved in life. He is quite invincible whenever he approaches that realisation.

'Camilla White Wine says Mille's a well-known singer,' he said.

'She's got three Danish grammies,' I said.

'She played me one of her CDs. *Hangover* or something it was called. Does she drink?'

'Not in the way you're thinking,' I said.

'What's her music actually like?' said Diana.

'How would you describe it, Mikkel?' said Søren.

He hadn't the guts himself.

'Clever pop,' I said. Søren nodded.

'Wouldn't cut any ice at Café Jernstangen, am I right?'

I asked the driver to go through the Grib Skov forest and then as we got closer to Tisvilde suggested we drive along the seafront.

The good weather had drawn out almost every type of potential visitor. The cabriolet crowd had opted for Tisvilde over Mallorca, the advertising boys held their PPMs and brainstorming sessions on the patios and deckings, and the intellectual left stood chatting in front of the fish van where they spent the best part of an hour buying thirty-two kroner's worth of smoked halibut. Then there were all the day-trippers, flocks of gay men cruising at Stængehus, trespassers from the deadly dull summer house areas of Smidstrup and Dronningemølle, families in sweltering hot cars.

It was all still the same. The kiosk was there, wasps hovering around the ice-cream wrappers.

'This is one of the poshest lanes in town,' I said as we rolled slowly down Nordhusvej. 'Unmade roads get you extra points.'

'Why's that?' said Diana.

'Everything original is high status. The old families have houses either here or on the side lanes leading down to the water. The town itself has become too vulgar. The finer people live out in Lundene and decline to venture out among the masses.'

'Oh, do they indeed?' said Søren. Diana chuckled with him and it was good the two of them could have a laugh together, but I found the occasion disturbing. It had been a long time since I'd been made to feel snobbish. I looked at Søren and feared that derisive smile of his, but all he did was smooth his hand over my hair soothingly.

Mille was conspicuously casual. Open shirt over a little bikini, tummy flab on free display. Her thighs had become rather round and her arse would be a mouthful. On the other hand, she now had boobs.

Nikolaj Krogh was in checked shorts and a closely knit navy blue polo with no logo patch. He had pulled up the collar, which could only have been by mistake.

It was an exceptional summer house. The main building was classic two-storey, but behind it a whole world emerged. The property was huge, about a hectare in all, and seemed to emanate from an enormous oak tree. All the fruit trees were represented, as well as raspberry bushes, a neat vegetable garden with all sorts of lettuce, potatoes, carrots, beans, courgettes and a myriad of herbs, from classic Mediterranean such as oregano, thyme, marjoram and sage to the more rare: three varieties of mint, lovage and red basil. Sun-bleached hammocks, a big campfire place. No trampoline, certainly not.

Four spacious, black-painted wooden cabins stood at the far end of the garden, each bearing the name of a late figure of Danish arts on little brass plates: Lean Nielsen, William Skotte Olsen, Dan Turèll and F.P. Jac.

'My parents always had people staying,' said Nikolaj Krogh. 'Lean Nielsen once bit my mother on the cheek.'

Mille had put us up in Skotte Olsen, and I told Diana that he had been a painter and a bohemian, and that his paintings were always either blurred faces in front of urban buildings or floating fish. He found his style and flogged it to the death.

Nikolaj Krogh grilled scampi and Mille put on a denim teepee and revealed her soulless approach to cooking.

A couple of years before, her repertoire had consisted only of Caesar salad and Swedish stew, but a downward-spiralling career and peer pressure exerted by the mothers of Taarbæk had given her delusions. The lettuce was freshly picked and delicately arranged in a faience bowl, but the dressing told all. It lacked zest and inspiration.

'What's your book about?' she asked.

'It's about the demise of coupledom and Søren's life at Floss,' I said.

'I was actually one of the thirty people who saw the Sex Pistols at Daddy's Dance Hall,' said Nikolaj Krogh, sounding out with a glance whether he had permission to go into detail.

'Not again, Nikolaj,' Mille said. 'You know how sick I am of hearing about that bloody concert.'

'Yes, sorry, I think I probably have mentioned it before.'

'Mention's not the word,' said Mille. 'Mikkel's heard it before, as well.'

It was true. The disastrous dinner in Taarbæk.

'Apologies,' said Nikolaj Krogh. 'In a way I still live on the energy from back then. Punk really was a revolution.'

'Punk was an unarticulated scream,' said Mille.

'It democratised creativity,' said Nikolaj Krogh.

'Thirty years from now punk will be remembered only for its hair-styles,' she said.

Nikolaj Krogh's cheeks sank.

'Name one thing punk ever did,' said Mille.

'DIY! Its whole approach to art,' said Nikolaj Krogh. 'All of a sudden you could just do it, without qualifications, there was no longer any precondition. It's still the way I work.'

'So you're without qualifications now, are you? You grew up surrounded by beautiful things and were spoon-fed qualifications from day one. It's hardly an accident you ended up working with aesthetics.'

Nikolaj Krogh leaned back in his bamboo chair. The air may have been alive with birdsong, but that just wasn't much use to any of us.

We all went down to the beach to swim in the evening, except for Nikolaj Krogh, who stayed behind to wash up.

'I used to have a body like that,' said Mille, as she watched Diana undressing. 'Well, actually, my boobs were never that good, and just look at this flab!'

Søren and I sat clutching our beers.

'What about we get our interview done after breakfast?' I said.

He didn't see the need to answer.

'I was afraid it was going to be all latte-farty and stuck-up here,' he said. 'But everyone's really nice.'

Mille and Diana tumbled about with the kids in the waves.

'Do you think they like me?'

'Definitely!'

'When exactly do you think they *began* to like me?'

'Don't get started, Søren.'

'Personally, I think it was about halfway through dinner, but no doubt you'll have your own idea about that,' he said.

'I told them you're a drug addict and advised them to hold on to their hats, seeing as how you don't know the difference between what's yours and what isn't.'

Søren put his hands on his hips.

'That's funny! Nikolaj Krogh told me they were going to take down Lean Nielsen and put a shiny new Søren T-shirt plaque up instead.'

I felt an obligation to introduce Søren and Diana to the Bio Bistro. I gave them the bare bones on the way: steak, red wine and pipe-smoking in the seventies, tittle-tattle in the eighties and clubhouse for the creative class since the nineties. The dew of evening brought forth aroma, honeysuckle especially, making a mockery of my rigmarole.

Diana dazzled in her sand-coloured Bottega Veneta suit. Søren looked like a fag-smoking troll, and you don't see many of them about these days. We were shown to a table in the corner and had just started on the white wine when a speckless girl from the sunny side of Copenhagen put her hand on my shoulder. She was drunk, as her type always are as soon as they put their law textbooks down.

'Sorry to interrupt,' she said, rather sheepishly. 'It's just that I read the interview with the two of you, and it inspired me to dump my boyfriend. We were together for five years and he was a seriously good catch!'

'Why did you dump him?' Diana asked.

'Can I have a glass of wine?'

She downed a glass in one and poured herself another.

'I've never been with a girl,' she said.

'Do you want to?' said Diana.

'I've got a good body.'

She got to her feet and ran her hands over her curves.

'Xander doesn't think my boobs are big enough.'

She squeezed them together under her little top and sized us up without blushing.

'Is he going home with you?' she said, with a nod towards Søren

T-shirt. 'You're quite a cool couple, but he's wasted. What do you want him for? Why don't you take me home instead?'

'We only go to bed with trolls,' I said.

'Don't say that!' she said. 'Xander's always calling me his little troll. Who the hell wants to be called that? He just bought us a house on Phistersvej. I don't suppose you'll know it. Aren't you from Vesterbro?'

'If you haven't got any coke you can share with us, get lost,' said Søren.

The DJ put 'Hot in Here' on and our friend knocked her glass over in her rush to get back to the dance floor.

'Since when were you so famous?' Søren said. I told him about the interview in *Berlingske Tidende* and furnished him with a simplified version of my views on coupledom.

'So you're going out with the world's most gorgeous woman, and yet you're talking about getting your end away with others instead. What's the matter with you?'

'We're not a couple,' I said.

'What the fuck are you, then?' said Søren. 'You snog and shag and go on holiday together. Of course you're a couple!'

'We're trying to do it differently, in a new way,' I said.

'What's wrong with the old way? You meet a gorgeous woman, shag each other stupid, and then have kids. That's just the way it is.'

'Have you ever wondered why you've had so many relationships?'

'I was a junkie, wasn't I, you daft twat.'

'You were bored.'

'I thought you were writing a book about my relationship. I prefer drugs! I'm sick. I can't cope with myself.'

He fell silent. Diana gave him a hug.

'Why the hell did we have to go and talk about that?' he said. His little piggy eyes were moist.

'Do you fancy dipping into the lucky bag, gorgeous?' he asked Diana, producing a pouch from his inside pocket. Pills of all shapes, sizes and colours. Diana picked one out.

'Excellent choice!' said Søren. 'But only one, mind.'

Diana blinked and swallowed.

They sat huddled together with their arms around each other. I droned on about the syncopation in 'In the Stone' by Earth, Wind & Fire, and then went to the bar to get another bottle of white when I couldn't think of anything else to do.

Diana was struggling to keep her eyes open. Søren had slumped into one of his classic postures, chin on chest.

'Mikkel wrote a piece about you,' said Diana, speaking through a druggy haze. 'He defended your right to be maladjusted.' She was talking about a piece I wrote in *Urban* seven years back.

'How can you remember that?' I asked her, but she'd shut her eyes.

Søren rallied for a moment. 'Gorgeous has had a Rohypnol and now she's tired. I'm as fresh as a daisy.'

His fag dropped from his hand.

'You're asleep, Søren T-shirt!'

'I'm thinking, that's all.'

It wasn't until we had arrived at the flea-market green that I realised how delicate my situation was. Partly because it had been my idea to leave the gorgeous softness of bed and venture out into the unbearably cheeping and twittering heat of day, and partly because to my horror I had realised that I was initiating Diana into a world to which I no longer wished to belong. The Sancerre of the night before repeated on me like slow-release medicine and I was sweating glycerine. I was also paranoid. The protest generation were laughing at me and waiting for their moment to pounce and put things in their correct historical context, to tell me all this free love stuff had been done before – and done better, at that. I bent over the first box of old LPs and flicked through them absently: Phil Collins and Dire Straits, but also Zambassa's *Mørkristet*, an Aarhusian Latin album that was near impossible to lay your hands on. A voice behind me began to sing a line from it:

I can't live without you. But you can live without me.

Levinsen was in narrow royal-blue shorts and a wife-beater of Egyptian cotton.

'The Japanese collectors would give you a grand for that,' he said.

Levinsen and Diana each did a funny little skip, and knocked their foreheads together in a bollocksed-up air-kiss.

'I've just sent the family back off to Aarhus,' he said.

'Are you here staying with people?' I asked.

'I'm checked into the Strandhotel. How about you?'

'We're with Nikolaj Krogh and Mille.'

He tried to conceal the flurry this put him in. If there was one thing Levinsen would love, it would be to sit and talk about Frieze Art Fair over a glass of white in Nikolaj Krogh and Mille's garden. I bit my tongue and abstained from making the casual invite he was anticipating, and he pretended he wasn't bothered.

A murmur went up and people stepped aside. Søren T-shirt came strolling across the green in cut-off jeans, Tuborg in hand. Levinsen was now clearly at a loss; how on earth did we know people like Søren? Was he some eccentric son of wealthy stock? An eighties poet?

Levinsen put his hand out in greeting, but Søren ignored him.

'See you later, then,' said Levinsen. 'Still the Bistro, is it?'

I had to stop myself feeling sorry for him.

'Who was that knobhead?' said Søren.

'Be nice to Levinsen,' said Diana.

'He looked like a guy who's had his hands in the biscuit tin,' said Søren.

'He's a gallerist,' I said.

'Like I said,' said Søren.

'We need to get back and do that interview,' I said.

'You can't be serious?' said Søren.

'You'll have a hangover tomorrow as well, Søren.'

'I need to relax a bit.'

'You've been relaxing since 1988.'

'I've been a drug addict since 1988. That's the equivalent of a stockbroker's career. Hard graft eighteen hours a day.'

'You're not a drug addict anymore.'

'I'm not a well man!'

A mousy stallholder interrupted us.

'Do you mind going somewhere else to discuss your personal problems?' she said.

Søren gulped down his beer and put the can down so hard on her table it knocked over her little Balinese deities. A big antique dealer bloke in a leather waistcoat came striding up with his chest out and laid his hands on our shoulders.

'I think it's about time you found somewhere else to go, don't you?'

'Get your grubby hands off, you fucking idiot,' said Søren, calmly removing the guy's hand and gripping him by the throat in a single seamless movement.

'Would that be all, Tarzan? Would it?'

Søren had never been the violent sort, but twenty years of hustling on Istedgade had taken its toll. The antique dealer began to whimper. Søren glanced about at the crowd that had gathered and let him go.

'Send a real man next time!'

I found it grotesque the way Mille constantly nagged Nikolaj Krogh and disheartening that he never answered back. That afternoon, it was his homemade bread she complained about. He had used wholegrain spelt, honey and Graham flour, and the result was definitely *not* satisfactory, that much I had to acknowledge, but someone really needed to have a word with Mille and tell her that not only was she humiliating her husband, she was also casting herself in a seriously unflattering light.

Later, when Diana and I biked over to Liseleje and were walking along the beach, I asked her whether Mille's behaviour bothered her.

She looked out over the water.

'Mille told me they hadn't fucked in two years,' she said. 'We must get them some sex.'

We cycled back through the woods and stopped at a secluded spot where I'd often foraged for chanterelles. I asked her to take her clothes off, then watched her walking naked among the trees and in the long grass. Gnats assailed her naked body, and when she bent over I could see her cunt open up. A branch snapped. A hundred metres away, a man was approaching.

'Just stay where you are,' I told her, and retreated.

The man passed close by, greeting her politely and pretending not to notice, but some way further on he stopped and looked back at her exposed cunt. I picked a swishy branch up off the ground with some withered leaves on it.

'Do you enjoy being naked?' I asked, and began flicking her with it.

'He's watching us,' she said. The man stood staring from behind a tree.

I whipped her bare bottom and drew blood, and she whimpered and began to play with herself. Her inner thighs trembled uncontrollably as she climaxed amid the anthills and the toppled trees, and I stuck my cock inside her and fucked her like a convict. We lay there, smelling of meat again.

That night I made an old-fashioned roast chicken with braised fennel and new potatoes. Søren asked Mille about the early days of her career. Diana stared out into thin air with a faraway look in her eyes. What lay in those absences of hers? She seemed to be in an almost meditative state, and I imagined our voices to be background music. Absences were usually ominous. What are you thinking about, darling? Nothing, darling. I never asked her. Diana returned to us with a smile. 'Can my friend Lisa come up and stay for a couple of days?'

Mille cast a glance at Nikolaj Krogh, who had no objections.

'Do you want me to look after the kids tonight, so you two can go out?' said Diana.

Mille gave her a big kiss, vanished into the bathroom for an hour and came back all flowing sleeves and swept-up hair.

Their marriage might have been strained, but Nikolaj Krogh and Mille still made a striking couple as they strode out along Nordhusvej that evening, tall and dressed in black, confident of their status as summer royalty.

Søren and I tripped along behind them, trying our best to keep up.

Tour disco, said the sandwich board outside the Bistro, and of course it was hardly suited to Mille, but before long Nikolaj Krogh was dancing awkward salsa steps to Ricky Martin. Everyone was dressed in white and the atmosphere was Bacchanalian. There was dancing everywhere. Chairs gave way and broke, tablecloths ripped under high heels, and the cordial local bar staff, who had grown up on edifying bedtime stories and soft alto saxophones, struggled to keep up amid the hoarsely delivered orders. Søren danced with his arms above his head and a wine-bar flourish of his hips and was immediately assailed by a twenty-year-old lad with briny hair and thick lips.

'Weren't you the one who got into that fight down at the flea market?'

'Yeah, that was me. I'm a bloody hero!'

'Can I get you a drink?'

Levinsen was standing just inside the door with a sloppy mojito. He clearly wasn't intending to play down how well we knew each other, and greeted me with a hug that was rather too prolonged.

'The Bistro's jumping! Life can only be understood backwards, but it's got to be lived on the two and four.'

He glanced with shameless insistence at our party, and before I managed to introduce him, he had thrown himself at Mille.

'I know we always talk work and career in Tisvilde, but I've had *The Görlitzer Hangovers Revisited* on repeat in my gallery for the last six months. It doesn't stop growing.'

He was right in her face. She took a small step back.

'It's a *mind*-blowing album!'

He flashed what he thought was a coy smile.

'Oh, sorry, I didn't introduce myself. My name's Morten Levinsen. Just a nutter from Aarhus who lives and breathes for those rare moments when the sky comes that little bit closer.'

He shook Mille and Nikolaj Krogh by the hand.

'You made all the right choices on that album,' he said. 'The sound of that snare drum! Where did *that* come from?'

Mille told him about the English producer who was always fucked up on coke but still managed to perform miracles when they eventually got him sat down at the mixing desk.

I wasn't in the mood, but I stayed put, buffeted by senselessly intoxicated upper-class kids.

Søren had become the night's novelty attraction for a group of Hellerup lads who plied him with whisky and fell about laughing at his slightest movement. I went home with Nikolaj Krogh and Mille. We sat in the garden drinking beer. The sun was on its way up.

'How are you two actually doing, anyway?' I said.

'Nikolaj?' said Mille.

'In the day-to-day run of things we work pretty well together,' said Nikolaj Krogh. 'We're very good at the practicalities, and we agree on the majority of issues. We don't spend a lot of time arguing about how things should be done, do we?'

'We haven't got a sex life,' said Mille. 'Don't you miss it at all?'

'Of course I do,' said Nikolaj Krogh, and I could tell just by looking at him that he only said it because he knew it was the right thing to say. He was completely out of touch with that side of himself.

'Do you even masturbate?' said Mille.

'Sometimes,' he said.

'Do you use anything? Do you look at porn on the Internet?'

'I've still got my stack of old *Playboy*s,' he said.

Mille laughed.

'Isn't he sweet? Even when he masturbates he keeps up a standard of aesthetics.'

'Why don't you just be friends?' I said.

'We are,' said Mille.

'If you agreed to keep living together as friends and allowed each other pleasure, as friends do, you wouldn't be frustrated anymore about your relationship not working. Then maybe you might be able to reclaim your sex lives. With others.'

'That's a very dynamic idea, Vallin,' said Mille.

N ext morning, Mille drew me aside after breakfast. 'The children are frightened of Søren,' she said. 'You'll have to talk to him.'

I found him passed out in his cabin, reeking of alcohol. I slapped him awake and dragged him out for a walk, and he insisted on bringing his fishing rod, babbling about wanting to catch a sea trout. Amazingly, he did catch one within a few minutes of casting his line into the sea, so we returned to the house to present this offering to Mille. It did the trick and gave Søren a stay of execution.

Mille and Nikolaj Krogh's kids, Knud and Druhde, sat on the counter in the kitchen, and Søren told them about which fish were to be found at the surface of the sea and which kept to the bottom. He showed them the gills and explained what they were for, and then they helped each other clean and gut the fish and get it ready for the barbecue.

The kids wanted a disco after dinner and Søren was the DJ playing the air drums. He dug out a best of Creedence Clearwater Revival and asked Mille up to dance, leading her like a gentleman, until he put 'Up Around the Bend' on for the fifth time and she took the record off, claiming that she wanted us to be able to hear the lovely local birdsong.

The kids wrapped themselves up in blankets and Søren told stories from his childhood, while Mille put a rhubarb pie in the oven and asked whether I'd like to read some of what I'd written out loud to them all. Søren's behaviour all evening had been impeccable, but I could tell he was getting steadily drunker and that things might end up going awry. He'd already absorbed a bottle and a half of white wine when Nikolaj Krogh produced a cognac from Jon Bertelsen.

I read the chapter where Søren and Signe go to the cinema and he does speed during *Jean de Florette*, and he whistled and bragged all the way through, but when I got to the bit about the psychological ramifications of the Internet he suddenly changed his tune and furrowed his eyebrows.

'What's all that pocket philosophy doing in a book about Søren T-shirt?'

'Let Mikkel read,' said Mille. 'In this house we respect people who have courage enough to lay themselves on the line. We shut up and listen when others have got something to say.'

Søren fumed and guzzled two glasses of cognac while Nikolaj Krogh went to get the rhubarb pie.

'This isn't crème fraîche, Nikolaj!' said Mille, pointing at the dollop of white that accompanied her slice.

'It's *skyr*,' said Nikolaj Krogh.

'*Skyr?*' said Mille. 'I am *not* having yogurt with rhubarb pie on my summer holiday. I want crème fraîche, and I want it oozing with butterfat!'

'Go in and get some, then,' said Søren.

'You're a guest here, Søren. Nikolaj and I converse as we see fit!'

'You're on his back constantly, the poor sod. It's excruciating!'

'No one's keeping you,' said Mille. 'You've been steeped in alcohol ever since you came, you've not so much as lifted a finger or offered to contribute even a penny. You're a joke, Søren.'

Søren laughed contemptuously.

'I heard your CD the other day. You've got fuck all to say, I'll give you that much!'

I went with Søren to the station and he seemed relieved.

'She's a dreadful woman,' said Søren. 'In the top five. Worse than the caretaker who used to puncture our footballs at break.'

I listened for reproach in his voice. The little yellow train rattled in.

'When I was in hospital the other week,' he said. 'It wasn't an accident.'

He narrowed his eyes and crushed his fag end underfoot.

'What was it, then?' I said.

'I'd run out of things to do.'

'What are you going to do now?'

'I think I'll go to Floss.'

'Why are you telling me this?'

'I'd promised myself I'd tell you while we were here.'

We gave each other a long hug, and he smelled of smoked mould.

'I love you,' he said.

I stood there until the train had gone from sight.

Next morning, Mille and the kids left for Anholt, and Nikolaj Krogh's reaction was not as one might have expected. He sat in the garden listening to Schubert's Fourth. Culturally conservative by upbringing, Nikolaj Krogh was always punctual and ever considerate, putting others before himself and striving to impart value into each and every day. His devotion to and admiration of Mille was touching. That she was treating him badly had probably only occurred to him that evening, the moment Søren T-shirt, a complete stranger, had brought it to his attention, and now he had been left to think about why he allowed himself to be trampled on, and then to decide whether it was a state of affairs he was willing to allow to continue.

I sat writing in the cabin, inspired by Mille and Nikolaj Krogh's situation. And yet it was hard to ignore his dejection; even Diana seemed affected by it. She had put a little folding table up in front of the cabin and was trying to draw, but I could sense that she was getting nowhere.

There was no communal lunch that day. We made our own sandwiches with no trimmings.

At a quarter to five I decided to cut through the misery and booked a table for Diana and me at the Helenekilde Badehotel. Diana put on her midnight-blue velour suit and I insisted we walk along the beach.

'Up there was where the Tisvilde Badehotel used to be,' I said, pointing up at the hill. 'The guests would be in dinner jackets and evening gowns and there was dancing to a proper orchestra. Kai Mortensen, the band leader, married a waitress here called Tytte.'

I dragged her up the steps and pointed into the cement.

'Tytte Kai Mortensen! He wrote that on their wedding night.'

I told her about the fishermen who moved out into their sheds in the summer so they could rent out their cottages to society people from Copenhagen, and I was just getting to the bit about the first par-celling out of summer house plots when Diana put a finger to my lips.

The sun was big and orange above the hotel patio. On the little lawn, a group of attractive children were playing, all in soft corduroy, angora and cashmere in the noblest of colours: royal blue, sand, lav-ender and Bordeaux red. Four Filipino girls were keeping an eye on them. One day, the children now running about so freely would all be sitting nicely on the terrace above them, like their parents were now. The restaurant seemed filled with light-hearted chatter as we entered, the diners having satisfied the anxious questions that always arose on arrival: who else is here? Who do we know well enough to say hello to? Will they give us a table befitting our status?

We arrived into this scene as though sent from heaven: not only did we legitimise, on the strength of our garb alone, their choice of Tisvilde as a rather alternative summer destination, more creative and relaxed than Hornbæk, less pretentious than Skagen; we also served as a welcome distraction from the excruciating intimacy of their own tables. A manicure-happy group of girl friends in their thirties decoded Diana's outfit and sent us bleached smiles, and a young solicitor-type even got to his feet, lauded the interview in *Berlingske Tidende*, which he had found *eminently entertaining*, and shook us both by the hand.

We were shown to one of the outer tables at the cliff, and I felt I was on the right track.

'You order for me,' said Diana.

I opted for langoustine, mullet and white Burgundy and was unable to refrain from instructing the waiter to make sure the chef was careful not to overcook the mullet. It was a difficult fish.

Maybe it was the surroundings. For the first time in three months I didn't know what to say to her, and with that realisation came the peculiar feeling of foreboding. At some point we would sit like this again. The same mood. Neither good nor bad. Just empty. Like staring into the kitchen sink after two days on speed.

'No, we're not going to do this!' I said. And then she was listening. I cancelled the mullet and we left the wine where it was.

We sang 'Sorry Seems to Be the Hardest Word' all the way home and woke up tightly entwined.

L isa got off the train in a bright yellow, gossamer-thin dress, and within fifteen minutes she had made the Dan Turèll cabin all her own. Her decorative dresses on hangers along the wall, a stack of books on the bedside table, vases resplendent with flowers and sprigs from the garden.

When Nikolaj Krogh showed her round the house it wasn't the Finn Juhl chair or the imposing Franciska Clausen canvas that grabbed her attention, but the big pile of jigsaw puzzles on the dresser.

'I was a strange child,' said Nikolaj Krogh. 'I'd do them all day. It doesn't make me very interesting, I know.'

'I *love* jigsaws!' said Lisa, picking up the one on top. The lid said two thousand and four hundred pieces.

I left them to it and made dinner: *pirogs* with courgette, fennel, onion, curry powder, coarse-ground black pepper, cream and lovage. Nikolaj Krogh lit a campfire after dinner and I found a dusty guitar and played some Parkering Forbudt:

On Gråbrødre Torv you can hang around
You can be yourself with time to kill.

At four in the morning we went down to the beach and swam in the dawn.

I woke up at half past eight and looked out on the dew-drenched garden. Nikolaj Krogh and Lisa crossed the lawn hand in hand, and it was striking how young they looked together. He put his arm around her and she leaned against his shoulder and fitted his height perfectly.

After breakfast they turned their attention back to their jigsaw and could not be reached. Diana went off into the woods to look for wild strawberries and I sat writing in Skotte Olsen, until Nikolaj Krogh suggested the two of us drive over to Gilleleje to buy fish.

I knew exactly how he felt.

On the first stretch we were silent, but as we approached Unnerup he pulled over, put the handbrake on and stared out across the fields.

Then he turned to me and laughed with every fibre in his body and didn't care that he was crying too. We bought a big turbot in the harbour.

There is nothing as peaceful as the hour between six and seven on a still evening in summer. Lisa lay with her head resting on Nikolaj's bare chest, Diana was drawing, and I sat with the guitar, trying to find the chord that best encapsulated the mood, and no matter how I tried to avoid it there was no getting around C major 7.

'Ever the melancholy,' I said.

'Brazil's like that too,' said Nikolaj Krogh.

'Have you ever had a physically demanding job?' Diana asked.

'Not really. Why?'

'The only thing you can think about in that sort of job is knocking off.'

Lisa had begun to kiss Nikolaj Krogh, and for that reason she was the only one of us who failed to notice that Mille had appeared in our midst. She stopped a couple of metres away and dropped her leather bag on to the dry grass of the lawn.

I tried to lean the guitar up against a chair, but it toppled over and let out an open chord. Lisa turned and saw Mille. Mille stared intensely at Nikolaj Krogh and Lisa narrowed her eyes to focus.

'He's needed it,' she said, and smiled.

Diana tossed away her charcoal and gave Mille a big kiss.

'I got the feeling it was important for me to be here,' said Mille.

She went and crouched down next to Nikolaj and kissed him, smoothed her hand across Lisa's cheek and looked at them both for a long time.

'Welcome, Lisa,' she said.

'Would you like a drink?' I said.

'Too bloody right I would!'

On my way in to get the spumante I glanced at Diana's drawing pad.

She had drawn a fat version of herself.

'Why don't we have a party on Friday?' said Mille.

'Of course, why not,' said Nikolaj Krogh. 'What sort of party should it be?'

'How about red?' said Lisa.

'Red it is,' said Mille. 'Who are we going to invite?'

'People who want to do more than just talk,' said Diana.

'Let's make it a shag-in, shall we?' said Mille.

Nikolaj laid his hand on the small of Lisa's back.

'We shouldn't forget the love part,' I said.

'Prim now, are we?' said Mille.

I picked up the guitar and sang:

Touch me now, so I may feel that I'm alive.

Take my hand and hold me by your side.

Diana and Mille swayed, arm in arm.

'A touch-me party,' said Nikolaj Krogh.

The guest list took a whole evening to compile.

We wanted people who were likely to contribute, which disqualified arm candy, male bimbos and professional mothers. Dull couples were ruthlessly excluded, and resumé-toting networkers went the same way. Film directors were either constantly sounding off or else talked about themselves to the detriment of everything else, for which reason we preferred their producers. We invited such actors as could have passed for tradesmen or waitresses, and instrumentalists were more coveted than lead singers, especially if they happened to play a brass instrument. Classical musicians and opera singers were invited across the board, and Lisa hand-plucked a selection of young designers, some imposing lived-ins, three wayward photographers, the most unpretentious of stylists *and* the most gossipy, a couple of has-been hairdressers and a make-up artist known to piss her pants when drunk.

Diana invited the Icelandic contingent from Jolene's, a few club promoters, DJs, a bevy of skateboarding models, and a cross-section of younger creative types still playing around with their careers, while Nikolaj Krogh and I put together an all-star team of single acid-jazz mothers, eighties models, assorted fops and dandies and a best of the old punks from Gammel Torv.

Visual artists were richly represented on the basis of our romantic notion of their combining the outgoing with unpredictability, and in their wake came senior hiphoppers of both sexes.

Authors were under-represented on account of their seldom getting any farther than fortifying themselves with drink. Male poets were included as they were always brazen, whereas their female counterparts were too serious by half.

The opposite was true of scriptwriters, the men tending towards Holbergian self-importance, while the women had a habit of tossing glasses over their shoulders. The communication crowd weren't even considered, not even ordinary journalists, though a couple of more flamboyant individuals managed to slip through the net.

Arts columnists were generally valued, especially the most pompous, whereas graphic artists, furniture designers and architects only got an invite if we knew their private lives were a shambles.

There were a number of chefs, foodies and wine people. And, of course, dancers, modern as well as classical. Few artist-craftspersons. Mathematicians and physicists we liked, and linguists working on obscure projects. A couple of wayward solicitors made the grade, as did a psychologist with an accelerating cannabis habit and two neuroscientists.

And then there were all those who seemed not to be interesting on paper, but who outshone everyone once the music kicked in.

We went for dinner at the Bistro and you could say we'd gone Brazilian. We kept touching each other and smiling, carried along on the tide. The party brought us together, and Nikolaj Krogh and Lisa were enjoying their new partnership with Mille's full support.

I looked up from my fish. A local artist had been allowed to hang their pictures up, and if nothing else they were certainly colourful. And then I saw Kreuzmann. He was on his own with a bottle of champagne. The same suit trousers, the same worn-out Adidas, but his cravat was small and grubby. He had grown a beard and sat blinking his eyes as if trying to recapture a memory. He got up and tucked the champagne bottle under his arm.

'The party's over,' he said.

Nikolaj Krogh got him a chair.

'What party?' said Diana.

'It's all over for Dave "Boy" Green,' Kreuzmann said in English.

He tipped to one side and nearly overbalanced.

'You're talking in code,' said Nikolaj Krogh.

'Our Adam's apple was better than a plate of chips!'

Sweat trickled down his brow.

'Chips?' said Nikolaj Krogh.

'Who's Dave "Boy" Green?' said Mille.

'A British boxer,' I said. 'KO'ed by Jørgen "Old Man" Hansen.'

'They've cleaned me out,' said Kreuzmann.

He smelled like a lion's cage.

'Spitting and fuming in their Learjets. They pressed the off button.'

'Who did?' said Mille.

'The Yanks, for Chrissake. They're shutting up shop.'

'I think he's talking about the financial crisis,' said Nikolaj Krogh.

'Have you lost money, Kreuzmann?' said Mille.

Everybody knew that Kreuzmann was made. He'd sold his firm to the Americans – something to do with mobile phones and branded entertainment – for a vast fortune.

'I put the whole caboodle on black,' he said.

'But you can't just lose two hundred million,' said Mille.

'Get rid,' said Kreuzmann, and ran his fingers through his filthy hair. 'Sell, sell!'

'Sell what?' said Diana.

'Your houses, your art. I'm the first man down, but you'll be next. Sell the lot, for Chrissake. Get rid, while you can!'

He tipped his head back and emptied the bottle in one.

'Kreuzmann's not feeling well. Kreuzmann needs champagne.'

'You're coming home with us,' said Diana, and kissed his brow.

I woke with Kreuzmann next to me in his pitiful get-up, snoring like a bellows. While that on its own might have been barely tolerable, the falsetto rattle of his throat was disturbing, his subsequent grunts came in uncountable time and the pauses in between were positively nerve-racking. Pathologically, it was like he was dead for about a minute at a time.

I recalled only a couple of detached scenes from the night before. There had been some dancing, and I could see myself rummaging through the DJ's CD collection. Mille and Diana had head-slammed tequila with the chef's crash helmet on. Nikolaj Krogh and Lisa must have gone home early.

I went into the main house and found Lisa in the kitchen.

'Will you make us some scrambled eggs?' she said.

'Where's Diana?' I said.

There was an original woodcut by Dea Trier Mørch in the hallway: a rear courtyard, a sun and a mother with two children in Icelandic sweaters. I went up the stairs, and in the first bedroom the homely, fluffy bedding was untouched. In the second I found Mille and Diana. They lay entwined, Diana with one brown leg on top of the duvet and a hand on Mille's full breast.

'Are you awake down there?' said Diana. 'I'm starving.'

I went round the garden and looked up at the sky, and just as I had located its great, white space, the wretched wood pigeon began its lament. Pure fucking Grundtvigian misery.

The eggs were fresh, their shells thin. A big knob of butter in the frying pan, eggs in, lots of coarsely ground pepper and coarse salt. A pinch of curry powder. Essential to stir just enough so as not to end up with an omelette, and then off the heat while the eggs still glistened.

'I always thought Café Victor's scrambled eggs were the best,' said Kreuzmann.

'They use cream,' I said.

Mille was in a flimsy dress, while Diana had taken a man's shirt from the nearest wardrobe and had her hand on Mille's inner thigh.

I put sandwiches in the oven: spinach, chilli, fresh mozzarella.

Mille and Diana didn't get as far as tasting them; they went upstairs again together.

Lisa and Nikolaj Krogh cleared the table and washed up.

'Everything under control, Vallin?' said Kreuzmann.

I shook my head.

'All shagging except you, are they?'

'Except you,' I said.

He sobbed with laughter.

'You got *me*. You got the dead man!' he said.

We laughed until we cried.

'When's Diana's exhibition opening?' he said.

'October the seventeenth.'

'Too late.'

'For what?'

'As soon as word gets out what dire straits we're in, they'll shut off the dosh. Art's going to be the first thing they stop buying.'

I watched *Weekend* from 1962, directed by Palle Kjærulff-Schmidt, script by Rifbjerg, a film that kicked up a fuss at the time. Men sporting well-groomed beards chased giggling women through the dunes.

When eventually Diana came in, I picked a T-shirt up off the floor and folded it neatly, even if it did stink of sweat. She put her hands around my neck and I did nothing to stop myself and held her in a tight embrace on the bed.

'There's something about women,' said Diana. 'You can keep on opening them up.'

'You looked like a Hamilton photo,' I said. 'Soft and gentle.'

'You're gentle,' said Diana. 'Mille's brutal.'

K reuzmann had put a tent up at the far end of the garden and I helped the beer man carry the kegs to the bar. Lisa made figures out of bright red cellophane, Mille made tomato soup and Diana ironed.

Levinsen came slinking in with two slutty-looking girls in their thirties.

Maybe they had once been dancers. Their dramatic curves were set off by skimpy clothes, and neither was wearing a bra.

Levinsen introduced them as the Sisters of Mercy, and they curtsied coyly.

'But we're not sisters,' one of them said.

Mille came out from the kitchen.

'Good idea, the tent,' said Levinsen, gesturing towards Kreuzmann. 'Do you mind if we put one up too?'

'If you promise to put your two gorgeous tarts inside it,' said Mille.

'It's not easy to put us in anything,' said one.

'We'd like to party with these two, wouldn't we, Mikkel?' said Mille.

I couldn't remember the last time I'd blushed.

'Let's go and buy a tent, girls,' said Levinsen.

'Let's get you to go and buy one,' said the first one.

Levinsen produced two bottles of Launois Millesime from his bag. 'This'll make you horny.'

The Sisters of Mercy swung their hips as they made off.

'It's going to be a good party,' said Mille, and put her arm around my shoulder. 'You're very handsome today.'

'I think we're all becoming more attractive,' I said.

Diana came with shirts on hangers.

'I've ironed your light blue one.'

'Men in light blue shirts can't go wrong,' said Mille.

She put her hands on Diana's hips and kissed her deeply. I refused to feel embarrassed and stayed put.

I gathered everyone together before the guests arrived, and there were nearly thirty of us: the bar staff from Jolene's, DJs, lighting crew, all of us, and various hangers-on.

'Anything can happen tonight, and we don't need to know where it's going to end.'

We stood in a circle with our arms around each other.

'Tonight we're venturing into something new, and we're doing it together!'

Lisa lingered at the bar afterwards; she was in a turquoise dress with long slits and in need of a glass of spumante.

'I'm absolutely mad about him, Mikkel!'

'He's mad about you, Lisa.'

'But I don't even know who's minister of transport,' she said.

'I'm pretty sure Nikolaj Krogh doesn't care in the slightest whether you know the names of the cabinet off by heart,' I said.

'He says he wants to have a baby with me.'

'He's very much in love!'

'Mille knows who's minister of transport.'

The temperature was still twenty-three degrees as the guests poured in.

Long days at the beach had made everyone loose-limbed and accustomed to the sight of bare skin. Hair was thick and crusty from the sea, and even the painters were tanned. The women were in airy dresses with loose straps, the men had loosened the top buttons of their shirts. A smell of musk hung in the air.

Nikolaj Krogh had designed and built it all, and everything was glossy red.

The DJ booth was set up under the big floodlit oak tree. The bar was an elegant curve and the bar stools were done out in red nylon. The big round rice-paper lamps were lit with red bulbs, the same as the fairy lights. Lisa's cellophane figures hung from the trees all around the edge of the garden.

By half past nine the party was two hundred strong. Selecting our guest list on the basis of capability and lifestyle verged on fascism, but any reservations I might have had were put to rest when it became obvious we'd got it right. The dance floor was packed and everyone wanted each other.

Clara was in an Elvira Madigan dress and looked spectacularly out of place.

Erik Brinch danced, squirming like a serpent in black leather trousers.

'What is this anyway?' Clara said.

'It's Noah's ark,' I said.

'And you remembered the sheep!' she said, with a nod in the direction of the Sisters of Mercy, who sat on display at the bar.

'Do you want a glass of spumante?' I said.

Erik Brinch was back and panting. He kissed her on the neck.

'We could do with that, couldn't we, darling?'

'You're sweating like a pig.'

'Come and sweat with me.'

She stepped away from him.

'Is this all going to end up in a sex orgy?'

'Who knows?' I said. 'That's for the party to decide.'

She looked at Erik Brinch.

'Why don't you say something?'

'You look ravishing tonight,' he said.

'You're showing me up!' said Clara.

'Me, darling?'

'Yes, you, writhing about with your dick hanging out!'

'It's a party, Clara. We're dancing, that's all. Having a good time.'

'I'm driving back to Asserbo.' She strode off with determination.

'Yesterday she accused me of flirting with the check-out girl at the supermarket,' said Erik Brinch. 'I was buying toilet paper and caustic soda.'

Clara came back.

'You needn't bother taking me into account anymore, Erik. We're finished! End of story!'

He said nothing, and Clara began to cry.

'I'm such a fool,' she said. 'I can see it's never going to work with us. Why do I even bother?'

She buried her face in her hands and sobbed for a minute.

'I'm not going to ask you to live a life you obviously don't want.'

She said goodbye and went quietly off towards the car.

'Are you selling whisky?' said Erik Brinch. 'I might need to work up a tab at the bar.'

I found Diana in the midst of a group of skater models and pulled her over to dance to Dusty Springfield. I buried my nose in her hair. 'I love you,' I said, to my own surprise.

'Do you want to walk down to the sea with me?' she said.

We went along the Skolestien path and the honeysuckle ought not to have been there.

She wanted to tell me something, it was that kind of walk. Why did the sea always have to be involved?

We didn't say a word all the way there. We went down the steps of the hotel hill and sat down with our backs against the big rocks. For the first time in three months we were behaving like a couple, which by definition meant it was over.

My body felt heavy and abandoned, and she looked at me intently, as if mustering the courage to say something I was going to find painful. She took my hand in hers.

'The cunts are no good, Mikkel.'

'What?'

'My exhibition, it's no good.'

I was overwhelmed with relief, and assured her that her tapestries were going to be utterly astounding. We lay down at the water's edge and gazed up at the stars.

The party was alive with stories by the time we got back; some would be told again at a dinner party the following winter, others would turn into sex, or the beginning of a friendship, or three notes in a trombone solo, but most survived only for that night. I fetched the old guitar and sang 'Touch Me', and when Mille stood behind Diana and put her arms around her breasts I maintained eye contact with her throughout the song.

Djuna Barnes DJ'ed and she could get away with anything, David Essex or Stravinsky, but then she chose 'Young Folks' and people jumped around like baby goats. I felt the thumping bass line and threw myself into the party with my arms above my head. In the middle of the dance floor Erik Brinch had his hands buried deep in a solidly built blonde. His pink neck seemed almost to be drooling from its folds.

'I don't suppose there's a little room or a cubbyhole somewhere where a couple might find a little privacy?' he said.

It wasn't the kind of party to refuse anyone anything.

'My cabin, Skotte Olsen, is empty,' I said, pointing him in the direction.

'I'm sure I can count on your discretion,' he said.

Levinsen waved me over to the bar and opened a Launois Millesime.

'Can you keep up, Vallin? Mad, isn't it?'

'Fancy a go in the tent with the Sisters of Mercy?'

'You haven't asked us yet,' said one of them.

'Didn't I just hear you say Mikkel was cute?' said Levinsen.

'We don't want you,' said the other. 'You can go and play with yourself!'

He struggled to keep a smile on his face and danced off into the throng with his Launois. I could tell he wasn't the sort who shook hands over the net after a hammering at tennis.

'Come here,' said a Sister of Mercy.

I immersed myself in bum, breasts and bare thighs.

She dug her nails into my cheek and we kissed this way and that. A spliff came by, and after a few tokes I was consumed by a feeling of indescribable truth. My head spun rather gently, and of course they had no knickers on under their skirts and were simply warm and serious cunts. We went in a little chain towards the tent, and I tumbled through twenty years of festivals into sauna-like heat, and through our sweat we metabolised into predatory carnivores and oysters. Our fingers became eels squirming upon exquisite cadavers, we dribbled and drooled like imbecile beasts of fable and wanted more, ever more of it all, further out, further up, and I whimpered as a finger was inserted into my arse, my throat rattling as I plunged towards blackout, veins quivering, face buried in cunt.

I woke up in a fug of sex and zipped the tent open to get some air.

All over the garden people lay in each other's arms. I'd had four missed calls from Clara and a text message:

Is he still alive?

I peered cautiously through the window of my cabin and saw an empty whisky bottle on the floor and Erik Brinch's fat bollocks. The solid blonde was talking and he tipped his head back and laughed, and I could see all the way into the murk of his insides.

I poked my head around the door. 'Clara's worried about you,' I said.

Her name was Miriam and she extended a ladylike hand across the duvet. I was about to say something polite when Erik Brinch put a finger to his lips.

'Hi, darling. Sorry I didn't call… Yes, we all had a lovely time… Mikkel was kind enough to put me up for the night. I just need to get ready here and then I'll jump in a cab to Asserbo… Herring! Delicious, marinated herring… Just what the doctor ordered. Don't forget the red onion, now, will you?… Looking forward to seeing you, darling.'

He gave us a wink as he hung up.

D iana and Mille lay curled up together in Skotte Olsen, and I looked at them for a long time and let my feelings run loose inside.

Diana opened her eyes and pulled the duvet aside.

'Were the Sisters nice to you?'

'Extremely,' I said.

'Tell me about it.'

'I want to sleep,' said Mille.

'See you over in the house in a minute, darling,' said Diana.

I told her everything in detail: the shape of their cunts, the look in their eyes, their heavy breasts and sweet-smelling alcohol breath. Diana took my hand and put my fingers inside her pussy.

I floated down to the grocer's on Købmandshjørnet with Nikolaj Krogh. We bought eighty-four eggs, twelve tins of baked beans, six loaves of rye and sixteen litres of juice, and after we'd fed the dishevelled masses, we all piled down to the beach and I coaxed people into the sea.

By five o'clock we had reclaimed half the beach from the intellectual left.

At half past five I called Andreas Møller and invited him up.

'Are you sure that's a good idea?' said Diana.

'I'd like God to be with us,' I said.

'God's already here,' she said.

'Why don't you like Andreas?' I asked.

'There's just something about him. It's the way he looks away.'

Andreas was sitting at the bar when Nikolaj Krogh and I came dancing across the lawn with two hundred people in tow. Now that word had got out, people who wanted to join the party had been arriving and putting up tents all day, and two chefs were getting the big barbecue started.

There was no sign of the Lutheran ruff, but Andreas Møller didn't need to exert himself to establish his position.

Once we read books, then we read mostly magazines and skipped the long articles to look at the pictures instead. Now it was film, and much rather a well-turned thriller than Truffaut or Bergman. Problems were not to be gone into in too much detail, conflict was to be quickly outlined and solved, and such an approach might even have been workable if only we hadn't been brought up to consider reflection to be better. We promised ourselves to spend the next holiday on the Russians or Mann, and we reserved tickets to the Cinemateket so that we at least might see every episode of *Berlin Alexanderplatz* on the big screen, but instead we ended up eating too much risotto and staying at home on the sofa. People punctured when they encountered a priest. They gasped for breath and staggered backwards. It wasn't just that studying theology involved reading Hebrew, Ancient Greek and Latin, it was also the fact that the seminary and an incumbency meant an obligation to sermonise week after week.

Nikolaj Krogh had the complete works of Kierkegaard at home, and let me put it this way, they weren't exactly hidden from sight.

Nikolaj and Mille held salons, the time they had been living in Christianshavn, and whether it was out of genuine interest for the major issues in life or just attitudinal relativism I was obviously unable to judge, but what was certain was that Nikolaj Krogh was determined to add to his work in aesthetics a superstructure of philosophical, ethical and religious dimension.

They had only just said hello to each other and he'd already invited Andreas Møller to occupy the F.P. Jac cabin.

'May I rename it Michael Laudrup or Johannes Sløk?'

'We've got chefs, we've got a doctor, and now we've got a clergyman,' said Nikolaj Krogh.

'Would you care to give a sermon tomorrow morning?' I asked.

'That'd be great,' said Nikolaj Krogh.

'Perhaps you've an idea as to what it could be about, Mikkel?' said Andreas.

'I'd like it to be about community,' I said, and walked him down to F.P. Jac.

The chefs were almost ready with the food, and I stood on top of a chair with the old guitar.

People were sitting on the lawn holding each other's hands and I didn't have to raise my voice.

'Maybe this party's never going to end,' I said to them. 'All my life I've believed I had to be part of a couple in order to function, but I'd much rather be part of you!'

I beckoned to Andreas Møller.

'This is Andreas and he's our camp priest. Tomorrow morning at ten he's going to give us his first sermon.'

I played 'Touch Me', and people stood in line to put their names down for cleaning up, refuse collection and dishes.

'What are you cooking up, Mikkel?' said Mille.

'I've got ambitions,' I said.

'Ambitions are good, sermons less so.'

'I invited Andreas to stay in F.P. Jac,' said Nikolaj Krogh.

'The girls love him,' said Lisa.

Andreas Møller was eating at the bar with two single acid-jazz mothers.

'He's been celibate for eleven years,' I said.

Diana and Mille looked across at him, and he looked away.

Kreuzmann was sitting outside his tent.

I sat down in front of him on the grass and the dew soaked through the seat of my trousers.

'How are you feeling?'

He squeezed me a glass of red wine out of his box. It tasted of scaffolding.

'Do you remember Arthur Ashe? He floated on the court! Connors was a powerhouse, and Borg was sly, but Ashe was on a completely different level. There was more to it. Do you see what I'm getting at?'

'Is there anything I can do?' I said.

'I'm short on red wine.'

'Do you want me to pop over to Vin og Grønt and fetch you a couple of bottles of Anjou?' I said.

'No thanks, no hocus pocus for Kreuzmann. I'd be happy with a new box from the minimart. There's a great tit on the front.' He turned the box towards me and there was the bird in front of a little waterfall.

It was midnight and there was no wind. Through the treetops you could sense the light in the north. A half-moon shone over the house.

There were about fifty of us around the campfire, and I sat between Mille and Diana and stared into the flame. A spliff went round, and a curly-haired guy with eyes that told of a twenty-four-hour binge played A7 and G major in 6/8 on the guitar.

A star comes falling down, and hardly makes a sound, now I believe in love.

We talked about our first experiences with sex. A pretty skater boy with welcoming body language and serious blue eyes told us about the girl from Vedbæk who had shaved off her eyebrows and begun to cut herself, and how they smashed up the house afterwards. A red-haired girl told us about her first boyfriend in the badminton club who slagged her off behind her back, and I told the story of my first shag, with Lotte in her white clogs from the Trocadero club.

'My first had a huge cock,' said Mille. 'I was Interrailing with a friend, we met this group of older Swedish boys in Estoril, and I fell very much in love with one of them, a tall tennis type. I asked him out and we had sardines and wine. I was impatient and wanted to do it, but I got the shock of my life when I stuck my hand down his shorts. I didn't think they could be that big.'

'What did you do with it?' said Diana.

'He had lubrication with him, but we still had a job getting it in. Once we did, we tore along at a grand old pace. I had the most amazing orgasm.'

'Where did Levinsen get to, anyway?' said Diana.

The Sisters of Mercy smiled.

'He's gone off to Skagen with that blonde DJ,' one of them said.

'Her father's an art collector,' said the other.

The spliff went straight to my dick and I stuck my hand down Diana's knickers. Her cunt was smooth and willing, she spread her legs and moaned in my ear. Mille's tongue was long and firm, and the pretty skater boy calmly watched as I walked off towards the cabin with a girl on each arm. The lawn felt as soft as foam rubber beneath my feet, and the universe was breathing all around us. We were souls together under the sky, and the world was hunky-dory.

We had just undressed each other when he put his head round the door.

'Do you mind if I join you?'

'Take your clothes off, gorgeous,' said Mille.

He was muscular, yet thin at the same time. His dick lay in an arc across his balls.

Mille lay down on the bed and put my hand to her warm cunt.

'Kiss his bum, Diana!'

Diana put her lips to the nape of his tanned neck, then kissed the myriad of tiny muscles along his back, eventually arriving at his pert little behind. Mille's clitoris was big and hard as a nut, and she grunted with every touch.

'Take hold of his hips and turn him over,' said Mille.

His cock stood erect, jutting out at the ceiling, his sack as tight as a tennis ball.

'Lick his sack,' said Mille, keeping my hand on her swollen clit. His stomach muscles contracted as Diana's tongue swirled at his scrotum, and his dick quivered, tiny spasms of delight.

Mille let out a heavy moan.

'Come here!' she said.

Diana led him over to the edge of the bed.

'Wank him off!'

Diana gently took hold of his cock and slowly pulled back the foreskin. Mille gasped at the sight of the glistening purple head. She had begun to cream, my fingers were soaked in thick, white secretion.

Diana stared in wonderment at the cock in front of her.

'Is it hard in your hand?' Mille said. 'Tell me!'

'Yes, it's hard,' said Diana.

He groaned, his chest blooming red. Diana began to masturbate him with long, lazy strokes of her hand.

'Stop!' said Mille. 'Put it in your mouth!'

Diana crouched down and placed her lips around the dome of his cock. Mille put two fingers inside her cunt.

'You're so turned on, Diana.'

She gripped Diana's hair, drawing her mouth further down the cock.

'All the way.'

Diana gasped through her nose as Mille finger-fucked her. My fingers slid around inside Mille's cunt.

'I'm going to make you come with his dick in your mouth,' said Mille.

Diana gasped for breath and whimpered.

'You're gagging on cock!' said Mille.

She pressed her hand against the back of Diana's head, pushing her down on to the guy's cock, and Diana whimpered again, her lower body trembling uncontrollably.

Mille raised her hips and thrust herself towards his cock.

'Make him come all over me!'

She rubbed her gigantic clit furiously as Diana took hold of his cock and began to jerk him off. Her cheeks were flushed, her eyes glazed over.

'He's coming!' she said.

The first burst was quick and modest, and splashed Mille's throat. The second fell heavily on her, and Mille roared like a weightlifter as waves of pleasure passed through her and Diana milked every last drop.

I heard the blackbirds outside. It wasn't going to get dark.

'Wow, look at them,' said Mille.

Diana and the skater were kissing passionately. His cock had not become limp, but waved promisingly in the air between them.

'What's your name?' Mille asked him.

'Mies,' he said.

I refrained from looking down at myself, at my little pot belly and spindly legs. In five years' time Diana might be the mother of children, and their father would not be a man with low-hanging bollocks and the first stages of diabetes.

Mies had his fingers up her cunt.

This wasn't just sex. It was about the survival of the species.

Mille patted the bed next to her and got Diana to lie down with her legs apart. She then went to work purposefully on my cock, sticking the fullness of her bum in the air and snuggling into place on the front row. 'Fuck her, Mies. I want to see you stick it up!'

She drew my cock inside her, and began to rub her clit again.

Mies got on top of Diana and she let out an intense sigh as he slid his knob inside her.

'Stick it right up,' said Mille. Diana's hands gripped Mies' firm buttocks.

'Hit me!' said Mille.

I slapped her bum and made its cheeks quiver.

Diana was immersed in her own breathing, drawing him ever deeper, and I watched the wave of her orgasm like a store detective staring at a surveillance monitor.

My only feeling was one of increasing annoyance at Mille's soundtrack: all the smacking and self-conscious grunting.

She pushed me away and turned her arse towards Mies.

'Fuck me with your big cock!'

He thrust it all the way up and she moaned and wailed and buried her nose in Diana's pussy. I was at a loss as to how I might join in. I could work his arsehole, but that seemed rather extreme, or else I could position myself in the vicinity of Diana's hand in the hope of getting a tug. I was beginning to feel like an insurance salesman, so I put a pair of jogging pants on and blew Diana a kiss on my way out.

There were people kissing by the fire, others sprawled half naked in the grass, and from the tents came the sounds of sex. I stared into the embers.

A knot in one of the logs exploded with a crack.

A Sister of Mercy appeared beside me.

'Do you fancy a snuggle?' she said.

I followed her into the tent where the other Sister lay reading a book, *Kritik der sogenannten praktischen Erkenntnis* by Alf Ross.

'What's it about?' I asked.

'He contests the notion of a fundamental, valid morality.'

'You mean a God? Good and evil?' I said.

'He believes in a morality of the moment,' she said.

'Like we're doing here,' said the first Sister.

'Are we moral?' I said.

'Certainly,' said the other one.

'I'm glad.' I said.

'Lie down and be quiet,' said the first.

I lay with my tongue in a Sister's pussy when Andreas Møller poked his head through the tent opening.

'You weren't thinking of letting me down, were you? I'm about to deliver my sermon. Come on.'

His sermon was about our duty to immerse ourselves in community, and it took as its point of departure a passage from Matthew. Andreas fulminated against false communities and argued for spirituality. 'We are all of us involved in many kinds of community, but more often than not we are part of those communities for our own gain. What do I get out of lying around meditating with others? What do people think of me when I write about myself on Facebook? These are vain delights! Jesus let his hands be nailed to the cross in order that he might show us the way. It is our duty to serve others, and such duty is no tedious obligation. One might word it thus: that we are all of us obliged to give ourselves up to community, and this is at once both true and misleading, for by putting others before us we lose nothing and yet gain ourselves. We become happy.'

Most applauded when he was finished, but Mille beckoned to me from the kitchen and locked the door behind us. Nikolaj Krogh sat at the little tiled table drinking tea.

'What we've got going here is fabulous,' she said. 'But duty? Obligation? I do *not* wish to be bloody sermonised in my own garden. It stops, right now!'

'Duty is such a provocative word,' I said.

'Don't you play the honorary citizen with me, Mikkel Vallin,' said Mille.

'No one's forcing you to attend his sermons,' said Nikolaj Krogh.

'Sermons?' said Mille. 'You mean there'll be more?'

'It can be quite uplifting to be given a moral kick in the pants,' he said.

A sleepy Lisa appeared with a duvet wrapped around her. She sat down on Nikolaj Krogh's lap. Three initials were embroidered on the slip: *E.H.K.* Edvard Heinrich Krogh, Nikolaj Krogh's grandfather.

Andreas was at the breakfast buffet, engulfed by twittering culture babes.

'Is there a problem?' he asked.

'It was a good sermon,' I said.

He sized me up.

'Let's go for a walk,' I said. People were coming from the train in their beach get-ups, a chatter of voices as they ambled their way down to the sea, and outside Stina's others were lounging around on Indian cushions, talking about the night before. We continued past them and turned right along the shore.

'You're a good man, Mikkel. Weak, but good,' said Andreas Møller.

'Why weak?'

'You know perfectly well.'

We had reached the nudist dunes. Men dawdled with their eyes peeled.

'Why are you celibate?' I asked.

'My expectations were too high.'

'You can go a long way without any, you know,' I said.

'Yes, that's an opinion I hear voiced a lot,' he said. 'I couldn't disagree more. It's pseudo-Buddhist hocus-pocus, if you ask me. A reflection of sloth and cowardice. We should expect something of each other.'

We walked through the dunes and into the woods of Troldeskoven where the trees were weathered by the wind. Gnarled, inky trunks and long, twisted branches reaching out like tentacles.

'Tell me about your book,' he said.

I told him how it had changed direction and was now about the dissolution of coupledom and forging a new path for human relationships.

'You're very much in love with Diana, aren't you?' he said.

I nodded, and a twig snapped under my foot.

'Isn't Mille complicating things a bit?'

'I've decided it's got to be viable,' I said.

'Of course,' he said. 'Otherwise your book will fall apart.'

'It's not about the book. It's about my life,' I said.

'Does it distress you, having to share her?' he said.

'Sometimes,' I said.

'Do you think her being so unattainable is what made you fall in love with her?'

'Are *you* in love with Diana?' I said.

'I don't know her.'

'Since when did that matter?'

'She's with you,' he said.

'She's her own person,' I said. 'But I do love her.'

I didn't see much of Diana in the days that followed. She was on the phone a lot, walking round and round in little circles at the far end of the garden, or else she was with Mille. They went riding together, dyed their clothes, or else went to flea markets in the surrounding area, and at night they lay naked together upstairs in the main house in grandmother Krogh's old linen. But otherwise our love for each other was seemingly unchanged. We hugged after breakfast, gazed into each other's eyes and parted feeling happy and secure. Naturally, I refrained from telling her how much I missed her.

New tents had been arriving and the camp was full of activity: there was a chess tournament at the campfire site, a yoga group, and a choir for the experienced singers. Most got up for the morning sermons, and Andreas and I spent a lot of time discussing and planning them.

We were sitting by the pond beyond the Horsekærlinien when he told me about his mother's suicide. She was a doctor's daughter and had grown up in an endlessly spacious apartment on Sankt Thomas Plads. She played Chopin, was fond of modern German theatre and had dreamt of one day seeing Matisse's garden.

She met his father at a Stan Getz concert at the former Montmartre jazz club and fell for his repartee and solid physical appearance. He was from Hedebygade, but had got stuck in at school and was reading law. He was devoted to his wife, but he both admired her classical upbringing and resented her for it. By the time Andreas was a year old, his father's law firm was doing good business, and when he wasn't working he frequented his clients' strip bars and various Vesterbro brothels. His drinking took over, he would throw his dinner in the bin if it wasn't to his liking, and bring girls home with him from the Kakadu Bar. He decided to move the family away from it all to Hørsholm and begin a new life. But Andreas' mother loved the city life, the theatre and the concerts, and she wilted in their new environment. Moreover, his father had sold the firm and conducted his business from home, and when he wasn't bossing the gardener about in his French Baroque gardens he terrorised his wife. She began to lose weight, became addicted to tranquillisers and stopped playing the piano. Having spent his entire childhood witnessing this brutal campaign against his mother, one day when he was a teenager Andreas finally lost it and went for him with a poker. His father lost his sight in one eye, and Andreas was sent to board at Herlufsholm.

Andreas' story was a horrendous lesson in how damaging it can be to grow up within the framework of a dysfunctional relationship. He had only ever had one serious romantic relationship, and although we talked without inhibition and could ask each other almost anything, I could sense it still pained him dreadfully.

They had moved in with each other when they were eighteen, and it lasted eight years. She was good looking and her name was Nathalie. That was all I got out of him.

We went to the Strandhotel and discovered an unoaked white South African Chardonnay, and it was the first time we had got drunk together. Andreas cursed the lounge DJ and wanted to hear the waves instead.

He became intense during the cognac.

'John Noyes was one man,' he said. 'We are two, Mikkel.'

'That's it!' I said. 'We'll have communal meetings before dinner.'

'Cadeau to Noyes!' he said. 'What shall we call them?'

'Assembly,' I said.

'Assembly's good,' he said. 'That's what we'll do. We'll assemble.'

He had begun to slur his speech rather affectedly and to bark out abrupt orders to the waiter.

'We'll take this a notch further, Mikkel. Are you in?'

'That depends.'

He was distracted for a moment by a pair of seventeen-year-old boobs walking by.

'How many people have we got in the camp now, Vallin?'

'About a hundred and twenty,' I said.

'Two hundred more and we buy a property!'

'You mean it, don't you?' I said.

He took his eyes off the boobs.

'Why did you phone me?'

'Because I wanted to progress.'

He put his hand on mine.

'It's all well and good people shagging left, right and centre, but we don't want to make do with just an exciting little holiday pushing the limits, do we?'

Mille and Diana walked in arm in arm. Mille was about to do a U-turn when she saw us, but then realised I'd already seen them. It was odd to see Diana in a dress. It was royal blue with a dazzling white collar, and reached about halfway down her thighs. She looked amazing, her legs were tanned and gorgeous, but at the same time it made her look like an expensive Tisvilde girl, and they were ten a penny. Mille had borrowed one of her ties, and that was even worse.

'We wanted to go dancing,' said Mille. 'But this lounge mood's going to drive me mad. How about the Bistro, Diana?'

'I don't see you at the sermons, Mille,' said Andreas.

'I don't see you either,' she said.

'Should we bike over to Hundested tomorrow?' said Diana.

'I'd love to,' I said.

'I thought we were going to the market at Græsted?' said Mille.

'We're not anymore,' said Diana.

Andreas fell into a hedge on the way home and went straight to bed.

The Sisters of Mercy were sitting by the fire with a group of slobbering young men. I got them both into Skotte Olsen and stuck my dick into every conceivable hole until eventually I was exhausted enough to sleep.

Diana and I biked off before the sermon. We went through Hegnet, passing the castle ruin and continuing on to Asserbo, before sweeping down on to the saturated fat of Liseleje's *croisette*, past the big white church at Melby, through Hald with all its little parcelled-out plots and standard houses of impregnated wood from the sixties, and eventually Kikhavn, a sanctuary of hollyhocks and the pastoral idyll of the intellectual left. We ended up with fishcakes on the quay at Hundested, and I sat swinging my legs like a little kid.

'I miss you,' she said.

'Should we kiss?' I said.

It wasn't the kind of quay you kissed on.

'Are you in love with Mille?' I asked.

She looked at me for a long time.

'What's the score with the Sisters of Mercy?'

'I feel like I know them,' I said.

'Do you know me?'

'You know I don't.'

She laughed and leaned into me. 'I'm meeting Moritz at the Tisvilde Café. He made it sound like it was important. Will you come with me?'

Moritz had at least made some sartorial concession to the fact that it was summer, and was wearing shorts and a straw hat. His opening gambit was studiously light hearted; they'd been having a terrible time with stones on their little beach at Rågeleje. He ordered mineral water and a *machiatto*, and just to spite him I asked for two safari suits.

Fortunately, the young waiter didn't know what it meant, which allowed me to add the words Elephant and Jägermeister to the long series of cultural markers the guests on the teeming terrace from then on would associate with Moritz.

'I hear you're staying with Nikolaj Krogh and Mille?'

'We're all bonking each other's brains out over there,' I said.

A twitch passed across his face, sheer disgust.

'Anyway, Diana,' said Moritz. 'I got this call from Stig Nissen.'

'He's so cute, don't you think?' she said.

'I haven't actually formed an opinion about that yet, but he was wanting to clear the rights issue.'

'Was it okay?'

'No, far from it, in my opinion. But he showed me a contract with your signature on it. Stig Nissen has no taste, Diana. But he does have money, and the drawings to which he now owns the rights are going to be plastered on to T-shirts and carrier bags and giant inflatables inside the shop.'

'At least it means people are going to see them,' she said.

'You're previewing your new work with a shopkeeper from the sticks.'

'Is that too vulgar?' she said.

'Stig Nissen made his fortune pissing on all notion of design and quality. Being associated with him is poison. All we can hope is for the journalists not to get wind of a story.'

I pictured the advertising.

'Our friend Kreuzmann claims there's a financial crisis on its way,' I said. 'Will that affect the market for art?'

Moritz found his expert voice.

'The abnormal prices for Warhols and Picassos might take a downward turn, but it won't affect contemporary art in general.'

'Jeff Koons' *Balloon Flower Magenta* just fetched thirteen million pounds at Christie's in London!' I said.

'Koons keeps his value,' he said. 'In a way, he has transcended himself out of the art sphere. What you're buying there is a piece of our age.'

I kept him going with this distraction from Diana's work, and he started talking about how pop art couldn't be judged in terms of isolated works, you had to take into account the way they engaged with contemporary society.

Diana waited until the Alfa Romeo had disappeared from view.

'Thanks for your help,' she said.

The following morning Clara called and invited herself and Kathrine to lunch. She sounded fine, though you never could tell.

I forced myself not to feel guilty, but it was a struggle: I'd known Clara since I was seven, and yet I had facilitated Erik Brinch's fling. Clara brought homemade chicken salad in a Tupperware bowl and mentioned three times that she'd used fresh asparagus.

'Kathrine's left Mosbeck now,' she said.

'Are you unhappy?' I said.

'I don't think so,' said Kathrine.

'We'll look after you,' said Clara, and almost fell over at the sight of the portable showers and loos, the great tent camp, the laundry waving from the washing lines, and the well-organised lunch buffet.

'This is brilliant!' said Kathrine, converting her *r* into a *w* in the eighties style.

'Everyone pays two hundred kroner a day,' I said.

'Is it like the old communes?' said Clara.

'They had the gender battle to deal with. We have fun.'

'Why don't we put a tent up too?' said Kathrine.

'Do you know the package-tour couple?' said Clara. 'They're the ones in the room next door when you go to Samos. They scrape their plastic chairs about on their balcony and you can hear them pour their retsina and inhale when they're smoking their fags, but they never actually say a word. All they do is clear their throats. Well, that's me. I'm the package-tour couple.'

I laid a table for us by the end wall. The chicken salad was bland.

'Of course, it's never nice when you're husband's unfaithful,' said Clara, reaching out for a piece of toasted bread. 'But I feel a lot better already.'

I was about to get up and give her a big hug when I noticed the look she gave me and stayed put.

'He told me everything,' she said.

I said nothing for a while. Clara went on:

'Who is she? I know he fucked some bimbo. Who is she?'

'You can't expect Mikkel to answer that,' said Kathrine.

'I've known him ever since he was in short trousers and had long hair. We were everything to one another. Who else could give me an honest answer!'

'Shall I toast some more bread?' I asked.

Kathrine put her arm around Clara.

'I lose my man. I lose my best friend.' Clara thumped the table and knocked the white wine over.

'This project of yours, it's sick, Mikkel. It's making people upset.'

I remained standing by the toaster. I thought of Clara in a mohair sweater and harlequin pants. Going halves on a chicken sandwich after the Survivors gig at the Montmartre, Clara in a tizz about the bass player with the curly hair. Gefilte fish balls at that Jewish restaurant in the Marais, Goya's black series at the Prado, En Vogue at the Hammersmith Odeon. All the telling looks behind the backs of successive girlfriends and boyfriends, the sense of having a person you needn't bother lying to. The toast popped up and as I returned to the table I resolved to stand my ground.

'It's a matter of principle,' I said.

'That's what they all say!'

'I can't help you,' I said. 'I won't.'

Levinsen came scurrying over.

'Ladies! We've the most amazing guest star in our midst. He's putting his couch up over in the corner by the pear tree and after dinner he'll be open for consultation! By day a chimney sweep, but in his spare time utterly devoted to his unique talent. Allow me to present: the Master Licker of Ørby!'

A stocky guy in a short-sleeved shirt and jeans presented himself with a folding seat under his arm. His hair was thick and cut in front of the mirror at home, and he was so ordinary in appearance you could sail across the Atlantic in his company without ever learning his name. The women applauded and whistled, and Master Licker bowed. Clara picked up her Tupperware.

'I'm going home. I've got weeding to do!'

Kathrine forced her back down on to her chair. 'You can't keep going home.'

Clara looked into Kathrine's brow and smiled.

'We need to start creating some new narratives for ourselves, Clara. It's yes or never! Say yes!'

'No, I bloody won't!'

'Say yes!'

Clara narrowed her eyes and frowned.

'Say yes!'

'Yes.'

'Louder!'

'Yes!'

'Shout!'

'YES!'

'Brilliant! Now let's drive to Helsinge and buy a tent.'

I had wilfully ignored the questions any other fool would have asked a long time ago, but on the Friday it all came crashing down around me. I can't find any other reason for it than weakness, and there is no doubt that the damage done was irreparable. I broke the spell. It was as simple as that.

It had all been going so well. The night before, Diana had slept with me for the first time in ages, and we had made love through all fourteen movements of *Music for 18 Musicians* – if, that is, the difference between making love and fucking is eye contact. The thing to do is to stick to your own course, and I was proud of not having attempted to compete with Mille. Her being in bed with me again was not a victory for my vanity, but a more spiritual kind of satisfaction, and for this reason my imminent fall would be all the more decisive.

After Clara and Kathrine left, I went back to the cabin to take a nap with Diana, and when I opened the door she was sitting on the bed with Levinsen, and while they may have been fully dressed, a room cannot lie. The intimacy was striking.

'I've just proposed to Diana,' said Levinsen.

I scratched my back so hard I drew blood.

'I want her! As a gallerist, Vallin.'

Diana asked him about his business philosophy and that sort of piddle, and he played the important man in the art world, until eventually they were both so exhausted from lying that Levinsen exploited a text message as a pretext to extract himself from the situation. She began to sort through her clothes.

'We need to clear the air,' I said.

'Is it dirty?' she said.

'How come you're on the phone so often all of a sudden?'

'What is it you want, Mikkel?'

'Did Levinsen come round while I was on Bornholm?'

'I can't remember.'

'Let me put it differently: has he ever been round on his own?'

'Stop it, will you, Mikkel?'

'He drinks Launois, a very particular kind of champagne, Diana, and there were two bottles of it next to your sink. You'd also had caviar. Surely you'd remember that?'

She stopped what she was doing.

'So what if he did come round?'

'Have you got a thing going on with Levinsen, Diana? Answer me!'

I had never seen her cry before. She sat on the bed with her face in her hands, and only then did I realise how terribly I had gone wrong. She held my head and kissed my cheeks and nose while the tears streamed from her eyes. I apologised repeatedly and cried just as much, and she caressed me and was small and fragile underneath her shirt.

That night we had dinner with Clara and Kathrine without letting go of each other's hands.

Levinsen stepped out of the dusk on to the tree stump in the middle of the camp and spread out his arms.

'The Master Licker of Ørby is now ready to receive his first client,' Levinsen pronounced. 'Number one, please approach the couch!'

Mille sprang to her feet and curtsied.

Diana's phone thrummed in her pocket and she stepped away.

Master Licker addressed the gathering with cheerful authority:

'This will require very little: you must take off all your clothes, you must breathe deeply, and you must relax and allow yourself to drift with the flow. It will take approximately twenty minutes, though some of you may have difficulty concentrating in front of an audience. How are we feeling?'

'I'd like them all to be here,' said Mille.

The entire camp had gathered.

'Right, now I want you to take off your clothes and lie down on the couch.'

Mille undressed quickly and made herself comfortable, and Master Licker of Ørby began to massage her face, his hands moving in delicate little circles as she breathed deeply.

After a couple of minutes he proceeded to her shoulders, collarbones and upper chest, making only the lightest of contact with her skin, gentle, sweeping strokes of his hands, while avoiding erogenous zones such as the breasts and abdomen.

After five minutes he took hold of her legs and began to massage the back of her thighs with both hands.

A couple of spliffs were passed round and a blackbird sang in the pear tree.

Master Licker now moved in between Mille's thighs and started licking from below: long, full strokes of the tongue, approaching the clitoris millimetre by millimetre. At the termination of each stroke he paused very briefly, as though to create suspense, before his tongue once more embarked upon its meticulous ascent. Kathrine watched every movement with baited breath. Clara stared the way a devout Muslim might stare at a suckling pig on a spit.

After some seven or eight minutes, Master Licker's procedure entered a new phase.

Placing one hand on her cunt, he moistened two fingers in his mouth and inserted them cautiously between her labia with his palm facing down. His fingers inside, he turned his hand a hundred and eighty degrees and caused it to gently vibrate in a series of small, circular movements, his tongue now proceeding towards the clitoris with rather more urgency.

She was wide open for him, her breathing guttural and imploring. Master Licker then abruptly stopped his licking and positioned himself at the side of the couch. The gathered fingers of his left hand drew small circles around her clitoris, his right hand exerting pressure inside her. Mille's breathing intensified as though she was about to climax, but Master Licker did not hasten as would the amateur. Instead, he maintained the steadiness of his pace, until Mille's arms suddenly began to twitch as though in spasm and she raised her legs off the couch.

A clear jet of fluid then spurted from her, and the grunt-like moan she expelled was so loud and protracted we almost feared for her health.

Master Licker slowly withdrew his wet fingers and allowed Mille to regain her composure. After a couple of minutes of recovery she climbed down, gave Master Licker a big hug and with glistening eyes rejoined the throng to spontaneous applause.

Master Licker of Ørby had a beer and a fag.

'Was that a squirting orgasm we saw there?' Clara asked.

I sat with a single malt at the bar.

'That's the most awesome thing I've seen since Caravaggio,' said Kathrine.

'I always turn the bedside lamp off during sex,' said Clara.

'I hope that's a metaphor,' said Kathrine.

'It makes me embarrassed. Have you ever noticed how sex noises are the same as when you hurt yourself?'

Kathrine grabbed my arm when Clara went off to the loo.

'I've put Clara's name on the list, but it's not her turn for another two hours. We've got to do something, otherwise she'll just crawl into the tent and sleep through.'

We agreed we'd head into town with Clara and get her drunk and we started at Le Petit Fer à Cheval. Like me, Clara was brought up to believe that rich people are bastards, and normally she upheld the prejudice as strictly as possible, but as soon as 'Africa' by Toto came on she dragged Kathrine on to the tiny dance floor, rediscovered her feet from her acid-jazz days and even looked like she was enjoying herself, dancing with a pair of stuffed dummies and sinking to her knees to 'Shackles' by Mary Mary. Eventually, Kathrine took me aside.

'Clara's appointment is in fifteen minutes.'

We made it back to Master Licker in the nick of time.

'Number eight,' he said, looking out over the gathered throng.

Kathrine found her little ticket.

'Is it you, Kath?' said Clara.

Kathrine handed the ticket to Clara, and I know for a fact that at any other second in her life she would have crumpled it up, but at that moment she accepted it and made her way to the front.

Self-consciousness did not kick in until she found herself hopping about on one leg with her knickers round her ankles, but Master Licker embraced her like a carport Buddha and directed her kindly yet firmly on to the couch.

Clara was ticklish, but Master Licker did not flinch, continuing to smooth his hands all down the pale fullness of her naked body. Kathrine squeezed my arm as he put his broad tongue to her cunt, and it was not exactly a sight I had been yearning to see.

'Breathe deeply, Clara,' said Master Licker of Ørby. 'You are surrounded by trees. Breathe with them.'

Five long strokes of his tongue towards the clitoris and she allowed her upper body to drop heavily back to the couch. When he moistened the fingers of his right hand, I cursed the fact that our old school photographs remained more vividly etched in my mind than Beethoven's violin concerto: Clara with a bowl cut and a woolly jumper with horizontal stripes.

And here she was now, stranded naked on a couch in Tisvilde. But her breathing had become heavy and regular.

Master Licker had proceeded through the round-tongued phase and had now positioned himself at the side of the couch ready to perform the decisive action.

It didn't take long before Clara was arching her voluminous frame and expelling a fountain of fluid.

It was another gorgeous morning and I'd got about ten metres from my cabin when the first buzz about Kreuzmann and the flea market reached me. I was waylaid by one of the single acid-jazz mothers:

'He's gone postal.'

'What's he doing exactly?' I said.

'There's enough gossip about us as it is,' she said.

'Is he running riot, or what?'

'He's sat down in the middle of the flea market. You'll have to go and see.'

'Let me get some breakfast first, all right?'

Clara and I had breakfast in front of the tent, and those who passed by stroked her on the head. She had neither sausages nor fried potatoes from the buffet and made do with a bit of fruit and muesli instead. She sat up straight and had a look of impenetrable serenity in her eyes.

'Welcome to the first day of your new life,' said Kathrine.

I went over to get some more mozzarella and ran into Miriam. She was wearing a bathrobe over her knocked-up boobs, and her make-up was almost offensive, given the time of day.

'Is that Clara?' she said with a nod towards the tent.

'Erik Brinch hasn't told her yet,' I said.

'I know,' she said.

I went back and sat down and tried to get as much of the green olive oil as possible to stick to the mozzarella.

'Who was that stripper you were talking to?' said Clara.

'You can ask her yourself,' said Kathrine.

Miriam came striding up.

'Hi, I'm Miriam,' she said.

'Hi, Miriam,' said Clara. 'You look like you want to say something.'

'I want your man,' said Miriam.

'Do you want your own hair colour too?' said Clara.

'He wants me as well, he just hasn't the courage to tell you himself!'

'Do you know her, Mikkel?' said Clara.

'Mikkel lent us a cabin,' said Miriam.

'What is this?' said Clara.

'And I slept in his summer house last night,' said Miriam.

'It's Clara's summer house,' said Kathrine.

'Have you been fucking in my bed?' said Clara.

'Sorry, Clara,' said Miriam. 'Facts of life.'

Kathrine leapt to her feet and gave Miriam a shove backwards.

'Get lost, before I smash your slaggy face in!'

Clara and Kathrine stormed off and I went back to Skotte Olsen to get a towel, then went for a shower in the Portakabin.

A single acid-jazz mother was in there with a skater boy, the water splashing from their tanned bodies. She had soaped his cock and was gently masturbating him, while he had his hands firmly around her buttocks. They were tongue-kissing as if they were never going to run short of variations.

I changed into a clean polo and a clean pair of shorts and went off to the flea market, Nordhusvej's dust kicking up under my feet as I went.

Kreuzmann was sitting about ten metres from the popcorn machine, and behind him two eleven-year-old girls were selling off their Bratz dolls. He had shorts on and a shirt that had once been white. He was seated with his legs out to the side, like a child who had only just learned to sit properly, and he wasn't wearing underpants.

His big hairy bollocks spilled out on to the sparse grass.

I sat down in front of him and tried to screen off his balls.

'You're losing it, Vallin!' he said.

'That's a rather categorical statement.'

'It's all right with those old herons from the acid-jazz days filling their fannies with young cock, but what the fuck are the church services in aid of? Are you starting a sect?'

A lady in her early seventies wearing braided-leather shoes smiled down at me.

'Good morning, Mikkel Vallin. I'd like to inform you that a large number of residents here have joined together and will be taking measures to put a stop to your filth.'

She was still smiling.

'How do you mean?'

'Exposing oneself in the presence of children, indeed!'

She gestured towards Kreuzmann's bollocks. He looked down at them.

'Sorry, my fault entirely,' he said. 'No balls without a cock!'

He pulled down his shorts, took his dick out and let it rest, fat and sweaty, against his thigh.

'Is that any better for you?'

'Measures will be taken!' she said. 'We're watching you, Vallin!'

People continued to arrive at the camp in their droves on the Saturday, and before long the front garden too was taken up by tents.

Levinsen had organised a big bash that night and some of the newcomers were his personal guests. *Levinsen Open Presents Love-In*, said the e-mail invite he'd sent round to his clients, and they were neither shaggy-bearded trumpetists nor mathematicians with an arty side, but people who read books about *blue ocean strategy*, divided their fellow humans into coloured categories and abbreviated 'return on invest-ment' to *ROI*.

My editor, Bernhard, called before lunch to check on the progress of my manuscript, and I told him I was researching my subject histori-cally and writing about the Ranters, an anarchist proletarian sect in seventeenth-century England who had gone in for drinking binges, partner swaps and public exposure.

'Sounds like you're on the right tack,' he said, and I agreed, though flinched at the nautical metaphor.

During lunch, an advertising photographer, well known for his arrogance, blew up in the face of one of the girls we had tending bar because we weren't accepting credit cards. I was concerned about the spiritual balance and direction of the camp and tried to speak to Nikolaj Krogh about it, but he was immersed in matters of a more practical nature: change for the till, the ice machine, power cables, and did we need to open another bar?

In truth, I was feeling rather done in and was missing the quiet moments with Diana on Lyrskovgade. She was either on the phone or else politely distant, and my mood was made no better by Mille constantly traipsing around in her wake.

Andreas and I went for an afternoon walk and sat down on the rock at Seksvejen.

'The sex is taking over,' I said.

'Wasn't that the idea?' he said.

'There's the idea, and then there's the sex,' I said.

'What does Diana have to say?' said Andreas.

'She's not saying much at all.'

'Are you afraid of losing her in all this?'

'You can't really talk about our relationship like that,' I said.

'Perhaps you've now met the woman you'd be most suited to make a couple with?'

'Yes, if that's what this was all about.'

'Isn't it?'

'Of course not,' I said.

'You're sticking to your guns. I admire you for it. It's very generous.'

'Thank Diana.'

'I will, once I get the chance.'

When we got back, Diana was sitting in front of the cabin, drawing. She put down her charcoal.

'Lift me up,' she said, and I danced her out into the camp and twirled her under the trees, and sang the first thing that came into my head.

L evinsen had a whole deployment putting a marquee up.

'What's that for?' I asked him.

'You're going to love it, Vallin. We've got acid rock, we've got joss sticks, we've got a light show! I've got two hundred spliffs of Svaneke pot coming in at seven o'clock. *I've hitched ten thousand miles and my speech is awesome, like the blowing of trumpets.* Total "Itsi-Bitsi", I promise you!'

'"Til Nashet",' I said.

'What?'

'The song. It's not "Itsi-Bitsi", it's "Til Nashet".'

'I want to hold an assembly,' he said. 'A reading and a little happening.'

'Good,' I said, 'I've got something important to say.'

A bout two hundred and fifty people came to the assembly. They were in suede waistcoats, Indian smocks and thin harem pants.

'I'd like to tell you all about a little experience I had earlier on today,' I said from the tree stump. 'Daniel, do you want to tell us about what happened at the bar earlier on?'

Daniel was wearing a number of expensive chains around his neck.

'What do you mean?'

'Daniel discovered he was unable to use his credit card here and decided to tear our bartender off a strip. You're a guest here, Daniel! Our shrubbery may be watered with piss, the lawn may be wrecked, but we love our little camp, and what I saw and heard today doesn't belong here.'

He tried to shrink back into the shadows.

'Don't go slinking away!' I said. 'Do you understand what I'm saying to you, Daniel?'

He nodded.

'I'm sorry.'

Andreas Møller nodded appreciatively as I stepped down.

'That's the spirit,' he said. 'Should we all give Daniel a hand?'

A sitar player struck a sinewy chord and Levinsen read out some of the raunchy bits of *Steppenwolf.*

I sat with Mille and Diana. Diana was wearing a thin yellow corduroy suit and leaned into me.

Levinsen stepped on to the stump.

'How insanely gorgeous everyone's looking tonight. What a magnificent evening. Can you feel the warmth? What say we all get our clothes off?'

He took off his shirt and threw it on the grass.

'Let's get naked, all of us together!'

Everyone stripped.

'Look at that cock!' said Mille.

Levinsen was circumcised, and his cock made his body look slight.

We had Indonesian *rijsttafel* and everyone laughed louder than usual. Levinsen had booked a young band who played acid rock, and it was like the Fælledparken in the seventies with bare boobs, clouds of pot and lyrics about elves and woodland. Levinsen danced with a spliff in his hand, gyrating like it was Woodstock, his dick slapping about on the off-beat.

Diana and I shared a joint at the bar and played chess with what was at hand: glasses, pepper pot, bottle tops. She took my hands and kissed my fingers one by one.

'Did you hear about the dyslexic atheist who didn't believe there was a dog?' she said.

I had to think about it for a second.

'Good, eh?' said Diana.

She laughed so much she fell off her bar stool. I lay down in the grass beside her and we rolled through the daisies and the four-leafed clovers with our dog, in the long, slanting rays of sun.

'Let's stay here,' I said.

'Nice doggy,' she said.

I felt a flat hand on my right buttock and looked up at Levinsen's dick.

'Showtime!' said Mille.

'Already?' said Diana.

They dragged her off and vanished into the marquee.

The Sisters of Mercy were sipping champagne and absinthe.

The band announced there was a show on in a few minutes.

'Levinsen's going to do something with his cock,' one of the Sisters said.

'What's Diana going to be doing?' I said.

'We kicked him out last time,' the other one said.

'You've no idea how stupid he sounds when he's having it off.'

The light was dim inside the tent, and we were surrounded by warm, tanned bodies.

After fifteen minutes a sitar began to play and a sweet smell of joss sticks filled the air. Four matches were struck and fat candles lit in a semicircle in front of the circular stage, in the middle of which were two black armchairs.

In one sat Mille, in the other Diana. Their legs were open wide and tied to the armrests, their arms were tied together above their heads with leather thongs, and both were blindfolded with black silk scarves.

Mille tugged on her tethers, her nipples jutting in the air.

People were kissing all around us, and I was sweating so much I was soaked. One of the Sisters put her tongue in my mouth.

Mille was clearly relishing being so powerlessly exposed. White fluid trickled from her cunt on to the black leather of her armchair.

Two younger guys entered the stage and kneeled down before Diana and Mille.

Moans were heard in the dark, and the pregnant smell of sex shrouded us like a blanket of cloud. The guys on stage now began to lick the two cunts in front of them, and the other Sister put my hand to her heavy breasts. I reached down and slid my fingers between her swollen labia and drank her spit, the first Sister caressing my balls, then putting my cock inside her wet mouth. Levinsen entered the stage behind Mille, his member fully erect.

'Is it true you like big cocks, Mille?'

'Yes,' she said, her voice trembling.

He placed his cock between Mille's tied-up hands and her fingers closed around it greedily. He made fucking movements, and Mille squirmed so much the guy with his tongue in her cunt had his work cut out just to stay on board. She grunted and squealed like a shed of pigs.

There was a look of insanity in Levinsen's eyes as he stepped down-stage gently masturbating. He looked down at himself as though to savour the moment, rubbing his thumb under the magnificent head.

'Would you like a huge cock inside you, Mille?' he said.

The two young guys stood up and left the stage.

'This is a love-in, everyone,' said Levinsen. 'Come up and pleasure Diana!'

Tongues and hands smothered her from all sides.

The second Sister thrust out her bum and I took hold of her hips and buried my cock inside her while the first rubbed her pussy and licked her tits. A young guy began fucking Diana, his muscular but-tocks a blur between her legs. All over, people were shagging and the air was thick with the sound of balls slapping against buttocks, an increasing hum of moans and groans, and tiny gasps.

On my way out, I saw a new, rather broader arse take its place between Diana's thighs.

The next morning, Diana and I cycled past Helenekilde and over the hill at Vejby Strand to the quay at Gilleleje, where we sat with a carton of chocolate milk and looked out at the fishing boats.

'Was he the second?' she said.

'Who?'

'Andreas Møller! Was he the second one who fucked me?'

'I couldn't see,' I said.

'It was him,' she said.

'He's celibate,' I said.

'It was horrible,' she said.

She took my right hand.

'I'm going home to my daughter!'

'You've got a daughter?'

'Nona. She'll be seven in October.'

'Where does she live?'

'With my mother in Budapest.'

'Is she ill?'

'She wants to see me.'

'When are you leaving?'

'Today.'

She went on ahead and had already packed by the time I got back.

'Aren't you going to say goodbye?' I said.

I followed her down to the yellow train and she gave me a long kiss.

'Look after our doggy,' she said.

I sat next to Lisa at dinner that night. 'I thought you knew she was leaving,' she said. 'She told everyone close to her.'

'Apparently I'm not, then.'

We sat down in the kitchen. I could have done with a whisky.

'Why didn't she bring her daughter with her to Denmark?' said Mille.

'Diana made a choice,' said Lisa.

'Between what?' said Mille.

'She knew she couldn't be a mother and an artist at the same time.'

'How old was her daughter when she left?' said Nikolaj Krogh.

'Four months.'

'How often does she see her?' said Mille.

'She hasn't been back to Budapest since.'

'*In defence of the mother who abandons the nest,*' I said.

'Who's defending?' said Mille.

'It was a piece I wrote once.'

'How despicable, leaving one's own little child,' said Mille.

'Let's drink our brains out, shall we?' said Lisa.

My popular science talk on the chemistry of love went down a treat at the assembly.

'Does anyone have anything they'd like to say under any other business?' I said.

A single acid-jazz mother put up her hand.

'Something needs to be done about Kreuzmann.'

'Could you be more specific?' I said.

'He's destructive, he doesn't involve himself, and he stinks!'

Widespread nodding.

'We must take Kreuzmann into the fold,' said Andreas Møller. 'Can you go and fetch him, Mikkel?'

He was sitting where he always sat, in front of his tent.

'You're an issue at assembly,' I said.

'What does that mean?' he said.

'It means you've got to come with me.'

He hesitated for a second at the sight of the two-hundred-strong gathering.

'Welcome,' said Andreas Møller. 'Would you care to repeat your point,' he said, raising his eyebrows towards the single acid-jazz mother.

'I'm finding your way of being here rather a problem,' she said.

'She doesn't think you're involving yourself, Kreuzmann,' said Andreas Møller.

'Why don't you wash?' said the single acid-jazz mother.

'Time flies,' he said.

'You smell really bad.'

'I can't smell anything myself,' he said.

'That's because you're drunk twenty-four hours a day,' she said.

A small red-haired woman stood up.

'It upsets me to see you like this.'

'Like what?' he said.

'My brother's a therapist,' said the red-haired girl. 'I'm sure I can persuade him to come.'

'Sounds like a good offer, Kreuzmann,' said Andreas Møller.

'I had a lovely childhood,' said Kreuzmann.

'Something obviously went wrong,' said the single acid-jazz mother.

'I've been a bastard for twenty-five years,' said Kreuzmann.

'You need to talk to someone about it,' said the red-haired girl.

'You must take the community seriously if you want to stay here,' said Andreas Møller. 'And you need to wash.'

'Can I have a word in private?' Kreuzmann said to Andreas Møller.

They spent two hours in the F.P. Jac and Kreuzmann came out with tears in his eyes and a set of clean clothes over his arm.

'What happened in there?' I asked.

'He emptied his soul and apologised,' said Andreas Møller.

'To whom?'

'He repented for having promised his wife he'd be faithful.'

The next morning, Kreuzmann was in a light blue shirt and his cheeks were white where his beard had been. No one was in any doubt that the day's sermon was in his honour.

Andreas began with a parable:

'A rich man's land had again brought forth so plentifully he had to pull down his barns and build bigger ones to store all his grain. And when he'd done that he leaned back to take his ease and enjoy the good life. But God said: "You're a fool! Tonight your soul will be taken, and who will benefit then from this great harvest?" *So is he that layeth up treasure for himself, and is not rich toward God.*

'Jesus says: "It is your Father's good pleasure to give you the Kingdom."

'That which we give away is ours to own for ever. The Kingdom is to give and to serve each other, and the Kingdom is here and now. We should not save our love, but share it freely. This is what we do here in our camp, and see how we smile. Amen.'

After breakfast, Kreuzmann took his turn doing the washing-up, and I went for a walk with Andreas Møller. We were at the edge of the woods, going in the direction of the church at Tibirke.

'Now is the time to stand firm,' he said. 'We created something unique here, but we need to take it further.'

It was the kind of rhetoric I could relate to.

'We can change people's lives, Mikkel. We can create something of lasting value to the whole world.'

When we got back, I called a meeting in the kitchen and spent all day with Andreas and Mille, trying to put our vision into writing.

'How does Next Love sound?' I said.

'Good,' said Mille.

Andreas made a pitch for: 'Next Love is a physical Christian community'.

'It doesn't sound even remotely sexy,' said Mille. 'It sounds like reading glasses and a little crucifix on a chain over a polo neck.'

'We're not virtuous,' said Andreas.

'It would be rather radical to get you to take Jesus seriously.'

'Jesus can deal with not getting a mention,' said Mille.

She proposed: 'Next Love is a devotional physical community'.

'The word *devotional* has lost its significance,' said Andreas.

After two bottles of Morelino di Scanzano we were all in agreement:

'Next Love is a physical and metaphysical community whose aim is to spread love and to achieve the greatest possible energy through work, spiritual enlightenment and new models of coexistence'.

I ran through our main principles:

Coupledom in the traditional sense was forbidden. Deep and

lasting relationships were good, but the closed unit was unwelcome and jealousy constituted grounds for exclusion. Members were obliged to put the community before themselves, and work was of the highest priority.

All problems were to be discussed and solved through group discussion.

The ambition was to create an autonomous society without isolating ourselves from the one surrounding us, with the aim of bringing benefit to the world.

The spiritual aspect was the backbone, and our point of departure was Christian Protestant. Each Wednesday and Sunday, Andreas would give a service. We dreamed of having our own cinema, a gym, playing fields, studios, writing spaces and a function hall. Sexual desire would underpin it all, whether we were in the fields, attending lectures, playing football or shagging.

We put our thoughts to the assembly that evening.

'Am I supposed to dump my girlfriend?' someone said.

'We are to love one another,' I said. 'And that's best achieved through openness.'

'How do we avoid getting jealous?'

'By rising above it,' I said. 'That may sound arrogant, but all it requires is to take a small step up.'

One hundred and twenty-seven put their names down, and Mille and I were elected joint chairpersons.

We rounded off with a communal hug and 'Touch Me'.

After the weekend people had to get back to work, so everyone was all in for the last party of the summer. Talk of the camp had spread, but we had stopped letting new people and tents in a while back. Our task now was to contain and sustain our success, and we made it clear that we all had to hold back on the invites.

'I've had a call from a journalist,' said Andreas. 'She's heard that we formed Next Love and wants to interview us before the party.'

'Who is she?' I said.

'Rie Becker. Do you know her?'

'I do. It's not a good idea,' I said.

'I'm a clergyman,' he said. 'I'm not in the media picture.'

'You could be.'

'If we do this interview right, Next Love will have five hundred members by Monday.'

'We?' I said. 'I think it's best you do this one yourself.'

'She expressly asked for you, Mikkel.'

O n the Thursday afternoon, I took the train back into the city to pick up Charlie, Helene and Tue Nissen at the airport, and I was struck by a rather unexpected emotion. For the first time in years I felt a connection with Helene.

I stood among the hordes at Terminal 3, light of heart and with an open mind.

Charlie's hair was bleached from the sun and his little arms melted around my neck. Helene had lost weight and her blue eyes sparkled against her tanned skin.

Tue Nissen greeted me vacantly and didn't know where to put himself.

'We're missing a leather suitcase, Helene. Aren't we missing a leather suitcase?'

'It's all here, Tue,' said Helene.

'I think we're missing a leather suitcase.'

'Everything's in order, Tue. Let's get home.'

'Right, we're going home and everything's in order. Is everything in order?'

Helene put her arms around him. He laughed and dribbled.

'Have you been tippling on the flight?' I said.

'We've been throwing it back,' said Tue.

'That's not like you two.'

'We're not like us two anymore,' said Tue.

'Did something happen while you were away?' I said.

Tue put his hand to his mouth.

'I don't know if I can talk about it, Helene.'

'Of course you can,' said Helene. 'Let's go home and make something to eat, then we can tell Mikkel all about it.'

Tue went out to get some shopping in, and Charlie ran upstairs to his toys. Helene had a short skirt on.

'You're looking good,' I said.

She turned to face me with a spoon in her hand. 'Thanks,' she said. She may have been going to say more.

I told her about our life in the camp, and about Master Licker and Clara, and she listened open-mouthed and howled with laughter. Tue came back with carrier bags in both hands. 'Fresh cod in the thinnest of slices for ceviche,' he said. 'Fresh-boiled Danish lobster, ta-da! A little bit of foie gras, yes? *Mousse au chocolat* for the Frenchman. What more have we got? Cheese, for God's sake, *Rødkit*, some sort of *bleu*, Gouda for the Jutland lass, which is me. A lot of vegetables that we don't really fancy.'

I read Charlie the one about Spot the Dog again, and as always he fell asleep just before the turning point with the crocodile.

Tue Nissen had set a table outside.

'So, tell me,' I said.

'What do you know about white Rioja?' said Tue, pouring a glass of Predicator. It presented itself becomingly and tasted like a superior white Burgundy.

'Extraordinarily good, don't you think?' he said.

'Let's eat,' said Helene.

'Sustenance, yes,' said Tue.

We had the lobster and the foie gras. Tue drank half a bottle of white wine in fifteen minutes and opened the champagne. The froth subsided in our glasses.

Tue Nissen stared obliquely into the air for a moment as though looking for a place to begin.

'Have you ever been to Deia?' he said.

'No. Isn't it a kind of reservation for rich bohemians?' I said.

'The house we'd rented was far too big, the terrace was enormous and commanded an incredible view of the Mediterranean,' said Tue. 'There are so many restaurants there you're spoiled for choice.'

'We were walking through the town,' said Helene. 'Charlie was in his buggy.'

'Deia's mostly Germans and Brits,' said Tue. 'People in the money, a lot of creatives, and we'd just been talking about how samey it all was when we passed this family with two kids. I happened to make eye contact with the father and nodded.'

Tue Nissen had tears in his eyes. He glanced at Helene.

'You know me, Mikkel,' said Tue. 'I mean, you were on the first row when I met Helene, weren't you? I'm mad about women.'

'But?' I said.

'I fell in love.'

'With the father?'

'I can't even begin to explain the turmoil.'

'What did you do about it?' I asked.

'Well, nothing. I was exhausted after the travelling. So I fantasised. It makes you hyper-sensitive sometimes, doesn't it? Hallucinatory, almost.'

'I noticed him, too,' said Helene. 'He's not that tall, but rugged-looking and sinewy, and he's got chestnut-coloured hair and these amazing green eyes. He looks like a sort of cat.'

'We found a splendid seafood restaurant and I was knocking back the wine,' said Tue.

'You weren't making sense on the way home,' said Helene.

'I woke up with a hangover and he was the first thing I thought about,' said Tue.

'I couldn't understand why he didn't want to come to the beach with us,' said Helene.

'I pretended I was in a deeply inspired writing phase and hid behind my computer.'

'There's only one beach in Deia,' said Helene. 'Anyway, I ended up having lunch with Aurelien and Julie and invited them to the house for dinner.'

'I've never made such dreadful food in my life,' said Tue.

'But we'd got lots of drink in, and of course they had to stay the night,' said Helene. 'We put the children to sleep together in a great big bed, and Julie's a real old-school Britpopper so we put some Oasis on.'

Tue put his glass down.

'I was sitting opposite him and my leg was burning under the table. At one point the girls were at the stereo fiddling about with some music and I looked at him, which got the both of us flustered, and we started talking about his job as an investment adviser with NatWest.'

'We wanted to dance,' said Helene. 'If they were going to talk about work, we thought they could just as well stay at home and keep an eye on the kids.'

'They went off together in high spirits and I took out a bottle of rum. Aurelien has also only ever been into women, and he was as terrified as me.'

Tue was drinking champagne like it was beer.

'After we'd polished off half the bottle I suggested we go outside on to the terrace. The night sky was incredible, stars everywhere.'

'We looked for them all over the house,' said Helene. 'Then after a bit we went out to the terrace and there were our men, snogging. I noticed Tue had taken his shoes off, and he never goes around in bare feet.'

'What did you do?'

'We put "Wonderwall" on again and tried to sing it all away.'

'How did it end?' I said.

'It didn't,' said Helene. 'Julie slept with me and the next day we held a meeting. Aurelien and Tue hired a car and went away for a week, and she moved in with me. We cried and comforted each other, but what can you do? It was out of our hands.'

'We drove around the island, staying at the loveliest little places, playing tennis and drinking wine on the beach, talking and talking,' said Tue.

'The last nine days we all stayed together,' said Helene. 'And it was fun, the way it often is after a funeral.'

'I'm moving to London,' said Tue.

'What?'

'I'm leaving the house as it is and I'll be paying all the bills,' said Tue.

'Because you want to be with Aurelien?'

'I have to find out what it is,' he said.

Tue Nissen smiled and began to cry.

'I'll get the cognac,' said Helene.

At 3.18 the next afternoon I was back in Tisvilde.

The asphalt was melting and I relished the breeze as I walked along Nordhusvej and assured myself that the black cat that crossed the gravel track in front of me had white paws. The groceries had come and were being lugged inside, and as I crossed the lawn it occurred to me that Helene hadn't asked about Diana and me. Presumably, she wasn't up to what she assumed would be a tale of joy and happiness.

'Now's not the time to run aground,' said Andreas Møller.

'What's that supposed to mean?'

'Rie Becker's coming in on the train in two hours and you reek of booze. Have a cold shower and meet me in the bar in fifteen minutes!'

Andreas Møller ran his way methodically through every conceivable question that might be put to us, and assigned us well-defined roles, with me handling the idealistic side and he the dogmatic. Rie Becker was bringing a photographer with her and I knew he or she would be going straight for the dancing, the kissing and the nudity, so for a balanced view the accompanying copy would have to be sober. We had to get Jesus in there somewhere, the notion of the great community, love rather than sex.

He adjusted my cravat as we walked to the station, and the change in him was almost creepy. Maybe the white shirt reminded me of school uniform, the way the monied classes went all tremblingly formal when something important was about to happen. His shoes were polished and shiny, his back straight and his language bucked up, tight and economical in the way of an army officer, little darts expelled from the foremost part of his mouth.

He bowed for Rie Becker and asked about her trip.

'I'm sorry about last time, Mikkel,' she said. 'I've felt so bad about slagging off your friend Jan's canvases like that.'

'He was asking for it,' I said.

It was plain that Andreas Møller's conviviality was pure manners, but there was nothing wrong with the effect. He spread a cloth over the table, on to which he placed a small vase of wild flowers, large wine glasses and a chilled Sancerre.

'If you'd prefer tea or something else, all you have to do is ask.'

Her eyes were framed heavily by kohl and appeared small and blinking, her skirt was thigh-length tartan, her jewellery obtrusive and silly, all infantile colours.

Andreas Møller began, and judging by Rie's note-taking it wasn't his CV or his theological diversions she had come to Tisvilde for. After fifteen minutes there were seven words on her notepad.

'Who is Master Licker of Ørby?' she enquired.

I fed her a small selection of sex stories from the camp so as to pre-clude any further questions of a more sensational bent, which seemed to work well enough. She began asking about what we were trying to achieve, and we were able to expand at leisure upon our thoughts as to setting up a large-scale commune, the ideas behind the daily sermons, and our hopes of finding a kind of love that was both great and accom-modating, and after about an hour of conversation Andreas Møller swept his arm across the view of the camp in front of us.

'Look at what a good time everyone's having,' he said.

People were milling about, and Rie Becker's photographer feasted on broad summer smiles and the effortless interaction of tanned naked bodies.

'They're here for more than just partying,' said Andreas. 'Can't you tell?'

'Are they here for Jesus?' said Rie Becker.

'We are all of us drawn towards eternity,' said Andreas.

Rie Becker put her notepad down on the tablecloth.

'Jesus is in the house and he's feeling horny!'

'There's your headline,' I said.

'Now I think I'll knock off for the day and party along with the Saviour,' she said.

Andreas Møller stood up and extended his hand.

'Nice meeting you,' he said.

I spent all Saturday under the duvet with the Sisters of Mercy, and the next morning I followed them to the train. Cars were in convoy on their way out of the town, rear windows jammed with luggage. Another summer in Tisvilde had drawn to a close. It was hot, but cloudy.

'I never thought the sun would stop shining,' I said.

'You're our boy, Mikkel,' said a Sister.

'I'm forty-two,' I said.

We hugged for several minutes without feeling sad.

I bought the paper and sat down on the bench outside Vin og Grønt.

A Bengali was sweeping shards of glass together in front of Le Petit Fer à Cheval, and Thomas was smoking a rollie and waiting for the bread van from Aurion.

Rie Becker had got a front-page teaser. The headline ran:

They've got it all and more in abundance – free sex and champagne in Tisvilde.

A collage of snapshots broke up the copy: Kreuzmann dancing, out of his head, paranoid fashion girls on their way from the Portaloos, men snogging, the Sisters of Mercy with their tits out.

Rie Becker had gone with the shabbiest of journalistic approaches: the tongue-in-cheek reportage. Falsely objective and cynically exposing its subjects to ridicule. It was a total massacre and improbably well written.

My phone rang, but I couldn't be bothered with Moritz.

Lisa sat down next to me on the bench. She had bought a packet of Tuc, a bottle of French mandarin juice and the English version of *Elle* for the train home.

'Thanks for letting me be a part of your dream,' she said.

'It may be mostly Diana's,' I said.

'I really hope you two stay together,' she said.

'Me too,' I said, and then burst into tears.

'It's so romantic, her going all the way to Amalfi just to meet you.'

I had no idea what she was talking about.

'Nikolaj's found somewhere for me to go to rehab,' she said.

'That's a good idea,' I said, distracted.

'Do you want to come?'

'No, I'm just going to try not to get drunk for the next few months.'

She looked at me like I was a lamp-post.

Nikolaj Krogh and a couple of jazz musicians were dismantling the bar, others had set about taking down the fairy lights, cleaning the barbecue and carrying bags of rubbish away. The garden looked naked and forlorn.

A dozen tents lay flat on the ground with holdalls and guitars on top of them, and I didn't hear what anyone was saying when they hugged and said goodbye.

By two o'clock everything was back to normal. Kreuzmann was sitting on his own in front of his tent at the far end of the garden and I was whipping some mayonnaise in the kitchen.

'Claudia rang,' said Mille.

'What did she want?'

'It's that photo in the paper. She's never seen him dance before.'

We had just got lunch together when Claudia appeared.

'Where is he?'

Ten minutes later she came back with the tent under her arm and a tight grip of Kreuzmann's hand. He didn't seem surprised.

'Thanks for everything,' he said.

I ate some shrimps without bothering to savour the taste, and Nikolaj Krogh finished reading the article and tossed the paper down in front of him.

'No one can ever take this summer away from us,' he said. 'All those magic moments. You made it happen, Mikkel!'

'Have you seen the ad?' said Mille.

It took up the whole of page three in the arts supplement. A big, grainy, black-and-white photo of Nikolaj Krogh with his hands on Diana's breasts.

Dusk – The Clothing of Emperors. Grand Opening, August 7th.

'It'll be nice to see the kids again,' said Mille.

Nikolaj Krogh smiled, and something at least was different about his smile, if nothing else.

'Fancy some coffee?' he said.

'No, thanks,' I said.

The wood pigeon began on cue as I lugged my bag down the infinite driveway. What sunshine is for the black earth, as Grundtvig wrote.

COPENHAGEN, AUGUST 2008

Anyone venturing out on the town on a Sunday night should be warned.

The usual upholstery of partygoers has all unravelled and gone, and what's left are the desperate, the misfits and the chronically inebriated, the sad and the sleepless. All who are out have reasons not to go home, and the reasons are not always cheerful.

It was half past one and I was seated in Andy's Bar with a Blå Nykøbing and an Arnbitter, hopelessly scribbling words into my notebook. I hadn't meant to end up there. When I'd put down my bag in the flat on Klerkegade at half past six, I was determined not to go out. Regrettably, however, it transpired that prohibition provokes the spark of its antithesis, and since it seemed pointless to waste an hour or two pretending to stand firm, only then to acquiesce, I decided to acknowledge my weakness straight away.

I never tired of looking at the Albert Mertz reliefs that Gunnar, the former owner of Andy's Bar, had bought at auction from Wivex, the old dance hall, and I loved the painting of the dizzy blonde with her knickers round her ankles, the one that Gasolin' had used for the cover of *Gas 3*.

'Hard at work, are we?'

Mosbeck, all of a sudden, in his tweed jacket.

'Can I get you one?' he said.

Where did he appear from, and why was he being so friendly?

'That article today was an all-out attack, wasn't it?'

'She caught us on the wrong night,' I said.

'She knew full well,' he said. 'And yet she decided to go with the story and turn you into a couple of pillocks going on about Jesus and doing the upper crust a service. Fly no higher than your wings can bear. That's the song we sing in this country, isn't it? Rather depressing, if you ask me.'

It transpired that as consultant physician at the Rigshospitalet, Mosbeck had been thinking about reforming the health service. He and an architect had delivered a proposal to set up a new department of alternative medicine, only to be obstructed and ridiculed.

'You showed guts, going to the papers with that project of yours,' he said. 'But it does place your own relationship under a certain strain.'

'How do you mean?'

'If you can't live up to your own ideals, you can hardly expect others to.'

'I've had my problems, but I'm over them.'

'Where's Diana now?'

'She's in Budapest.'

He smiled faintly, positioned his beer and asked whether I'd like to hear a story about a man called Donald Crowhurst, and before I could object he had begun.

In 1968, the *Sunday Times* announced a competition. Who would be the first person ever to sail single-handed and non-stop around the world? The paper had its eye on the stunt's immense publicity potential, with its steady flow of stories about one man's battle against the elements, and elected for the sake of balance and excitement to make the competition open to anyone. Nine European men entered, among them Donald Crowhurst.

Crowhurst was a thirty-five-year-old British businessman and father of four, happily married and a devoted family man. He was also a dreamer. His small electronics company wasn't doing as well as he would have liked, but he was convinced that an invention of his, a marine navigation system he called Navicator, would make him rich if only it received due attention in the press. Moreover, he was intent on bringing honour to his family by winning the five thousand pounds sterling offered in prize money for the fastest circumnavigation.

Crowhurst lived in Bridgwater, a small market town in Somerset, where he was well liked for his cheerfulness and optimism. He was in no doubt that he would win, regardless of his relative lack of experience on the sea, including the fact that he had never at any time sailed farther than the Bay of Biscay. His wife admired him for his grand designs, and since it was highly unlikely that Crowhurst would be able to raise sufficient funds to build the kind of boat that would be necessary for such a venture, she willingly lent him her full and enthusiastic support. But she underestimated his enthusiasm.

Crowhurst got the backing of a local factory owner, who paid a boatyard in Norwich to construct a high-spec tailored trimaran for Crowhurst's voyage.

The rules required that all competitors depart no later than 31 October and in order to get the trimaran ready in time, certain corners were cut in the construction process. A fortnight prior to deadline, Crowhurst drove to Norwich to collect his boat. The champagne bottle used in the launch ceremony failed to break, an omen Crowhurst took with a smile. Nor was he discouraged by the fact that the journey from Norwich to his departure point, Teignmouth in Devon, took almost two weeks rather than the expected three days.

On the day before the final permitted departure day, Crowhurst said goodbye to his family and a gathering of several thousand well-wishers and left the harbour. Ten minutes later, when his sail jammed, he was towed back in again. Local sailors gave him little chance. To their minds, his boat was far too flimsy, but the worst thing was that Crowhurst himself had begun to have doubts. On the evening before his departure he broke down crying in his wife's lap, and the fact that he sailed at all was perhaps only a matter of his stiff upper lip British upbringing.

In Crowhurst's teenage years, his father went bankrupt and died soon afterwards of a heart attack. Now Crowhurst found himself in what he considered to be a perilously similar financial position. His benefactor, the local factory owner, had made his support conditional upon Crowhurst being personally liable, which meant that his family would have to sell their beloved house in the event of Crowhurst dropping out or his boat being wrecked at sea.

On the afternoon of 31 October, Crowhurst finally set sail. It didn't matter that his competitors had left weeks earlier: the prize money was for the fastest circumnavigation. The first week passed without event, Crowhurst making progress, though nowhere near as quickly as expected. On the eighth day, however, his boat began taking in water, and a number of bearing screws were lost to the Atlantic.

The short cuts taken by the shipyard began to show, and while he was able to bail the vessel manually he knew he would find himself in rather more serious trouble after rounding the Cape and entering the Indian Ocean. The waves there would reach some thirty metres in height and tear the screws from the hull, and it would no longer be possible for him to bail by hand. The boat would sink.

Crowhurst now faced an impossible choice: either he sailed on into the Indian Ocean to meet his death, or else he gave up and returned home to disgrace and financial ruin. He loitered, dragging out the decision for days without solution.

After a week of brooding, an alternative gradually presented itself.

During his deliberations he had shut down his radio, causing much consternation to the press and his family. Their joy when finally he made contact again knew no bounds. He even had good news. He had entered the Indian Ocean and was making excellent speed. In fact, he was sailing so quickly he was now the fastest of the nine competitors.

The press sensed a sensation. Crowhurst's children were proud. What they didn't know was that Crowhurst had begun to keep two logs: his actual navigation log and a second that was false. By intricate calculation he succeeded in accounting for his false position, while all the time remaining in the South Atlantic. Crowhurst had a plan.

He would slip into the wake of his competitors for the return leg, but since this was still some considerable time off he decided, in order not to be discovered, to shut off his radio once again.

For eleven weeks he loitered off the coast of Brazil. The only things he saw were the sea and the sky. He lost all sense of time and place, finding it increasingly difficult to distinguish himself from his surroundings and penning madly escalating torrents of prose about a higher cosmic order.

By the time the others crossed his position, the competition was considerably reduced. Five had given up in the Indian Ocean, while one had sailed on with no fixed destination, and when Crowhurst, after almost three months of isolation, broke his radio silence he was finally able to state a position that accorded with the truth.

His wife was delirious with joy and the press had a field day with the story of the happy amateur now vying for the prize.

Robin Knox-Johnston would be first home, but he had been the first competitor to leave and would not be the fastest man. That honour would befall another Briton, Nigel Tetley, which suited Crowhurst admirably.

The winner's log would be subjected to the severest scrutiny, and though Crowhurst had been meticulous in his falsification he would surely be exposed. For that reason he proceeded at a leisurely pace with his eye on the second place that would secure him honour and reunite him with his family and home.

Tetley, however, felt himself to be under pressure and forced the pace beyond his boat's capabilities, and two days before finishing, his vessel broke up and sank. Crowhurst, realising then that victory was unavoidable, gushed out twenty-five thousand words and then threw himself overboard.

Twelve days later, his empty boat was found.

We avoided eye contact as Mosbeck concluded the story. I stared at a radiator, he downed his beer in two gulps. 'I hope you work it out, Mikkel,' he said, curling his lip in what was supposed to be a smile.

It had been eight days since Diana had left for Budapest. I had started listening to Schubert's String Quintet in C major and was proceeding sideways through the days with an ache in my chest. The night before, I'd had dinner with Charlie and Helene, and she had been positively quivering. The initial shock at Tue's betrayal had turned into grief and bewilderment. But as is so often the case with those who are abandoned, something in her was already anticipating better times. Her hair had taken on a sheen, her eyes were bright and energetic, she had begun to lose weight without trying, and to voice whatever thoughts occurred to her, like how nice it would be to re-locate to Mozambique, the destructive honesty of Thomas Mann, or getting her boobs done. I prayed this openness would last.

A couple went by the window of the bar, their pram laden with carrier bags from the supermarket. You looked after your offspring, made sure the home was warm enough and there were clean sheets on the bed, and cooked the meat until it could be eaten. You did the washing-up, and from the kitchen window noticed a plane in the sky, recalling what it felt like to be on your way into the unknown. A train, a boat, a plane. Then you opened the bottom cupboard and put the salad bowl back in its place, and there were voices coming from the television in the living room, and every step towards it seemed like a bad decision.

On the Wednesday morning Diana called and said she'd be land-ing in the evening at sevenish. I knew she wasn't capable of put-ting feeling into the transfer of practical information, so I didn't take it personally that her tone was mechanical, bordering on the abrupt, but I did decide right away that I would cook her a welcome-home dinner of *Pappardelle ai funghi porcini* – porcini mushrooms lightly fried with shallots, garlic, a nip of rosemary and a dash of cream to bring it all together.

There was no doubt that a cup of strong chicken stock would add to the dynamics, and so I went to Irma on Borgergade and spent the last of my money on a young cockerel, a kilo of organic onions and the same of carrots. I got the stock on the go and then cycled over to Helene's office and borrowed a thousand kroner. As we hugged I couldn't help but notice that she didn't put her hands on my shoulders as she normally did, but instead slid one hand around my hip. The Italian on Lille Trianglen had *pappardelle*, but was out of fresh porcini, and while he was kind enough to enquire with Supermercato in Sydhavnen, it seemed I was out of luck. In the old days, the grocer's on Rosenvænget would have saved the day, but all they had was a little basket of dry-looking chanterelles.

Mad og Vin had cultivated oyster mushrooms and those brown beech mushrooms that taste vaguely of chlorine, as well as some chanterelles that looked like they were from Chernobyl, but no porcini, and Røde Claus over at Restaurant Gammel Mønt reproached me for not having given word earlier, sending me over the road to Bo at Restaurationen, who, though he had copious amounts of forest mushrooms, albeit mostly brown birch boletes, could spare no porcini at all. I rang round a few Italian restaurants, one of which actually served *Fettucine ai funghi porcini*, but they used the dried variety.

It was one o'clock when I got hold of Kreuzmann. He hadn't got the Range Rover, but he could borrow Claudia's car, and twenty minutes later he picked me up in a white Mini at Klampenborg Station. 'We're going up to the castle ruin at Asserbo,' I said. 'Head for Hillerød, Helsinge, then turn off towards Frederiksværk.' I made no efforts towards polite conversation and stared stiffly at the glove compartment.

Three days of heavy rain had compensated for the lengthy dry spell and the woods were dotted with mushrooms: orange blankets of freshly emerged chanterelles, flourishes of sweet tooth, birch boletes and honey fungus in their hundreds, but, after an hour's intense searching, only three porcini, of which two were too sloppy in the cap.

I sat down on a tree stump and stared at the forest floor.

'Has she got a man in Budapest?' Kreuzmann said.

'She's got a child,' I said.

'Presumably there's a father,' he said.

'Do you know "Borderline" by Madonna?'

'The only one I remember's the one with the tits.'

'Do you know when a song opens up for you because someone you know is mad about it?'

'How many fingers have I got?' said Kreuzmann, holding up four in front of me.

'You used to have two hundred million, now you've got none.'

'Listen, mate, I may be broke, but all it means is I'm temporarily on Mâcon instead of Meursault.'

A short distance away, an elderly woolly jumper of the intellectual left came crawling through the tall grass trailing a basket on her arm, her busy, ceramic artist's fingers sifting every centimetre of soil.

'Why don't we just buy your rotten fungus off Granola Woman over there?' said Kreuzmann.

'It's not the done thing to converse with other mushroomers,' I said.

'Do you want to make Diana the porcini or not?'

He trampled a mat of chanterelles underfoot on his way over.

'Good afternoon,' said Kreuzmann.

She looked up at him with an indignant expression. She was the type who used a knife, of course she was. Her basket was filled to the brim and contained at least three hundred grams of porcini.

'Sorry to bother you,' said Kreuzmann.

'We usually don't,' she said.

'My friend Mikkel here is in a bit of a jam.'

'I'm not sure I wish to hear the rest,' she said.

Her trousers were dyed at home, and her chunky, striped cardigan looked prickly. Her boots were the kind with wooden soles.

'Mikkel's a chef, you see, and tonight he's preparing the food for a small and rather exclusive charity dinner for which he has announced there will be porcini. I know it's quite unheard of, but we've been all over the city and are complete novices when it comes to mushrooming. You know your woods, I see.'

'You could say. I've been coming here almost fifty years.'

'How much do you want for your porcini?'

'Oh, we never sell.'

'Of course we wouldn't be purchasing them,' I said. 'But we would very much like to compensate you for your efforts.'

'How about a hundred kroner?' said Kreuzmann.

'I'm sorry, but I do find this all rather intrusive.'

'Two hundred,' said Kreuzmann.

'Personally, I've always valued the porcini more than the chanterelles,' she said.

'We couldn't agree more,' I said. 'And that's exactly why I'd so much like to serve porcini this evening. If the dinner proves as successful as we hope, we shall have collected in the region of two hundred thousand kroner for victims of the war in Afghanistan.'

'Of all the meaningless wars,' she said.

'Four hundred?' said Kreuzmann.

She lowered her basket.

'Well, just this once,' she said.

K reuzmann burned rubber as we tore off in the direction of Asserbo.

'Fucking old hippies,' he said.

We had fifteen porcini on the back seat.

'A dried-up fanny like her with a great big house on Emiliekildevej and a summer house up here to the tune of five million, still voting socialist and serving her guests nettle soup.'

We reached the T-junction outside Helsinge, the grim video shop.

'You've ruined their paradise back in Tisvilde,' said Kreuzmann. 'Monster knob Levinsen's forever in and out at Krogh and Mille's.'

'Levinsen and his wife have got an open relationship,' I said.

'She kicked him out six months ago.'

'Who told you that?'

'Our kids go to the same school.'

'Everyone lies,' I said.

'I lied first,' he said.

'And then you went Christian?'

'The only difference is it means putting your lies into a system,' he said.

The herbs tumbled about in the simmering chicken broth, and I skimmed off the top and strained the stock through a cheese-cloth. On Dronningens Tværgade I bought two bottles of Mongeard-Mugneret 2002, an earthy, graceful wine I had sampled at Sollerod Kro.

Kreuzmann took me to the airport, and as we stood in arrivals at Terminal 3 waiting for her to come, I visualised Diana's kitchen counter. The red bowl to the right of the sink: garlic, perhaps a lemon or two, and hadn't there been some shallots as well? How long could they stay fresh? And if they couldn't, or there weren't any, would I be able to cook the dish without? I saw myself peeling the skins off them, putting them down on the chopping board. If she wasn't hungry, I could make it a late-night meal instead, but was the red wine in that case a mistake? Why hadn't I bought a spumante or a light white? And then I looked up and saw her come trundling with her purple trolley suitcase, and I'd never seen her looking so tired. Jan was walking at her side in new clothes, she wasn't listening to him. I immediately went up to greet her, and she was surprised to see me. Maybe it was just me feeling shy and awkward, but I was acutely aware of people around us waving their paper flags, their provincial accents. I pulled her into me, but it was hardly a kiss, more like a collision of lips. It would have been too odd to shake hands with Jan, and when I hugged him instead I saw how easily Diana embraced Kreuzmann.

'I came back via Berlin,' she said.

Mies appeared from the throng.

'Mies showed us round Kreuzkölln yesterday,' said Jan.

Mies had a new hairstyle; fair and closely cropped to his head. It accentuated the purity of his face, and he greeted me like it meant something.

Diana chose the passenger seat next to Kreuzmann.

Mies had lived on Grafestrasse since 2006 and worked as a photographic artist, traipsing round the flea markets finding old family photos from the former East Berlin, then Photoshopping himself in at the tiled coffee table at Uncle Günther's fiftieth birthday in 1976, or beside the Christmas tree in cheerless flats with confusing wallpaper and electric organs.

Everyone got out on Lyrskovgade, and I had my hands full of porcini, red wine and stock as Mies said goodbye.

'Why don't you come up?' I said.

I was frightened I'd be alone without him.

'I'm meeting someone,' he said, and obviously wasn't.

Kreuzmann wanted to see Diana's apartment, and she told him the first tapestry would soon be arriving from Vietnam. There *were* some shallots.

'Do you sell to friends?' he said.

'All sales go through Moritz,' she said.

'Are you hungry?' I said.

'Not just now,' she said. 'We've brought some absinthe home.'

Jan lit the torches on the rooftop terrace and put some Balkan remix or other on the stereo, and it was just all too strenuous with all those wind instruments and his going on about the breakfast at Ankerklause and the little garden at the Literaturhaus and the Gerhard Richter exhibition and the men-only *Lab-oratory* at Berghain with shit on the floor and stiff cocks waving about at lip level.

'Berlin's nothing but gays and artists,' said Kreuzmann.

'You're forgetting gay artists,' said Jan.

'I've always preferred Hamburg,' said Kreuzmann. 'The Lime Tree Terrace at the Hotel Louis C. Jacob, where the shipowners come to watch their ships sail past. Berlin is lukewarm canned beer.'

'I'm hungry,' said Jan.

Kreuzmann followed me inside before he left.

'Get rid of spunkface, so you can get her clothes off.'

I opened one of the bottles of Burgundy and it tasted of Grand de Luze, like all red wines do if they haven't been properly attended to. I worked mechanically towards my objective, chopping the shallots, lightly frying them with the garlic, then chucking in the chopped mushrooms, the chicken stock and reducing it all down before finally adding the rosemary, but I wasn't engaged in the various processes. The shelves on the wall were something I could relate to and understand, the way they were just there. The water came to the boil and I dropped the fresh pasta into it and got three plates.

Jan smothered his with freshly ground pepper and Diana only ate half. I couldn't taste a thing. There were sirens below.

'What was it like seeing Nona?' I said.

Jan got up and took our plates.

'It was fine,' she said.

'Can I see her?'

'She's in Budapest.'

'I meant a picture.'

'I haven't got one.'

'You didn't take a picture of her?'

Jan screwed the top back on the absinthe.

Later, in bed, she lay looking at me as I lit the chunky candles around the room. I felt obliged to speak, so I started to tell her the story about Tue and Aurelien. I'd only just got to them making eye contact on the street when Diana interrupted and took my hand.

'I need a father.'

'What do you want a father for?'

'To decide.'

I searched for something to say.

'Will you be my dad?' she said.

I managed to get her pants off before she fell asleep. Her little round bum filled out her small panties and I made the effort not to press my dick against her. She was twenty-seven and had just met her daughter for the first time. Of course she was exhausted.

W e woke up half an hour before Dusk's grand opening.
'Have you got any money?' she said as we sat in the taxi.
'I've got five hundred.'
'Ida-Marie wants the rent.'
We stopped off at Kongens Nytorv.
'How much is fifteen biggies?' she said.
'Fifteen thousand,' I said.
'Stig Nissen wants to give you fifteen thousand for a talk. Can't you make sure he does?'

Nikolaj Krogh had shaped the Dusk logo in wood, the lettering was a metre and a half tall and coated in piano varnish. The door handles were black and looked like oversized claves, and the front facing out to Østergade was all glass. Inside the large, airy store, the flooring was matt black, and all the organically rounded shelves were as glossy as mirrors. In the far corner was Nikolaj Krogh's signature chair, the Black Egg, surrounded by black Eames chairs and a primly designed black leather sofa. All the clothes racks were transparent plexiglas. Diana's cunts had been blown up into giant photostats.

'Is this *spitzenklasse* or what?' said Stig Nissen.

He was in a narrow black suit that accentuated his stubbornly bandy legs, and on his feet were a pair of silly designer sneakers. Black-clad waiters served champagne from trays, and on the great glass counter a deconstructed brunch had been laid out, foie gras, crème brulée, millefeuille of slow-baked pancetta with whisked egg whites, melon shots with freeze-dried crumbs of ham, and black blintz with caviar.

Lisa was on mineral water and standing on her own.

'He's ruined my design!'

She took a boiler suit off a rack and held it out in front of us.

'Do you remember what this looked like in the sketches, Diana?'

'Is it the one that was tight at the top and baggy at the bottom?'

'Look at it now,' said Lisa. 'It's just a catsuit.'

'What happened?' said Diana.

'He's had his bollocksing-up team in Brande editing my styles.'

She picked up a sunshine-yellow blouse from a shelf.

'This was mustard before.'

'I was wondering about those colours,' said Diana.

The label at the neck said *Dusk by Lisa Zöllner*.

Stig Nissen tapped his glass.

'Yeehah, Duskies! In a minute we're going to be opening the doors to the public and the story of Dusk will be under way.'

The queue outside the store was several hundred strong.

'Let's get set for an amazing day and a bloody gobsmacking night. In a bit, the bus'll be here to pick us up and it'll be showtime and party over at Custom House. Then once we're all fired up and dancing, it's on to Jazz House to rip the place apart!'

The black-clad doorman opened the doors and took the coupons all the teenage girls had cut out of their fashion mag. *Free Brunch with the Dusk Team*. Stig Nissen waylaid Diana.

'Cunt counter!' he said, steering her towards a big pile of white T-shirts with Diana's cunts on the front. He pressed a black marker pen into her hand, and for the next half-hour she was signing T-shirts. The quality was so poor she had to be careful not to tear through the material.

At twelve o'clock, a black bus with tinted windows drew up outside the store to take us on to the next phase of the party.

Stig Nissen went speed-talking from seat to seat. I looked out at the cyclists pedalling along in the bike lanes, noting firstly how foot-wear lost its dignity as soon as there was a child seat on the back, and secondly that I was plainly in more trouble than I realised if thoughts like that had begun to occupy me. No one wanted to be the ordinary guy with the child seat anymore. We were only what our lust made of us. When the luxury hippies of sixties California developed a taste for Zen meditation they sent for a Japanese master.

His instruction was simple:

'Sit down on a chair and close your eyes.'

'Okay, and then what?'

'Just sit there.'

'What do I get out of it?'

'You get sitting on a chair with your eyes closed.'

Stig Nissen danced his way up and down the aisle with two serving girls.

Nikolaj Krogh took Lisa's hand and they still looked like a pair of besotted teenagers.

'I've spoken to my solicitor,' he said.

'Stig Nissen is in breach of your copyright by altering your designs without permission. All we have to do is compare your sketches with the clothes in the store.'

'I haven't got the sketches.'

'Where are they?'

'Stig's got them, of course.'

The bus pulled up outside Custom House and Diana, who had spent the journey gazing out of the window absorbed in thought, put her hand on mine and looked me in the eye for the first time since she'd come back from Budapest. I wiped a tear from the corner of my eye after we kissed.

I wandered about backstage with a smile on my face. Flocks of small-breasted teenage girls were getting their make-up done and having their hair arranged, people with headsets and bewilderment in their eyes kept bumping into each other, and any attempt at communication was drowned immediately by the deafening onslaught of house music. No one loses their head as efficiently as the fashion business. On the big terrace facing the harbour, rental chairs had been lined up in rows, and Nikolaj Krogh and I were right at the front.

'Andreas has found a property for Next Love,' he said.

'Look at all this,' I said. 'Isn't it great?'

The pleb celebs were pouring in, girls with dead hair attachments, hideous designer handbags and inflated boobs, guys with shiny waxed hair, locked hips and excessively pumped biceps.

'We were talking about going up to have a look at the place next week,' said Nikolaj Krogh. 'It's an army barracks.'

I waved one of the girls over and took yet another glass of champagne from her tray. There was too much resilience in me to get drunk, it was that kind of day. Mille and two guys in sloppy muso attire stepped up on to a small stage. She had sunglasses on, a straight up-and-down pink dress from the collection and tall boots.

'Do you want to come along?'

Two bimbos with neat holes in their jeans and little dogs in their shoulder bags sat down next to us. The harbour was at our feet, the spire of Vor Frelser Kirke glittered in the sunshine across the water, and of course I wanted to go with them to see the barracks. A tight chord was struck and remained suspended in the gentle breeze, followed by a heavy, dragging beat, banjo and bass. Mille took the mic and sang:

This is the day. This is the day. This is the day we were longing for.

A large schooner came drifting in towards the quayside. Seven fashion models stood posing at the gunwale, and the audience rose from their gold-coloured chairs and applauded. *This is the day. This is the day we were longing for.* Not a bad tune, actually, a lot of minor key. Repeating a lyric over and over can be quite effective, it lends something ominous. Another wooden ship came sailing in with another seven models. The music stopped, a drum roll sounded, and out on the water five speedboats approached in formation. Mille switched from the airy flutter of before and sang from her chest, shifting an octave higher. *This is the day.* She screamed out the words and the beat returned, only in double time now. People got to their feet again and started dancing all around us. There were three models on each of the boats, arranged according to clothes and colour, and after they passed by, one of the musicians switched to accordion and picked up the theme while the other played the chords on the banjo. Mille leaned towards her audience. *This is the day.* A gondola came sailing some ten metres out in the harbour, and in the bow stood Diana in a fishing net like Kráka. *This is the day we were longing for. Dusk!*

The music stopped. People whooped and yelled, and Mille bowed.

'No expense spared,' said Nikolaj Krogh.

Stig Nissen was jumping up and down with excitement.

'Congratulations,' I said. 'They've never seen that before.'

He threw his arms round my neck.

'We bloody well showed them how to do it there, didn't we, eh? Bloody hell! Your missus, the bride in a fishing net! Are you proud or what?'

I wondered whether I should take advantage of the buoyant mood to confirm my fifteen-thousand-kroner talk in Brande, but decided it would be inappropriate to distract him in his moment of triumph.

'Come over here and give us a hug, Nikolaj Krogh!' Stig Nissen cried, and roughed him about.

'Who'd have thought a stuck-up city snob and a backwoodsman like Nissen here could get together and make miracles!'

Lisa clearly wasn't on the wagon anymore and stood propping up the far end of the bar. Mille had slipped into something black. 'Here she is, the lady herself!' Stig Nissen cried. 'You tell her to write a song called "Dusk" and what do you get? A smash hit off another planet. If that's not going to get your career going again, I don't know what is!'

I went inside to the restaurant arm in arm with Diana. Lisa was dancing on her own now, and she smiled a distant smile when anyone tried to compliment her. Waiters came and went with dishes of seafood and the crowd thinned out. Stig Nissen called the assembled guests to order. 'It's only the superstars left now! And do you know what? We're going to give ourselves a bloody great pat on the back and get stuck in to all this good bubbly, that's what!'

The bartender opened three bottles of Dom Perignon.

'We'll be popping off,' said Nikolaj Krogh. 'Vibskov's got a party on.'

It was a quarter to ten and I was sitting in a taxi heading for Jazz House, a stomach-churning slalom through the city: Skt. Annæ Plads, Bredgade, Dronningens Tværgade, Borgergade, Gothersgade.

Something repeated on me. It tasted like the tarragon from the mussel soup and I tried not to dwell on it.

'Did you ask Stig Nissen?' said Diana. My cheeks were cold and I didn't know where to look. Diana was too close up, and why did the driver have so much heat on? I opened my jacket. Store Regnegade, Bremerholm, Antonigade, Pilestræde. Every time he made a turn I got thrown against the door.

'About what?'

I felt a rush of nausea. Kronprinsensgade, Valkendorfsgade. Don't read the signs.

'About your talk, Mikkel!'

And then at long last Niels Hemmingsensgade. Air, for Christ's sake. Air!

'I'll ask him later,' I said, plonking myself on the wall of the Helligåndskirke. 'You go on in, Diana.'

There was a huge queue for the Dusk after-party and as far as I could see, no one was over eighteen. I lay down on the wall and looked up at the stars. They swayed like the Viking ship in the Tivoli Gardens. I jumped down to the other side, bent forward, stuck a finger down my throat and emptied my stomach of lobster, oysters, mussels and champagne, and since I could hardly just go in stinking of vomit I staggered over to the kiosk on Klosterstræde to get some chewing gum but it was closed, so I had to go all the way up to Gammel Torv.

Luckily, Søren T-shirt was at Floss.

'Where have you been all this time?' he said, and I told him the truth, that I was turning into Diana's puppy dog, and he said she was mad about me, but he knew the feeling, and even if I didn't believe him it was a tonic running into a friend who was so unconditionally on my side.

'I'm wasted,' I said. 'Have you got any hard drugs?'

'No, but I can get some,' he said.

'Lovers come and go,' I said. 'Friends remain.'

'I'll need seven hundred,' he said.

By the time I got back to Jazz House the queue had disappeared. The bouncers were sitting around in their black coats drinking coffee.

'Is the party finished?' I asked.

'What party?' said one.

'Everyone's gone to Vibskov's,' said another, looking the other way.

A couple sat snogging on the long sofa against the far wall and the two bartenders stood arsing about behind the bar. Music thumped up from downstairs. On my way down I ran into Rie Becker.

'Diana never went to Magyar Képzőművészeti Egyetem.'

'Are you talking backwards?' I said.

'The Academy of Fine Arts in Budapest.'

'So what?' I said.

'It says in her CV on Moritz's website that she went there from 1999 to 2002, but they've never had any student by the name of Diana Kiss.'

'Clear the front page,' I said, and carried on down the stairs.

'How much did she get for destroying her name?' Rie Becker called after me.

Stig Nissen had his own little VIP area sorted out; it was even roped off and there was a tablecloth on the table, whole bottles of booze and ice buckets. He was immersed in conference with a couple of his people, and Lisa sat slouched in the corner asleep. A crowd of drunken sixteen-year-olds were dancing an improvised routine to a sugary beat, and the bar seemed to be far too long. Diana was seated at its far end.

'How nice of you to come,' she said.

'Time to talk business,' I said.

'Wipe your mouth first,' said Diana. 'There's something white on your lip.'

Waves of warmth passed through me and I put my hand on her shoulder.

'It's such a release when things don't get complicated,' I said.

Things? Ladles, tennis balls, paper clips. Things?

'I mean, you not getting annoyed,' I said.

'What would I get annoyed about?'

'About me going off like that.'

'Go off any time,' she said.

My eyes clouded with tears and I wanted to cast myself into the dirt, to sink down before her feet and propose to her, but then the last bit of coke I'd done wore off, and my mood descended suddenly through a deep and filthy shaft. The DJ did a clumsy mix of 'The Power' by Snap and at once it became all too obvious that there were sixteen of us inside a discotheque with a capacity of four hundred.

'I wonder if they've still got Galliano shots here?' I said.

Diana came with me to the VIP table.

'Did we kick ass, or did we kick ass?' said Stig Nissen.

'We couldn't have asked for more,' I said.

'Total impact, am I right?' he said.

'Do you still want me to do that talk?' I said.

'Here we go!' he said. 'First write-up, Berlingske.dk,'

He read the headline out loud from his mobile:

'*New high-street label falls short*,' he said. 'What do they know? Brilliant photo! You've a right to be proud of her, Mikkel.'

He handed me the phone, and of course it was Diana as Kráka.

'Dusk is Berlin,' said Stig Nissen. '*Berlingske* is Rungsted.'

'No one takes *Berlingske* seriously anymore,' I said.

'I don't understand this country, said Stig Nissen. 'When were you last in Singapore or Rio? Innovation is king! Why are those markets out there all booming? Because they believe in people like me who think outside the box, that's why!'

The bartender shouted out last orders.

'What sort of bubbly have you got?' said Stig Nissen.

It was a hostile crémant from Alsace.

'That talk you mentioned,' I said.

'The one you turned down?' he said.

'That was a mistake,' said Diana.

'Isn't he supposed to be writing a book?' said Stig Nissen.

'I'd be more than happy to come over and talk a bit about Copenhagen,' I said.

'What's the book about?' said Stig Nissen.

'It's a rallying call against coupledom,' I said.

'What does Diana say about it?'

'Mikkel has some very entertaining theories,' she said.

'All right, listen here,' said Stig Nissen. 'We've got this little arts society in Brande for the town's bigwigs, you know: the mayor, the chairman of the retailers' association, the magistrate, Chopper the butcher. The wife's just texted me, that lifestyle fella with the wavy hair can't make it tomorrow. Shall I put you on instead?'

I couldn't find my legs when the alarm rang. Diana had to throw water in my face and I've absolutely no idea how I managed to get through the necessary procedures and on to the right train.

The first swig was horrendous, the second was okay, and when we got to Roskilde after half an hour I bought two more beers, got my notepad out and began to draw up an outline of my presentation, with my relationship to Helene as the main example. Best to draw pictures rather than try to be subtle.

I suddenly found myself thinking about Helene's hand on my hip, and the thought of it precipitated an erection of the insistent kind and so I went to the toilet with a jumper round my waist. I stood there feverishly tossing away until someone knocked on the door. I got off at Brande with a talk ready on my notepad, and Stig Nissen was waiting for me on the platform.

'Tax-free beer on the ferry, thank God,' I said.

'Very funny. Welcome to the mainland,' he said, and we drove off in his black Audi.

We pulled up outside the Hotel Dalgas. There were fifty people in the hotel restaurant. The men were drinking beer, the women white wine, and all of them looked like couples.

The host couple showed me to a little room at the back.

'I'll introduce you in ten minutes,' said Stig Nissen.

I took my notepad out of my bag and made a couple of last-minute adjustments to my outline.

The paper trembled in my hand and I could hear them laughing on the other side of the door. There was a copying machine in the corner, a whiteboard and an overhead projector with its cord neatly wrapped around one leg. The notes from the last meeting could still be picked out on the whiteboard, a circle drawn in thick blue marker pen and inside it the words *Where we are now*, then an arrow pointing to another circle: *Where we are going*.

Thud, thud. Stig Nissen tapped on the microphone.

'Good evening and welcome once again to the Brande Arts Society. Now, I can see most of you have brought your better halves along with you, and I can tell you now you'd better keep tight hold of them, because tonight we've got with us a writer from Copenhagen who questions what all of us here have to get up and face in the mornings, and I'm talking about good old-fashioned coupledom. So please give a nice round of applause for Mikkel Vallin!'

There was nothing wrong with the applause apart from the fact that it stopped abruptly while I was still some ten metres from the stage. From there on, only the sound of my creaking footsteps could be heard and I had to narrow my eyes in order to maintain some kind of grip on reality. But once I was standing in front of the mic with the flimsy pages of my notepad in my hand, staring out at the audience, I realised that the lights had been dimmed and everyone present was a cuddly toy.

'Five years ago I met the woman of my dreams,' I said. 'We had a baby together and I was crippled with guilt when two years later we split up and got divorced. But then one day I was talking to a friend of mine about it and I heard myself say: "The only thing standing between me and true love is couplehood."'

A ripple of laughter passed across the tables and the beads of their little eyes were so cute. I made them laugh, the women mostly, and the Q&A afterwards overran the allotted time by fifteen minutes. 'But doesn't it all get samey if you can be with whoever you want?' a woman asked.

'I think it makes it all the more significant,' I answered. 'I'm not advocating just sleeping around, but granting each other the best in life.'

'Personally I'd lose focus entirely,' she said.

'We can handle a lot more than we think,' I said. 'As I see it, most couples lost their focus a long time ago.'

'I'd live in constant fear that my husband would fall in love with someone else,' she said.

'In that case, I wouldn't advise you to make the experiment. Obviously, it requires both parties to be in agreement and to trust each other completely.'

'I feel the exact opposite,' another woman said. 'Everything's so fleeting and stressful these days, I actually think a lot of people are very happy to promise each other fidelity.'

'I'm not talking about irresponsibility,' I said. 'I'm talking about the opposite, and I think it's a fine thing indeed to love each other until death do us part. But I don't understand why it should rule out loving others as well.'

'But what about the children?' she said. 'Isn't it confusing for them?'

'I believe children are happiest when they're given as much love as possible, and I'm certain it's better for them to grow up in a loving environment rather than one that is disharmonious. I'd say they'd be more confused growing up in the confines of a relationship that is defined by conflict.'

'If you're in love, you don't want anyone else,' someone said.

'Well, that's what they say, at least,' I replied. 'In my own personal experience I've found myself wanting all sorts of other people even when I've been in love. But because we're brought up to go for the one and only, I've always fought against it.'

'What about you?' said a thickset woman with glasses on a cord around her neck. 'Have you found yourself a new partner?'

'We don't call each other that.'

'But you're in love with a nice girl?'

'Very much in love, yes.'

'Then you'll want to marry her and have children with her, won't you?'

'We haven't thought about it.'

'She could be in bed with someone else right now, then?'

'Possibly, yes.'

'Doesn't that hurt?'

'Not after three glasses of wine.'

The women were so interested in talking to me throughout dinner that I had to lift my glass to their husbands every now and then to reassure them. I met Stig Nissen in the gents and he dug his elbow into my side.

'You carried it off, Vallin. We're all lined up now for a big night at the Kvium Bar.'

'Kvium Bar?'

'It's not for kids,' he said, and took me by the arm. 'The difference between us and you is that you Copenhageners write books about it. Here we just do it. Are you with me?'

He laughed and breezed out through the door without holding it open for me.

At exactly eleven o'clock, everyone got to their feet, found their coats and went back out to their cars. Stig Nissen led the convoy and the Kvium Bar turned out to be housed in a wing of Nissen's vast house: black carpets, black walls, three big canvases from Kvium's black period on each of the long walls, the fourth comprising a curved panorama window facing out into the darkness.

The lights were dimmed over the cosy sofa areas, and the long bar at the end of the room was softly illuminated and enticing with Grey Goose vodka, Curaçao rum, a selection of whiskies, grappa, Poire Williams and some unfamiliar gin labels.

'And you haven't even seen Nissen's cognac collection yet,' said Chopper, a large man with a moustache and blotches of perspiration encroaching from under his waistcoat. The girl waiting on us smiled and pushed the sliding door of a cupboard to one side.

'Some of them are up to a hundred and fifty years old,' he said.

He nudged me in the side and winked. 'I sense a certain hospitality among the local wives.'

'How do you mean?'

'You can put two and two together, surely? Or three and three, for that matter!'

He laughed, somewhere between baritone and falsetto.

Another girl came round with white bathrobes.

We went through a black door into a wellness area worthy of a five-star German health resort. To the left was a large steam bath with glass doors, to the right a sauna, and five steps down was a twenty-five-metre indoor swimming pool. I went into the sauna, which was packed with glistening, middle-aged flesh.

Stig Nissen drove me to the station the next morning.

'So now you've seen Brande by night. Not as dull as you'd think, was it?'

He handed me an envelope.

'Make sure it's all there.'

I opened it and there were five one-thousand-kroner notes.

'I thought we said fifteen?' I said.

'It would have been if you'd given a talk to my staff. Five's the going rate for the Brande Arts Society. Besides, we look after our big city guests, don't we?'

I got out with the envelope still in my hand and he rolled his window down.

'Put the word about!'

And with that he turned the car sharply, sounded the horn twice and sped off with a wheel-spin.

I couldn't sleep on the train and kept mixing things up in my mind: the great bales of straw in the fields, the special-price offer on Haribo Starmix, a conversation between two men on their way to Fredericia to give a seminar on innovation for the local authority and who kept assuring each other how much better it was to take the train. I had to walk up and down the aisle to stop myself from going mad.

When we reached Vejle I tried to recall the names of their football team's former captains. I could remember Iver Schriver, the Tychosen brothers, Ulrik le Fevre, Knud Nørregaard, but what was that other one's name? Frizzy microphone hair and a beard. A sweeper.

I woke up at Fredericia and realised someone was standing over me, staring at me intently. It was my old colleague from the newspaper, Blismann. We had shared an office for five years and seen more of each other than our families. We had both overestimated our importance in the Danish media landscape and been conceited enough to imagine our turn had finally come to be opinion-makers. He'd ended up teaching in some backwater, and here he was, wearing a protective little smile as if both of our falls from grace had all been my fault. He was in a cheap anorak and looked like someone from the Faroe Islands. His short hair exposed a receding hairline and his smooth cheeks made me think of a tranquilliser pill.

'Knud Herbert Sørensen,' I said.

'You what?' he said.

'Former captain of Vejle. Have a seat. Where is it you're teaching these days?' I said.

'In Ribe.'

'Are you enjoying it?'

'I read that interview Kiest did with you for *Berlingske*.'

I assumed that wasn't the only information he wanted to impart, but it was all he said. I had to drag the insults out of him.

'Anything else you've read recently?' I said. 'A brochure, perhaps?'

'Where's fat Tove supposed to go for free sex?' he said.

'How about Weight Watchers? Fat people aren't exactly in short supply.'

'You're manning the barricades for the right to grope each other in trendy hangouts.'

'It's not my fault you had to get out of the city in a hurry,' I said.

He looked down at the floor.

'Where are you going anyway?' I said.

'A Thåström gig in Malmö.'

'Still into him, then. Thåström.'

'I'm going to be a dad,' he said.

'You're not? Who's the lucky lady?'

'Her name's Kirstine.'

'Where did you meet?'

'At a folk concert.'

'What's she like, this Kirstine of yours?'

'She's not a DJ, and she doesn't blog about shoes. She's a school-teacher and she looks like someone called Kirstine who comes from Ribe.'

'So you're not in love with her, is that what you're saying?'

'No, funnily enough. You know how useless I am when it comes to being in love.'

He might have changed, but he could still soften up when I made an effort. I began to tell him about the humiliations I had suffered the night before in Brande.

'I've never seen a cunt as voluminous as the mayor's wife's. She had me in a vice between her flabby thighs, and her labia were so big you could have sewn them together behind my ears. And when finally I was finished with her there was Chopper's wife to attend to, big as a house and strong as an ox. At some point I managed to escape, soaking wet with sweat and cunt juice, then knocked back the drink until I passed out. Which was a big mistake.'

'What happened?' he said.

'I came to when a pair of glasses fell down on my cock, and when I looked up I realised it was the magistrate's wife, her Coke-bottle specs. I'll never forget the look in her eyes, that intense, bewildered way short-sighted people stare when they haven't got their glasses on. She was lying on her side on the sofa with my cock in her mouth, and she was wearing this long, knitted sleeveless coat.'

An announcement said next stop Odense.

'Fancy a beer?' I said.

Blismann wanted to convince me of how enriching it was to live in a place that was quiet in the evenings, where you could see the stars at night, hear the birds and go for long walks in the marshland, and I respected his courageous attempt to sustain this story about how happy he was, even as it evaporated beer by beer. By the time we reached Høje Taastrup, the table between us was littered with bottles and Blismann was restored to his old cynical self, and while Floss was still too much for him, thankfully there has never been anything wrong with the Jernbanecafé. I felt sure that all bad feeling between us had been swept aside and that we would be able to sit down and play a game of dice while talking about nothing in particular, absorbed temporarily into an environment of pill-pushers, errant businessmen from Jutland, semi-hot student girls from teacher-training colleges and the usual drunks in denim jackets and cheap boots, and everything was in Blismann's words *dismal!* or *super-dismal!* or even *super-duper-dismal!*

I had four sixes in hand when Diana called and I stepped outside on to Rewentlowsgade and still couldn't make up my mind whether I liked the Hotel Astoria's architecture as she told me the first of her tapestries had arrived from Vietnam and asked me to help her carry it home from Moritz's at nine.

You can allow yourself to be romantic when you're with Blismann and I waxed lyrical on the bells of the Rådhus and opined that they, and the gleeful shrieks of joy from the Tivoli Gardens, were the sounds of other people's childhoods.

We had decided on the obvious idea of having dinner in our old canteen at the newspaper; the chef was the same one as before, and Blismann naturally remembered his name. He opted for the meat loaf and I had happily forgotten how sloppy he could be with gravy. I chose a well-topped open sandwich and had just flicked the slice of orange from the pork when Peter, our former editor, came down for a diet Coke. He was all 'bloody hell' and 'to what do we owe the pleasure', but he was nervous and had good reason to be.

'Have a seat!' said Blismann.

'There's nothing I'd rather do than sit here and have a few beers with you, but I've got Saturday's arts section to see to,' said Peter.

'Just sit yourself down with your old mates here and ask how they're doing,' said Blismann. 'After all, it was you who gave us the boot.'

Peter placed a cautious hand on Blismann's shoulder, only to be brushed away and stared down for ten very long seconds before beating a quiet retreat with shoulders drooped and eyes fixed on his commute back to Værløse.

'What time does your concert start?' I said.

'It's six months since I met Kirstine and this is the first time I've been away from her.'

'What's that got to do with it?'

'Thåström isn't playing in Malmö tonight.'

I can't actually remember which of us suggested going upstairs to wind up Rie Becker, but I do know she wasn't in her office. Some plastic case folders lay fanned out on her desk: *Lauritz.com*, *Valby Galleries*, *Collectors*, and then, furthest to the right: *Diana Kiss*.

'Super-duper-dismal!' said Blismann, and picked it up.

A printout of Diana's CV from Galleri Moritz's website, a photo of Diana as Kráka from the Dusk launch, the ad from the paper, a list of phone numbers, including the long one of the Hungarian fine arts academy and another for Minna Lund, a page of notes from our evening out at the Tivoli Gardens.

The door opened and it was Peter.

'You've no business here,' he said.

'What do you mean?' said Blismann.

A security guard stepped forward.

'I ought to report you to the police,' said Peter.

'Look at him,' said Blismann. 'I much preferred the bourgeoisie in the old days. At least they had style.'

Blismann was received with applause and confetti at Floss and it was all hugs and kisses until Søren T-shirt turned up and he and I descended into an epic reminiscence about the night at U-Matic in 1987 when Søren got hold of some real Bolivian coke and Signe thought she was ill because her tongue had gone numb from kissing him.

'Søren T-shirt! Still on the fiddle, are we? Keeping dismal?' said Blismann, butting in and making Søren spill his beer.

'Watch what you're doing, you fucking idiot,' said Søren.

Blismann narrowed his eyes.

'I've not seen my mate Mikkel here for over a year and we happen to have more important things to talk about than you being off your head on coke at U-Matic twenty-one years ago.'

I glanced at my watch.

'I've got to go,' I said. 'I promised to help Diana.'

'If he's in a free relationship, then all I can say is that free relationships sound exactly like ordinary ones,' said Blismann.

'There he goes, with his tail between his legs again,' said Søren T-shirt.

I said my goodbyes to Søren and was about to do the same with Blismann.

'I'm coming with you!' he said. He recited Strunge in the taxi:

'Berlin, maybe a never-developed image exists of a girl on Kurfürstendamm who for a second saw me as human in the world.'

I stared at the city lights without speaking.

'Berlin, my head is so unclear.'

He was so close to me I felt his spit in my face. His voice slowed:

'How can I find her lips in all that dust?'

I shifted away from him.

'He could have looked somewhere other than a building site.'

Diana was standing with her shoulder against the wall outside Galleri Moritz. She was in a slim-fitting grey suit, matt red and terra-cotta-coloured golfing shoes, purple shirt and a dark green tie.

'She looks like a Hopper painting,' said Blismann.

Diana hadn't seen Moritz since the photo shoot for the ad and the fashion show. The situation required some subtlety, and I had with me Blismann, a person who possessed none.

'Super-dismal, Vallin! First the Jerbanecafé, then Floss and now

Galleri Moritz! We're like knights in a game of chess, two squares forward and one to the side, all the way through the city!'

I put my hand on his arm.

'Best keep your head down here, Blismann.'

'What are you on about?' he said.

Blismann pogoed into the expansive premises and roared at the top of his voice:

'Squatters in our hearts!'

'Squatters in our hearts, Comrade Blismann!' Moritz repeated, placing his hand to his chest.

They embraced warmly. 'What the fuck have you been up to, Moritz? Last time we met, you were booking some Belgian industrial band.'

'That was the nineties, Blismann.'

'Art for art's sake! Money for God's sake,' said Blismann.

'Bowie?' said Moritz.

'10cc,' I said.

Diana's tapestry was rolled up in bubble wrap.

'It'd be great to sit and talk about old times,' said Moritz, 'only I've got some matters to discuss with my favourite artist.'

'They can stay, I don't mind,' said Diana.

Moritz fetched a bottle of Sune's nature spumante, raised his glass politely and pulled up a chair for Diana. Blismann sat down in the deep window recess three metres away and I just hung about.

'Before we unpack the tapestry, we need to talk about your involvement in Dusk, Diana,' said Moritz, pulling out a drawer. 'What the hell is this?'

He held up the ad in front of her.

'It's a good photo,' she said.

Moritz gave her an indulgent smile, which was a mistake.

'Minna Lund didn't buy your work because you've got a good body, Diana. She wants to support a serious working artist.'

'Minna Lund lives in a palace,' said Diana. 'I live in a plumber's storeroom.'

'Super-duper-dismal!' said Blismann.

'Your prices have risen three hundred per cent in six years, Diana. Your tapestries aren't the kind of thing people buy on a whim, and maybe that slump everyone keeps whingeing about is actually going to come down on us all of a sudden. The art market is jumpy and this isn't the right way to go about making it stable again.'

He held up Diana as Kráka on *Berlingske*'s front page.

'Why don't we have a look at my tapestry?' said Diana.

Kaspar Moritz skidded across the floor on his office chair.

'For Christ's sake, Diana! I'm trying to put it nicely for you.'

'Then put it not nicely instead!' she said.

'Next time, you're out of Galleri Moritz. I've got a brand to think about too, and I can't have artists displaying that kind of idiocy.'

We unpacked the tapestry in silence.

'The colours are good,' said Moritz.

Diana's cunt lay open before us. And Peter Borch-Jensen's semen.

'Sick!' said Blismann. 'Is it your own cunt?'

'I'm not comfortable with this,' said Moritz. 'The age of provocation is gone. Do we agree not to include it?'

Fifteen minutes later, Blismann and I were walking through Vesterbro with the tapestry across our shoulders. Diana was silent.

'I'm a brazen hussy with a great big pussy!' Blismann sang.

We had to keep stopping to reorganise ourselves after his fits of laughter.

'Let's go to Blomsten,' said Diana.

We sat there with ninety thousand kroner's worth of cunt under our feet, and Blismann went to the bar for more safari suits.

'I've got to give Ida-Marie ten thousand six hundred tomorrow,' said Diana.

I reached into my pocket and pulled out some crumpled notes.

'Where's the rest?' she said.

'I only got five thousand and I've spent some of it.'

There were two thousand seven hundred left. Diana sat staring into the clouds of tobacco smoke until Blismann stepped in.

'Can't you see she's upset?' he said, pulling up his chair and putting his big arm around her. She leaned her head against his shoulder. How come everyone else could comfort her better than I could?

I used to drink to have a good time, now I just wanted to be drunk. I had no anecdotes I was desperate to tell, and I couldn't be bothered listening to those of others. I was too unfocused for serious discussion, too weighed down to have fun. I wanted to feel something, and alcohol was the only thing that would let me.

'Have you got Kreuzmann's number?' said Diana.

She came back ten minutes later.

'Let's get this cunt home, then you can come back.'

There was no doubt that the latter was an order and sadly it suited me fine. I had already written Diana off for the night. Café Sommersted was my idea, on the basis of an assumption that our Faroese binge would befit the gloomy interior. I didn't want to be seen and I didn't want to see anyone. All I wanted was to be left alone to drink.

It's the summer, and outside the season, hoola hoola, I love that cola cola.

Blismann had got a jug in and there was nothing I fancied less than stout, aquavit, lemonade and Pernod all mixed together. 'How can it be summer and outside the season at the same time?' I said.

I took a sip and nearly threw up.

'Is it June, I wonder?' I said.

'This is August, mate,' said Blismann.

'In the song, I mean. Johnny Madsen lives on the island of Fanø. Perhaps he's singing about a holiday place before the hordes arrive. But what's *cola cola*, and who would drink it?'

'Should I have that kid?' he said.

'What?'

'Should I have a kid with Kirstine?'

'No, I don't think you should.'

He got that defiant look in his eye that I've never cared for.

'And why would that be, my fine friend?'

'You asked and I gave you an answer,' I said.

He put his hands down hard on the table.

'This decision, Mikkel, is going to determine the rest of my life, and with that in mind I honestly think you could pull yourself together a bit and give the issue rather more consideration. We're not talking about a glass of wine, you know!'

'I find it sad that there's such an obvious lack of passion involved.'

'It's me, Blismann, you're talking to. You've seen how I react when there's passion involved.'

I reran a couple of his impossible love affairs in my mind, fast-forwarding to what they would have been if they'd lasted, and saw Blismann stuck in some hinterland about to put a rope around his neck or else apply for a mortgage.

'I can learn to love her,' he said.

'That sounds sensible.'

'Is it wrong?'

I made the mistake of looking down at the floor and it came lunging up into my face. I put my glass down and tried to focus.

'I'm going for a piss and then it's either yes or no, okay?'

I hit my shoulder against the door frame as I went out.

I tried splashing my face with water, but it didn't help.

A tubby guy with his wallet in his back pocket waddled his way to the urinal.

'That's the bastard thing about drinking ale,' he said. 'It gets lost! It goes in all right, but when it comes out it's all diluted!'

Of course Blismann had to have that kid.

I staggered back, preparing to toast his impending fatherhood, only he was nowhere to be seen. Sønder Boulevard was deserted on both sides.

He must have legged it down one of the side streets, and that was the most surprising part of the whole situation: Blismann running.

A ndreas Møller and Nikolaj Krogh picked me up in Krogh's new Volvo at ten on the dot. I hadn't seen Andreas since he had left the camp just over a fortnight earlier and being always on the lookout for somewhere to park his disappointment, he chose at first to ignore me completely.

We were off to the Sjælsmark Kaserne barracks and I was in the back, emitting two odours: one was sweet bordering on sickly and issued from my pores, that were hard at work separating glucose from alcohol; the other was so rank it made my eyes sting, came from my stomach and was channelled out through my mouth into the confined space of the car's interior. I had a serious hangover.

As we passed B 1903's training ground the first sentences and images of the night before began to crop up and trouble me. After Café Sommersted I had lurched off in the direction of Lyrskovgade, and as so often happens when changing location in a state of total intoxication, that state escalated with each step I took. Diana was sound asleep when I began pounding at the door with the flat of my hand. Five minutes, ten minutes, a quarter of an hour perhaps, passed before she opened up. I delivered a speech, a jumble of indignation, sudden accusations and self-pitying tears over the unconditional nature of my love for her, and the worst thing was that along the way I not only paid emotional tribute to myself for being honest, but also completely confused the concepts of passion and loss of control.

She did the cruellest thing and heard me out.

'What is it you're hiding, Diana?'

She wanted to sleep, it being night-time, and yet she may have been amused by my behaviour. At any rate, she joined me in a straight vodka.

'What do you want to know, Mikkel?'

'We can't have a relationship if you refuse to talk to me about the things that matter, Diana. Nona, for instance. You went to Budapest and saw your daughter for the first time. That must mean something to you! But you're completely closed about it. There isn't a single photo, a single story you've told about meeting her. Nothing!'

'She's like me,' said Diana. 'She's exactly like me.'

'Where does she live?'

'With my mother.'

'How can you be so unmoved?'

'It was a mistake to visit her.'

'Do you miss her?'

She knocked back a gulp of vodka.

'Why does your CV say you went to the Academy of Fine Ats in Budapest?'

'It was my uncle's fault I didn't get in.'

'In what way?'

'He was vice-chancellor there until the Wall came down. He was a party loyalist and it reflected on me.'

'What's his name?'

'István Kiss.'

I got the laptop and googled him:

István Kiss, vice-chancellor of the academy 1985–9, sculptor, responsible for a number of monumental works of socialist bent.

'Everyone knew I was his niece. They didn't even look at my drawings, they just sent out the letter of rejection as a matter of course.'

I poured us some more vodka.

'Did you go to San Cataldo in order to meet me, Diana?'

'Yes.'

'Why? And how did you know who I was?'

'The first piece of yours I read was your interview with Bjarne Riis in *Euroman*. My Danish teacher, Jørn, had his sister go to the library in Copenhagen and dig out everything you'd written. Have you ever been to Budapest?'

I shook my head.

'My mother works fourteen hours a day doing people's laundry and still our flat was cold and damp. Budapest is porn, Serbian gangs and Albanian pimps. Everything's dirty: the way people treat each other, their clothes, the streets. It all smells of wet dog, and without my Danish connection I'd have gone down with the rest of them.

'I imagined what your life was like. Your style of writing is very personal and I soaked up all the information: what you thought about various things, your travels, your opinions. You belonged somewhere

and to me you represented something secure and infinitely attractive.
I did go to San Cataldo just to meet you. I know it sounds funny, but
I thought of you as my crowning glory, and at long last I felt up to
making a go of it.'

'How did you know I was there?'

'You mentioned it to Christian Finne and he happened to mention
it to me one day when we were talking about where to find some
peace to work.'

'What was it like meeting me?' I said.

'It was wonderful right from the start, Mikkel, but I was surprised
by how much it taught me about myself.'

'Like what?'

'Everything I was so eager to find in you is exactly what tears us
apart.'

'Such as?'

'You have a history, Mikkel, and you keep on adding to it each day.
I felt it so strongly that evening at Clara's, all the things you don't need
to talk about. You know what she looked like as a child, you know
your friends' parents, your language is all slotted into place, the music,
the opinions, the furniture.'

'But you not being a part of all that is exactly what's so fantastic,
Diana.'

'I've met your friends, Mikkel, and in the space of half an hour
they'll tell me things you've never talked to them about. It's to do
with me being the way I am, of course, but it's more than that: I don't
count, I'm an outsider.'

'Of course you count.'

'If I went away, you'd all miss me for about a month, and maybe
you'd miss me again at some dinner a year later, but I don't have the
history. Do you understand how hard it is for us to be together? I keep
having to start again from scratch.'

'I'd like to start from scratch, too.'

'I know you would, Mikkel.'

It all just followed on once we got under the covers. Each and every

thrust felt overwhelming to me, and with everything being so intoxi-
catingly sad, it just had to be head-on, so we could look at each other.

K reuzmann woke us up the next morning. He was wearing a tie
again and put a thick envelope down on the table.
'Forty big ones.'
'What's going on?' I said.
'Claudia wants some art on her walls,' he said.
'Kreuzmann's bought the spunky cunt,' said Diana.

A s Nikolaj Krogh drove he gave us the low-down on the firm of
architects who were in the picture to take charge of doing up
and refitting the barracks for Next Love, and Andreas Møller fired
questions at him.

'We're going to be spoiled for choice,' said Nikolaj Krogh. 'There
were nearly seven hundred in our Facebook group this morning.'

'That crappy article did the job,' said Andreas Møller.

Sjælsmark Kaserne was not so much a barracks as a small town.
The main building was stately and the myriad of low buildings that
surrounded it looked like they could relatively easily be converted
into small apartments. Andreas Møller had a source high up in the
Ministry of Defence and knew that the barracks was to be shut down
for good imminently.

I took part in the general enthusiasm on the way home and had
loads of ideas, leaning forward between the seats in front like a child
that keeps pestering his parents.

Andreas Møller swivelled round.

'Did you give Levinsen carte blanche to misuse our name? Nikolaj
didn't spend two days creating our logo just to rub shoulders with
Tiger Beer.'

'What are you talking about?' I said.

'He can't remember his own promises,' said Andreas Møller, and handed me a printed invitation:

Levinsen Open and Next Love present: The Next Party.

At the bottom were four logos: Levinsen Open, a vodka brand, Tiger Beer, and the stringent pen strokes of Next Love.

Nikolaj Krogh paid special attention to his hug when they dropped me off on Lyrskovgade. Andreas Møller made do with a handshake.

'There's an old friend of mine, a woman I'd like you to meet.'

'Sounds interesting,' I said.

'It's entirely up to you.'

He handed me a business card, on the back of which was written *21 August, 11.30 a.m.* The front said: *Xenia Leth-Hansen, Alcohol Coach.*

Helene, Charlie and I had started having dinner together every other evening, and it was amazingly hassle-free. We met outside the fishmonger's on Gammel Kongevej, to show Charlie the ferocious porbeagle before we grilled it. We went to Chinese restaurants and practised eating with chopsticks, or else we cooked fine dinners at home and teased the queen with our bad table manners. It was nothing like when we were living together and I could get stressed out just thinking about her late-afternoon phone calls. She had this supernatural ability to phone me just as I was biking across a busy crossroads.

'Milk, butter, porridge oats.'

Or maybe:

'Washing powder, bacon, freezer bags.'

Now and again I'd say:

'Pork scratchings, hessian, dual carriageway.'

And she never laughed.

I realise she had to give me messages, of course.

Should she have done so in verse, or perhaps put them to music? I'm not fond of everyday life, and I realise that is where the problem lies.

It was always a contrast to go to Diana's rooftop terrace after these quiet evenings with Helene and Charlie.

'Can't we do without street art soon?' Jan might say. 'I'm sorry, but forty-three-year-old blokes in hoodies enlarging cartoons and spraying a little skull in the corner? What's it doing in the galleries? "Hey, man, I can like really get up your nose! I can drink out of the bottle and stub my fags out in your ketchup!" No, actually, we're not in the slightest bit provoked, so why don't you sod off home and tidy your room while you're at it? And hey, take your whoopie cushion with you!'

Diana was sick of his ranting, but she could almost never be bothered to argue and preferred to change the subject.

'I'd like to meet Helene,' she said. 'How about that party of Levinsen's? Maybe you could invite her?'

'We could go out for a meal first,' I said.

'Or we could just drink,' she said.

It could be that uncomplicated, I supposed, and so I put it to Helene one afternoon when I was bringing Charlie back.

Helene was sunbathing and had filled the paddling pool.

'You look tired,' she said. 'Why don't you go up and have a lie-down?'

I felt the urge to tear off her bikini.

'Do you want to come to a party on Friday?' I said. 'Diana would like to meet you.'

'What about you?'

'I'd like you to come, too.'

I had at last managed to get hold of Søren T-shirt to do some more interviews for the book, and I wasn't in the mood for his eternal attempts at avoiding the subject. Besides, I didn't much care for his new stories. They used to be about having a good time and perhaps pulling a fast one on some fruit-and-veg wholesaler at the billiard table, but now they all seemed to involve raw physical violence. I interrupted him in a loop of uppercuts and prescription fiddles.

'Tell me about your first dealer, Søren.'

'That's not something I do at the drop of a hat.'

'You've got to.'

'I didn't think that book was going to come together!'

'Of course it is.'

'I thought it was going to be all latte-farty, a lot of wind about relationships.'

I got a notepad out of my bag.

'Let's sit down and get started.'

'You couldn't buy me a sandwich, could you? I haven't eaten in three days.'

We went to the little joint across the road.

'I've got this dodgy stomach,' he said. 'Everything goes right through me.'

We sat down on a step. His grey-green features were glazed with perspiration and he took his sandwich apart and ate the lettuce first.

'You haven't exactly been holding back of late,' he said.

'No more than usual,' I said.

We got out of the sun and went into the darkness of Floss.

'I need to be pissed if I'm going to talk about it,' he said.

I got him a double Arnbitter and two Gold. I had a coffee.

'Do you remember what the tables looked like?' I said.

'Of course I do. They had mirrors on, all broken.'

'A bit obvious as metaphors go,' I said.

Søren was never interested in this kind of sixth-form talk.

'Okay, so this new bloke had started over at Huset. Jimmy, his name was, and I sussed right away he was on drugs and began to score off him. I was giving him all my wages every month and then eventually I told him I wanted to see his dealer.'

'Tell me about the dealer.'

Søren's mouth crumpled.

'Now you're being hard on me.'

'Where did he live?'

'Second-floor flat on Lille Colbjørnsensgade. You always had to go up to the third first.'

'How come?'

'The pigs used to lie in wait and you'd have to shout the alarm so he could stick his stash up his arse. His bags often smelled of shit.'

'What did it look like, this place of his?'

'It was just an ordinary two-room flat. His girlfriend was on the game, she used to wave from the bedroom with some old git on top of her. He was known for good-quality white Pakistani. Istedgade was very sharply divided in those days. White smack was the stretch between the main station and Gasværksvej, and the dealers there were Danish. After Gasværksvej it was all foreigners and they sold the brown stuff.'

'What's the difference between white and brown?'

'The white's more of an upper. You can snort it, or you can add a few drops of water and then shoot it. The brown's heavier and has to be mixed with citric acid and heated up on a spoon until it goes sticky and caramelises. It's got to be down to thirty-seven degrees before you can inject it, but if you buy it on the street to shoot in a gateway and the pigs come, then you've got to do it straight away while it's hot, and your whole arm feels like it's on fire then.'

Søren knocked back his second Gold and ordered two more and an Arnbitter to go with them.

'Where did he used to sit?'

'On his settee, like they all do. Great big, ugly leather jobs. With a big mirror flat in front of him on the coffee table. He was always sitting there cutting dope. He only ever used one arm.'

'Why was that?'

Søren looked up at the ceiling and then at me.

'He had gangrene in his other one. A big seeping wound it was. It stank so much he had to keep holding it out of the window.'

Søren's hands tightened around his bottle.

'One time, he pulled his arm back in and started picking great big scabs off it. I can't describe the smell of it, but it was like rotten cheese. Once he'd picked off all the scabs he got his tackle and injected himself straight into the wound.'

Søren got to his feet and went outside. People were sitting out at

L'Education Nationale eating their French lunch dishes; there were bottles of rosé on the tables and knives with proper serrated edges. He gasped for breath. I fetched him a big glass of water and left him alone for a bit.

'When was the first time you shot heroin?' I said after a while.

'There was a group of us around here who messed about with smack, but we only used to snort it. Then one day one of the hard lads said I was going to have to make my mind up – if I was going to just mess about or do it properly. One of the worst things was the day Signe said to me: "I don't know you anymore, Søren. Have you met someone else?" And I had, too, in a way, but I couldn't tell her that, could I?'

'Tell me about the first time you did it properly.'

'Do we have to?' he said. 'I'm having a hard time here, in case you hadn't noticed.'

'Okay, we'll start with your first fix next time,' I said.

'So that's what I've got to look forward to, is it?' he said.

Søren caught sight of the gnomish guy with the pointy beard and immediately made a deal involving two hundred kroner from out of my pocket.

'Are you going to be all right?' I said.

'Course I am, I'm Søren T-shirt!'

Bernhard had arranged for me to meet the marketing department, but insisted that Helene and I have lunch together first, 'to iron out any differences of opinion'.

I ordered the pâté again. Hopefully because of the sour pickles.

Helene was in a flimsy short skirt and was wearing lipstick.

She had a salad and looked like she regretted it.

'Have you written anymore about our private life together?' she said.

She winced as I read her the bit about the negative tendencies in our relationship and didn't agree with me that *Once Upon a Time in*

America could be dismisssed as a tacky Scorsese pastiche.

'All right,' she said, extending her hand across the table. 'I hereby give you permission to publicly humiliate me.'

'Let's have a glass of white wine and drink to it,' I said.

To my surprise, they had a Leon Beyer Riesling.

'I'd have lost my job if I'd gone against this book of yours,' she said.

'What?'

'You remind Bernhard of the intellectual left in its more scandalous days. As a publisher he's very old-school. Above all else, the word! It makes him amazing to work for. He would have chosen your book over me if he'd been forced to decide.'

'So you're only giving me your permission under duress?'

'I'm very proud of you.'

We parted with a prolonged hug, conscious of each other's bodies, separated only by our flimsy summer clothing.

The meeting with marketing took place in the most exclusive room in the building, all wood panelling and the finest herringbone parquet. Unfortunately, the furniture was from the early nineties and horribly unmusical in design. A busty girl whose name started with Ka – Kamilla? Katrine? Katinka? – closed the window and shut out the pleasantness of late summer that had been drifting in from the street outside. There were eight of us around the table, and Mark's name was the easiest to remember. He was the new man in charge, headhunted, in his own words, to at long last bring the illustrious publishing house into the present. He had come from a similar job with Carlsberg and was wearing a grey suit that I judged to be Calvin Klein because of the unbecoming salesman's crotch.

The others only spoke to comment on the coffee.

'You've got a great product, Mikkel!' said Mark, his eyes darting from face to face. 'Some people in the business don't like me calling books products, but before we know it your auntie's going Christmas shopping and we need to make sure she buys a book and leaves that new electric kettle well alone. Henrik, will you give us the good news?'

A guy with ponderous eyelids picked up a computer printout.

'We've struck a deal to go on the buses.'

'Bus ads?' I said.

'You're an old Østerbro lad, aren't you?' said Mark. 'Can you see yourself all along the side of a number fourteen bus? All right lads, remember me?'

Bernhard entered and tried not to attract attention.

'We put out dozens of titles in the run-up to Christmas,' said Mark. 'We've got to make priorities, it's no good chucking a heavy marketing budget at a poet who's never going to lift more than two hundred copies. You're our number-one priority this Christmas, Mikkel. With the right backing you could go a long way.'

He looked at Bernhard and something was clearly going on.

'Would you like to take it from here, Kamilla?' said Mark.

'We've been discussing your title,' she said. 'If we're going to go out there with guns blazing it's vital we communicate unambiguously.'

'*The Ballad of Signe and Søren T-shirt* is unambiguous,' I said.

'Nobody knows either Signe or Søren,' said Mark. 'Do you see where I'm heading?'

'Not really,' I said.

'You get on the S-train and it's a war zone,' said Mark. 'Dog eat dog, everyone scrapping for your attention. You've got TV screens in all carriages and ads all over the shop. It's all about sticking out and making an impact.'

'Get to the point,' I said.

His teeth were beginning to annoy me.

'Farewell coupledom and thanks for nothing!' said Mark. 'Bang! You got my attention. Farewell coupledom? Hey! What's he mean by that?'

'The divorce rate in Denmark is over forty per cent,' said Kamilla. 'And that's only those who are actually married. If you add in those who never bothered making it official we're well over the sixty per cent mark, at least.'

'All good communication contains an insight,' said Mark. 'You go straight to the heart, because we've just been arguing over breakfast, haven't we? Who's taking the kids to school, who's picking them up? Packed lunches, all that shit.'

Bernhard cleared his throat and took the floor.

'You've got a book coming out which everyone here is extremely excited about. But it's worth considering whether your loving portrait of Søren T-shirt needs its own platform.'

'You want Søren out?'

'I want to make sure both projects are accorded the best possible opportunities for success. I see you as a writer with a host of books inside you waiting to get out, and Søren's story could be an arresting and very different follow-up.'

Bernhard stood up and everyone else followed suit.

One of the women said she'd put feelers out to the monthly magazines, another suggested some dates for a photo session and a third wanted to know whether I could spend fifteen minutes on the eighth of October filling in some booksellers on the idea behind the book.

'Looking forward, *big-time*!' said Mark, the adverb in English.

He clearly thought we should hug, but I had to draw the line somewhere.

Maybe it was the thought of my impending appointment with the alcohol coach, but whatever the reason, I had succeeded in keeping my drinking in check for a week.

Diana was in a sort of limbo and had told herself she couldn't make any kind of step forward until the exhibition kicked off.

'Can I give you a job?' I said.

I missed seeing her hunched over her drawing paper.

'I'd like you to do some illustrations for my book,' I said.

'What kind of illustrations?'

'Draw what we do. Draw people and situations.'

'There you go. You see, you *can* be my daddy, no problem,' she said.

'Whatever, just get started,' I said.

She had done the first four drawings by the time Jan called us to dinner. Her pen was black and tremulous and picked out all the right details: Mille with her bum in the air, looking libidinously over her shoulder. Lisa's way of holding her champagne glass at an angle. The quiet couple at the Helenekilde Badehotel and the slight look of surprise in the eye of the au pair.

Jan had prepared a Korean barbecue and definitely hadn't held back on spending Diana's money: the meat was organic and we drank the hysterically overestimated cult wine of the Lebanese Château Musar.

He studied each of the drawings for a long time.

'You're playing about, Diana!'

'They're for Mikkel's book.'

'Set me free! I want a job like that too.'

They talked about how imposing restrictions could be inspiring and I pictured Charlie's bedroom; stuffed full of games, cuddly toys and clothes for dressing up, but did any of it make him happier than the kids in an African village playing with a ball made of rolled-up elastic bands? How could I argue that something as loosely defined and as unpredictable as a relationship between two human beings restricted self-realisation? Were all these thoughts of uniting socialism, Christianity and free love just a distraction from the truth that monogamous coupledom might be the greater challenge? If restriction could be liberating, then Søren T-shirt's way of thinking made some sense: you meet a woman, fuck her and have kids. Just to break that statement down: who do you meet? How do you fuck? What kids come out of it? And what do you do then?

'Why aren't we a couple, actually?' I said to Diana.

'He is rather cute, our Mikkel, isn't he?' said Jan.

Xenia Leth-Hansen ran her practice from Bredgade where she shared a premises with a fashion photographer, a firm of architects and some kind of investment company. The nameplate was polished brass. I'd just washed my hair and was in a pair of grey trousers, brown Clark's and a dark blue Smedley polo neck. Perhaps it was the hyphen, but I had imagined a detached, rather stooping blonde and encountered a small brunette in trousers that were somewhat on the tight side. We sat under a Richard Mortensen lithograph and on the low table were a jug of iced water with mint leaves and a vase of wild flowers.

'So you're no longer reviewing restaurants?' she said.

I told her about my big come-down and she said *aha* in the middle of all my sentences and always with a marked exhalation.

'I absolutely loved your writing,' she said. 'I still do, I suppose.'

She asked me about my upbringing and I felt shame at not having run away to sea at the age of sixteen or carved out a career in the armed forces.

'Was it usual for the family to have red wine at dinner?' Xenia wanted to know.

'Yes. And nebulous waffle for dessert,' I said.

She laughed, clearly aware of how charming she looked when she narrowed her eyes.

'Don't I know,' she said, and proceeded to tell me her own backstory: daughter of a GP from well-to-do Trørød and parents who never missed their drinks time; pot smoking with the older lads and later coke at On the Rox. Xenia could remember that Phillipe Starck had designed the toilets at Isis. Her parents had died within six months of each other and after a four-month binge she opted for treatment and was now into her twelfth year on the wagon.

''That was a very entertaining interview you did for *Berlingske*,' she said. 'You certainly thrust your hand into the hornets' nest there.'

'I'm not doing it to stir up trouble,' I said.

'What about you and Diana? What did you do yesterday, for instance?'

I told her about Diana's new drawings and mentioned that I had been fairly restrained in my drinking in the week that had passed.

'I find it interesting that Diana doesn't want a partner,' she said.

'And that everyone else does,' I said.

'It's certainly high time we re-evaluated traditional relationships,' she said. 'I'm just not sure you're the right person for the job.'

'It happens to be my idea,' I said.

'I think you're taking on far more than you're capable of dealing with.'

'You mean I've got enough on my own plate, is that it?'

She uncrossed her legs and straightened her back.

'Diana drinks too much as well, Mikkel. She is well on her way to fulfilling her potential as an alcoholic.'

'On what do you base that assumption?'

'The signs are so very easy to spot. I still like to go out. In fact, I was at a certain party in Tisvilde recently.'

'I didn't see you.'

'I don't suppose you saw anything in the state you were in, Mikkel.'

'Did Andreas invite you?'

'Andreas is concerned too, if that's what you mean.'

'Too? Who else are you talking about?'

'Me, said the dog.'

'You?'

She accentuated the pause with a smile.

'I've been watching you these last couple of years, Mikkel.'

'How do you mean?'

'Byens Kro, Andy's Bar. I like to do the rounds.'

'Fishing for clients?'

'You could look at it like that, if you want to. But I see it as my job to help people before they go over the edge.'

I made a point of not folding my arms.

'You're an alcoholic, Mikkel.'

'I certainly drink too much, that's true.'

'That's what alcoholics do.'

I was already lost in thought as she began to outline a possible course of treatment involving a series of therapy modules and multimedia support. I went straight to the nearest bar after leaving her office.

I thought I had managed to avoid having any kind of expectations ab
out Helene and Diana meeting each other, but then I realised
there was at least one thing I *hadn't* expected, and that was Helene in
a polka-dot dress.

The Toldbod Bodega was my choice, a classic drinking-house
interior with tablecloths, low-hanging lamps and the kind of furniture
you sank back into. Despite the bodega's reassuring wood panelling,
Helene seemed completely out of sorts, so her new dress seemed well
chosen, and of course polka dots are a cliché of the same rank as the
bowler hat, the use of oft-cited quotations in speeches to the bride,
and the French generally.

She wanted to know too much about Diana's life as an artist
and made no bones about how stark a contrast it made to her
own existence; the regular salary and the des res in Frederiksberg.
Diana was forthcoming in a measured kind of way, cutting a
natural figure in her midnight-blue suit. Helene seemed to be con-
tinually poised with her next question at the ready, interrupting
Diana mid-sentence, or finishing them on her behalf. Diana smiled
when Helene played her riff about the artist standing on the shoulders of art history, and at that point I realised it was my life, too,
that she was holding forth on.

Helene and I had both been brought up in the force field between
Freud and the Irma supermarket chain. Neither of us had ever crossed
Albanian mountain passes to flee our country, we had never risked our
lives for revolution. At best, we had turned our backs on white flour
and empty carbohydrates, or found the guts to wear cowboy boots
two weeks before everyone else. And tonight Helene seemed set on
reducing herself in Diana's eyes to some kind of generic arts worker
whose only detour from the straight and narrow was her husband
running off with someone else. Diana seemed to sense this and came
to the rescue:

'Is that from Commes des Garçons?' she said.

'The most expensive mistake I've ever bought,' said Helene.

'It looks gorgeous on you.'

I've always despised all that rubbish about men not understanding women, but I was still surprised by how little it took to turn the mood around.

Helene suggested Irish coffee, and after that we were getting on like a house on fire.

'Have you read what Mikkel has written about our sex life?' said Helene. 'It's true, he always did the same things with his hands. Why couldn't you try something else once in a while, Mikkel?'

'Why did you treat my dick like a gear lever?' I said.

'What's *your* sex like together?' said Helene.

'Mikkel can be rough with me,' said Diana.

'Mikkel? Rough?'

'He's quite the man!' said Diana.

Helene looked me up and down.

'I think you two would fuck brilliantly now,' said Diana.

'What about us two?' said Helene.

We walked along Esplanaden and Helene indulged in a rape fantasy involving a dark room full of unfamiliar cock.

'Will Andreas Møller be there?' said Diana.

There was something forced about the torches that lit up the outside of Levinsen Open. They were playing Stereo MC's and there were quite a few people there, albeit surprisingly few I actually knew. Andreas, Nikolaj Krogh and Lisa had positioned themselves centrally in the large space and looked like delegates at a conference. I found myself not wanting to notice them. It was a do dominated by men, all off-piste, shooting party and leased cars, and laughing loudly at nothing. Diana and Helene headed straight for the dance floor.

I went and found Andreas Møller. 'We met with the solicitor and the accountant today,' he told me. The formal tone annoyed me.

'The architects have given us a fantastic concept,' said Nikolaj Krogh.

'Do you know the *trulli* in Apulia? Think conical huts strewn across the landscape.'

'You've been busy,' I said.

'We need a board meeting. We need clear directives,' said Andreas Møller.

Couldn't he hear how tedious he was?

'We're millimetres from making this real,' said Nikolaj Krogh.

He tried to make a toast.

They were playing 'I Love Your Smile' by Shanice.

'We'll have none of your standing around looking like you're too good for the place, if you don't mind!' It was Levinsen and his smile was all wrong. 'May I give you all an eye-opener?'

He nudged us on through the oblong space and opened a sliding door.

'Have a look round,' said Levinsen. 'World-class art everywhere you look.'

Great oil canvases hung from the walls, the style keenly realistic.

Scenes from an eligible residence in the Bredgade district: no furniture, light pouring in through the classic tall windows, a mattress, paraphernalia on the parquet flooring – empty sachets of heroin, tinfoil, a candle. The young man on the mattress with his back to the observer, seated in a corner with his hands in front of his face, or lying stiffly on the floor.

'The artist is Henrik Høeg Müller. Is he good? Is he mind-blowingly good?' said Levinsen. 'I just sold two of the big ones to Deutsche Bank. Olafur paved the way in Berlin, now Henrik's ripping them apart. They're at eighty grand at the moment, but Next Love is meganice karma. Fifty thousand for you, lads. Tonight only.'

'He's good,' said Nikolaj Krogh, 'but I OD'd on disillusion in the eighties.'

'No light without darkness,' said Levinsen.

'I only watch films with a happy ending,' said Nikolaj Krogh.

'What say, Andreas Møller?' said Levinsen.

'Thanks for showing us,' said Andreas.

They were playing 'Sexy Motherfucker' by Prince and the girls were swaying their hips out of time to the music.

I didn't care for all the attention.

'Levinsen's finished,' said Andreas Møller.

'What makes you say that?' said Nikolaj Krogh.

'My family fortune is founded on bankrupts.'

I stepped aside and disappeared. Mille was at the bar.

'I never actually thanked you,' she said.

'For what?'

'It was your idea for me and Nikolaj to just be friends. It's changed everything. Did you know we're having a baby?'

'Are you pregnant?'

'No, Lisa is.'

'And you're okay with that?'

'Yes, and the kids are ecstatic. And you've got Helene back now, I see,' she said.

'I'm not sure about that,' I said.

She steered me towards the dance floor and in the midst of a group of wanton acid-jazz mothers, Helene and Diana stood kissing.

'The waters meet,' said Mille.

People stepped aside for me.

'What do you think you're doing?'

'We're kissing, that's all,' said Helene, drunk as a student.

'Let them kiss if they want to, leave them alone!' said a peripheral acid-jazz mother who had once been reasonably gorgeous.

'Mind your own business!' I said, and the long intro of the 'Dream Come True' remix kicked in with its wallowing percussion.

'I thought we were partying for Next Love?' the acid-jazz mother said.

'That's not love,' I said.

'What kind of a faker are you?' she said.

The next morning I was woken at quarter past eleven by someone pounding on the door. It was Søren T-shirt, with his hair combed.

'Are you on the Rohypnols again?' he said. 'I've been standing out there the last half-hour!'

I tried to claw my way back to reality.

'What the hell have you been doing?' he said. 'Your eyes are like slits.'

I tried to tell him, but was too incoherent to convey an accurate account.

'I've not touched a drop of alcohol in three days,' he said.

'What have you been doing instead?' I said.

'Reading the papers, eating salad, push-ups.'

I put the kettle on.

'It's for our sake,' he said.

'How do you mean?'

'We'll never get the book finished otherwise.'

I poured the boiling water over the ground coffee beans and put a pair of mugs out on the table.

'Everyone at Floss keeps asking and the other day it dawned on me I had to keep a clear head to tell the story properly, so I went home.'

I poured the coffee into the mugs.

'I can't remember when I last had three days on the wagon,' he said. 'I was still in flares, though. That much I do know.'

His shirt had been ironed.

'I've started remembering the maddest stories. Did I ever tell you about the time I painted that Jehovah's Witness girl's kitchen? You'll be rolling about. Put the tape recorder on, I can feel it all wanting out!'

'I've just had a meeting with the publishers,' I said.

'And?'

'They love the book about you, but they want to put it on hold.'

'You mean it's not going to come out?'

'It's been put back a bit, that's all.'

'That sounds exactly like when you used to send your demo tape in to some prick at a record company. There was always something in the way all of a sudden.'

He put his jacket back on.

'Fuck this. I'll think of you when I stick the needle in my arm.'

Diana knew the big dinner at Minna Lund's was going to be an ordeal and I sensed that my job was to pretend everything was all right.

It was always the first Thursday in September and the menu had remained unaltered since 1988: first escargots, then borscht and finally Spanish almond cake.

The beverage was champagne and only champagne, always a Pol Roger. Moritz told me F.P. Jac had once been shown the door for bringing his own Elephant Beer in a carrier bag.

We met up outside the gallery and strolled towards Amalievej.

Moritz was wearing a tie, I had on my trench coat from the flat on Klerkegade and Diana was in Loden knickerbockers and mustard-coloured stockings. Moritz could easily have chosen to distance himself from the event with reference to bourgeois suffocation of the arts, but this was his tenth year running on the guest list and he had gained, as he liked to say, a more balanced view of the business community.

Minna Lund was far and away the most prominent of Danish art collectors and her annual dinner was partly a self-interested celebration of a new season commencing, and partly an opportunity to do a stocktaking of the Copenhagen art world. Those on their way down or going nowhere were absent.

She was seventy-two years old and her fortune stemmed from her father's cannery business. Originally a graduate in librarianship, she began buying up works of the Cobra movement as a hobby in the seventies, but in May 1982 she happened to attend the opening of *Kniven på Hovedet*, the seminal exhibition of De Unge Vilde, and their breakthrough became hers too.

She soon developed a taste for a certain kind of contemporary art, and a reputation for being first among buyers. She visited the artists in their studios, attended lectures on semiotics at the university and was always present at any opening. When the nineties came round she embraced installation art, expanding her territory. London became a particular interest, and she discovered Britart long before any other Danish collector. She was a veteran of the Frieze Art Fair, VIP guest at Art Basel and a fixture on the invitations lists of all the important Berlin galleries.

We turned down Bülowsvej and entered that peculiar blend of musty banknotes, Greek mythology off-pat and hat-doffing in appreciation of the Wagnerian tenor that is so characteristic of the inner core of Frederiksberg.

'Diana is one of the few domestic artists Minna Lund buys no matter what,' said Kaspar Moritz, anticipating events. It was imperative Diana talk up her exhibition at Minna's dinner. The tapestries had turned against her the moment she sent the drawings off to Vietnam. The exhibition was an enemy and the way Diana saw things, it was all about damage control. Apart from that, her work was going better than ever. She was producing six drawings a day and they were as inspirational as they were true to life. We had reclaimed our days together, albeit in somewhat modified fashion, insofar as I was no longer doing my writing on the bed, but shopping and cooking instead. The place smelled of meat when we woke up in the mornings and I enjoyed being the one she leaned on, and starting again each new day.

A maid in black ticked our names, another took our coats and a third offered champagne. In the hundred square metres of garden room, Minna Lund held court with magnificent froideur. As far as I could make out, Erik Goldschmidt was the only collector invited. His body language signalled remoteness, his face was straight out of an early Scorsese film, his mouth petulant in every movement.

'May I show Mikkel and Diana some items from the collection?'

said Moritz.

Along the stairs leading to the first floor were a dozen or so draw-ings by David Shrigley. The first room contained some Billingham photos from *Ray's a Laugh*, a disturbing and evocative Kirkeby, a Tracey Emin embroidery and stills from that video of Peter Land's where he falls off a bar stool. In the next there was a big Gary Hume and a Chapman piggyback sculpture.

'Are you ready?' said Moritz.

We stepped inside a third, spacious room.

'This is the only place in Denmark you can see a spot painting!'

Minna Lund had a tendency to overburden her wall space, but here she had accorded due reverence to a gigantic canvas comprising rows of circles in every conceivable colour.

'Damien Hirst. She got this in 1994 for ten thousand pounds. Two years later one of the others in the series made the front page of Christie's catalogue. His assistants have done hundreds of them since then, but this is assumed to be one of the very few he did himself. One nowhere near as good as this just went for 1.8 million pounds!'

De Unge Vilde had their own corner room and Moritz stopped at a large canvas incorporating foam rubber and tar.

'I checked the seating plan for dinner,' he said. 'We've got the main table again. Let's agree that your exhibition is going to be a resounding success. Now's the time to stay the distance, Diana. Now!'

There were some two hundred guests for dinner, by all accounts dividing fairly evenly into artists and others.

The male artists preserved their integrity by coming directly from their studios in old Carhartt pants, caps and Kansas workman's jackets, whereas their female counterparts tended to have made a plucky effort in the form of dresses, clutch bags and good shoes.

Minna Lund sat at the head of the table with Goldschmidt at her side, and since we were following Emma Gad's guide to etiquette, Diana and I, being an unmarried couple, had been placed next to each other, with me seated to the right of the hostess. The rows of tables snaked their way through the rooms and the cheap seats at the end were noisiest. Black-clad waitresses came with aromatic escargots oozing with garlic, and Goldschmidt did his duty as dinner partner to the hostess and gave a brief speech in her honour.

'The art season has never commenced until Minna's borscht has been served.'

Minna Lund had no intention of wasting time.

'Have you been adapting to the crisis, Kaspar?'

'A crisis is what we make of it, I'd say,' he said.

'You'll have to think again about that, I shouldn't wonder,' said Goldschmidt. 'The American pyramids are tumbling, it's all a matter of hours.'

'A good friend of mine claims the art market's going to bottom out,' I said.

Minna Lund studied me inscrutably.

'The galleries have had their seven years of plenty,' said Goldschmidt. 'They'll be doing the rounds for custom now.'

'Some of us recall the austere eighties,' said Minna Lund. 'When the men were separated from the boys. How many artists of the day survived? A handful, if we're feeling generous.'

'You overbought, Minna,' said Goldschmidt.

'True,' she said. 'I learned a lesson. A lot of those purchases would have done better to be binned.'

Goldschmidt laughed drily.

'What are you doing to prepare your artists for recession, Moritz?' said Minna Lund. 'How are you advising Diana, for instance?'

He was saved by the borscht and a prolonged chin-wag about the recipe, which the Lund family chef had developed during World War II.

I stared into the thick white tablecloth and saw Donald Crowhurst. He was loitering off the coast of Brazil, and there was nothing but sea and sky.

'I hope we'll see you at our opening next week,' said Kaspar Moritz. 'Ida-Marie has been working hard on a new track all summer and I'm pretty sure she's going to come out guns blazing.'

'May I be indiscreet?' said Minna Lund.

'Do I have a choice?' said Kaspar Moritz.

'How could you allow one of your artists to become an advertising display for clothing in all the leading papers?'

'I needed the money,' said Diana.

'Haven't the two of you been getting on?' said Minna Lund. 'I did wonder if Diana was seeking new pastures and whether her new gallery would be one with which I did not wish to be associated.'

'It's no secret the matter gave rise to a certain disagreement,' said Moritz.

'I suppose the next thing would be seeing one of the tapestries at the Bruun-Rasmussen auction house,' said Minna Lund.

'Would there be anything wrong with that?' I asked.

'Your call, Moritz,' said Goldschmidt.

'A gallerist will always go for optimal placement and for obvious reasons that's out of his hands in the case of auction.'

'Where would they go ideally?' I asked Moritz.

'To serious collectors like Minna or Erik, or to the museums. And then there's the price: I take great pains to find the right price and auctioneers don't always see things the same way.'

'It would be annoying, to say the least, if I were to buy a painting from Kaspar only then to see something very similar go for half the amount at Bruun-Rasmussen,' said Goldschmidt.

'How can you stop people putting a picture up for auction?'

'A conscientious gallerist is selective at all levels,' said Goldschmidt. 'He does not serve Bull's Blood at his *vernissages*, nor does he include daubers in his stable. And he makes sure his buyers are serious.'

'A work may on occasion escape one's control, though thankfully it doesn't happen very often, touch wood,' said Moritz. 'I've got a little list of people not to sell to.'

'How would you react, Diana, if one of your works were to be cast into the no-man's-land of an auction?' said Minna Lund.

'It's never going to happen,' said Moritz. 'We know exactly where Diana's tapestries are placed, and they're all hanging very happily indeed where they are.'

He indicated one of them on the wall, a classic helmsman in sou'wester, his beard spattered with semen.

'I've always envied you that one, Minna,' said Goldschmidt.

The Spanish almond cake arrived and it was quite as dry as I'd expected.

Minna Lund whispered some words to one of the waitresses. I began to look forward to escaping her clutches and gave Diana's hand a squeeze under the table.

Moritz mustered the last of his strength and smiled at me.

I had just checked to make sure my jacket still hung from the back of my chair when the waitress came back and handed Minna Lund an envelope.

'What have you got there?' said Goldschmidt.

'Bruun-Rasmussen's latest catalogue,' said Minna Lund.

She flicked through the pages until she found what she wanted and handed the catalogue to Moritz.

'How would you explain this?'

Diana Kiss, Untitled, said the caption. Peter Borch-Jensen's spunk dribbling from Diana's cunt. Estimated price: 50,000–70,000 kroner.

'I don't understand,' said Moritz.

Diana let go of my hand under the table.

'I sold it,' she said.

'So I see,' said Moritz. 'But to whom?'

'His name's Kreuzmann and it was for his wife.'

'I went to school with him,' I said. 'He's on the level.'

'Thomas Kreuzmann?' said Goldschmidt. 'We've a number of loose missiles whizzing about at the moment and Thomas Kreuzmann is almost synonymous. He couldn't buy a cucumber without being asked to show some ID.'

'I can get him to withdraw it,' I said.

'The damage is already done,' said Minna Lund. 'Neither Moritz nor I can accept one of our artists being presented at cut price.'

Diana introduced me to a whole new sound when we got home. It came from the diaphragm, at once deep and guttural, and between each eruption she reached for something on the shelves and smashed it against the wall. I had a feeling she blamed me for bringing Kreuzmann into her life and landing her in a situation that threatened to end her career. I was reluctant to put my hands on her shoulders and poured her a whisky instead, which she promptly dashed to the floor, causing the glass to shatter into a hundred pieces.

'Do you want me to stay?' I said.

'Do whatever the hell you want!'

I biked over to Klerkegade and slept like it was the nineties again, without cause to even turn in my slumbers. I was almost grateful when Kaspar Moritz rang at a quarter past nine.

'Can you meet me over at Minna Lund's place at ten? We need a plan of action.'

'Have you spoken to Diana?'

'She's got enough to think about as it is.'

Moritz was waiting outside the house in a suit. The remains of the dinner from the night before had been consigned into bin bags neatly placed beside the path.

'What day is it?' I said.

'Friday,' he said.

'It feels like it's Tuesday,' I said.

'Aha,' he said.

'It must be the light,' I said.

A maid showed us into the garden room and tea was served in thin cups, along with some biscuits that didn't make much difference one way or the other.

'Diana's tapestry is due to be auctioned on the seventh of October,' said Moritz. 'A fortnight later I'm showing eight similar works. These have been priced at ninety thousand. We simply can't operate with the kind of uncertainty that exists on the free market.'

'What are you getting at?' I said.

'We need to make sure that tapestry doesn't come cheap.'

'How do we do that?'

'Do you know anyone, male or female, a person who can dress well and who at the same time is rather more reliable than Thomas Kreuzmann?'

'What would she have to do?' I said.

'She would attend the auction,' said Minna Lund.

'And bid for the tapestry?' I said.

'More precise instructions will be forthcoming,' said Moritz.

I knew exactly who I had to ask, and headed round to Clara's.

'What do you want?'

Clara was in a pair of old Levi's and a purple college sweatshirt. Getting straight to the point would be suicide.

'Sorry,' I said.

She was listening to Joni Mitchell and I recognised her mood all too well.

'Sorry's only a bit better than nothing,' she said.

She was in the process of reupholstering an armchair in pink material and had once again decided to become a tea drinker.

'I've got Erik's stuff together.'

She nodded at a tote bag in the corner.

'See if there's anything you want.'

A tie was poking out. Black satin.

'No, it's okay,' I said.

'Kathrine ran into them at the theatre,' she said. 'He used to take me to the theatre. She's got blue veins on her tits, hasn't she?'

'What was on?'

'A comedy, at FÅR302. According to Kathrine, he fell asleep.'

'Are you glad you got rid of him?'

'Does it look like it? You gave him a bed to fuck in, Mikkel. I know he's a drunken freeloader, and he's not exactly the height of intelligence, but I do actually miss him.'

She held my gaze. 'She's as thick as a plank. I'm better-looking than her, aren't I? I've got better taste, anyway. But she bribes him with blowjobs. Why are men such bloody imbeciles?'

'That's a bit simplified,' I said.

'I've never understood the attraction of a dick in your mouth. It's where I put my food.'

She put the kettle on.

'I've tried to despise you, Mikkel, but I can't. You just can't be hated. Why is that?'

'Maybe there isn't enough of me,' I said.

The cushions on her sofa were in bright colours, the way she imagined they were supposed to be.

'You look like shit,' she said, making me a coffee. 'Why do you never see white dog shit on the pavement anymore? Wasn't it poodles? Did they put chalk in their dinner, or what?'

'Things are going wrong with Diana,' I said.

'What did you expect with that stupid project of yours? Next Love! As if, Mikkel! As if!'

'I don't know what's going to become of me and Diana, but I do know I'm never coming back to this.'

'So it's all going to be young girls from now on, is it?'

'She's opened everything up for me, and once you've seen the big white room it's impossible to go back into a little dark one again. Do you see what I mean?'

She pressed the cafetière's plunger down.

Diana and Jan were shelling prawns on the rooftop terrace and she didn't return my kiss. Jan was coming down on Damien Hirst. Something about a solo auction at Sotheby's and what was it exactly Hirst had done that was so amazing, and blah, blah, blah about that bloody skull with all the diamonds in it.

'I know you saw a genuine spot painting at Minna Lund's place,' he said. 'But Povl Gernes was doing much better spot works in 1968, and what's more, he did them all himself.'

'Do you know what that shark thing he did is called?' I said.

Jan smothered the prawns in mayonnaise, dill and lemon.

'It's called *The Physical Impossibility of Death in the Mind of Someone Living*. The title on its own is a work of art,' I said.

'I'm going for a lie-down,' said Diana.

Jan moved his chair into the sun and leaned back with his eyes closed. He took his T-shirt off and rolled his shoulders.

'She's been crying,' he said.

A seagull landed on the ridge of the roof opposite.

Jan looked up at me for a second, then leaned back again.

'She hardly stopped when we were in Berlin,' he said.

'It must have been hard on her, leaving Nona,' I said.

It was annoying that he kept his eyes closed. It was like talking to blancmange.

'She seems to be all right about Nona,' he said.

A drop of sweat ran down his chest and settled in a fold of his belly.

'What was she crying about, then?' I said.

'It was all that business about Mies,' he said.

'What business?'

'You're not jealous, are you?'

'Didn't she go to Berlin to meet up with you?' I said.

'You'd have to ask her about that.'

'You're the one who brought it up!' I said.

'All I did was tell you she'd been crying in Berlin.'

'I'm not stupid,' I said.

'Anyway, I've got work to do,' he said, getting to his feet.

'What work?' I said.

His eyes went yellow with rage.

'How's the book coming along?' he said.

'Fine, thanks.'

'Face it!'

'Face what?'

'You've ripped it all off from Diana.'

'I've exploited her energy,' I said. 'The ideas are mine.'

'You can go on as much as you like about unrestricted love, but the fact is, you're not up to it,' said Jan.

Diana was sweeping up the smashed plates and shards of glass. Bewildered dust particles whirled in the air.

'Tell me about you and Mies,' I said.

She carried on without looking up.

'Are you in love with him?'

'Give me the dustpan,' she said.

'Why haven't you said anything, Diana?'

'Give me the fucking dustpan and shut up!'

It was leaning up against the pillar. I snatched it up and hurled it across the room and it smashed into an African figure on the shelving. Diana rushed over to it.

'You've killed Fela!'

She held it up. The head had been separated from the body.

'Get out!' she said. 'Just get out!'

Ida-Marie appeared from her room.

'Can you keep it down a bit?'

She went over to put the kettle on.

'Why don't you mind your own business?' said Diana.

'This is a place of work,' said Ida-Marie. There was a knock on the door and she composed herself and went to answer it.

Moritz was in a checked Sherlock Holmes suit and behind him cowered the three curator girls with shoulder bags full of densely written A4. Lea brought up the rear and didn't so much as glance in our direction. The two others smiled sheepishly, cheeks blushing becomingly.

'Thanks for taking the time to see us,' said Lea.

'It's no bother,' said Ida-Marie, holding the door.

So as not to make a drama of it I packed a few items of clothing and had just zipped up my bag when they came out again with smiles on their faces.

'I'm speechless,' said Lea, too audibly. 'It's so confident, Ida-Marie! Anyone would think you'd been working on it for years.'

I followed them out, then patted my pockets as if I'd forgotten my keys and stayed back on the landing. Their chatter reverberated around the stairwell and rose metallically back towards me.

I might have agreed with Diana on a lot of things, but apart from that, I understood nothing about her. Never had I spent so many hours with another human being without getting any closer. I had no history to give me a clue, no inkling of what might have been motivating her, and I was never anywhere near guessing her thoughts or what she was going to say next.

Whether it was infatuation or an advanced form of dependence I was unable to judge, but I did know that my supreme intoxication had reversed and turned against me.

It came as a surprise to me that beyond my own vanity and banal fear of losing her, I had cultivated a veneration for Diana Kiss as a person, and felt profound and unfalsified tenderness for her.

It began outside Bang & Jensen, because once you've become a part of Vesterbro, returning to the centre of the city seems so regressive. It was early afternoon and half the bands in the country seemed to be going past, and producers and DJs with expensive headphones around their necks. Inside, people sat with their laptops and soft-boiled eggs. I was outside among the more experienced crowd, Vesterbro newcomers to a man, of course, but with the privilege to criticise the newer arrivals and to withdraw from Bang & Jensen when evening closed in and couples from the provinces claimed the stage.

Vesterbro has always had a frivolous and hearty tone about it, and while the majority of the original population has moved on, died or are simply claiming their pensions, this atmosphere lives on. The new generation of Vesterbro inhabitants are well read and intellectually inquisitive, they love explaining and discussing things at length, and as I shared my frustrations about Diana with the sympathetic assembly, the analyses came pouring in.

She has an unresolved issue with her father, one opined. She's put you in his place, but that means she becomes her own mother and that you're a boy. She wants a man and you want a mother. It can't ever join up.

I had just asked for elaboration when Mies came walking along with that erect posture of his and a tight little rucksack on, and as always it was disarmingly easy to be convivial with him. He had come home to play a gig with his electronica duo and when he asked whether I wanted to come along to see them at Jolene's I was already hatching a plan, so I invented a story about a big birthday bash in Charlottenlund.

It was a regrettable lie, though one I was compelled to tell.

The light was fading as I sat myself down on a bench in the little park that gave me a view of the entrance door to Diana's building. I had brought a couple of beers with me, from the Herslev Bryghus, and my theory turned out to be right. At a quarter past eight Diana came out dressed in a new suit.

Mies had been heading towards Lyrskovgade and while I credited him with the best of intentions and felt certain he had invited me to his gig out of the sheer goodness of his heart, I was equally sure that Diana had received word of my impending absence with relief. It was one thing her reserving the right to decide for herself who she wanted to share herself with, but it was quite another that she couldn't be doing with the difficulty of me.

I waited three minutes before following her, and I knew which way she'd gone because she always took Flensborggade no matter what. I stuck to the other side of Sønder Boulevard, keeping an appropriate distance. She turned into Kødbyen's meat-packing district at the corner by the Chicky Grill and I watched her until she went into Jolene's.

An electronica duo usually play only one set, forty-five minutes, give or take, and since going in would be too risky I retreated some sixty metres and sat outside Karriere Bar with a glass of white and my legitimising notebook on the table in front of me in order to survey the situation from a comfortable vantage point. Bands were always set up by the DJ booth at the far end, and my plan was to slip in once they were finished. I wanted to hit the half-hour when friends and hangers-on were milling around the band, and I was in no doubt about where exactly I would find Diana.

I had just got started on my second glass when they began to play, and judging by what seeped out they were relatively tuneful: heavy bass and drums, and high, almost falsetto vocals that almost certainly belonged to Mies. The idiom was simple and melancholic and the songs were short. The windows steamed up inside and people applauded longer than politeness decreed.

'Come on, old mate, that's Menu Rabbit on in there, and you're coming in with me.'

Levinsen had grown a moustache and it suited him.

'I'm fine here,' I said. 'They're good, though. Great name.'

'Isn't Diana in there?' he said.

'Don't tell her you've seen me,' I said.

Levinsen smiled, clueless.

'It's a surprise,' I said.

He gave me a hug and I tried to relax into it.

'Vallin, for fuck's sake! You're so mega old-school!'

At ten o'clock the crowd were chanting for the encore and I went and got a double whisky, knocked it back in one and went over. I scanned the bar area through the big window and once I'd made sure Diana wasn't in the first bit I opened the door and went in. My timing was perfect. I stood in a corner by the exit from where I could survey the stage area and still remain hidden among the punters.

Behind the DJ booth was a makeshift backstage area and Mies and a dark-haired guy with wolflike features, his bandmate, I supposed, stood all but surrounded by a thick wedge of admirers. Directly in front of them were the genteel, older crowd: family and long-standing neighbours, perhaps; behind them a garland of friends and professionals. Diana was in the third tier with the journalists, hangers-on and oversexed girls, but was making her way through the ranks, and I reckoned she was focused enough on that for me to close in a bit. I made note of some strategic points on my route: blind spots, groups behind which to duck. My goal was the little smokers' recess with the front-room furnishings to the right of the DJ booth. It would be perfect, allowing me a close-up, side-on view of the parties involved without much chance of being discovered.

I had just sought cover behind three guys in sweatshirts and Palestinian scarves when I felt a tug on my trouser leg.

'Vallin! Have you got a sec?'

Levinsen was seated in the company of three eccentrically clad teenagers in turbans and sunglasses.

I smiled and waved him away.

'I was just telling the girls here about our summer hols. They refuse to believe Mies was running around starkers in Tisvilde.'

'We'll be there next year with no clothes on,' said Sister Turban.

At that moment Diana turned round and I ducked and crouched down.

'Have you heard of Diana Kiss?' said Levinsen.

They nodded and their jewellery rattled.

'Vallin's here to propose to her.'

The Turban Sisters clapped their hands.

'Go, tiger, go, go!' Levinsen said in English, and slapped my behind.

Diana had made sufficient progress to nearly be at the front now, and rather boldly I decided to leave my hard-won refuge in favour of standing behind a tall guy in the crowd so as to bring myself within earshot.

It all took place a metre and a half in front of me.

Diana was now standing in front of Mies with a big smile on her face and only then did I realise I hadn't thought things through to their conclusion. It was no surprise to me that she threw her arms around his neck and whispered words in his ear, or that it hurt to see them so intimately together, but I had no idea whatsoever as to what exactly I was to do next.

I couldn't blame her for falling in love, and certainly not with a person like Mies, the thoroughly decent, physically perfect and in every respect promising young man that he was.

I looked down at my scuffed leather shoes and then at all the open faces that surrounded me, all of them fifteen years younger, if not twenty. I thought about being that young again, that all-consuming excitement of leaving an unfamiliar flat with a new scent lingering in the nostrils.

I had just resolved to beat a retreat when Mies abruptly raised his voice:

'Get lost, Diana!'

The throng parted and her eyes were lowered to the floor as she left. She passed so close I could smell her shampoo.

The next time I took Charlie back to Helene, she had just got out of the bath when we got there. She was all steamy under her robe and fragrant with wild rose moisturiser as she cubed and diced a lump of butter. On the chopping board were two chunky fillets of turbot, and in the pot some shallots were simmering away in white wine.

'Is chocolate mousse still the king of all beasts?' she said as she opened the fridge. The dessert was all prepared in little glass bowls.

'I didn't think you liked oysters,' I said.

There was a whole dish of them on the bottom shelf.

'Tonight I do,' she said.

'Are we celebrating?'

'I spoke to Tue without crying today.' Tears welled in her eyes, not grief, but because grief was subsiding, or so I assumed, and we hugged without thinking too much about it first.

Tue's wine cellar comprised several hundred bottles: there was a section devoted to red Burgundy, another to the Italian wines, mostly Barolo, a large selection of German white, a slightly smaller one of white Burgundy, and about fifty bottles of champagne, including a dozen Krug Grand Cuvée, and I went with a Weissburgunder from

Bernhard Huber.

Helene went to get dressed and came back in a thin petroleum-blue trouser suit, bare feet in delicate high heels, and a necklace of big, bright red beads. I put Charlie to bed, then dug out the dub version of Horace Andy's 'In the Light'. We sat facing one another across the table amid the glasses, plates and cutlery. I considered saying something about the fact that although we'd sat in exactly the same way hundreds of times before it now somehow felt different, but in the end I decided to let the situation exist on its own terms.

Twelve oysters glistened in the space between us and we toasted with the Krug and sipped cautiously: it was like drinking a state of mind; the bass line repeating over and over, the elongated echo of the snare drum. We took an oyster each and enjoyed the shock of suddenly being immersed in the sea. She may have been wanting to say something, but until she did or didn't I was acutely aware of my own body, seated on the chair with my feet on the floor.

We fried the turbot and swayed together as the heat turned the flesh white. I removed the leaves from twenty Brussels sprouts and steamed them meticulously while Helene worked the butter into the saturated onions, and all of a sudden there was no sound but music and the rhythm of the wooden whisk.

'You're glowing,' I said.

She ran her hand through her hair. My phone thrummed in my pocket. It was Diana.

'Mikkel, darling, would you be kind and come over?'

The ingratiating tone did not become her.

'Where are you? Ida-Marie's dinner party?'

I gave Helene a smile and stepped out into the garden.

'I'm on my way,' I said.

'Was that Diana?' said Helene, and I nodded. The music had stopped.

Ida-Marie's dinner party was in the part of the gallery that was normally the back office for Moritz and his secretary. Six round tables
for eight had been brought in, with white tableclothes, proper napkins
and chunky candles. Diana had been placed between Goldschmidt
and a Dutch artist with a fringe and I had to interrupt their conversation to give her a hug.

Her crisis seemed to be over, and counter to expectations I realised that I was enjoying myself. The conversation was engaging and
people forgot to drink.

My name had been written on a place card in a personal, cursive
hand and I had been put diagonally opposite Diana with Nynne, one
of the curators, on my right.

Ida-Marie was in a long, cobalt-blue silk dress and sat between
Goldschmidt and a film director with a long square beard who made
commercials.

'Has she sold anything?' I asked.

'From what I hear, there are only two canvases left,' said Nynne.

'Did Minna Lund buy anything?'

'Four.'

'What's she been painting?'

It was asking for it.

The beholder this and the beholder that, the forcefulness of
naivety, and, hey, in came Bourdieu again. I'm making it sound bad,
but the truth is that I was quite content with Nynne's flow and even
encouraged her by asking questions, and after a bit we crossed over
on to the subject of the big women's exhibition that had now finally
come together, and the name, *Athena 08*, was predictable enough for
me to picture the logo straight away, but I found it interesting, nonetheless, that they were including a special tribute section in honour of
Dea Trier Mørch, and it was hardly a coincidence that a commitedly
socialist artist from the seventies would now come to the fore again.

'There's an aesthetic aspect, of course,' I said. 'Woodcuts are
modern again, that rather awkward black-and-white mode of expression that was so very much hers, but the ethical side is more important.'

'We've talked a great deal about ethics in our meetings,' said Nynne.

'It'll soon be okay to say *solidarity* again,' I said.

'I do very much admire what you're doing with Next Love,' she said. 'I hear you've got your eye on an army barracks.'

We continued our exchange of utterances, gradually moving towards the point at which the women's exhibition and spiritual love would become two sides of the same coin, and had I not made eye contact with Diana we would undoubtedly have ended up in consensus. Her look was a glare.

Goldschmidt was explaining something to her and was so wrapped up in himself he didn't notice that she wasn't paying attention. I frowned with bewilderment and Diana nodded towards the exhibition space, simultaneously acknowledging Goldschmidt's concluding point with a smile.

Moritz tapped his glass lightly with a spoon and got to his feet.

'When Ida-Marie presented her new works to me at the end of July, I knew immediately that she had found her way. Never before have I showcased a debuting artist so certain in her endeavour, and fortunately I am not alone in that appraisal. At half past two this afternoon, I received a phone call from Nynne Willer, one of the three curators of *Athena o8*. Nynne was able to disclose to me that Ida-Marie has been selected to take part in that exhibition. And this is just the beginning! Congratulations!'

Diana did not applaud. The waiters served Gateau Marcel and I crouched down beside her.

'What were you trying to say just now?'

'Ida-Marie's canvases.'

'Aren't they any good?'

'I came too late, but Goldschmidt just told me about them.'

She stood up and took my hand.

'Let's go in and have a look.'

There were seven big oil canvases along the main wall, five on the end wall. The seven all shared a dazzling white background, the five were pigeon blue, and all the subjects were in shades of brown. The exhibition was entitled *Put Your Worries in My Pocket* and it was the meat-packing district, Kødbyen, by night, snapshots of people having a good time together, glasses in hand, and it was easy enough to imagine Ida-Marie sitting there with her sketchpad at Jolene's and Karriere Bar.

The figures were touching: an arm around a shoulder, holding hands in the balmy nights of summer, laughter and hugs at the bar. Stylised humans with a decidedly sculptural quality, and so pleasingly painted as to approach decoration.

Diana let go of my hand and moved in a slow arc around the big white space.

She pursed her lips and muttered irascibly under her breath, clicked her heels together like a soldier, then strode purposefully back to the dinner.

People were chatting over their chocolate gateau when she returned to the table.

'You stole my idea!'

She pointed a finger in Ida-Marie's face.

'What, did I paint your cunt, Diana?' said Ida-Marie.

'We were sitting on Jan's terrace,' said Diana. 'I said I wanted to sit myself down on the street and paint people.'

'There is actually a rather long tradition of painting popular scenes, if I may say so,' said Goldschmidt. 'L.A. Ring portrayed the impoverished land workers, and Willumsen painted a host of street scenes in Italy.'

'You were painting souls, Ida-Marie,' said Diana. 'You told us you didn't understand what you were doing. Where did this new idea come from?'

'I don't need to answer to you, Diana. I've got nothing to defend,' said Ida-Marie.

'Mikkel heard you,' said Diana. 'Didn't you, Mikkel?'

'Diana said you could sit yourself down on the street and paint the people, and Ida-Marie mentioned Søren Hjorth-Nielsen,' I said.

'I was thinking out loud,' said Diana. 'And you stole my thoughts. Without a word!'

The room was silent. Moritz stepped in.

'I don't think this is a matter we should be discussing in the present forum,' he said, placing a hand on Diana's shoulder. She shrugged him off, furious.

'You've got nothing to paint, Ida-Marie! I wasn't going to tell anyone, but now you've forced me!'

A woman with a pile of rags in her hair and some pleasant smile lines put her oar in:

'We all understand your frustration, Diana, but my daughter can hardly be blamed for the curators ignoring you, can they, my dear? Envy is a very human emotion, though hardly one to air in public.'

She led Diana calmly back to her seat.

'We think you're a very talented artist, Diana. We wish you the best, we all do. Come and sit down, we're having such a lovely evening. Did you get some dessert?'

Diana looked down at her gateau.

'It's heavenly, I can assure you,' said Ida-Marie's mother.

Diana picked up her gateau and raised it slowly towards her mouth:

'Do you want me to put it in my mouth?'

'Sit down, dear. Don't be so silly,' said Ida-Marie's mother.

Diana pressed the gateau into her face:

'Where's my mouth?'

She began to laugh and repeated the gesture.

'Where did my mouth go?'

She rubbed the gateau all over her face and all down her neck.

'Can anyone say what on earth all this is in aid of?' said Ida-Marie's mother.

The Dutch artist got to his feet and applauded as Diana was escorted to the door. Everyone else tried to pretend it hadn't happened.

I couldn't tell Andreas Møller apart from the horseradish. We were having lunch at Schønnemann's and I hadn't slept for two nights. My brain kept skimming through sounds, smells and visual impressions and stopping randomly wherever it chose. I had got so used to Diana's bestial howls they had become a permanent background noise, but the effervescent fizz of mineral water in my glass and the restaurant's busy choreography was enough to drive me up the wall: waiters whizzing back and forth with plates and glasses, not to mention the mindless wanderings of its customers from the tables to the toilets and back again, and what was it with those shirts everyone was wearing? Why did we need to see their skin through such thin, white material? The sounds were insufferable: the throaty laughter punctuated by fits of coughing, the clatter of plates, the chinking of glasses. I felt like I was at every table, under the greasy ceiling, on the floor in the midst of miserably neglected footwear.

'I think we need to talk things through,' said Andreas Møller.

I picked up my knife to cut into the beef on my plate, then put it down and picked up my glass of water instead.

'I've been suspended,' he said.

'That doesn't sound nice,' I said, passing in my mind through the corridor between Diana's and Jan's apartments with a removal box in my arms; the grey paintwork flaking off the dry wooden floor, the feeling of dust in the throat, and Jan, waddling along in front with the crack of his arse on full display and the smell of his fat, sweaty body mingled with aftershave.

'Fortunately, I now have something meaningful to be getting on with,' he said, slowly putting down his knife and fork. 'I want to thank you for having thought of me.'

He was trying to sound genuine, but I suspected he had prepared this speech in advance, considering his words, playing the scene through in his mind. His thanks rang hollow and I was too far gone, too fragile, to accord his words any sort of value anyway. Instead I just stared at him blankly.

'We need some beer,' he said.

He asked about the book and couldn't have cared less about the answer. He seemed to think the book represented something solid in my life, and I waffled on about the polyamory movement in the USA and the Ranters in the UK, but refrained from telling him about my meeting at the publishers the day before.

Bernhard had invited me in for coffee and it took him three minutes to figure out how things stood. 'The machinery's up and running,' he said. 'If I have to press stop, I want you to say so now.'

'Is a hundred pages enough?' I said.

'Yes, but no less. How much have you got?'

'Without Søren I'm down to about thirty or forty.'

'You're not going to be done by October the first,' he said. 'My suggestion is we get you installed in our writers' cottage at Vejby Strand, and that you come home with a complete manuscript under your arm.'

'I want to change the world,' said Andreas Møller.

'I'm with you,' I said, which I most certainly wasn't.

'Do you even grasp the magnitude of our mission, Mikkel? It's so immense, so tremendous that we are unable to fully comprehend its scope with such a feeble apparatus as ours. There is only one way forward.'

'And what's that?' I said.

'Faith!'

We stared at each other for a long time.

'You must sweep away the banalities,' he said.

'How do you mean?'

'You will never mean anything to Diana.'

'I do mean something to her.'

'The Third Testament is ours to compose, Mikkel Vallin! It is a task requiring complete submission, years of life spent in blinkered dedication, and you aren't even here! You've vanished. You're fiddling about, contemplating your navel like some neurotic housewife. Pull yourself together, man!'

Lunch was over, and if nothing else, at least I had woken up.

Andreas Møller paid the bill and put on his seaman's jacket.

'Mille's stepping down as chairperson at the next meeting,' he said. 'Perhaps you should consider doing likewise.'

The cottage was on top of a ridge and was an ordinary summer cabin with two bedrooms and big panoramic windows that wanted to be posh but looked out on to a cluster of pine trees and a neglected lawn that was riddled with molehills. The whole place stank of mice. Leaves had begun to fall from the trees and lay scattered about the lawn. Usually I was fond of September, the way the air seemed to cleanse and make everything new, but I didn't find any of this particularly inspiring.

The previous incumbent had left behind half a bag of onions and a green pepper and I went to the shop to get red lentils, coconut milk and curry powder. 'A little party tonight, is it?' said the shopkeeper guy, with a nod in the direction of my twelve cans of Classic. 'Don't forget the crisps.' I made enough dal to last me a few days and on the radio all they talked about was a huge firm called Lehman Brothers going bankrupt in the States. I'd never heard of Lehman Brothers. Maybe it was just someone else's turn to keep hold of the money.

I had three notebooks full of events from the summer camp, little scenes and considerations I'd penned while completely out of it. By half past eight I had drunk four cans and written a page and a half about Emma Goldman, a motherfucker of a Russian-American Jewish battleaxe who stood up against everything and everyone at the beginning of the 1900s and who said:

'I demand the independence of woman, her right to support herself; to live for herself; to love whomever she pleases, or as many as she pleases.'

The sun had gone down when I heard the mouse for the first time.

284

There was a scratching in the cupboard under the kitchen sink. I went over and counted to five before opening the cupboard door abruptly. A field mouse leapt into the air and vanished down a crack. It had chewed holes in the bin bag and littered the cupboard with droppings and crumbs. I went online and read that mice seek refuge indoors in September and after half an hour it got started on the bin bag again. I had a whisky with the fifth can and wrote about Emma Goldman getting deported to Russia, but why was that relevant to my book? I deleted half a page and lay down to sleep on the sofa-bed in the living room. The noises under the sink intensified with the darkness. All through the night I kept waking to the sound of scratching.

'We've got an offer on Fernet Branca,' said the shopkeeper the next morning. 'A nice little glass to keep off the chill in the evenings. Can't be beaten,' he said.

I went for a walk and the sea had consumed the beach.

The mouse was pluckier now. Perhaps it could tell I was a man of peace. It ate the breadcrumbs off the counter and darted back behind the wall. I read they could go completely flat and pass through cracks seven millimetres wide.

They were still going on about Lehman Brothers on the radio and I needed to get to the shop again before they closed at seven.

'Always better to get too much in than not enough,' said the shopkeeper, as he scanned my six-pack of Classic. 'Staying at the writers' place, are you?'

I nodded.

'I thought you looked the type.'

I got into the habit of knocking on the cupboard door before opening it to get to the bin and tried to reinfuse the book with some kind of passion by introducing the scene with Master Licker of Ørby. I was finally getting myself immersed in orgasms and treetops when I saw the mouse out of the corner of my eye.

It scurried across the living-room floor and disappeared behind the bookcase. There, up against the skirting board, was a little nest dotted with droppings and lined with dyed wool that looked like it was from the blanket that lay draped over the armchair.

I pulled the duvet up over my ears to escape the rustling. At three o'clock in the morning I gave in and retreated to the freezing cold bedroom.

The next morning it had shat on the counter again.

It was testing me. This was no longer about having a furry little friend about the house, it was a merciless battle for territory.

The shop had two kinds of mousetraps.

One was familiar from cartoons, the other was Swedish and made of plastic and ventured claims of efficiency, killing the vermin humanely and without suffering.

It was shaped like a little pipe and in the middle was a guillotine. You lured the mouse inside with a bit of sausage and as soon as it touched the bait the guillotine deployed and broke its neck.

'We've got Easter brew on offer,' said the shopkeeper.

'Easter brew?'

'Beer like that'll keep for years, even if drinking it now means thinking creatively.'

I gawped at him.

'With it not being Easter anymore,' he said.

'It'll come round again,' I said.

'Can't be sure of anything these days, can you?' he said.

Apart from an aggressive wasp or the occasional gnat I had never killed anything in my life. Would I be able to do it?

Was I going to take a life just to be able to write about the demise of coupledom?

I decided to investigate its behaviour when left alone, and so I crept up to the house and peered in through the kitchen window.

The mouse was pattering about on a plate, and that was where I drew the line.

I raised the guillotine, attached a little piece of salami to the trigger and placed the contraption in the cupboard under the sink. I pretended to be absorbed in the singular skills of Master Licker and froze at the slightest sound. I was waiting for death.

The trap went off after half an hour. First the abrupt snap, then three seconds of silence, followed by several minutes of thrashing about. I imagined the little creature's agony in its final throes and not until I'd had three stiff whiskies later in the evening did I venture to open the cupboard and peep inside. The stiffened corpse lay outstretched in the trap. I shook it out on to the dustpan, went out to the bin and dropped it next to an empty tin of chickpeas and the plastic wrapping from the six-pack. Peace descended. I lit candles and wrote until I conked out on the sofa.

At 1.24 I was woken by a sound outside the window.

I held my breath and heard the wind in the trees. There it was again.

Someone was walking round the house. Someone was peering in from the darkness.

I rolled down on to the floor and crawled across to the wood burner. I picked up the poker, deciding to confront whoever it was in the open, where I could utilise my weapon to the full.

I opened the back door and stood for a second in the dark until my eyes adjusted.

I went left with the poker raised like a baseball bat, making sure to tread where the ground was soft and there were no twigs or leaves to make a sound beneath my feet.

My heart filled my entire frame. I paused briefly before turning the front corner. A person was standing by the door.

I shouted out, producing some incoherent sound, and charged forward. The figure jumped and shrank back in fright, almost falling down the step.

Helene had a basket on her arm, full of delicacies from Løgismose, and I gorged myself on blue cheese with egg yolk and raw onion for the first time since the eighties and talked incessantly before finally asking why she had come.

'For dick and scrambled eggs,' she said.

We drank a brutal south Italian red wine and half a bottle of Minervois, and then had uncomplicated, cheerful sex for an hour and a half.

'I really like you,' I said.

'It's mutual,' she said, and looked down at her scrambled egg.

And then a whole lot went on without words.

'Next time give me a ring first,' I said as we stood by the car.

She looked like she was going to say something, but didn't.

I knew the damage Ida-Marie's success had done to Diana. The real-life drawing project had shown her that she could take a different artistic direction if she wanted to, but that particular avenue had been closed off – no one would ever see that work as original now that Ida-Marie had got there first. Since work meant everything to Diana, Ida-Marie's betrayal crushed her, and of course rational arguments could have been put forward to convince her that the end of the world was not nigh, but it wouldn't have helped in the slightest.

We had talked three or four times on the phone while I was up at the cabin, albeit with nothing really to say, apart from breathing at each other, and now that I was back things didn't seem to be any better. I missed her, even when she was sitting in front of me. She made an effort and asked about the book and I said I'd written eighty-two pages and needed another eighteen, and she refrained from commenting on my lack of enthusiasm.

'My tapestry's being auctioned tomorrow,' she said.

'Are you nervous?'

'No, why should I be?'

I wondered whether I should tell her what we had planned for the auction the next day, but it had gone too far for me to be able to get my head round the consequences and I was stricken with fear at the thought of Moritz perhaps ringing while she was within earshot, and so I muttered something about getting some things in to make veggie burgers.

I phoned Moritz as soon as I was out on the street.

'About time!' he said.

'Did you know Damien Hirst just raked in more than a billion kroner at Sotheby's!'

'He uses diamonds,' I said.

'The auction kicked off at the same time as the Lehman Brothers crash!'

'And somewhere in Jutland a cow had a calf.'

'Don't you see what this means?' he said. 'The crisis is giving contemporary art a swerve! We're too strong for it!'

'What are we going to do about the auction tomorrow?' I said.

'The tapestry's under the hammer at half-past six.'

'How high do you want us to go?'

'Minna and I have agreed to stop at ninety thousand.'

'What if no one else bids?'

'Diana's a star. Of course they'll bid.'

'Do you want me in a suit?'

'I want both of you well dressed but discreet. And another thing: don't go in together and don't sit next to each other. Someone might recognise you and we don't need any rumours going around.'

'Is what we're doing actually against the law?'

'Your friend can buy as much art as she wants.'

When I got back, Diana was listening to 'At Seventeen' and washing up.

'I thought you were going shopping?' she said.

I'd forgotten all about the veggie burgers and had to make up a story.

'I ran into Blismann,' I said.

'Isn't he in Madrid?' she said.

'What would he be doing there?'

She rummaged through a pile and handed me a postcard.

It was from the Prado, one of Goya's grizzly Black paintings, Saturn devouring his newborn son.

I picked my way through the scrawl of his handwriting.

'Thanks for the tussle, gorgeous. My son will be named Bob Blismann.'

A shudder went through my body and tears welled in my eyes.

'You've got friends who can make you cry,' said Diana.

'You've got Jan,' I said.

'He's a champagne friend.'

'Lisa?'

'A nice girl from the provinces.'

'You've got me,' I said.

We stood and hugged, keeping hold for a long time, until eventually she stepped back and gripped my shoulders with her arms outstretched.

'Did Helene go to see you in the cottage?'

'No,' I said, and I was a bastard to lie to her.

'You don't want to start from scratch anymore,' she said.

'What do you mean?' I said.

I picked my jacket off the back of the chair.

'What about those veggie burgers?' she said.

Clara's outfit was perilously close to parody. She had been through Laura Appelgreen's wardrobe and borrowed a dark blue cardigan, loafers from Tod's and a prim city skirt, topping it off with a splashy silk scarf, done up like a yacht-club wife.

'Spot-on, don't you think?'

At Krut's she went with a glass of white while I had two large beers.

'I followed the auction online yesterday,' she said. 'It was their big Cobra night and it didn't go well at all.'

'Cobra numb the optic nerve,' I said. 'All that colour.'

'Cobra always sell, but three out of four got pulled and they had to send thirty-five Jorn canvases back.'

'I wonder what'll happen if no one bids for Diana,' I said.

'Danish shares dropped eleven per cent yesterday,' she said.

I tried to calm us down with a couple of cognacs, but to no avail.

It was a gorgeous evening otherwise. The air was still and relatively warm, and the trees showed their hues in the soft light. It was my fault that Clara felt so uncomfortable walking through Kongens Have, and so I told her about my old hippy friend, Franz, who back in the sixties had done a turn as a snake charmer on the lawns in front of the Herkulespavillon, stark naked, playing his pipe and making his dick rise to the music.

Normally she would have laughed.

'I noticed the auctioneer started very low,' she said. 'He may kick off asking forty thousand, in which case I'll bid, but I can't go straight for ninety.'

'Moritz says the crisis isn't hitting contemporary art,' I said.

'Do stop saying *contemporary art.*'

People were standing around in clusters outside Bruun-Rasmussen and Clara gave my arm a little squeeze and went in. Judging by the chatter on the pavement, the day's auction had carried on where yesterday's disaster had left off.

All seats were taken, so I joined those standing at the rear. Retired doctors and solicitors were richly represented, people who played swing jazz with the old boys and collected Burgundy. There were a couple of furs, but otherwise the place was short on flamboyance.

Clara had seated herself in the third row. There were three lots before Diana's tapestry.

First there was a recent Chinese painting, a big thing depicting a young couple not doing anything. The style was photographically precise and the soft lighting gave it a nicely apathetic touch.

'Do I hear twenty-five thousand Danish kroner for this excellent painting by Xioao Wang-Lee? Twenty-five thousand, surely! Fifteen. Do I hear fifteen thousand kroner?'

A hand went up in the second row.

'Fifteen thousand bid. Twenty? Do I hear twenty?'

The auctioneer peered out at the assembly with a look of resignation and raised his gavel.

'Sold for fifteen thousand kroner.'

Then came two works by Olafur Eliasson.

The first was a photograph showing a dead Icelandic landscape with a hot spring and was quite incomprehensibly valued at seventy-five thousand, which it made by the skin of its teeth. The next up at least had a little house in it and went for eighty-five, and I couldn't make up my mind whether following Eliasson would be to Diana's advantage or not. I was still none the wiser when I noticed a platinum blonde with something strangely familiar about her. It was Rie Becker, sitting nine rows back with a gormless look on her face.

Two assistants held Diana's cunt up so everyone could see.

'Our next lot is a tapestry, not many of these on the market. The artist is Diana Kiss and the piece is dated this year. She's represented by Galleri Moritz. Shall we begin at thirty thousand Danish kroner for this exceptional work?'

Clara raised her hand and was immediately outbid. As far as I could make out, it came from one of the assistants, which presumably meant an anonymous buyer had put down a maximum bid beforehand.

'Forty thousand?' said the auctioneer.

Clara bid again and the auction gathered momentum.

Fifty-five thousand, sixty, sixty-five, seventy thousand.

'Eighty-five thousand I have!' said the auctioneer. 'Do I hear ninety?'

Clara made her final bid and the auctioneer peered out again.

'Ninety thousand Danish kroner for this vivid tapestry by Diana Kiss, straight off the loom. Ninety thousand for the first time, ninety thousand for the second…'

A new assistant entered the fray with a mobile phone pressed to her ear.

'I'm now bid ninety-five thousand,' said the auctioneer. 'One hundred thousand.'

The bidding ebbed and flowed between the two anonymous buyers and my fists were clenched in excitement. A hundred and five thousand, and the air was thick with tension. A hundred and ten!

Diana's tapestry went for one hundred and seventy-five thousand kroner and I reeked of sweat as we came out on to Bredgade and Clara threw her arms around me.

'What the hell happened there?' she said. 'They went mad!'

'You were really good,' I said.

'Are you satisfied?' said Rie Becker.

She had her fussy journo's notepad in her hand.

'Who's this?' said Clara.

'So you were wanting to buy a Diana Kiss tapestry?'

'She's a brilliant artist,' said Clara.

'Are you a collector?' said Rie Becker.

'Sorry, Rie, we need to get going!' I said, taking Clara by the arm.

We made off through the Sankt Annæ Passage and didn't stop until we got to Byens Kro and ordered two sets of Urquell and old Caribbean rum.

'Selling above valuation like that will be a fantastic PR boost for Diana's work,' Clara said. 'Her gallery prices will seem like a snip now.'

The thought occurred to us both at the same time and I went outside and rang Moritz.

'Was that you? You and Minna Lund?'

'What are you talking about?' he said.

'You bumped up the price, didn't you?'

'Tomorrow you can read all about how Diana rode Olafur off her wheel. She deserves the success, Mikkel. What about your mate Kreuzmann? He'll be rubbing his hands together, don't you think?'

I bought the paper the next day and read through the first part of Rie Becker's new series of articles under the title *Art: From boom to doom*. They'd made it a big feature, with its own graphics and a photo of the star journalist herself. The article was a broad-spectrum account of the art-world crisis, the controversial bit consisting in the rumour that the Valby galleries were about to go bust. The auction at Bruun-Rasmussen was cited in support of the general prophecy of doom, but Diana's tapestry wasn't mentioned.

Jan was up in arms. For one thing, he couldn't bear the idea of one of Diana's works pulling in a hundred and seventy-five thousand without her profiting from it, and for another he was jealous of her having stepped up on to the established stage with such success.

Diana herself was relieved and pretended we were getting on, while I went to prepare the talk my publishers had asked me to give to the booksellers in advance of my book coming out.

Clara called me.

'I just got back from the classroom and sat down to lunch and there's five messages from that Rie Becker. You've got to do something!' said Clara.

I called Moritz.

'Any anonymous purchase from Bruun-Rasmussen is always going to be shrouded in mystery. Rie Becker knows that full well. She hasn't got a thing to go on.'

I biked down to the harbour and the exercise helped. It was still warm enough to sit out in the Design Museum's garden. I had quesadillas and mint tea and had just regained some measure of calm when Clara rang again.

'She's waiting outside the school.'

'Just smile and say nothing.'

'She knows we went to school together.'

'I'll get Kreuzmann to pick you up,' I said. 'He owes us a favour.'

Five minutes later Moritz called.

'I've just had Laura Appelgreen on the phone.'

'What did she want?'

'Rie Becker has somehow got wind of the fact that Laura and your friend Clara know each other, and Laura didn't know Clara was going to Bruun-Rasmussen yesterday.'

'Did she tell Rie Becker that Clara had got done up at hers?'

'You've got to get out there and shield Clara,' said Moritz.

'Kreuzmann's just got in the car to pick her up.'

'Kreuzmann the swindler? What were you thinking?'

I pedalled hell for leather all the way out to Christianshavns Gymnasium.

Rie Becker was guarding the arched gateway with her notepad in hand.

'What's with the tabloid approach?' I said.

'I called Moritz from the auction yesterday,' she said. 'His number was busy all the time.'

Kreuzmann rolled up in his white Mini, parked halfway up the pavement and jumped out with his mobile pressed against his ear.

'Is this the one?'

'Who are you?' said Rie Becker.

'Someone with nothing to lose.'

'They're the ones I'm writing about,' she said.

Kreuzmann went through the gate.

'That tapestry's from her new series, right?' said Rie Becker. 'I didn't realise Moritz was that desperate.'

Kreuzmann escorted Clara to his car.

'What was your name again?' said Rie Becker.

Kreuzmann opened the door for Clara and turned round. He looked straight at Rie Becker, holding her gaze for maybe half a minute until suddenly he snatched the notepad out of her hand, tossed it on to the pavement and urinated all over it.

'Pity. Nice jugs,' he said, and was gone.

I called Moritz and told him what had happened as I biked across the Knippelsbro bridge.

'Rie Becker thinks you got Diana's tapestry put up for auction so you could pump her prices up ahead of the exhibition.'

'But that wouldn't be against the law,' he said. 'In the business world, that sort of thing is a punishable offence, but the law still views art as philanthropy. Rather arrogant of it, wouldn't you say?'

'You're being rather laid back about it.'

'I'll call her editor and let him know I'm familiar with the law on libel. That ought to shut her up.'

B ernhard took my hand in both of his and didn't ask about the manuscript, because this was booksellers' night and it was the job of the illustrious publishing house to promote Danish culture as it had done for centuries. The booksellers got stuck in to the tapas buffet.

Bernhard was first to take the floor. Helene was sitting with a couple of colleagues.

'I haven't prepared anything,' I said.

'You don't have to say much,' she said. 'Use your charm.'

This was a sales push for the spring catalogue, but as Bernhard put it, there would also be a couple of explosive surprises ready for Christmas. I jotted down an outline while a well-preserved woman talked articulately about her upcoming biography of Tom Kristensen, then started from scratch when a much-loved writer from an outlying region held forth on his crime-thriller pastiche set in Sønderho.

Bernhard gave the floor to Mark, who opined that my book was set to be the big eye-opener that Christmas, and he added weight to his words by opening his Mac and giving the assembled booksellers a sneak preview of the ambitious marketing campaign.

The rear wall transformed into a big screen and the art department had put together some realistic visualisations: there I was on a billboard in between Samsung and Mentos at Nørreport Station, and there on the side of a bus. *Farewell coupledom and thanks for nothing! – the book you don't want your partner to read!*

Helene gave my hand a squeeze under the table and I stepped up amid a round of applause.

I talked about the perpetual motion machine first, then gave examples of regular dysfunctionality, explained that the book was based on my own life and then rounded things off by reading the bit about Master Licker of Ørby.

Mark glowed with enthusiasm.

'Do you know how totally wicked that came across, Vallin?'

We adjourned to the Byens Kro and Helene pressed her bum against me, accepting shots from the skilled bartender and getting drunker than she intended.

'Is this not good?' she said as we sat in the taxi.

'Everything's fine,' I said.

'You know what I mean,' she said. 'I'm sorry,' she went on. 'I'm imtim . . . in-timi-dat-ing you. You're with someone, for God's sake. A gorgeous woman you're mad about.'

I put my arm around her shoulder, but I missed Diana like hell.

'Should we eat together tomorrow?' I said as she opened the car door.

'We like our food, you and me,' she said and kissed me. 'Food!'

Diana's side of the bed was empty by the time I woke up. The pillow had lost its pillowcase in the night, and the sheet was scrunched up at the bottom of the bed. Jan was snoring and the only other sound was the faint hum of traffic.

Three suits and a pile of shirts lay on the floor in front of Diana's clothes rack. She had started examining herself in the mirror, or maybe she had always done so, just not in the kind of way you noticed.

'How about this one?'

It was lavender-coloured, a suit.

'Are you going somewhere?' I said.

'I've got to get dressed!'

'It's only Monday,' I said.

'Why do Danish people always say *only* in front of everything?'

It was probably true.

'You look very nice,' I said.

'There's something wrong with the collar,' she said.

'Not as far as I can see.'

'I mean inside. It prickles my neck.'

She did a little jig, anger and irritation.

'Perhaps it's just my neck,' she said. 'Here, you try.'

'It won't fit me,' I said.

'You don't need to put your arms through,' she said.

She wriggled the jacket on to my shoulders and dragged the collar back and forth across my neck so that I might feel whatever it was that had bothered her. I tried to concentrate.

'Nothing yet,' I said.

'Walk about a bit while we do some breakfast.'

I put some bread in the toaster and Jan watched me with his eyes half shut.

'You should wear lavender more often,' he said.

I took the jacket off and handed it back.

'There's nothing wrong with it.'

'Give it a chance to work first!' she said.

'The itching powder, you mean?' I said.

'Perhaps they use a lot of chemicals at the dry cleaner's,' she said.

'Your other jackets don't prickle.'

'How would you know, Mikkel?'

'You've never mentioned it if they do.'

'You don't tell *me* everything, do you?'

It had started with her feet a few days before. They had grown, she said, and now all her shoes pinched. Maybe it was some kind of fluid build-up in her body. I didn't know how to tackle it. Diana could be annoyed or angry, but she was always herself, and this new darkness seemed to come from somewhere else. It came to a head in Irma.

She had stopped cycling and went for endless walks instead. We had tramped all through Søndermarken and then Frederiksberg Have, and my feet automatically headed for the Irma supermarket on Gammel Kongevej. I suggested something Vietnamese with chicken, lemon, mint and chilli, but she turned her nose up at the prospect, as well as at my alternative involving mushrooms and tofu.

Her only suggestion was spinach.

'They've got frozen whole leaves at the end of the display over there,' I said. 'It's even on offer this week. Grab three.'

'Is this where you shop with Helene for your meals together?' she said.

I didn't have the chance to talk my way out of it, or even to be honest, as Moritz stepped out from behind the bread counter wearing a rather clingy trench coat.

Diana's eye began to twitch as she dug into the potatoes.

'You like your spuds, I see,' said Moritz. Diana had filled the bag almost to bursting point.

We exchanged the standard air-kisses.

'I was just thinking about you, Diana,' he said. 'Should we drop that collectors' dinner and throw a party instead? We're tired of sitting down, aren't we?'

Diana nodded and was miles away. 'All right,' she said.

'I'll invite the collectors for champagne beforehand.'

'I'm sorry,' she said, and wandered off.

Moritz picked up a pack of Portobello mushrooms. I found her a few minutes later, hiding in a doorway.

'I can't breathe!'

A young mother walked past with two children, and a shuffling pensioner trundled a tartan shopping trolley along in the other direction. Diana clutched her chest and battled against a panic attack. I tried to teach her the breathing exercises I'd learned from the drama project on Suhmsgade, but they were no help whatsoever. Fifteen minutes later we began to slowly make our way home.

The next evening I went up to Taarbæk for help.

I wanted to borrow some money so Diana and I could go to Rome once we'd got everything out of the way, and I had a feeling Nikolaj Krogh had already decoded the purpose of my visit. Only a small minority of those involved in the arts had money enough to lend, and it clearly wasn't the first time he'd been asked.

Mille was folding clothes on the long dining table, Nikolaj Krogh was cooking dinner and Lisa was slouched in a futuristic armchair, flicking impatiently through a Dutch fashion magazine.

It was an evening like any other in Taarbæk, and choreographed down to the way the big white bath towels had been stacked in the bathroom.

We had oxtail stew.

'She's always nervous before an exhibition,' said Lisa.

'She lies awake all night,' I said. 'Big round eyes staring into the darkness.'

'It's anxiety,' said Mille.

'You say that about everything,' said Lisa.

'It'll stop once the exhibition gets started,' said Mille.

'Should we have the meeting here instead tomorrow?' said Nikolaj Krogh.

'What meeting?' I said.

'The Next Love meeting,' he said.

'The distraction will do her good,' said Mille.

I helped Nikolaj Krogh with the washing-up.

'How are you two getting on, anyway?' he said.

'Apart from all the disasters, we're not,' I said.

'We can't have that!' he said. 'What should we do about it?'

I came clean. 'I want to show her Rome,' I said.

'Always a good idea to get away,' he said. 'I've got a partner down there. Do you want me to make a call, see if I can get you fixed up with a flat?'

'We can stay with a guy we met on Capri,' I said.

'Do you need to borrow some money?' he said.

'If you could, I'd be grateful.'

'How long were you thinking of staying there?' he said.

'Four days,' I said.

'About twenty thousand, then?'

I nodded and hung a little copper saucepan on a hook.

'And you were out for lunch with Andreas, I believe?' he said.

I noted the introductory conjunction. It meant he linked the two things together. First he told me about some hurdles that had cropped up regarding the Sjælsmark purchase, and then he hit me with it:

'Have you thought about your role in the organisation, Mikkel? Wouldn't it be a relief to hand on the chairmanship to Andreas?'

I hung my tea towel up.

'We've already got some funds in the kitty,' he said. 'The summer camp at Tisvilde came out rather well in that respect.'

He took off his blue apron. It looked expensive. 'You must have forked out quite a bit of your own money on that account?'

I was about to say I hadn't.

'Let's say we're quits,' he said.

Jan insisted on making dinner for the meeting at Diana's flat the following day, partly because he wanted to impress Nikolaj Krogh, and partly because the organisation was footing the bill, including the twelve-year-old balsamico, the new olive oil from Sicily, and the grappa, delicacies purchased exclusively from the finest of retailers.

Diana volunteered to lend a hand and it didn't seem to bother her that Andreas Møller would be among the guests. They were listening to Erasure and spooning spinach filling into home-made ravioli when I got home, and there were canapés with chicken-liver pâté, pickled plums and salmon tartare with peas and tarragon.

Andreas Møller arrived on the stroke of seven with his cheeks aglow. He was wearing a blazer and had brought flowers for the hostess.

Mille drank three glasses of spumante in fifteen minutes and Nikolaj Krogh insisted on the prolonged and heartfelt hug. There was a delicious garlicky smell from the lamb slow-roasting in the oven and the biodynamic Beaujolais was chilled and went down a treat. Nikolaj Krogh took it upon himself to call the assembly to order before things got out of hand. He pulled a xeroxed agenda from his sumptuously patinated leather briefcase.

'Are we quorate?' he asked.

'I thought you'd never ask,' said Mille.

'Why don't we give Jan a vote?' I said. 'He and Diana have been cooking all day.'

'I don't think I've ever had one before,' said Jan. 'It feels rather nice.'

'And let's all agree on Lisa voting *in absentia*,' said Nikolaj Krogh. 'She's at home feeling sick.'

The first item was electing an executive committee.

'Neither Mikkel Vallin nor Mille Cortzen Krogh are seeking re-election,' said Nikolaj Krogh. 'Andreas Møller has put himself up for chairman.'

Andreas Møller gave an inappropriately formal speech of acceptance and I observed the way his jaw muscles worked in forming his words, the way he angled his hands and bared his lower teeth.

'Which brings us to the most important item on our agenda tonight,' said Nikolaj Krogh. 'Our line of direction. I suggest we identify five components of our work: love, finance, property, membership and God. Let's start with love, shall we?'

'What a marvellous meeting,' said Jan. 'Love!'

'Our primary inspiration is from John Noyes,' I said. 'At Oneida, fixed coupledom was forbidden, and in my opinion that line of thinking is fundamental to what we are trying to achieve.'

'What's *fixed coupledom* when it's at home?' said Mille.

'It's when you turn yourselves inward and confine each other,' I said.

'What if a couple were to allow each other freedom within that construction?' said Nikolaj Krogh.

'Then there's no shortage of nice houses in the suburbs,' I said.

'You're not addressing the question, Mikkel,' said Andreas Møller.

'Do I have to?' I said.

'Isn't that what we're here for?' said Mille.

'I was pretty sure our ambition was to break down the norm,' I said. 'I thought the very idea was to liberate energies and let them flow freely, to elevate the common mass on to a higher level of consciousness.'

'Where did I put those joss sticks?' said Jan.

'Okay, so what if Diana fell in love with someone else?' said Mille.

'Then I'd probably feel down about it,' I said.

'And what if you got jealous and did a lot of stupid things?' said Mille.

'I'd like to think I wouldn't,' I said.

'But you are quite jealous, Mikkel,' said Jan.

'Should couples live together, too?' I said.

'I'd like to be able to sleep in the same house as Lisa and our little baby,' said Nikolaj Krogh.

'I understand that, but aren't we now reducing it all to communal living? What would set us apart from your average house-share?'

'God would,' said Andreas Møller.

We debated the issue for half an hour and it was me against Andreas Møller, Nikolaj Krogh and Mille. Jan was impressed by our seriousness. Diana drew doodles on her agenda.

'We need to put this to the vote,' said Nikolaj Krogh. 'First, the most far-reaching proposal: all those in favour of prohibiting couple-dom raise their hands.'

'Hang on a minute,' I said. 'The most far-reaching proposal would be to allow couplehood. That's never been the intention.'

'Mikkel has a point,' said Andreas Møller.

'Okay, so all those in favour of allowing coupledom.'

Nikolaj Krogh, Andreas Møller and Mille raised their hands.

'And those against?'

I raised my hand, as did Jan and Diana.

Nikolaj Krogh took a piece of paper from his briefcase:

'Taarbæk, October fifteenth. I hereby inform the general meeting that I vote in favour of Next Love permitting couplehood. Signed: Lisa Zöllner.'

'How ruthless!' said Jan with a laugh. Diana carried on doodling.

'Now, let us proceed to the issue of finance,' said Nikolaj Krogh.

'That sounds logical,' I said.

'Don't sulk, Mikkel!' said Mille.

'I'm distraught,' I said.

'Why don't we have a break and get some fresh air?' said Nikolaj Krogh.

I went out on to the terrace and stared up at the grey sky.

'I respect you for sticking to your guns,' said Andreas Møller.

He'd brought his drink with him.

'I thought you didn't compromise,' I said.

'I've always considered John Noyes' weakness to be his idiosyncracies about free love.'

'You should have told me that before.'

'You didn't ask.'

'What's your motivation here?' I said.

'A qualified congregation,' he said.

Nikolaj Krogh called to order.

'We need to discuss something tangible,' he said. 'Therefore, I've altered the running order a bit, so our next item will be *property*.'

He handed out some photocopies. They were in colour.

'As you all know, we had reached a rather advanced stage in our negotiations regarding the purchase of Sjælsmark Kaserne, but it turns out the local authority have decided to make use of the facility themselves, and for that reason Andreas and I have gone on to Plan B.'

'What a magnificent place,' said Jan.

The handout was from an estate agent and detailed a manor house in Odsherred: the main building comprising some two thousand square metres, a picturesque lake, a number of small cottages dotted about the property's perimeter, and a seventeenth-century church. And all of it but two hundred metres from the sea, private access.

'The main house can relatively easily be turned into about forty separate dwellings. Then there's the cottages, and on top of that plenty of acreage on which to build in the longer term. It does mean going for about one hundred dwellers rather than the three hundred we were looking at before, but we're actually rather happy about starting off with a smaller congregation. It should allow us to be more focused.'

'It looks expensive,' I said.

'The place has been on the market for two years and they've offered us a considerable reduction on the advertised price if we jump in now,' said Nikolaj Krogh.

'We signed the papers today,' said Andreas Møller.

'You've bought it?' I said.

'Imagine being able to buy a manor just like that,' said Jan.

There seemed to be no point in further objections, and one by one the details were passed by vote.

Nikolaj Krogh and Andreas Møller began the process of picking out the strongest possible group of one hundred members from all the potential candidates, and the socialist requirement that each resident contribute five hundred kroner a month to the kitty was agreed. There would be religious services on Sundays and Wednesdays.

I think it was obvious I no longer wished to be associated with the organisation, and I was on the verge of drawing attention to the fact that I should at least get some credit for having thought up their name when I remembered that Nikolaj Krogh had just lined my pockets with twenty thousand kroner. I decided to remain silent.

'Right, let's have some food, shall we?' said Nikolaj Krogh. 'It smells absolutely delicious.'

My defeat was so comprehensive it didn't seem to matter much. We gave Jan and Diana and their slow-roasted lamb a well-earned round of applause, and everything was oddly okay.

'Pass the potatoes, would you, Diana?' said Andreas Møller.

She handed him the dish.

'Thank you.'

'What did you say?' said Diana.

'I said thank you,' said Andreas Møller.

'Get out!' she said.

'What?' said Mille, and giggled.

'I want you all to go, now!' said Diana.

'Whatever for?' said Jan.

'Put your cutlery down and get out!'

She snatched the fork from Andreas Møller's hand. 'I knew you were a bastard.'

Nikolaj Krogh and Mille stood up. Andreas Møller was the first one through the door.

'Don't we get some sort of explanation?' said Mille.

'Later,' said Diana.

The roasted baby potatoes with rosemary were still steaming.

'What was all that in aid of?' said Jan.

'He said thank you,' said Diana.

'Who did?'

'Andreas Møller said thank you after he fucked me at Levinsen's party in Tisvilde,' she said. 'It *was* him! He was the second guy who fucked me.'

I drew her towards me, but she wrestled free.

'It's best you go, too, Mikkel.'

She took my hand.

'I need some space, is that okay?'

I nodded.

'See you Friday,' I said.

Bernhard's secretary had been calling and I couldn't put it off any longer. I took a long soak, washed my hair, shaved, and decided on the dark blue suit, white shirt and a tie.

The secretary out front announced my arrival.

'They've been waiting for you, Vallin,' she said. 'Bernhard's got a little surprise for you.'

I passed through the mahogany; he was in a pullover the colour of egg yolk.

On the desk was a bottle of champagne and three glasses.

'Our golden goose, at long last!' he said.

Mark knocked and came in.

Bernhard uncorked the bottle and poured the bubbly.

'The booksellers have given us the most amazing response,' said Mark.

'*Skål!*' said Bernhard, peering over the the rim of his raised glass in cultivated fashion.

'The book's off,' I said.

'How do you mean?' said Bernhard.

'My relationship's on the rocks.'

'So what?' said Mark.

'And I want to save it.'

'Right,' said Bernhard. 'I've got my fortieth anniversary in the publishing business coming up next year, Mikkel. The problem that you're outlining is one of the most frequent of all, and it is especially common in the case of authors coming out for the first time. The vast majority find separating the writer from his words to be a cause of great anxiety, to say the least. You are not your book, Mikkel. Your words are your book.'

'Exactly!' said Mark. 'It's only a book, for Chrissake!'

'I'm trying to live my thoughts. I don't want them broadcast.'

'I thought you had balls, Vallin,' said Mark.

'I hope you realise that you are not merely letting yourself and us down, Mikkel,' said Bernhard. 'You are letting down your entire generation. And here I was, thinking it finally had something to say.'

The day before Diana's opening began with Rie Becker's article on the front page of the arts section. A big portrait photo of Diana in a Marilyn pose with flirty eyes and a pout, and the caption:

Kiss-ing the boom goodnight.

Followed by:

'Diana Kiss, feted during the contemporary art boom, now cast aside as crisis separates wheat from chaff.'

They made her out to be the very symbol of the 'fashionable middle', a group of artists who, according to Becker and her team of experts, had emerged through the symbiosis of the financial boom and greedy gallerists. Demand had pushed prices skyward, in Diana's case they had trebled, but art purchases among the well-heeled middle classes had plummeted with the financial downturn and the fashionable middle were left to adorn the gallery walls at prices no one was prepared to pay anymore. The first of the Valby galleries had shut up shop and more would follow. Artists would be without an outlet and gallerists were already displaying the first clear signs of desperation. The piece had obviously been vetted by the paper's legal department, and the story of Diana's surprisingly high auction price at Bruun-Rasmussen teetered on the brink of libel, littered as it was with phrases such as 'puzzlement all round' and 'several recent examples of artificially inflated auction sales abroad'. The conclusion could hardly be misunderstood: Galleri Moritz and Diana Kiss had been greedy and failed to see the signs, and the italicised information at the foot of the article seemed almost sneering:

Diana Kiss, 'Runaway Girl', Galleri Moritz, 17.10–16.11.

I went over to the house on Ceresvej before the opening and found Helene and Tue Nissen in a tight embrace in the kitchen. He had started doing cross-fit and his chest and cheekbones looked chiselled. He was in town to meet up with his editor. His new novel would be called *Carrer Es Clot*, after the lane on which he and Aurelien saw each other for the first time.

'I've been thinking about you,' he said.

'What have you been thinking?'

'Diana could be just a transition for you, Mikkel.'

'A transition towards what?' I said.

'Why don't you move in here?'

I could tell from the look on Helene's face that the suggestion had not come out of the blue.

'How strange that the thought never occurred to me,' I said.

'There's plenty of room, for a start,' she said.

'It mustn't be for Charlie's sake,' said Tue. 'It would have to be because you want to. Will you think about it?'

'I'll take it with me to Rome,' I said.

My mind was racing as I biked off towards Galleri Moritz.

It had been raining and the street lights reflected in the puddles.

The exhibition had stood between us ever since we first met, and in twenty-four hours we would be sitting on the Piazza Madonna dei Monti drinking Pinot Grigio. Our tickets for Rome were tucked inside my pocket and the keys to Maurizio's apartment were waiting to be picked up at the Caffè Il Cigno. The name was enough on its own.

I assigned myself a single task: to help her over the final hurdle of this evening.

Moritz was pacing about in cobalt blue and two girls in black uniform were opening champagne and lining up glasses. 'Just go with some Latin the first hour,' Moritz instructed the DJ.

'What about that article?' I said.

'Sod it,' said Moritz, handing me a glass. 'The art world doesn't care about journalists.'

The eight tapestries were beautifully set off by the space around them. Diana herself was all in white.

'I'm proud of you,' I said.

She tried to smile.

'Tonight I'm your dad, Diana.'

Her laugh was a snorted spray of saliva.

'You can ask anything of me,' I said.

Minna Lund and Goldschmidt arrived on the dot with a big bouquet. The collectors fell into two groups: an older crowd who were familiar with the menu at Søllerød Kro and knew Florence better than Aarhus, and a younger lot, a number of whom I recognised from various nightclubs, the kind who navigated the gates of Frankfurt airport with world-weary detachment and spent far too little time in their Bulthaup kitchens.

The division of the creative class who had au pairs, so to speak.

Nikolaj Krogh and Mille air-kissed the majority.

'We're in town to buy up some art,' said Nikolaj Krogh.

'I think we'll have to be quick,' said Mille.

She turned casually and indicated the half-open cunt in the corner.

'I'll get hold of Moritz,' said Nikolaj Krogh.

'What on earth got into you, darling?' said Mille.

Diana told her about Andreas Møller crossing a line and I caught sight of Moritz and Minna Lund. Judging by their gestures something interesting was going on. They had stepped out into the office area and

I positioned myself at the champagne buffet and managed to catch enough of what was said to piece together a scenario. Minna Lund was offering a hundred thousand for two tapestries, almost half-price.

I sidled closer.

'We both know the others are awaiting my move,' she said.

'Is that a threat?' said Moritz.

'I won't pay more than they're worth.'

'I can go down to a hundred and twenty. That's thirty-three per cent!'

'Careful, Kaspar. If you persist in being stubborn you will sell nothing.'

'I've just sold one for the full asking price, Minna.'

'May I remind you that we were the only bidders at Bruun-Rasmussen. Diana's work no longer sells itself.'

Five minutes later Minna Lund left the gallery without saying goodbye.

Moritz busied himself pouring champagne to keep hold of those who remained, but the effect was the exact opposite. The creative upper class, ever in search of that exclusive experience, shunned failure in its every form. The DJ struggled blindly to find a foothold: jazz was too spacy, and anything with a groove served only to remind those who were still there that it wasn't a party.

At seven the exhibition opened officially, and it was neither the sight of Inger's slightly stooping frame, her bony cheeks reddened with splodges of rouge, or the dandruff on Peter Borch-Jensen's collar that prompted the winner types to beat a retreat: it was the cheap plonk Inger cradled in her arms, and specifically the red cellophane that was wrapped around the bottle.

'We're staying,' said Mille.

'Are you pleased with how it's turned out, Diana?' said Inger.

'Thanks for the wine,' said Diana.

'It's Argentinian,' said Peter Borch-Jensen. 'The grape is Malbec and originates from France.'

Diana maintained her smile.

'You're on the champagne, I see,' said Peter Borch-Jensen.

'Sorry, I forget to get you some,' I said.

'I won't claim the honours,' said Peter Borch-Jensen, 'but I am rather gratified by the small part I played in the creation of these magnificent works.'

'Nonsense, Peter Borch-Jensen!' said Inger. 'He's been boasting his head off about it this past hour and a half down at Vinstue 80.'

'90, actually,' said Peter Borch-Jensen. 'Odd that it calls itself a wine bar when everyone goes there for the beer.'

'What part was it you played?' said Mille.

'That would be rather indiscreet of me to divulge,' he said.

'He photographed the cunt!' said Inger. 'I would never have the guts to paint mine. It's not sufficiently photogenic.'

Diana wasn't smiling anymore.

'But I did paint my cat once!' said Inger.

'And what was the underlying message there?' said Peter Borch-Jensen.

'There wasn't one,' said Inger. 'It was just a pussy cat.'

'Peter Borch-Jensen is one of Denmark's foremost Holberg scholars,' I said, and Nikolaj Krogh picked up the cue in cultivated fashion.

Diana tugged on my arm and we went over to a corner.

'Is it too much for you, Inger and Peter Borch-Jensen being here?' I said.

She put her hand on my arm.

'Am I cold?'

I smiled and she didn't.

'I don't know,' I said. 'Do you feel cold?'

'Just tell me,' she said.

By half past seven it was just an ordinary reception with students from the academy and the university, curators, architects and hangers-on who drank whatever was swilled into the trough while doing their best to combine being utterly unique with not saying anything out of place.

Mille and Nikolaj Krogh adjourned to Karriere Bar along with the more upper echelons of art-world aristocracy, while Peter Borch-Jensen was becoming bolder.

I placed Diana at a small table and did not move from her side. It was, I felt, less stressful for her to be stationary.

Peter Borch-Jensen pulled up a chair and sat down.

'How's your csardas coming along, Mikkel Vallin?'

'Csardas?'

Diana reached for her glass.

'Hungary's answer to the tango,' he said. 'Liszt was hugely inspired by the csardas in his *Hungarian Dances*. You're familiar with Liszt, of course. All pianissimo to begin with and then all of a sudden your heart leaps out of your chest: vroom! The scales explode and syncopated torrents rain down.'

'I thought the mazurka was Hungarian,' I said.

'Did you really? Well I never.'

'Mazurka's Polish,' said Diana.

Borch-Jensen reeled over to the DJ and a tango struck up.

'We never did have our dance, Miss Kiss. May I?'

The lumberjack shirts made space and Peter Borch-Jensen didn't see the indulgent smiles. He placed his right hand against her upper back and his dark brown lace-ups glided across the floor with purpose and determination. Diana let go of her inhibitions after some sixteen bars and Borch-Jensen didn't seem to care about anything in the world apart from leading her in the dance. His long hair stuck to his cheeks, the tails of his jacket flapping and swaying.

Diana came back blushing.

Peter Borch-Jensen produced a leather-encased hip flask.

'Our history extends beyond time and geography, Diana.'

He tossed his head back and the cognac ran down his chin and dribbled on to his sweat-soaked shirt.

'You mustn't bask in the glow of your potential, Diana Kiss.'

I saw no reason to hide my smile.

'You must never succumb to being realistic! Elevate your ambition and throw caution to the wind! Mediocrity's path is paved with ill turns and questionable services.'

The thought occurred to me that he might be addressing me through Diana, but it wasn't the case. I was just a piece of furniture with fingernails.

'What are we even doing here, Diana Kiss?'

I was outclassed, not by his wit or his sonorous articulation, but by the sheer force of his words. How often do you meet someone who fearlessly embraces the power of language?

'Diana, how I sense you! You may be untruthful in action and in thought, but against the heart you stand defenceless.'

He was invincible until his next swig of cognac.

He leaned forward and put his hand on her thigh.

'You are as yet one photograph short!'

'What do you mean?' she said.

'The consummation!'

He removed his hand and glanced up at me.

'I saw you through the lens. I saw you tremble as I entered you.'

'I don't need this,' said Diana.

'Have you told him how much you enjoyed it?' he said.

I handed him his coat.

'It's time you were going!'

He gave my cravat a look of disgust.

'Once a pleb, always a pleb.'

I led him through the gallery by the scruff of the neck and he was anything but the leading man as he stood there outside trying to find his sleeves. He'd have a long journey home.

Diana and I went for a walk and had Peking soup at the Chinese by the main station, and when we got back to the gallery we were met by an insane conceptual artist and had a drag of his spliff. Galleri Moritz was bouncing now.

Jan stood in the doorway kissing right and left. His poncho was bright turquoise. A photographer from one of the fashion magazines stopped us in front of the entrance and I could feel how good the picture would be. The music stopped when she entered, and two hundred people whooped and applauded.

Who was Rie Becker to say whether Diana was a success or not?

The crowd were the kind who had first met on the skater scene and had gone on to become designers, feted architects, producers, artists and actors, and all still stuck to the old rule of capitulating totally to the party.

'You were a good dad,' said Diana.

The DJ played Tone-Loc and a flock of sirens pulled Diana on to the dance floor.

I leaned my head back and for the first time in what seemed like an age my calf muscles untensed.

'That was it, wasn't it?'

Levinsen in a Hawaii shirt.

'What was what?'

'The art business. You need to move on, Vallin.'

The DJ was mixing Kurtis Blow.

'I'm off to Istanbul,' he said.

'To do what?'

'Content.'

'What?'

'Content.'

Diana came back perspiring and I licked her armpits.

In the little room behind the office were three orange nylon sculptures and an archive of smaller canvases. We clashed teeth and my lip was bleeding as she contracted. I came so forcefully I had to support myself against a mountain-bike version of Duchamp's bicycle wheel. Moritz had stashed two bottles of champagne at the back of the little fridge. We drank straight from the bottle and shared with everyone around us.

Jan was giving his flabby arms some air in a chalky tank top.

'It'll turn out all right, you'll see,' he said.

'As the actress said to the bishop,' I said.

'What will?' said Diana.

The old hip-hoppers were battling and people crowded round and clapped their hands.

'Haven't you heard?' Jan said. 'I got a friend of mine to play the interested buyer.'

'And?' I said.

'He could take his pick. There's only one been sold.'

ROME, OCTOBER 2008

We gazed up at the pink sky, facing away from each other. The cupolas and spires didn't matter, and the Pantheon was at our feet. On a little glass table was a bottle of Pinot Grigio and the air was just warm enough not to be noticed. I always wanted to sit on the rooftop terrace of the Hotel Minerva, and the mood was hard to describe. There was no passion, but no reproaches either. Nor was it much like staring into the sink after two days on speed and noticing the congealed toothpaste. It wasn't at all as dramatic. It was more like Blegdamsvej, perhaps, on a Sunday in July, when everyone else is out of town. I might have known she would hate Rome.

There was nothing wrong with the set-up, though.

Maurizio's apartment was situated in the well-to-do area below the Villa Borghese. The streets were airy, the apartments high-ceilinged and expansive. It was a penthouse on the Viale Parioli, two storeys in a mix of styles, with a wealth of peculiar arrangements and interesting art. There was a roof terrace with an automatic watering system, and a little note written with a fountain pen: 'Sleep in, sleep out. Eat at Molto. Have a drink at Gotha. Make yourself at home. Avoid Saint Peter and enjoy love. Yours, Maurizio.'

The weather was warm from the early morning and Diana took her book out with her on to the terrace while I popped down to the street. There was a shop that only sold work clothes for domestic staff, and outside Il Cigno an elderly lady in a pink Chanel suit and big sunglasses sat engrossed in the day's share prices.

The deli was huge and well assorted and I bought *proscuitto crudo*, bread, freshly squeezed grapefruit juice and *mozzarella di buffala* from Campania.

I found a grassy-green Umbrian olive oil in Maurizio's arsenal and arranged the food on two plates. Small birds hopped about and twittered in the lemon tree and there was a distant hum of traffic from the centre of town. Diana put down her book and smiled.

'I think I could lie here all day.'

'I thought we might go and see *Saint Teresa in Ecstasy*,' I said.

We went through the Villa Borghese and I relished the way she took in the Piazza del Popolo: the large and prominent cafés with their waiters dressed in white, stately Roman men with the day's newspaper under their arm, the overly made-up women in hats, accompanied by little dogs. We turned down the Via Margutta and passed by the painters with their colourful figurative canvases.

'They work on the street like prostitutes,' I said.

'They're just trying to scrape a living, that's all,' she said.

'That's what I mean,' I said.

We negotiated the hordes of school classes on the Piazza di Spagna and continued along the Via Condotti, and then Diana wanted a look inside the Brioni store and came out with a tightly knitted light blue polo that set her back four hundred euros.

I wanted us to celebrate our arrival with a traditional lunch and had picked out Da Gino. We went in circles for half an hour before finding the place, and when we did, it turned out to be *prenotazione* only.

'Can't we just grab a sandwich?' she said.

'There's a good place on the other side of the Corso,' I said.

We scoured the side streets along Via Babuino, weaving a slalom through the tourists, and my shirt was plastered to my skin.

But the Romans were queuing outside the Hostaria al 31.

'We'll go to La Pollarola instead,' I said.

And so we crossed the Via del Corso again, and I could sense her patience ebbing away. I took pains to avoid the maze-like lattice of backstreets, sticking instead to the Via Ripetta, which was so long and straight she couldn't help but realise how far we had to walk.

'Caravaggio used to do his carousing around here when he'd been painting,' I said. 'He came here the same night he killed a man.'

She wasn't listening.

'Look at that scene over there,' I said, pausing on the Via della Scrofa. The chicken man and the ham man had come out on to the pavement in their white aprons and stood with their arms around each other's shoulders, engaged in banter.

'It's like that here every day at lunchtime.'

'How sad,' she said.

La Pollarola was exactly the same as always, nothing had changed.

Mario draped a camelskin coat over the shoulders of a regular customer who was about to leave and I went through the menu and recommended the *spaghetti alle vongole* and the turbot, ordered a white Sergio Mottura and lost my head completely:

'Coming here always makes me so happy.'

She looked me in the eye.

'How did you find the place?'

'Helene and I had been at the Campo dei Fiori…'

'And then you were hungry?'

'Yes, we were hungry.'

It was a joy to watch the man fillet the turbot and I cajoled her into trying the whipped sabayon with wild strawberries.

We had coffee and a beer at the Bar del Fico and a flock of nuns went by.

In the taxi to Santa Maria della Vittoria I told her about the Spanish nun Teresa and her radical practice of her faith: long, meditative sessions in which dream, reality and prayer merged into one with orgiastic force.

We went to gaze at the Bernini sculptures and were dizzied by the way he made marble levitate and bronze burn.

'He must have been a pretty amazing guy,' Diana said.

I told her the story on our way to Monti. Bernini was handsome and highly intelligent. He landed all the most prestigious commissions, was a friend of the Pope and presided over an army of minions. Mario was one such minion, married to Constanza, a beautiful young woman of good family.

In those days, only the nobility were immortalised in marble busts, but Constanza inspired Bernini to break with convention. For months she sat for him, and he kept the finished work for himself: the sensual smile, the slightly parted lips, the unbuttoned blouse that allowed the beholder to sense the fullness of her bosom.

Bernini became obsessed with Constanza, and Mario allowed it to pass. To be fucked by Maestro Bernini bestowed honour indeed.

Bernini had a brother, Luigi, equally good looking and one of Italy's most promising mathematicians. Like so many others in Roman society, Luigi, too, found himself taken in by Constanza's beauty. Bernini noted how the two often came together at parties, and their intimacy ultimately betrayed them. One day Bernini announced that he would be out of town to oversee a commission. But he stayed home instead. The next morning he lurked outside Constanza's house, and as daylight came she and Luigi emerged in the doorway and kissed each other goodbye. Bernini chased his brother through the streets of Rome and beat him senseless with an iron bar. He hired a servant to go after Constanza. The face he had studied for hundreds of hours to eternalise in marble was slashed beyond recognition with a sharp blade. Constanza was jailed for her infidelity, and Luigi, who miraculously had survived the attempt on his life, was forced to flee. By papal order, Bernini married a becoming young woman from one of Rome's wealthiest families, and the bust of Constanza was removed to Florence.

But that wasn't the end of it. Bernini's career, until then an unbroken line of success, began to falter. Even the Pope vetoed his ideas, and Bernini had all but slid into oblivion when a benefactor commissioned him to produce a sculpture of the newly canonised Teresa.

I led Diana through the narrow lanes of Monti, once the haunt of ruffians and prostitutes, now of artists and intellectuals. It was half past six and we strolled across the Piazza della Madonna dei Monti.

People were sitting on the steps around the fountain with wine and panini, kids played football up against the walls, and clusters of locals stood passing the time of day. A nice-looking couple left us their table on the terrace of the Bottega del Caffé, one of the better ones in the corner, and I ordered a bottle of Pinot Grigio from a broad-shoul-dered waiter, who flirted with Diana.

'I've been so wanting to come here with you,' I said.

All the time, new faces to look at.

'I can see why you're so mad about Rome,' she said.

'Everything looks and tastes good,' I said.

'How many times have you been here?'

'This is the seventh.'

'And all the other times have been with Helene, right?'

I smiled and nodded.

'Am I sitting on her chair?'

I saw myself wake up in the house on Ceresvej, the feel of the soft blue stair carpet under my bare feet. I put the kettle on, got the corn-flakes out for Charlie, fetched the paper from the hall and put the bread in the toaster.

'Would you order me a grappa?' said Diana.

She took out a sketchpad and drew an elderly couple.

'Are you an artist?' said the broad-shouldered waiter in Roman English.

She gave the drawing to the couple and they insisted on getting us some spumante. Then the people next to us became curious, and an hour later our table was groaning with wine, beer and grappa.

'You make a drawing of me too?' said the waiter. 'If your boyfriend will allow, of course.'

'I haven't got a boyfriend,' said Diana.

'He won't understand that,' I said when he popped back inside.

'Of course he will,' said Diana.

He reappeared with his hair combed and slicked back.

'I finish work now,' he said.

'Have a seat,' said Diana.

Marco was a maker of documentary films, albeit by name only.

He had no end of pretentious ideas. He wanted to re-establish Italy's conscience and clean up after Berlusconi. His opening scene was all lined up and none of it made sense. He said it was going to be hand-held.

'Where do you go after work?' said Diana.

They frequented a gay club behind the Colosseum, he said. Not that he was gay himself, but a lot of girls went there too. Diana shaded his right cheekbone.

'You look like a model,' she said.

'Actually, I was a model,' he said. Dolce & Gabbana, Prada, Bottega Veneta. He had lived the life for two years and earned a packet, but it was a superficial world, he said. No substance.

Marco looked sideways at my cravat:

'But I learned to get along with gay people.'

In the round-the-world yacht race, the Frenchman, Moitessier, looked set to win, but sailing had become for him a philosophical, existential project, and on his way towards the prize he altered his course and sailed on without destination.

Marco treated us to the best grappa in the house and marvelled at how much of it Diana was able to consume. We went on by taxi to Coming Out, a lively, bustling place with pretty boys in white tank tops dancing to plastic house. Marco introduced me to a guy who was familiar with most of the classics of world literature and displayed a keen sense of humour, and in any other situation he would have made rewarding company.

I finished my beer and went over to Diana.

'I'm going back to the flat.'

She kissed me on the cheek.

'I think you should come with me,' I said.

She said nothing.

'Do you hear me, Diana?'

'I'm staying here to dance,' she said.

I found a bottle of white in Maurizio's fridge, dropped my glass on the floor and got another. All of a sudden I wanted to get on with writing about Søren T-shirt again. I carried on drinking and filled half a notebook before passing out in the deckchair.

I woke up in a blaze of sunlight and was so dizzy the plants were all over the place, but although everything swirled together, one thing was crystal clear to me: I wouldn't be moving into Helene's house on Ceresvej.

Diana rang at half past two and the only place I could think of to suggest we meet was Bar della Pace. The Borghese park was teeming with birds. The sky they populated was a static expanse of sunshine and I found it depressing that the grass was in such a poor state. There were scooters and cars. The smell of coffee and ice-cream cones with scoops of many colours.

I took a break at the Bar della Scrofa, whose beer provided the perfect tonic until a fatigued pair of Danes plonked themselves down at the next table and began to squabble over converting euros into kroner. Diana arrived at Bar della Pace on the back of Marco's scooter and they kissed before he sped off round the corner.

'Do you know where I can find a toy shop?' she said.

It was not what I'd been expecting her to say.

She bought a little cuddly horse by Rudi in the fine old shop on the Piazza Navona, and afterwards I insisted on living out my dream of a drink on the rooftop terrace of the Hotel Minerva.

We sat for half an hour without saying a word.

'What do you want the horse for?' I said.

'It's Nona's birthday the day after tomorrow and I'm going to Budapest.'

On our last day together I hired a bike and bombed down the Via Veneto, across the Piazza Barberini, through the tunnel to Monti and along the Tiber to the right-angled streets of Testaccio. I have always been drawn by church bells, but never so beguiled as by the bells of the Basilica San Paolo. I listened with all my being to their deep and sonorous clang.

When the final tone faded away, I understood there was nothing to fear.

I was on my way to dinner at Helene's and I knew I would have to be honest with her. In moments of weakness I was tempted by the prospect of giving Charlie a home with a mum and dad, and lazy summer evenings in the garden, but I never got far into that world before I felt what a deception it would be.

For the past two days I had lived like a tramp, writing about Søren and Signe without any idea of what the time might be, eating oats and rice milk, fried eggs and baked beans.

Diana floated above it all like a dream, and now and again it all became tangible: a sudden sinking feeling in the abdomen when I woke up alone; a shirt that kept her smell. And yet I felt nothing.

Perhaps Helene was afraid of coming on too strong. Tonight there was no fish or seafood, just spaghetti bolognese and elderflower cordial.

I read Charlie his bedtime story and carried on even when he began to snore.

She had opened a bottle of Irma's Chardonnay from the south of France and I knew there was champagne waiting in the fridge.

'Cheers,' she said.

'I've given it some thought, Helene,' I said.

I took a deep breath, but before I could speak she pre-empted me.

'Do you mind telling me what this is all about, Mikkel?' she said, and produced what I could see were a child's drawings. 'I emptied Charlie's drawer at the kindergarten.'

A drawing of a man with a pint in his hand, an ashtray.

'Did you take Charlie to a bar with you, Mikkel?'

She put her hands flat on the table and got to her feet. 'Have you been out drinking and taken Charlie with you?'

'He had a very nice time at the Borgerkroen,' I said.

It wasn't an utterance I felt that good about.

'This stops here, Mikkel! It stops here!'

For me it didn't stop until Andy's Bar closed.

My fellow traveller at the sausage stand on Gothersgade was a Greenlander.

'What do you miss most about Nuuk?'

'Minced seal meat,' he said.

'Can you get that in the supermarket there?'

I woke up with the sound of Diana's new answering-machine message in my head:

'You've called Diana. Leave a message.'

The first time I rang was from outside Chicos Cantina, I remembered that much. Had I sung? How many messages had I left? I saw myself sprawled on the steps in front of the music institute, but what had I been singing?

I called Jan, but he knew nothing and had no idea what Diana's mother was called, or where she lived.

'She's not coming back,' I said.

'How do you know?'

'I can feel it.'

'You're pissed,' he said.

'I'm going to find her,' I said.

'If she'd wanted you to go to Budapest she'd most likely have asked.'

BUDAPEST, OCTOBER 2008

I asked the taxi driver to take me into the centre of town and after a quarter of an hour the motorway and the exhaust-blackened concrete buildings that lined it gave way to a boulevard of grainy apartment houses and shops that bought gold and sold sex.

I arrived in a city whose architectural splendour and cultural wealth had flourished in the late nineteenth century, only to be ravaged by two world wars and Soviet invasion. It was now notorious for its right-wing radicalism and large-scale porn industry, but all I was interested in was my own story.

I had come to Budapest to find my ending.

The driver stopped on Erzsébet tér, a park-like expanse hemmed in by finance and international hotel chains. I was convinced that somewhere among all those bank logos I would find Diana.

The closest hotel was Le Méridien. The lobby was full of the usual American pensioners in floppy sunhats and trainers who all seemed to be suffering from spinal collapse. There was an atrium garden, *Hungarian Night* every Saturday, and a blown-up photo of smiling Gypsies, the very same Romani the skinheads were so fond of chasing through the city's streets.

The glossy reception was all fake wood, the furniture conveyor-belt rococo, the plants an unnatural green, and the tame mediocrity of it held me together.

I paid for a room, and after I'd dumped my bag on the bed and taken a shower I sat down at the little desk with a notepad. My information was sparse and Budapest was almost twice as big as Copenhagen.

I had a good likeness of Diana saved on my phone and was

intending to show it to all the right people. I made a list of possible lines of enquiry and went down to see the concierge, who drew a circle round the smart part of town on a map and marked the Academy of Fine Arts with an X.

The Jewish ghetto was unusually photogenic.

The buildings along Király Ut were low and poetic, and behind the gateways lay the quaintest courtyards with little dwellings, uneven cobblestones and wild flowers, the kind of places that in Copenhagen would have been cultivated to death by well-meaning architects and awarded little brass plaques from the council.

A design shop was followed by a place selling skateboarding gear and then a café with futuristic lighting and a smartly dressed younger clientele. I showed the owner my photo of Diana and he told me the place had only been going for three years and shook his head.

Was Kiss a Jewish name? I had the feeling I was on the right track and braced myself to run into her round the next corner. Part of my plan was to visit every laundry on my way. The first one was run by Chinese. I called Diana's number, only to get her answerphone again. From a third-floor window came the purest of scales from a violin. A couple of side streets further on, an opera singer was practising. There were spacious bookstores and shops selling musical instruments and classical records.

The second laundry was Hungarian-owned. The woman was wearing a white coat and took time to study the photo. I got my little notepad out that I'd taken from the hotel and wrote the name *Kiss*, endeavouring by means of gestures and drawings to explain that the woman I was looking for was the daughter of a woman who ran a laundry business. The woman's face lit up and she handed me a stack of flyers advertising a good deal on shirts.

In a basement drinking place all I got was filthy innuendo, and the dreadlocked bartender in the anarchist café eyed me suspiciously. I had goulash soup at Menza, a smart restaurant in the flashy street called Liszt Ferenc tér that messed around with a kitsch aesthetic for those in the know. The waiters didn't know Diana, but then I started on the bars one by one. At the scruffiest of them they were playing The Doors and airing the place out after the excesses of the night before. 'Yes, I remember her,' an Australian bartender said. 'She used to come here all the time, but it's been years.'

'Do you know where she lived?'

'Can't say I do, mate. A bunch of girls, you know.'

'Do you remember any names?'

'Arhhh… Maria was another. They used to hang out all the time.'

'You wouldn't know her last name, would you?'

'Sorry, mate. Never any time for proper introductions here.'

I left the Jewish quarter and found Andrássy Ut, a surrogate Champs Élysées with dashed hopes. Posters advertised concerts by Vaya con Dios, Kiss and Paul Anka. The shops still had their high ceilings, but were now full of crap and cheap mobile phones.

The Academy of Fine Arts was at the top end, and the girl at reception was helpful enough:

'We have the files from 2000 and 2001, but I'll have to go through them manually. It could take a week.'

D inner at the hotel restaurant was a definite mistake. The table-cloths were damask, the tables themselves placed too far apart, the diners few and far between. The waiters in full get-up struck all the right poses, but the lobster soup tasted of stock cube, the salmon mousse had a perilous smell about it, and the steak had been overdone by about half an hour.

I decided to go for an evening stroll and have a beer before bedtime. The hotel's back entrance led out on to a quiet side street and a hundred metres further on two girls with a map stopped me and asked the way. They were from Pécs in the southern part of the country and were going to a hairdressing fair the next day on the other side of the river.

They were interested to learn of my endeavour and we walked together towards the Danube. They were about twenty-five years old, one rather short and provincially broad-bottomed, the other somewhat taller and decent looking, both of them bright, uncomplicated and good humoured. I suggested a generic English pub, but they were more for the place next door, a bar advertising the best cocktails in town, and it looked like the kind of place that would get lively later on.

The doormen hung around at the bar and inside were two couples on dates, high-backed chairs, black candles in rectangular glass candlesticks and dreadful high-tech art on the walls. The way they studied the cocktail menu was rather ravishing.

I made do with a Heineken served in a tall, thin glass with a blue base and stem, most likely to justify bumping up the price.

Rebecca and Olga wanted to hear all about my romantic mission and couldn't get enough of my and Diana's relationship. In Hungary, they said, it would be unthinkable for a man to engage in such a project.

The sexes had drifted apart after the dissolution of the Eastern bloc.

Women now took an education, were ambitious, industrious and outgoing, while men carried on as they had done under communism: they drank too much, were lazy and incapable of providing any kind of qualified sounding board.

Olga was a good example. She had her own salon, went on courses in London and Amsterdam and had got a divorce the year before.

I asked about the hairdressing fair and she told me about the competition.

The theme was extensions, and she knew most of the other competitors and reckoned she had a fair chance of winning. Rebecca was always her model. They had both been talented sports dancers in their teenage years.

It was half past eleven. I asked for the bill.

'Have you got a picture of Diana?' Rebecca asked.

She studied it intensely and said something to Olga.

The bill was a hundred and eighty-eight thousand forint, about four hundred and eighty kroner, expensive for Hungary.

The girls seemed to be arguing and had raised their voices. I got my money out and realised I didn't have anywhere near enough. I did the sums again and this time it came to four thousand eight hundred kroner.

'I think there's some mistake,' I said to the bartender. 'We had six cocktails and three beers. The bill's way too high.'

I showed him, only he didn't bother to look. 'I made it out myself,' was all he said.

'You're charging me a hundred euros for a cocktail. I never saw prices like this anywhere in the world. How do you explain that?'

'This is a VIP bar,' he said.

'This is illegal.'

'The price list is on display in the window,' he said.

I was just another horny middle-aged punter.

'There's a cashpoint on the other side of the street, sir.'

Rebecca was unable to look me in the eye. Olga was as cold as ice.

'Listen, I'm a journalist from Denmark and I'm writing about Budapest.'

The black doormen fronted up.

'If you don't have the money in cash, I will allow you to go to the cashpoint on the other side of the street, sir. No problem.'

The girls got up and left.

'I thought you were nice,' I said.

The bartender and the three doormen accompanied me over to the cashpoint.

I had a good look to make sure I remembered the place, then strode purposefully off back to the hotel to report the incident.

Rebecca was waiting at the entrance.

'I'm sorry,' she said. 'I know Diana. You can meet me tomorrow at twelve o'clock.'

She handed me a note that said Café Csiga and the address.

The place was in Józsefváros, a district I'd have been worried about visiting in the dark.

She was seated at the bar. Her hair was tied in a ponytail. She looked older without her make-up and there was an almost dejected air about her. Her name wasn't Rebecca at all, but Maria, she said, and she had never been a hairdresser's model in her life.

She handed me forty-seven thousand forint, her share of the spoils, and I tried to ease the situation by praising her acting skills, but the previous night's events had been no one-off performance and tonight she would be back at work.

I ordered two beers from the Irish bartender.

'Can you show me where Diana's mother lives?' I said.

'Just around the corner,' she said.

She told me she'd lost contact with Diana in 2000.

'Diana got involved with Mr Jørn.'

'Her Danish violinist?' I said.

'He's a jerk,' she said. 'He fucked up her mind.'

She and Diana had been inseparable since Year Three.

'I miss her,' she said. 'It was so funny to work with her.'

'What did you do?'

'Diana was a *consumer girl* like me. The best! Every night she invented a new story.'

'She's an artist now,' I said.

'Diana can be anybody,' she said.

We drank up and turned down the first side street.

Maybe Maria was ashamed of not getting on in life. She pointed towards the laundry and shook my hand.

'You're a nice girl,' I said.

'I do bad things,' she said.

The street was cobbled and the house was small and consisted of two storeys.

Diana's mother was short and stocky with jet-black hair. She was wearing a pink smock and her calves were a criss-cross of varicose veins. I introduced myself as a friend of Diana's and explained that

Maria had shown me the way.

'Diana?' she said.

'Is Diana here?' I said, twirling a finger in the air to indicate the home.

'Diana not here,' she said.

'Diana out with Nona?' I said.

'Diana not here.'

'And Nona?'

'No… na?'

'Her daughter. The child.'

I mimed a child in my arms.

'Child?' she said.

'Yes. Nona.'

'No Nona,' she said.

She beckoned for me to step behind the counter.

'Come, come!'

We went up some narrow, crooked stairs and through two small rooms full of bric-a-brac and embroidered cushions.

She opened a low, brown-painted door and smiled.

'Diana!' she said.

There was no sign of habitation. The room had been left untouched.

'May I?' I said, stepping inside. A bell tinkled downstairs in the shop.

'Look, look,' she said, and left me on my own.

The room was bigger than the two through which we had passed, and faced out to the street.

In the corner was a three-quarter-width bed with a black cover on it, and the little art deco lamp on the desk looked like something she might have saved up for. Bjarne Riis smiled down from the centre of the noticeboard, the gleaming white teeth and lean, tanned face. Next to him was a photocopy of the piece I'd done for *Urban*: *In defence of the mother who abandons the nest*.

There was a Polaroid of Diana on her bike with a silver medal draped around her neck, and another of her and Maria taken at the

Carnival. But where was Diana if she wasn't here?

Had she gone somewhere with Nona?

The bookcase was full of books in Danish: *Gift* by Tove Ditlevsen, several of Suzanne Brøgger's and Henrik Stangerup's, *Lykke-Per* and *Kongens Fald*. *Den Store Danske Encyklopædi* took up the bottom two shelves and above it was a row of VHS cassettes: *Pelle Erobreren*, *Café Paradis*, Helle Ryslinge's *Sirup* and all twenty-four episodes of *Matador*.

Diana's mother came back upstairs from the shop.

'Where is Nona's room?' I said.

She frowned and threw up her arms.

'Look!' she said, then mimed cycling and pulled out a drawer under the desk. The first ten pages of the scrapbook were full of cuttings from local papers and were all about Diana's road-racing victories. After that, it was empty.

I noticed a folder with my name on it. The xeroxed pages inside were articles, interviews and columns I'd written, all in chronological order and dating back to the beginning of the nineties and my time as a music reviewer.

'Do you know Mr Jørn?' I said.

She mimed playing the violin and I nodded.

'One moment,' she said, then went away and came back with a little phone book.

I thanked her and rang the number as soon as I was outside again.

Hypodermics littered some basement stairs and his voice sounded younger than I'd expected.

I called Diana's number again from the taxi.

Jørn Schelenius lived in a beautifully tatty palatial building on Szófia Ut and was hardly older than me, average height, thick, dark brown hair greying at the temples and insistent furrows that ran between his nose and the corners of his mouth. His feet splayed outwards when he walked, his shoulders were a gentle gradient and his eyes were blue and moist.

He was in pre-washed Replay jeans, a white-and-blue-striped Ralph Lauren shirt and ordinary black leather shoes.

His living room was high-ceilinged and from the little bay window he could look down and keep an eye on what was happening on the street below. The walls were covered in art: there was a collage of Birkemose's, a pair of non-figurative oil canvases of debatable quality and a quirky woman in urbane surroundings by Seppo Mattinen. He poured a beer into two glasses and sat down in an armchair with a little sigh of discomfort.

'My knees tell me it's autumn,' he said.

The furniture looked like heirlooms from a bygone bourgeois home.

'How long have you lived in Budapest?' I asked.

'Twelve years this May,' he said.

'When did you meet Diana?'

He laughed loudly, but not because it was funny.

'It was at an opening over in the ghetto. She found out I was Danish, and you know what she's like, of course.'

'How do you mean?'

'Over the years I've met quite a number of the world's great solo-ists. These are people who practise twelve, fourteen hours a day. But I dare say none comes anywhere near focusing the way Diana does. After two months of Danish lessons she could make herself under-stood. After six months she spoke the language better than most.'

He scratched his chin as if he had a beard.

'That requires two things! A brain bordering on the autistic, and overriding ruthlessness. She keeps her head down and doesn't look up. Diana *never* looks up! Because if she did, she would see only her victims, writhing around in the ditches in agony.'

He took a sip of his beer and I felt sure he had been eating bread made of rye and wheat flour.

'Diana Kiss has a personality disorder,' he said. 'It took me a long time to realise it, and it was not a welcome admission, but it did make things clearer.'

'When did you last see her?'

'The same day she left for Copenhagen. She just upped and went.'

'Now she's left Copenhagen in the same way,' I said.

'I knew you were next in line.'

'We've had a lovely time together,' I said.

'You don't need to tell me. Of course you've had a lovely time together! She lifted you up out of your bag of bones and the only thing you could think about was wanting more. Am I right?'

I refused to indulge him with so much as a nod, and his embittered laughter was getting on my nerves so much I had to look away.

'It's a pity we can't learn from others' mistakes,' he said. 'We must all learn the hard way, I'm afraid.'

He had to go and teach, and showed me to the door. A children's drawing hung in the hall.

'Is that one of Nona's?' I asked.

'Ah, she told you about Nona.'

'She came here for her birthday.'

One of his knees appeared to buckle and his eyes glazed over.

'She'll be seven tomorrow,' he said, and breathed in deeply to hold back the tears. 'We'll always have Nona, at least.'

'Are you Nona's father?' I said.

'You could say.'

'How do you mean?'

'Nona has yet to become manifest in the physical world.'

I took a taxi back to the laundry and explained to Diana's mother that I needed to use her phone.

Diana answered immediately.

W^e agreed to meet at the Würgeengel on Dresdener Strasse. I
came straight from the airport and got there an hour early.

It looked like a place that had been open since 1924.

The long bar curved elegantly and in front of it were twelve bar
stools with red leather upholstery. The ceiling was latticed glass and
the dim lighting came from candelabras and a chandelier. A lot
could go on in that semi-darkness. The bartender was in a shirt and
waistcoat and had tucked his tie between two buttons. I studied the
comprehensive menu: the classic cocktails set out according to key
ingredient, a large selection of rum and whisky; indeed, just about any
alcoholic beverage the heart might desire and all expertly selected.
They even had mescal.

I ordered a glass of Grauburgunder and seated myself at the bar.

The girls were pretty starlet types and preferred their drinks strong
and tart rather than package-holiday sweet, while the guys, in suit
trousers, plain shirts and Hush Puppies, went for American classics.

I was on my second glass when she ran her warm fingers down my
neck. Her hair was cut short to the roots, accentuating the beauty of
her features. People turned their heads to look at her.

She was wearing an anorak.

'What happened?' I said.

'I've found my face.'

It was an utterance that would have frightened the life out of me
in the nineties.

'I was at this heavy bar in Friedrichshain with chains hanging from
the ceiling and Jack Daniel's as far as you could see. The bartender was

this big girl with dark red hair. She kept looking at me and I couldn't work out if she wanted to get off with me or if she was annoyed with me because of my clothes. But then at one point she came round the tables collecting empties and put her hand on my shoulder as she went past. It was her smell that did it.'

'What did she smell of?'

'Geraniums.'

We ordered Moscow Mules and I told her about my trip to Budapest in chronological order, and now and then she had to interrupt to ask about Maria. She told me the hairdressing story was one she had made up ten years earlier, and then she wanted to know what I thought about her mother and whether I'd noticed how she never touched the ground when she walked.

'Jørn told me about Nona,' I said. 'Why did you invent her?'

'Jørn took Nona for himself. I should never have told him about her.'

'How did he find out?'

'I couldn't conceal my happiness.'

'You were happy about a child you'd made up?'

'It wasn't me who invented Nona.'

'Who was it, then?'

'You did.'

I looked at the walls. They were Bordeaux red.

'I needed a child to abandon,' she said.

'*In defence of the mother who abandons the nest…*' I said.

'I would never have got away without it.'

Of course, it was 'God Only Knows' that I had sung into her answerphone. I told her I was finishing up the Søren T-shirt book and she said a number of galleries were showing interest in her drawings. It didn't surprise me in the least that Mies turned up just before midnight, and as the clock struck twelve we were sitting arm in arm at the bar with a bottle of champagne, singing for Nona.

'Why exactly did you go to Budapest?' she said.

'To say thanks,' I said.

'For what?'

'I'm not sure yet.'

I went with them to Graefstrasse and the three of us slept together in the double bed.

The way we held each other's hands on top of the duvet felt so incomparably restful, and I woke up with violins in my arms and legs.

COPENHAGEN, 24 DECEMBER 2008

S øren knocks on the door as only he can.

I'm already pressed and have spent fifteen minutes going through the old CDs without finding anything suitable. He's wearing a tight-fitting black jacket which he refuses to take off and is very obviously in the kind of mood where nothing is good enough. He opens the fridge and there's a jar of piccalilli, some rather bewildered pickled cucumber and half a packet of yeast.

'Where's the duck?' he says.

'We're having dal,' I say.

'Dal? Dal?'

'I just need a tin of coconut milk,' I say.

'I hope you can hear yourself.'

'Have you even tasted dal?' I say.

'A goose would have done,' he said. 'But I'd rather have duck.'

I put Skousen & Ingemann on to shut him up.

It's so hard to get through! It keeps on disappearing inside itself.

'I knew I should have gone up to my mum and dad's,' he says. 'She'll already have the gravy on the go. She takes it very seriously. Which is the least you can expect. They always have a great big nosh-up first, with pickled herring and fried fillets of fish, then it's flat out on the sofa with a glass of wine while the duck's in the oven.'

'Christmas dinner here was your idea,' I remind him.

'Have you got a beer?' he says.

He knows I haven't.

'I've got tea with ginger and lemon.'

He puts on his black leather gloves.

'I had hoped that this one day in the year I could avoid having to break the law, but someone has to do something.'

He opens the door and is already on his way out.

'Wait a minute, where are we going?' I ask.

'Irma on Borgergade,' he says.

'I've got no money.'

'Who's the prehab here, you or me?'

He swears all the way along Klerkegade, stops outside Irma and gives me a handful of change. His nails are yellow and bitten down.

'You buy a red cabbage, right? When you get to the check-out you ask a load of questions. Can you manage that?'

It's almost closing time and the few customers are spread about the shop: a pensioner with a Zimmer, a disturbed woman in a quilted dressing gown, a dad sent out for browning and a packet of almonds.

'Should I pretend I don't know you?' I ask.

'It's not Robert de Niro. It's ordinary shoplifting.'

The red cabbage costs 14.95 and I take it to be a good omen.

I've got exactly fifteen kroner and Søren is circling by the meat counter.

'They've got quail breasts and seventeen kinds of chicken, but where the fuck's the duck? It's fucking miserable, this is. What are they doing out back, are they all stoned out there or what? I'm so livid I've gone blind. You look.'

'Fresh duck's sold out.'

'We'll have to get a frozen one, then, won't we!'

'It won't have time to thaw,' I say.

'We'll chuck it in the oven for a couple of hours first.'

So Søren lifts this big organic duck from Lindebjerggaard.

'Where are you going to put it?' I say.

'Just go away and let me get on with my work!'

He glances about, to make sure there's no detective.

'Right, you go to the check-out.'

I turn round to do as he says, only for female hands to stop me in my tracks.

The Sisters of Mercy in form-fitting coats.

'How come you weren't at the Next Love meeting?' the first one says.

'I'm not in it anymore,' I tell her.

'There was only the Taarbæk crowd there,' says the other.

'Where was it held?'

'Gammel Strand Gallery of Contemporary Art,' the first one says. 'You had to write a formal application stating your reasons for wanting to be considered. With a photo and curriculum vitae attached.'

'We're busy here, Mikkel,' says Søren.

'This is my best friend, Søren,' I tell them.

Søren shifts the duck over to his left hand for the introduction.

'I'm making my way over to the check-out,' he says.

He loiters at the crisps, and the duck is so cold he has to change hands every five seconds. I'm number three in line, and when an elderly woman queries her receipt with the check-out girl I make a rash decision and change queues, only then I notice the little sign on the conveyor saying *Till Closed*.

Back in line again and Søren's biting his hand in rage.

The Sisters of Mercy get behind me.

'We could start our own Next Love,' says one.

'How's that?'

'We just threw our lodger out.'

Søren moves towards the unmanned check-out. It's my turn now.

'Is your red cabbage Danish?' I ask.

A big bloke with a moustache wearing an Irma fleece jacket starts filling up the display cabinet to the left of the till with cigarettes. Søren picks up speed.

'Is our red cabbage Danish, Peter?'

A metre from the check-out, the duck slides out from under his coat, hits the floor with a hard clack and skids away to be halted by a metal display.

The bloke in the fleece blocks the exit and a colleague comes to his aid from the other side. Half a minute later they're leading Søren away.

'What's going on?' a Sister says.

'Merry Christmas,' I say.

The lino on the floor is grubby and worn. Empty cardboard boxes stamped flat have been piled in a corner next to half a pallet of corn on the cob. Søren is sitting on a black chair in the opposite corner and the bloke in the fleece, the biggest of the two, is standing next to him with his mobile in his hand.

'What do you want?' he says to me.

'I'm spending Christmas with my friend here,' I say.

'Not where he's going, you're not.'

'What are you going to do?' I ask.

'We're calling the police. That's what we do in these cases.'

'Piss!' says Søren, raising his voice. 'Bollocks!'

'You just stay calm,' the bloke says.

'Do you have to call them?' says Søren.

'I'm afraid so.'

'But it's Christmas Eve. Please.'

'You should have thought of that before,' the other one says.

'People like you always say that,' says Søren. 'Boneheads.'

'I don't think we need to discuss who the bonehead is,' the big bloke says.

'All right, so it's me,' says Søren. 'But if you let me go you'll have one shoplifter less to be worried about. I'll never steal from here again. Promise.'

'You'll just go on to our next store instead.'

'I swear on my mother's grave I'll never steal from Irma again.'

The smaller guy looks at the big one.

'We've got a zero-tolerance policy here and it's in force all year round,' he says. 'You'll be back home in time to dance round the Christmas tree. They won't keep you in for a minor offence like this.'

'But they will!' says Søren. 'I know they will!'

His voice cracks.

'I've got previous. They'll put me away. Please! Please!'

'It's not up to us,' says the big bloke. 'I'm calling them now.'

The Sisters of Mercy enter.

'You can't come in here,' says the smaller guy. 'Everyone out!'

The big bloke puts the flat of his hand against my back and moves me gently towards the door.

'Can we ask why he's being detained?' the first Sister says.

'He was caught trying to steal a duck.'

'How can you be sure?'

'He was on his way out through the check-out with it. That's why!'

'It's not theft until he's passed the last chance to pay, and he hadn't at that point.'

'He had a duck under his coat,' says the big bloke.

'There's nothing illegal about that,' the second Sister says.

'It was frozen,' Søren says. 'I was keeping it warm.'

'So you were intending to purchase this duck, were you?'

'Of course I was,' says Søren. 'I'm not going to go out stealing on Christmas Eve, am I?'

'Would you care to show me what you were intending to make this purchase *with*? Would it have been debit, credit or cash?'

Søren grimaces.

'I'm the one with the money,' the first Sister says, and produces a thousand-kroner note.

'I always let her hold on to my dosh,' says Søren.

The Sisters are all smiles.

'All right, let them pay,' the big bloke says.

S øren has been asleep on my shoulder since the gospel.

'You can tell he's a good boy,' the first Sister says.

The Ballad of Signe and Søren T-shirt is tucked between my feet in a carrier bag from the minimart and it doesn't matter in the slightest that he'll never get round to reading it.

The organ strikes up and the Marmorkirken lifts in song: *Dejlig er jorden.*

Fair is Creation.

It's almost a year since I lifted my arms above my head, and perhaps I shall never fly. But the others do.

I can feel Søren's breath against my hand.

'You're lovely when you cry,' the first Sister says.
'We know it's not because you're sad,' says the other.
I kiss their cheeks and clasp my hands, and sing as loud as I can.
Tider skal komme, tider skal henrulle:
Ages are coming, ages are passing.

ACKNOWLEDGEMENTS

For all the artists, gallerists, collectors, curators, journalists and auction-house staff who shared their knowledge and personal views with me.

The Danish Centre for Writers and Translators at Hald Hovedgaard for repeated residencies and kindness.

The Danish Institute in Rome for residency.

Bente Clausen for support in good time.

Mads Nørgaard for friendly encouragement.

The Danish Arts Foundation and the Danish Public Lending Right programme for financial support.

The Danish Writers' Association's *Autorkontoen* for financial support.

Jakob van Toornburg for wanting to do his best and doing so.

My mother, Elisabet Kongstad, and Uwe for all manner of support.

Roxanna Anne Albeck for inspiration.

Lars Worning for insight.

Malene Kirkegaard Nielsen for excellent advice.

Sørens Værtshus for noble hospitality.

A particular thanks to Nicolai Wallner for putting me in touch with David Shrigley, and to David Shrigley for the Danish edition's cover art.

And most of all to Rufus, Alma, Coco and my beloved Linda for sticking it out.

Copenhagen, June 2013